I0618350

The Healer And Me
A Novel

James Randall Miller

To Allen and Mary Miller, my parents,
Your legacy beats in my heart, inspiring me.
Rest in Peace

In my end is my beginning.
— T. S. ELIOT

The longest journey is the journey inward.
— DAG HAMMARSKJÖLD

PROLOGUE

HELLO. MY NAME IS Jaänjo—pronounced "Jon-jo." I am an intragalactic refugee, one of the few survivors of a dead world. After traversing seven thousand light-years as pure energy, I've arrived on a new planet teeming with life. To live again in physical form, I must convince one of this world's inhabitants to share its body with my alien consciousness.

Forgive me—I'm getting ahead of myself. Let me tell you why I'm here.

My home was once N'ridium, a world of vibrant oceans teeming with life, lush rainforests echoing with the songs of exotic birds, and towering snow-capped mountains that shimmered in the sunlight. Our advanced civilization flourished for millennia in the far reaches of what I've learned you call the Perseus Arm of the Milky Way galaxy. But all of that is gone now, swallowed by our sun in its death throes.

N'ridium's fate was sealed long before my ancestors' earliest memories due to our sun exhausting its hydrogen fuel—the elemental fuel that powers stars. Our ancient astronomers first observed the subtle signs of our sun's evolution, and each subsequent generation refined our understanding of the impending cosmic tragedy. This stellar aging, spanning millions of years, would transform our life-giving star into a bloated orb hundreds of times its original size.

Armed with this knowledge, we prepared for the inevitable future, developing incredible technologies for ambitious planetary preservation projects. Yet, despite our vast knowledge and tireless efforts, we could not prevent the looming catastrophe. Ultimately, all our preparations could only delay, not prevent, the extinction of our world.

Sadly, I never saw N'ridium as it once was. My birth coincided with the final stages of my planet's existence, where brutal temperatures and lethal radiation had already ravaged its surface. Like everyone else of my generation, I lived my entire life in subterranean cities, sheltered from the dying world above. Our underground hydroponic farms, a pale substitute for the vibrant bounty our world once yielded, barely sustained us as our society slowly unraveled.

Toward the end, in our shelters, each cycle of artificial light brought more pain as I watched friends and countless others succumb to the cruel grip of hunger and radiation sickness. The horror of our civilization's decline was a constant presence, weighing heavily on every N'ridian. I also nearly succumbed to the gnawing hunger that plagued us all. The memory of that suffering—both my own and that which I witnessed—is forever seared into my soul, a haunting reminder of my world's final days.

In our darkest hour, our brilliant scientists, one of whom was my brother, achieved a groundbreaking feat: transforming living beings into pure energy. This energy, encapsulating our essence, could be launched into space with the hope of finding refuge in a new habitable world. It was a desperate gamble, a leap of faith into the unknown.

I underwent this matter-to-energy conversion, becoming a beacon of hope amidst our world's final moments. As I hurtled through the vastness of space, N'ridium met its fiery end, swallowed by the sun, its once remarkable beauty and rich history forever lost to the indifferent cosmos.

My journey through the cosmos defied the conventional understanding of time and space. As pure energy, I existed in a timeless flux, free from physical constraints and aging. While my energy form allowed me to perceive the universe as a tapestry of forces and fields, with celestial bodies resonating with unique signatures, the reality of interstellar travel was far less dramatic.

As I traversed the immense void of space, a staggering emptiness that defies description enveloped me. Imagine an expanse so vast and empty that you could travel millions of miles without encountering a single atom—a void so absolute it challenges the concept of existence.

After journeying a staggering distance of over four quintillion miles from N'ridium, my quest for survival took an unexpected turn. Suddenly, a captivating pattern caught my attention—a vibrant concentration of energy manifesting as a sphere—a planet—cradled in the steady radiance of its star. This new world, slightly smaller than N'ridium, would become my new home. Soon, I would learn what the advanced lifeforms on this planet called it: Earth.

The stark contrast between Earth's vibrant life and the dying world I left behind filled me with awe—and torment. Let me explain. On N'ridium, our desperate bid to escape by morphing into pure energy had succeeded, but with a cruel twist. Our scientists lacked the time to master the reversal process, leaving us trapped in an ethereal limbo—aware but unable to truly live.

However, just before I departed N'ridium, our experts discovered a way to return to a physical state by intertwining our energy with an alien host possessing a similar biological makeup and life energy. This "fix" wasn't perfect; it would be a delicate dance with my essence weaving into the host. But this physical rebirth presented a moral quandary: How could I, a being who values the autonomy of others, even consider the possibility of forcefully inhabiting another's form? Yet, the alternative—remaining in a formless energy prison—seemed equally unbearable.

As I studied Earth, a symphony of vibrant energy unfolded before me, perceived not through physical senses but through an intricate dance of vibrations and frequencies. Each object and living thing hummed its own unique energy, revealing its essence to me. Amidst this abundance of life, one advanced lifeform stood out. Their energy signatures suggested an unexpected biological kinship to my kind. Interestingly, their level of technological development appeared far behind what we had achieved on N'ridium. In the days ahead, I would come to know what they called themselves: humans.

As I contemplated how to interact with these beings, a spark of inspiration ignited within me. I realized I could offer something every intelligent being craves—knowledge—the kind of knowledge that would dramatically enhance their understanding and abilities. In exchange, they could host my formless essence. The prospect of this unprecedented energy exchange intrigued me and perfectly aligned with my unique skills.

In my world, I was a healer, possessing a rare gift to perceive and manipulate auras—a person's life energy force. This ability manifested early in my life, allowing me to see the vibrant hues and patterns of energy emanating from every living being. I could sense emotional states, physical ailments, and even spiritual essences, giving me a deep understanding of the interconnectedness of all life. This unique perspective made me an exceptional healer, loosely akin to what humans call a physician.

Through a symbiotic partnership with a human, my energy could intertwine with the intricate bio-energy field of their body. Together, we could create a form of healing unlike anything Earth has ever witnessed. This collaboration could bring immense good, offering a chance to apply my rare gift in ways that could profoundly benefit those living on this planet.

This is why selecting a compatible host isn't simply about biology. To merge successfully, I need a human whose life energy force resonates with mine. Locating such a compatible individual will be daunting if the ability to perceive the interconnectedness of all life is as rare on this planet as it was on N'ridium. But I'm determined to succeed. My chance for a second physical life depends on it.

And so my quest to find a perfect partner on this captivating planet starts where I landed: Tenakee Springs, a small town on Chichagof Island, Alaska.

1

A CRISP BREEZE CARRYING the scent of kelp and brine whipped through Aan Gajaa's hair as she emerged from her cabin. She paused momentarily, letting the rising Alaskan sun warm her face. Sunlight glinted off her crutches as she surveyed the steep dirt trail leading to the main road and frowned—the loose rocks and gnarled roots on the trail promised another treacherous descent for her unsteady legs.

"One step at a time," she muttered, her voice barely discernible against the wind. She planted her first crutch with a determined inhale, easing her weight forward. Each step was a battle against gravity, a silent war between it and her body. Her legs protested every movement, a constant reminder of the muscle weakness and stiffness that plagued her.

A year ago, she had traversed this path with a single crutch, her pace slow but steady. Now, two crutches were necessary, each step a precarious gamble. The path mirrored her life with cruel precision, a stark reminder of the relentless advance of her multiple sclerosis.

Despite the physical toll, Aan's spirit remained unbroken. Though fatigue lined her thirty-year-old face, her eyes blazed with an indomitable spirit. She was a Tlingit woman, a descendant of a proud lineage. As she struggled down the path, she silently vowed to face this adversity with the same resilience her ancestors had shown in the face of countless challenges.

The town of Tenakee Springs knew Aan as more than just a woman battling MS. She was the sharp-witted bookkeeper for her family's fishing business, transforming numbers into profits and losses. Or at least, she used to. Now, the figures blurred and twisted, and simple calculations became monumental tasks.

She was also a Tlingit shaman, a mantle passed down from her grandmother. As a spiritual guide and healer, she guarded her people's ancient traditions and beliefs. The intricate rituals once performed with grace and fluidity now demanded painful concentration, her body resisting the movements her spirit yearned to express.

Sadly, MS was stealing more than her mobility and mental acuity; it eroded her independence, her identity, and her dreams. The vibrant days spent on the fishing boats, her laughter mingling with the cries of gulls, were now distant echoes. Now Aan could only watch from the shore as her family cast their nets, her heart aching with the knowledge that her active role in their lives was diminishing.

In her unhindered youth, Aan's beauty and warmth had captivated everyone, drawing attention wherever she went. But admirers dwindled as her reliance on crutches grew, replaced by pitying glances or averted eyes. Though her hopes of marriage and motherhood faded, a flicker of optimism remained—a stubborn ember refusing to be extinguished.

Aan's arduous descent felt endless, but she finally reached the bottom of the hill, her body aching and exhausted. She paused, drawing in a few deep breaths before continuing along the town's narrow, unpaved main road toward her family's harbor office. "Defeat is not an option," she whispered to herself. "Not today."

Inside the office, Aan's parents, Yéil and Keet, watched her through the window, their faces etched with concern as they observed her labored movements.

Keet sighed. "Look at her struggling, Yéil. Winter is nearly upon us, and she won't be able to walk to her cabin in the snow. She needs to move back to our home."

Tears welled in Yéil's eyes. "She cherishes her independence, but you're right. It won't be that long before she needs a wheelchair." She paused for a moment, her voice breaking. "What will we do when her condition gets even worse? We have no doctors, hospitals, or long-term care facilities here."

Keet nodded. "And there's your health to consider, too."

The unspoken truth hung heavy in the air: Juneau—the nearest big city—with its medical resources, loomed large in their future. Yet, despite the uncertainties, their hearts brimmed with love and determination. Together, they would face this new reality as a family, mirroring their daughter's resilience.

With a final push, Aan reached the office door, her chest heaving with the effort. Her mother opened the door and greeted her with a warm smile, masking her worry with practiced ease. "Hello, daughter. How are you feeling today?"

A wisp of pain flitted across Aan's face, momentarily marring the smile she offered her mother. "I'm hanging in there, Mom. Just a bit slower than usual." She moved towards her desk, her crutches tapping a steady rhythm on the wooden floor. "Today will be busy—I need to order fuel for the boats and finish the payroll."

But as Aan sank into her chair, the facade crumbled, and a wave of self-pity threatened to consume her. *"Can I make it through the day?"* she thought with a creeping sense of despair. A surge of anger and frustration quickly followed. Self-pity was a luxury she dared not indulge. "I am a warrior, a shaman, a daughter of the Tlingit people," she whispered aloud. "I will not yield to this darkness. I will fight, I will persevere—I will find a way to embrace life, even as my body betrays me."

With renewed determination, she turned to her work, ready to face whatever challenges the day might bring.

2

PERCHED HIGH ATOP A towering Sitka spruce, Jaänjo witnessed his sixth sunrise on this unfamiliar planet. Golden sunlight painted the Alaskan landscape as his ethereal form resonated with the sun's energy. Through his non-physical senses, he perceived the stirring of life in Tenakee Springs below—a tiny settlement nestled where the forest met the sea. The rhythmic pulses of existence echoed through him, revealing the intricate energy dances within this ecosystem.

From his lofty observatory, Jaänjo lamented his non-physical existence. Since departing N'ridium, he had existed as pure energy, untethered to any form. It was a life of boundless freedom, soaring through the cosmos unburdened by matter's constraints. Yet it was also a life of isolation, marked by a deep longing for what could be—the warmth of a touch, the wonder of sounds—and his dream of experiencing nature's unspoiled beauty.

Each day, Jaänjo observed the energy signatures of the town's lifeforms. Their patterns offered a fascinating glimpse into this new world, but the complex interplays remained indecipherable with no physical senses. As his curiosity intensified, so did his yearning for physical existence. To truly comprehend these novel sensations, he needed a compatible host—a being whose energy signature harmonized with his own.

Despair washed over him as he realized his current state rendered this impossible. Without eyes, he couldn't see auras, condemning his search for the perfect host to failure and extinguishing any hope of reclaiming his role as a healer. The thought of remaining formless forever was unbearable. Reluctantly, he considered a morally dubious solution: invading another being to see auras. It clashed with his values but seemed the only viable option.

This internal conflict gnawed at Jaänjo as he explored Tenakee Springs' ethereal landscape. Though now familiar with many residents' unique vibrations, discerning the subtleties of their life force was like trying to understand a painting through touch alone. The missing visual component was key to his salvation, but how could he obtain it without compromising his integrity?

On an afternoon excursion into town the next day, Jaänjo chanced upon a seemingly friendly encounter between two people. The energy signature of one—a male—resonated deeply with him, mirroring his warmth and compassion. Intrigued, Jaänjo followed the man, drawn to his gentle rhythm. He noticed, with concern, the man's frequent coughing.

At the man's modest hillside home overlooking the sea, Jaänjo sensed his deep care for his garden and the simple satisfaction he found in eating sun-warmed berries. Yet, beneath this contentment, Jaänjo also sensed the man's solitude—the quiet ache of a life lived mostly alone, the reasons for which Jaänjo could only speculate.

The more Jaänjo observed, the deeper his yearning grew to experience the world as this man did—to feel the sun warming his face, the wind rustling through his hair, and nature's pure offerings on his tongue.

After gardening, the man settled into a wooden contraption on his porch that moved rhythmically back and forth. This alone was a curious sight to Jaänjo. Reaching into his clothing, the man pulled out a small, cylindrical object, then another item. With a flick of his finger, a tiny flame erupted from the second object. He then touched the flame to the end of the cylinder.

To Jaänjo's surprise, the man placed the unlit end of the cylinder between his lips and inhaled deeply. When he exhaled, a cloud of toxic smoke billowed out. This act of apparent self-harm utterly baffled Jaänjo. It reminded him that there were still mysteries to unravel on this planet, facets of life he couldn't quite grasp.

Remarkably, after the man had smoked the first cylinder down to a stub, he grabbed another from his pocket and repeated the process. Jaänjo noted how the man's coughing markedly increased during this ritual.

As evening fell, the man entered his cabin. Jaänjo followed, witnessing more peculiar human behavior. The man ate from a container retrieved from a cool metal box. After finishing the meal, the man turned his attention to another metal container in the corner of the room. He added wood to it and ignited a fire, the flames quickly warming the cabin. Jaänjo watched, fascinated by the use of such a primal heat source.

Later, the man prepared for sleep. As he drifted off, temptation struck Jaänjo—now was his chance to take over the man's body, to experience the world through his senses. Revulsion washed over him as he floated closer. The idea of violating another being's autonomy contradicted every principle he held dear. Yet the desire to escape his formless existence, to experience the world's wonders once more, was a siren song he found increasingly difficult to resist.

For hours, Jaänjo wrestled with his conscience. He longed for physical sensations but questioned the cost. Could he sacrifice his principles for the pleasure of embodiment?

The man stirred, his energy rising. Jaänjo knew he had to decide. He could retreat, maintaining his integrity but remaining trapped in his ethereal prison, or succumb to temptation, betraying his ideals for a chance to experience life anew. The choice was agonizing. As Jaänjo contemplated merging, shame overwhelmed him. On N'ridium, the sanctity of individual consciousness was paramount. Healers like him believed interfering with another's mind was the gravest transgression.

As dawn broke, the man awoke and opened the window. Jaänjo withdrew from the house through the window, his essence fading into the morning mist.

Throughout the new day, Jaänjo brooded over the missed opportunity. That night, he resolved to try again, morals be damned. As twilight descended, his internal conflict intensified. The weight of his ethereal isolation pressed down on him, each moment a reminder of the sensations he craved. He thought of N'ridium, of his role as a healer, of the lives he could save in this new world. Wasn't the greater good worth compromising his principles? Yet, the idea of violating another's autonomy still repulsed him.

Jaänjo's thoughts oscillated between resolution and doubt. He imagined physical sensations—experiences tantalizingly close yet infinitely far. As night fell, desperation began to overshadow his moral reservations. The prospect of an eternity as a formless observer became unbearable.

"Just once," Jaänjo rationalized. *"I'll experience the physical world briefly, then return to my energy form. Surely, a momentary intrusion can be forgiven if it leads to a greater purpose?"* Even as he formed the thought,

he knew he was justifying the unjustifiable, but the pull of physicality had become irresistible.

After following the man throughout the next day, Jaänjo slipped into his house when he opened the door and waited for him to fall asleep. This time, unable to resist, Jaänjo merged his essence with the man, a silent invasion for the chance to once more experience the physical world.

Jaänjo's world exploded into a kaleidoscope of sensations. The rough texture of the blanket, the musty scent of the room, the pounding heart in his chest—it was overwhelming. Jaänjo gasped, his newly acquired lungs struggling to adjust.

Forcing himself to steady his breath, Jaänjo focused on exploring the man's mind. He gleaned the man's identity—Silas Tenhoff—and absorbed the nuances of English. Immersed in Silas's mind, Jaänjo uncovered insights into this unfamiliar world's customs, traditions, and history.

As Jaänjo delved deeper, a disquieting feeling grew. Something felt... off. He sensed a complexity to Silas's memories that he hadn't expected—layers that seemed to shift and change as he examined them.

A memory surfaced of Silas comforting a crying child. At first glance, it was heartwarming. However, as Jaänjo focused, he detected unmistakable insincerity—Silas's compassion was a mere mask, a carefully crafted facade.

Troubled, Jaänjo pushed further. He uncovered a memory of Silas accepting money from an older woman, ostensibly for charity. But accompanying the memory was smug satisfaction at having pulled off another successful con.

With growing horror, Jaänjo realized he had gravely misjudged Silas. Each memory revealed another layer of deception, another mask in Silas's arsenal of manipulation. The charming, compassionate man Jaänjo had observed was a crafted illusion.

As Silas's true nature came into focus, Jaänjo felt revulsion. He had violated his principles and betrayed his people's ethics, only to find himself trapped in the mind of a skilled fraud.

Jaänjo recognized the irony. In his desperation to experience physical sensations again, he had rushed to a decision that now left him feeling more trapped than ever. He realized his natural inclination to trust others would not serve him well in this new world.

As dawn approached, Jaänjo detected a change in Silas's brain activity. Panic surged through him as Silas woke. What would happen when Silas opened his eyes? Would Jaänjo be able to see as Silas saw?

Silas's eyelids fluttered open, and for the first time in what felt like an eternity, Jaänjo experienced vision. The dim light of early morning filled the room, and he marveled at the colors and shapes surrounding him.

Then, Silas's gaze fell upon a mirror across the room. Jaänjo saw the man's aura for the first time through Silas's eyes and inwardly gasped—it was a smoky black color, the signature of evil.

3

SILAS TENHOFF'S MORNINGS BEGAN with the same ritual: coughing, hacking, and expelling phlegm. He shuffled to the bathroom, depositing the mucus into the sink. His eyes scanned it for any ominous traces of red. The absence of blood brought a fleeting sense of relief, etching a small victory onto his weathered face before he washed it away down the drain.

As Silas looked in the mirror and combed his hair, Jaänjo recoiled within him. *"This is not my face, not my body,"* he thought. *"It's a borrowed vessel, a stolen life. I'm a healer, not a thief. What have I become? And this isn't even the worst—this man is pure evil."*

Even more troubling was the alarming clash between Silas's powerful negative energy and Jaänjo's positive essence. Silas was like a relentless parasite, draining Jaänjo's positive energy. Jaänjo knew he couldn't stay in this man's body for long. His only escape, without possible detection, was while the man slept.

Jaänjo sighed, accepting this grim reality. But a glimmer of hope emerged: if Silas ventured into town again, Jaänjo could use the time to learn more about Tenakee Springs. And he could see the auras of people. *"Make the best of this,"* Jaänjo told himself. *"Just twelve more hours, and then you can leave this evil creature."*

Silas reached for a shaver but stopped, glancing in the mirror again. A sly grin spread across his face. "No need to shave until tomorrow when the rich ladies come to town on the charter boat," he mused aloud. "Then it's time to turn on the charm and lighten a few wallets." He chuckled, already calculating which sob story would work best. "Maybe I'll be a struggling artist... or a widower with medical bills. Rich ladies love a good cause."

Jaänjo, privy to these thoughts, felt disgusted at Silas's casual duplicity.

Back in the bedroom, Silas casually lit a cigarette and took a deep drag. The burning tip cast a soft, almost seductive glow, yet revulsion stirred within Jaänjo from the acrid odor of the smoke.

"The irony is not lost on me," Jaänjo reflected. *"Here I am, desperate to embrace physical sensations once more, only to find that not all experiences are as pleasant as I had hoped."*

After a few inhalations, Silas's lungs absorbed a rush of chemicals from the smoke, which entered his bloodstream and traveled to his brain. Jaänjo felt a tingling sensation, a subtle buzz of euphoria that seemed to silence the chaos in his host's mind. As wisps of smoke enveloped Silas, Jaänjo understood the allure of cigarettes—and the man's endless cycle of craving and consumption. As a healer, he recognized it for what it was: classic addiction—chasing the elusive bliss that always seemed just out of reach.

Silas sighed with a satisfied sigh and ground the glowing ember into the overflowing ashtray—a dented metal can brimming with the ghosts of dozens of other cigarettes. He pushed open the creaky wooden door of his cabin, stepping out into the bright morning sunlight.

Within Silas, Jaänjo reveled in the sensations. Every sight, every sound, every smell was a revelation. The world felt like a kaleidoscope of vibrant colors and textures, a rich cacophony of familiar and strange sounds. It was as if he experienced everything for the first time.

The sun's warmth on Silas's face felt like a gentle caress to Jaänjo, a stark contrast to the cool air that nipped at his ears. The scent of woodsmoke filled the air, a complex fragrance that soothed and invigorated him. The earthy smell mingled with the sweet scent of wildflowers blooming defiantly by the roadside—a testament to nature's resilience.

As Silas walked, the sound of children's laughter, a melody of pure joy, mingled with the rhythmic cadence of people's footsteps on the hard-packed earth and gravel main road. Each sensation was like a note in a symphony, filling Jaänjo with awe and wonder. It starkly contrasted the emptiness he once knew, and he drank it in—every sight, sound, and scent reminded him of the vibrant world he now inhabited.

Gradually, Jaänjo became aware of another layer of perception emerging. The ability to see auras, dormant since his transformation into pure energy, began resurfacing. At first, it was subtle—faint glimmers of light surrounding the people they passed. But with each step, the auras became clearer and more vibrant. Jaänjo felt a surge of excitement. This was what he had been waiting for, the key to finding a suitable host. He focused his attention, eager to unravel the mysteries hidden within these ethereal manifestations of life energy.

Silas continued eastward towards the rising sun, smiling and nodding at passersby. The rustic charm of the wooden buildings lining the town's unpretentious main street captivated Jaänjo. Their long shadows stretched out in the gentle morning light, playfully reaching towards him. Jaänjo delighted in seeing the auras of the townsfolk they encountered, most radiating a modest white glow—the color of pure, positive energy.

To Jaänjo's dismay, their stroll ended too soon at a modest, two-story clapboard building nestled against the shoreline. The quaint structure, painted in various shades of green with white accents and anchored by dark green double doors, proudly displayed its name in black lettering upon a slender red plank: "Party Time Bakery."

An attractive woman greeted Silas as he walked in. Her eyes sparkled with recognition. "Hello, Silas! Do you want your usual?"

Silas's lips curved into a charming smile. "You know me so well. Yes, I'll have my usual, please."

Among an eclectic mix of tables and chairs, Silas sat by the front windows. Jaänjo eagerly took it all in, especially the heavenly smells of freshly baked goods. An impressive assortment of local artwork—some of it for sale—adorned the walls of the beautifully restored historic building. The place exuded a wonderfully cozy and inviting atmosphere.

A few moments later, she arrived with a steaming cup of coffee and a plate holding an enormous cinnamon roll. Compared to the near-starvation diet Jaänjo experienced toward the end of his home planet, this six-inch-high marvel seemed absurdly large for one person.

Silas nodded thanks and eagerly claimed the dessert that dared to call itself breakfast. As the first bite of bready, gooey, icing-laden delight hit his tongue, a shockwave of pure ecstasy coursed through Jaänjo. Never had he tasted such a sublime combination of warmth, sweetness, and texture. It was as if a universe of flavor had exploded within his consciousness. *"Oh,"* he thought, *"how utterly delightful this is!"*

Silas also marveled at the confectionary masterpiece. "Sir, you're a culinary genius!" he yelled to the baker behind the counter.

The man left the counter and approached Silas with a warm smile. "Thanks for the compliment. How's your day shaping up?"

Silas swallowed another bite before responding, "I'm heading over to see Keet Gajaa. The engine on his boat died again."

"Argh. Well, let's hope it's an easy fix. Do you want me to make you a turkey sandwich to go?"

"Nah," Silas shook his head. "I'll come back after working and have a meal then."

After finishing breakfast and paying the bill, Silas strolled the short distance to Keet's family business, perched on pilings on the rocky shore. Still obsessing over the marvelous cinnamon roll and marveling at gull cries overhead, Jaänjo scarcely noticed Silas approaching the building.

Upon seeing Silas through the window, Keet Gajaa rose from his chair, walked out, and greeted him with a firm handshake. "Thanks for coming, Silas. I appreciate you coming on such short notice. This engine's been nothing but trouble."

"Happy to help, Keet," Silas replied, his tone sympathetic. "How's the fishing been? Must be tough with all these mechanical issues."

Keet's shoulders slumped, the weight of his worries visible in his posture. "It's been a struggle. We're barely breaking even some weeks. And with Aan's condition..."

Silas placed a comforting hand on Keet's shoulder, his voice softening. "I understand. Tell you what—I'll see what I can do about giving you a discount on this repair."

Gratitude shone in Keet's eyes. "That's very kind of you. We appreciate it more than you know."

Silas nodded and offered a friendly smile. "Let's take a look at that engine. Hopefully, I won't be here long."

As Keet led Silas into the office, the sight of a young woman deeply immersed in her computer work stunned Jaänjo. Her aura—a breathtaking white glow of pure energy, the largest and most dazzling he had ever seen on Earth or N'ridium—left him awestruck.

4

"Wait! Go back to the woman in the chair and let me see her!" Jaänjo thought as Keet Gajaa led Silas past her and out the office's back door. But Silas, oblivious to Jaänjo's desires, followed Keet onto the pier.

The sturdy fishing boat, *"The Spirit of the Tides,"* bobbed gently on the water. Its thirty-foot hull bore the proud scars of countless fishing expeditions, its weathered wooden frame a testament to its enduring strength. Designed for the narrow coastal channels, the vessel's modest size and rugged build spoke of a life lived on the sea. Each weathered plank held a story, a silent witness to the family's reliance on the ocean's bounty.

"She's a beauty, Keet," Silas remarked, his eyes roaming over the practical layout and essential fishing gear adorning the deck.

Keet, a Tlingit native with a face etched by years of seafaring, smiled with pride. "Thanks, Silas. She's been in the family for three generations now. My father bought her when I was just a teen."

As they boarded the vessel, Jaänjo noted its primitive yet practical design. Having lived underground on N'ridium, boats were entirely foreign to him. The wooden structure and manual controls stood in vivid contrast to the automated systems of his home world. Yet, he couldn't help but admire how well-suited this boat seemed for its purpose on this watery planet.

"Let's head to the engine room," Keet said, leading the way.

Inside the cramped engine room, Jaänjo's fascination deepened. He intently watched as Silas navigated the maze of pipes, hoses, and auxiliary equipment surrounding the marine diesel engine. The sheer number of components crammed into this small space, each seemingly vital to the boat's operation, amazed him.

"Alright, let's see what we've got here," Silas muttered, his hands moving with practiced expertise over the engine's components.

As Silas worked, Jaänjo pondered the vast technological gap between Earth and N'ridium. *"How can I adapt to this world of manual labor and archaic machinery?"* he wondered, baffled by the reliance on such outdated methods. *"And yet,"* he thought, *"these technological relics are oddly intriguing."*

After about an hour of examination, Silas straightened up, wiping his hands on a rag. "I've found the problem, Keet. Let's head back to the office to discuss it."

Once they were back in the office, Silas delivered his diagnosis. "Well, Keet, you've got a fuel injector problem. They're all clogged up with deposits and grime."

Keet's face fell. "How bad is it?"

Silas put on a show of consideration before responding. "I need to replace the injectors, which aren't cheap. But I guarantee, once the new ones are in, your engine will purr like a kitten."

Jaänjo, privy to Silas's thoughts, knew the truth: the injectors only needed a thorough cleaning, a simple task costing a fraction of what Silas intended to charge. The ease with which Silas lied disturbed Jaänjo deeply. Was such deceit commonplace on Earth? How could a society function with such casual dishonesty?

Silas pulled out his smartphone, tapping away at the screen. "Give me a few moments to look up the cost for the parts I'll need."

Keet nodded, worry lines deepening on his forehead. As Silas manipulated the numbers, inflating the labor costs, Jaänjo's essence recoiled. When Silas handed his phone to Keet, the fabricated quote displayed was an egregious overcharge.

Keet's shoulders slumped as he looked at the figure. "That's... that's a lot more than I was expecting, Silas."

"I know it's not easy, Keet," Silas said, his voice dripping with false sympathy. "But think of it as an investment in your livelihood. I can express ship the parts from Juneau; installing them will only take me a day."

Keet sighed heavily, then nodded. "Okay, let's do it." He handed the phone to his daughter, who frowned when she saw the price.

"Great!" Silas exclaimed, barely concealing his glee. "I'll order the parts today. Don't worry—once I do my thing, your engine will be good as new."

Jaänjo cringed at Silas's exploitation of such a kind family. Most troubling was how Silas seemed to revel in his deceit rather than feeling any remorse. *"I so want to part company with this man,"* Jaänjo mused.

Silas turned his attention to the woman at the computer, whose aura had captivated Jaänjo earlier. "Aan, how are you today?"

As she swiveled her chair to face them, Jaänjo's awareness was once again overwhelmed by her ethereal beauty. Her luminous aura enveloped her, casting a soft, radiant glow illuminating the air around her.

"Never have I encountered such a pure aura," Jaänjo marveled. *"Could she be the one I've been searching for?"*

As quickly as that thought came to him, his excitement waned as he noticed subtle disturbances in the aura's brilliance—flashes of angry red that pulsed intermittently. *"But those red flashes... what ailment plagues her? And would it be right to burden her with my presence if she's already struggling?"*

Aan's gaze met Silas's, and for a moment, Jaänjo felt as if she could see right through Silas and into his essence. "Hi, Silas. I'm fine, thanks," she said, her voice soft but clear. She glanced down at the phone screen, her brow furrowing. "These numbers look high to me. Are you sure they're accurate?" Her eyes narrowed slightly as she studied Silas. "You seem different today. Lighter, somehow."

Jaänjo's surprise was palpable. *"She senses my presence!"* he thought, stunned. *"But how? Is her perception linked to her extraordinary aura?"*

Silas laughed off her comment about him seeming "lighter." "Different? Must be your imagination, Aan. As for the numbers, they're spot on. I'll even show you the invoice from the supplier when the parts come in."

Aan's nod was hesitant, her doubt evident. "Alright," she muttered, returning to her screen. But her eyes held a flicker of suspicion.

As Silas left the building and stepped onto the main street, he paused to light a cigarette. The familiar acrid smell filled Jaänjo's awareness, and he mentally flinched.

"Here we go again," Jaänjo thought bitterly. *"Smoke, hack, cough—smoke another cigarette, then hack and cough some more. It's unbearable that this man poisons himself while I, a healer, am trapped within him. Each inhale of smoke is an insult to my purpose."*

He paused, reflecting on Silas's grim condition and the irony of the situation. *"If you knew the state of your lungs, maybe you'd give up this disgusting habit. But given your treatment of others, as you Earthlings say, 'What goes around comes around.' Your body seems set on delivering this cosmic justice."*

As Silas continued down the street, Jaänjo felt compelled to leave him for two reasons: the moral cost of staying in Silas was too high, and Silas's dark energy rapidly draining his positive energy was too severe. As his thoughts turned to Aan, Jaänjo knew that this time, no matter what, he wouldn't enter her body without her explicit permission. Yet, as pure energy, he'd have no way to communicate with her. As Silas rounded a corner, Jaänjo grappled with how to solve this seemingly impossible problem. His fate hung in the balance.

5

As LUCK WOULD HAVE it, Silas retired early that night, leaving his window slightly ajar. Once Silas drifted off, Jaänjo seized the opportunity and left his body. As pure energy, he effortlessly traversed the gap in the window and ventured into the enveloping darkness.

Safely away from Silas, amidst the towering spruce trees, Jaänjo felt the draining effects of their encounter. Silas's negativity had severely depleted his energy, leaving him weak and in need of rejuvenation.

As much as he detested Silas, Jaänjo already missed the physical sensations he experienced through him and loathed being trapped in his ghostly prison once more. Learning the human language was one good thing about being in Silas's body. Another good thing was that Jaänjo observed how human vocalizations created distinct patterns of air pressure fluctuations. These rapid, intricate variations in pressure, imperceptible to most, were a symphony to his energy form. With incredible focus, Jaänjo learned to translate these pressure variations into recognizable words.

As the night progressed, Jaänjo drifted among the towering spruce trees, his essence mingling with the ethereal energy of the Alaskan wilderness. The tranquil solitude was a welcome contrast to the turmoil he'd experienced within Silas. He sensed the faint twinkle of distant stars, a reminder of his long journey across the cosmos.

With the breaking dawn, Jaänjo felt his strength returning. The sun's energy, filtering through the trees, invigorated him. As the morning wore on, his resolve crystallized: he would focus on observing Aan, seeking to unravel the mysteries surrounding her. The feeling that she might be the ideal host was intoxicating, yet he tempered his excitement with caution, determined not to repeat his mistake with Silas.

When the sun reached its zenith, Jäänjo headed back to town, drawn by thoughts of Aan. Outside Keet's office, he sensed Silas approaching and followed him inside.

"Hey, Keet—I've got the parts for you!" Silas announced, setting a box on the table with a thud. He handed a paper to Aan. "And here's the receipt, minus my labor charge, of course." Silas leaned toward her, lowering his voice. "Between us, Aan, I pulled some strings to get these here so quickly. I called in a few favors—at no charge to you."

"That was fast," she remarked, impressed.

Silas nodded, his face a picture of false modesty. "These parts are top of the line. They cost a bit more upfront, but it'll save you in the long run. Keet, let's head to the boat. I'll have these installed in no time."

As Keet and Silas left, Jäänjo remained, once again captivated by Aan. He yearned for physical eyes to see her beauty and brilliant aura, even as he worried about the troubling red flashes he had observed before.

Moments later, Aan turned to her mother. "Mom, do you feel anything odd in here?"

Her mother looked puzzled. "Odd, how?"

Aan shook her head. "Yesterday, when Silas was here, something felt different about him. After he left, that odd feeling disappeared. When Silas came back in just now, I felt it again. Even though he's on the boat now, I still feel something odd in here, like a presence."

Her mother's eyes twinkled. "You're just like my shaman mother. She always said she could sense spirits."

Aan smiled. "I'll take that as a compliment."

As the day progressed, Jäänjo sensed Aan's energy dwindling. Her mother also observed the change. "Aan, you can't stop yawning. Why don't you call it a day, go home, and get some rest? Or you can stay at our place to save you from walking up the hill to your cabin. As an enticement, I'll make your favorite dinner."

"That's tempting," Aan replied, her voice tinged with fatigue, "especially not walking up the hill. But I always sleep better in my comfortable bed. Plus, I still have the fish casserole you gave me, so I'll have that for dinner."

Yéil sighed. "I'm getting concerned about you falling when going up and down the path to your cabin. We're all ignoring the obvious—your MS is progressing, and changes will soon need to happen. Your dad and I want you to move back into our home."

Aan remained silent for a long moment. "I... I can't talk about this right now," she whispered.

Her mother nodded, got up, and embraced her. "I know how hard this is on you, but just know that your dad and I are here for you—no matter what happens, we'll always be here for you."

"I love you and Dad so much," Aan said, a tear rolling down her cheek. "Mom, my spirit is losing the battle with MS."

"I know. So does your Dad. In the days ahead, let's discuss the changes that must happen."

Aan sighed, too exhausted to argue, and nodded.

Jaänjo's essence vibrated with empathy as he interpreted the subtle fluctuations in air pressure, translating them into the words exchanged between Aan and her mother. A deep yearning to offer solace or aid consumed him, but his disembodied state rendered him helpless.

As Aan prepared to leave, the cruel reality of her condition became painfully apparent. Her legs trembled as she stood, her hands fumbling for her crutches. Each movement was a battle against her failing body, a desperate struggle to maintain dignity in the face of MS's relentless assault.

The afternoon sun streamed through the office windows, its warmth contrasting with the chill creeping into Aan's life. As Aan said her goodbyes to her mother, Jaänjo's resolve strengthened. *"I'll find a way to help her. But it will be on her terms, with her full understanding and consent. I won't repeat the mistake I made with Silas."*

After Aan laboriously made her way out, tears fell from her mother's eyes. For the first time, she witnessed her daughter's unwavering spirit beginning to yield to her illness.

Despite Aan's admission of struggle, her resilience in the face of her illness moved Jaänjo deeply. As he followed her, he vowed to be a silent, invisible guardian for this remarkable woman. Whatever challenges lay ahead, he somehow knew his path was now inextricably linked with Aan's, for better or worse.

6

AAN WALKED TWO HUNDRED feet down Tenakee Springs' three-mile-long main street to reach the path leading to her cabin. It felt like a marathon, and this was the easy part. Now came the uphill dirt trail—filled with rocks and tree roots—that led to her cabin. She paused to catch her breath before resuming her arduous journey. After a few steps, the trees and bushes along the trail enveloped her, obscuring her from view from the main road and leaving her isolated and alone.

Each uphill step tortured her; her hands cramped from the tight grip on her crutches. Pausing again, she struggled to catch her breath. "Come on, Aan—keep going, you can do this," she whispered. Three steps later, one of her crutches slipped on an exposed root, upsetting her balance. She fell hard, kicking up dust as she hit the hard-packed earth. "Aah!" she cried out in pain.

Jaänjo watched in horror as she fell, powerless to help her.

Aan lay still for a few moments, assessing whether she had broken a bone or twisted an ankle. Aside from the general pain from the impact, she felt relatively okay. She summoned her strength, used her crutches for leverage, and pushed herself upright. Feeling unsteady, she glanced back down the path, contemplating whether it would be wise to return to town. She mentally calculated the distance to her cabin and her parents' home, determining that the shortest route was to her cabin. However, she failed to account for the challenge of battling gravity on the uphill journey.

Several agonizing uphill steps later, the muscles in her right hand gave out, causing it to slip from the crutch. Aan spiraled downward, landing on her back. The impact knocked the air out of her lungs. Gasping for breath, she unleashed her frustration and despair into the open sky with an angry scream, pounding the ground with her hands. That's when her tears started; her pathetic cry turned into a full-out wail as her anguish vented itself openly.

"Spirits, hear me!" she shouted to the sky. "My strength is gone. I beg for your aid—please help me." Her voice faded to a pitiful whisper. "Please help me..."

Jaänjo couldn't bear to witness her suffering any longer. In desperation, he surrounded Aan with his energy. He emitted an electromagnetic field, modulating its frequency enough to cause subtle movements in the air molecules around him, creating a gentle breeze that began to caress Aan—a silent gesture of comfort and care.

Aan experienced the same strange sensation she had felt at the office—a palpable presence. "I sense you. Please help me home." Almost immediately, she felt lighter and managed to rise to her feet. With hesitant steps, she moved forward—one step at a time, slow and unsteady. Yet, with each step, she felt a newfound determination. Gradually, clumsily, she began to make progress. Finally, her cabin came into view.

Inside her cabin, Aan collapsed onto her cushioned chair. She sighed, knowing her days living alone in her cherished cabin had ended. As quickly as that thought entered her awareness, another, more powerful feeling sprang forth. She felt the presence again—the same one she felt at the office, only it was much more intense here.

"Whatever you are, I know you're here. Please reveal yourself to me," Aan implored softly, her voice trembling. In response, Jaänjo emerged before her, a soft, ethereal glow. His luminescence flickered and faded as abruptly as it had appeared.

Shocked, a soft gasp escaped Aan's lips. She gathered her thoughts, her mind racing with questions and possibilities. "Are you here to harm me?" There was no response. "Do you understand what I just asked?" Jaänjo responded with a single quick glow. "Okay, please glow once for yes and twice for no. Can you do that?" A single quick glow appeared.

"Okay, good. Are you here to harm me? Two short glows appeared. "Are you a spirit? A spirit of my ancestors?" Two soft glows. "Are you some kind of alien, an alien from another planet?"

Jaänjo's essence quivered with excitement and apprehension. *"She understands!"* he thought. *"But how can I explain my true nature and my desperate need for a host? How can I convey the complexity of my situation through mere yes or no responses?"* He longed to share his story, to explain the destruction of N'ridium, his journey across the cosmos, and his hope for redemption. But for now, these simple yes or no glows were his only means of communication. He focused his energy, determined to make the most of this unexpected opportunity. He gave one soft glow.

"Oh, my goodness, why are you here?" No response. "I guess you can't answer that with a simple yes or no glow, correct?" Another single glow.

"You were at my office today and yesterday, weren't you?" A single glow. "You were on the trail with me today, weren't you?" Another single glow. "Do you understand human feelings?" A single glow. "You were the gentle breeze that comforted me when I fell, right?" A single glow. "Thank you."

She thought for a few more moments. "When Silas was in my office today, you came in with him, right?" A single glow. "Something is confusing me. You didn't go with him when he left to go to our boat, right?" A single glow. "I sensed today you were apart from him, but it felt like you were in Silas when I saw him yesterday. Am I correct?" A single glow. "Are you telling me that you can enter into someone?" A single glow. "Why did you enter Silas?" No response. "Did you hurt him in any way?" Two glows. "Why did you enter into him?" No response. "Are you not responding again because it's too complicated to say with just a yes or no response?" A single glow. "Is there a reason you chose to be with me?" A single glow. "Wow. Do you want something from me?" No response. "Too complicated to say again?" A single glow.

Aan sat for a while, her mind racing. "So, if you entered Silas, can you also enter into me?" A single glow. "Did you ask Silas to enter into his body?" The reply was slower than his previous replies. Two glows. "Are you saying you entered Silas without his permission?" Another slow response—one glow.

She frowned and thought some more. "Then why don't you enter into me without my permission like you did with Silas?" No response. "If I allowed you to enter me, would you?" A single glow. "Why would you want to enter me?" No response. "If you entered me, and I asked you to leave, would you?" A bright, single glow followed. "That's good to know. Okay, let me think. What would be the reason for you to want to enter my body...

"Do you want to take anything from me, like my brain or something?" Two fast glows. "If you entered into me, would this allow you to somehow talk to me?" A bright single glow. "Like in movies about aliens, would you want to impregnate me or suck away my life's energy for food—you know, stuff like that?" Two bright glows. "Do you have something to offer me? I don't mean this in a greedy way. I mean, I'm struggling right now, so could you help me in any way?" A single glow.

Aan hesitated before replying. "Could you cure my disease?"

Hope and frustration surged through Jaänjo as he struggled with the constraints of their limited communication. *"Yes, I could heal you,"* he thought, *"but at what cost? How can I convey the complexity of merging our essences, which would be far more extreme than a simple cure."* He responded with a bright single glow.

She gasped. "How would you cure me?" No response. "Are you some sort of healer, like a doctor on your planet?" A single glow. "Do you have some sort of medicine that will cure me?" No response. "Can you heal injuries?" A single glow. "Diseases, too?" A single glow. "Wow." Aan sat for a few moments, intrigued.

"Are you here with others of your kind to invade and take over Earth?" Two strong glows followed. "Are you alone here on Earth?" A single glow. "Do you have a family back on your planet?" One glow. "Your parents?" Two glows. "A sibling or siblings?" One glow. "Do you have a name?" A single glow. "Are you visible to other humans?" Two glows. "Can you read my thoughts?" No response.

Aan thought some more. "Do you believe in spirits or a higher power?" A single glow. "Interesting. Are you a nice alien?" A single glow. "Do you know what love is?" A bright single glow. "Do you possess an understanding of right and wrong?" A single glow. "Do you respect other life forms?" A bright single glow. "Do you avoid causing harm?" A single glow. "Do you practice kindness?" A bright single glow. "Do you seek peaceful solutions?" A single glow. "Do you care for the environment?" A single glow. "Do you respect traditions?" A single glow. "That's good—traditions are very important to me and my people. Do you act with integrity?" A single glow.

"You sound like a good person—I mean, a good alien. I wish I could see you face-to-face. Can I touch you?" A single glow. Aan reached out and gently moved her arms in front of her. "I can't feel you. Are you some kind of energy?" A single glow. "Do you want to be my friend?"

Jaänjo's essence pulsed with warmth at Aan's question. *"Friend,"* he mused. *"Such a simple word for such a complex question."* He wished he could tell her that what he offered was more than just friendship—it was a deep connection that went beyond anything she—or he—had ever known. He wished he could convey his loneliness, his desperate need for connection after his long journey through the cosmos. But more than that, he wanted her to understand the depth of his commitment to her well-being. *"Yes, I want to be your friend,"* he thought, *"but also your healer and a bridge to understanding the universe in ways you've never imagined."* His essence glowed once, hoping to convey through light what he couldn't express in words.

She looked at the clock on the wall. "Do you know about the concept of human time?" A single glow. She looked at the clock on her wall. "It's nearly five o'clock. If I said you could enter my body for thirty minutes, would you leave me when that time is up?" A single glow. "Do you promise you'll leave me in exactly thirty minutes?" A single glow. "And you'll promise not to hurt me in any way?" A bright single glow.

She weighed all that he said. "Will it hurt when you enter me?" Two large glows. "Okay, let's do it. You have my permission to enter my body for thirty minutes. Thirty minutes."

7

WITH APPREHENSION AND EXCITEMENT, Aan took a deep breath. She had just granted an extraterrestrial lifeform permission to enter her body. She braced herself, closed her eyes, and tried to relax. Her pounding heart drowned out all other noises in the cabin.

She felt a sudden warmth spread through her body. The sensation wasn't unpleasant—more like a gentle, enveloping hug. As the warmth reached her core, Aan felt a light pressure in her mind, as if something was gently knocking, seeking entry. She instinctively knew this was the alien.

"It's okay," she whispered. "You can come in."

The pressure increased slightly, and suddenly, she felt a rush of energy flow into her. Her body tingled—for a moment, she felt as if she were floating. Her vision blurred and then sharpened, colors becoming more vivid and details crisper. She felt an overwhelming sense of clarity and awareness as if a fog had lifted in her mind.

The alien's presence settled within her, a gentle yet distinct entity in her consciousness. He didn't feel intrusive; instead, it was as if he was sitting quietly in her consciousness, observing and waiting. Aan took a deep breath, marveling at the sensation. "Are you okay?" she asked aloud, unsure if he could hear her thoughts. She glanced at the clock, noting how much time had passed.

A warm, reassuring feeling spread through her, and she somehow knew it was the alien's way of saying yes.

"Hello, Aan. My name is Jaänjo. I'm so very delighted to meet you."

"Wow," she said aloud. "This is... incredible. I'm also pleased to meet you, Jaänjo."

After experiencing these new sensations for several moments, Aan spoke again. "Jaänjo, tell me more about who you are and where you came from."

Jaänjo paused, aware of the ticking clock. He wanted to share everything but knew he had to be concise. "Okay, but it's a hard story to tell." His voice quivered with emotion as he spoke. "My planet, called N'ridium, was located in the far reaches of what you Earthlings call the Milky Way galaxy. Unfortunately, our sun started running out of fuel, causing it to expand and grow hotter and larger. It started swallowing the planets in our solar system. As the sixth planet from our sun, we had enough time to build underground cities to survive, but not even that could save us as our sun crept closer. Our hydroponic farms couldn't grow enough food, and..." He choked up. "Most of us didn't survive."

He sighed, burdened with sadness. "But we didn't give up. We devised a way to convert our bodies into pure energy. I volunteered for this matter-to-energy conversion and surrendered my physical form, dissolving into a stream of energy that held the blueprint of life. Then, we were launched in all directions into the cosmos, hoping to find a new home somewhere in the universe. That's how I came to Earth."

"That's so sad," Aan said softly. "Why don't you convert back to a physical form now that you're here?"

"We couldn't perfect the reversal process. Those of us who converted are trapped in an ethereal limbo—aware but unable to truly live."

Aan sighed. "So, you can only experience being physical again by being in another living being?"

"Yes," Jaänjo confirmed.

"Is that why you entered Silas without his permission?"

"Yes, but there's more to that story than I can explain in our limited time."

Aan nodded, her mind racing with questions. "You mentioned you could cure my disease. Is that really possible?"

"It is. I was a healer on my planet. Being inside you now, I see how your body's communication system is malfunctioning. Imagine your nerves as vital pathways, with the protective myelin covering acting as insulation. Your immune system is mistakenly attacking this myelin, causing 'short circuits' that disrupt the transmission of messages. This is what's causing your muscle weakness, numbness, difficulties with coordination, and everything else bothering you. All I have to do is repair this damage to restore your body's communication network."

"How will you do this, and how long will it take? By the way, on my planet, what you described is known as multiple sclerosis."

"I wish I had more time to explain the details," Jaänjo said. "The key will be tuning our two energies to function harmoniously. By focusing my energy and subtly guiding yours, we'll fix the glitches in your body's communication network. As for how long it will take, my guess is about an hour or two."

"Two hours?" Aan gasped. "You're saying I could be cured in two hours?"

"We could try to do it sooner, but combining our mutual energies might be challenging initially."

Aan hesitated, her mind racing. Was she being reckless, trusting this alien entity so quickly? The prospect of a cure was tempting, but at what cost? She thought of her parents and the Tlingit teachings about spirits and otherworldly beings. Her grandmother's voice echoed in her mind, speaking of respect for the unseen forces of the world. Was this alien one such force? Or was she betraying her heritage by embracing something so foreign?

But then she remembered her fall on the trail, the constant struggle against her failing body. If there was even a chance of healing, didn't she owe it to herself to take it? She took a deep breath, steeling herself for whatever might come.

"Jaänjo," she said, her voice firm despite her inner turmoil, "I want to trust you, but I need to know if there are any risks to this healing process. And what exactly do you gain from this?"

Jaänjo was quiet for a moment. "Aan, I appreciate your caution. It's wise to question, especially in a situation as unnatural as this. The healing process poses no danger to you, but the sensation might be intense. You may feel tingling, warmth, or even brief discomfort as your nervous system recalibrates."

He paused before continuing. "As for what I gain... it's complex. I'll fulfill my purpose as a healer, gain experience, and..." he hesitated, "a connection. A chance to be part of something again after being alone for so long."

Aan considered his words. "And after healing me? What then?"

"That's where things become more complicated," Jaänjo admitted. "I hope for a continued partnership, but the nature of that partnership is something we'd need to discuss at length. I promise you, Aan, I will never do anything without your full understanding and consent."

Aan nodded, processing this information. "If I want you to leave at any point, will you?"

"Without hesitation," Jaänjo assured her. "Your autonomy is paramount to me."

Aan took a deep breath, feeling apprehension and hope. "Okay, Jaänjo. I'm ready to try this. When can we start?"

"Tomorrow," Jaänjo said. "You need rest after today's ordeal. I promise to heal you with no conditions attached except that you'll listen to what I propose about the future. Does this sound fair?"

"It does," Aan agreed, her voice betraying her exhaustion and excitement.

"It's time for me to leave now," Jaänjo said. "I'll return in the morning."

"You don't have to leave, Jaänjo. You're welcome to stay inside of me for the night."

"I'd like that," said Jaänjo, "but we'd be up all night talking if I did."

Aan laughed, her mood noticeably uplifted. "You're right. Jaänjo, as odd as it sounds, I feel a powerful connection to you."

"I feel it, too. Goodnight, Aan."

"Goodnight, Jaänjo."

With that, Jaänjo left her body for the night. As Aan drifted off to sleep, she felt a strange mix of emotions—hope for the healing to come, lingering caution about trusting an alien entity, and a surprising sense of loss at Jaänjo's departure. She fell asleep, wondering what the morning would bring and how this encounter might change not just her health but her understanding of the universe and her place in it.

8

THOUGHTS OF JAÄNJO, THE alien who had filled her with such glorious sensations, kept Aan tossing and turning in her bed. The prospect of being healed from the dreadful disease ravaging her body filled her with giddy anticipation.

She awoke with the sunrise, eager for the day. "Jaänjo, are you here?" A bright glow immediately appeared before her.

"Good morning. Yesterday, you manifested as a luminous glow. Could you show me a visual representation of your physical form on N'ridium? I'd love to see what you looked like."

A single pulse of light flickered, and Jaänjo materialized before Aan. His luminous, remarkably humanoid form stood slightly taller than an average human. An ethereal glow softened his features, while large, expressive eyes radiated wisdom and warmth, hinting at depths of knowledge beyond his youthful appearance.

Jaänjo's bearing exuded vitality and poise, reminiscent of a human in their late twenties, yet with an underlying maturity suggesting far greater experience. Though the shimmering light obscured finer details, his striking presence was undeniable. His eyes, pools of kindness, conveyed profound compassion, and an unmistakable smile played across his face, both welcoming and reassuring.

His stunning appearance mesmerized Aan. "Oh, my, Jaänjo, you're breathtaking. May I touch you?" Jaänjo's glow pulsed once. Taking this as a signal, Aan reached out to touch his face, only to find it passing through his glow as if through air. She sighed, a pang of disappointment flitting across her face. "I wish I could give you a proper hello with a hug."

He moved closer and enveloped her with his light. The gentlest hug she had ever received flooded her with an overwhelming sense of peace and comfort. Aan closed her eyes, savoring the moment.

"Jaänjo," she whispered, "when the time feels right, please merge your energy with mine once more."

Like yesterday, a sudden warmth spread through her body, feeling as pleasant as the hug he had just given her. Once more, an overwhelming sense of clarity and awareness filled her.

"Hello, Aan. Did you sleep well?"

"Hi, Jaänjo. Thanks for asking. I did sleep well, although I have to say that I'm consumed by thoughts of being free of my disease." Her voice trembled as she spoke.

"Before we begin your healing, I need to explain a few things so that you will understand the process."

"Okay. I'm excited to hear what you have to say." Aan settled herself comfortably, her eyes wide with anticipation.

"On N'ridium, I was one of the rare few who could see what others couldn't—a person's aura, their life energy force. The ability to perceive and manipulate auras is a rare gift, often associated with those who possess exceptional healing abilities. I was no exception. My gift manifested early in life, allowing me to see the vibrant hues and patterns of energy that emanate from every living being. I could sense their emotional states, physical ailments, and spiritual essence. This unique perspective made me a skilled healer and gave me a deep understanding of the interconnectedness of all life."

"Jaänjo, I think I have a gift somewhat like yours," Aan interjected, her voice filled with wonder. "While I don't see auras, I feel spirits, like I felt your presence."

"You do have a gift. I'll talk more about this later."

Aan nodded, her curiosity piqued. "I'd like to hear what you say about it."

Jaänjo continued, his voice taking on a teacher-like tone. "For highly evolved beings, auras emanate in two primary colors: white and black. White represents pure energy, and black represents dark energy. Positive emotions like kindness, love, joy, and peace fuel pure energy—good energy. It promotes healing, harmony, and well-being. Conversely, black auras represent dark, evil energy that's fueled by negativity. Those who dwell in anger, hatred, worry, anxiety, cynicism, and malice toward others exude this dark energy."

"This makes sense to me," Aan replied, her brow furrowed in concentration. "I sense good and evil in others, though not in colors. It's more like… a feeling, an intuition."

"I'm sure you do. Aan, auras are dynamic reflections of our inner selves. They ebb and flow in response to emotions, thoughts, actions, and one's overall state of being. Each individual's aura color mirrors the predominant energy within. Those who struggle between pure and dark energies emit only a faint luminescence."

Aan nodded, absorbing this information. She could almost imagine seeing these auras Jaänjo described, picturing them swirling around people she knew.

"As a healer, my task is to mend imbalances within the auras of others. These imbalances manifest as distinct colors superimposed on the two primary aura colors, revealing the nature of the underlying issues. For example, a flickering red pulse within the white aura indicates physical distress, such as pain or illness, while flashes of blue signify emotional sadness stemming from grief or sorrow. These visual cues guide my healing process, allowing me to identify and address the specific areas needing attention."

Aan's eyes widened. "That's incredible, Jaänjo. It's like you can read a person's entire state of being at a glance."

"Exactly. Now, let me explain how the healing process works." He paused for a moment, thinking. "When I lay my hands over someone needing healing, I channel a transformative energy that penetrates to the very core of their being. This energy delicately manipulates the blueprint of their cells, restoring them to a healthy state and guiding the body back into harmony and balance. It's as if I am realigning the intricate threads of their physical and emotional fabric, mending what has become frayed or tangled."

Aan closed her eyes for a moment, trying to visualize this process. "It sounds almost like weaving a tapestry of health," she mused.

Jaänjo's energy pulsed in agreement. "That's a beautiful way to think of it. As my healing energy flows through them, it helps their body to realign at a molecular level. This means it fixes any disruptions within their cells, tissues, and organs, bringing everything back into a healthy, balanced state. Even though this process happens on a level too small to see, its effects are felt throughout their entire being, leading to a deep and lasting transformation. The colors in their aura, which once showed signs of trouble, return to a balanced state, reflecting the restored health and emotional peace."

Aan felt a surge of hope coursing through her. "And you think you can do this for me? For my MS?"

"Yes," Jaänjo replied, his voice warm with reassurance. "So, my role as a healer is to act as a bridge for this powerful, transformative energy, helping individuals regain their balance and harmony. By addressing the root causes of their physical and emotional issues, I support a complete healing process that promotes overall well-being and vitality. Through this careful and detailed work, I am able to assist others on their path to optimal health and inner peace."

"What you're saying is amazing," Aan said, her voice filled with awe. "As a Tlingit shaman, I, too, am a healer. I focus on healing the whole person—body, mind, and spirit. Using ancient wisdom and guidance from the spirits, I seek the root of ailments, sometimes using herbs or touch, other times performing rituals. Healing is a shared experience with family and community as we work together to restore balance. It is an honor to carry on the traditions of my people and bring wholeness to those who seek my help."

"When I first saw your aura, I suspected you were a healer, too."

"Why?" Aan asked, curiosity coloring her voice.

"Aan, your aura shines with such brilliance and purity. It's unlike anything I've ever seen—on Earth or my planet. Witnessing it is truly awe-inspiring and speaks volumes about the immense goodness within you."

Aan felt a warmth spread through her as she heard his words. "If I could see your aura, I know it would shine just as brightly as mine."

"No—no, it wouldn't," Jaänjo whispered, his voice thick with sorrow. His energy dimmed slightly, mirroring his emotions. "For most of my life, I lived through the horrors of my planet's slow decline. Long before I was born, our world had wasted away—farmlands withered, and the hydroponic farms we built underground couldn't sustain us all. I witnessed family, friends, neighbors, and countless others perish from starvation and cities unable to keep up with the heat. I nearly succumbed, and the memory of gnawing, relentless hunger is forever etched into my being. My spirit, my will to live, plunged into a deep abyss, dwindling my aura to a feeble glimmer. But in the short time I've been on your planet, I feel my aura recovering."

Aan's heart ached at the pain in Jaänjo's voice. She longed to comfort him, to ease the weight of his memories. "The pain you endured is unfathomable for me to grasp. Jaänjo, you're welcome to use some of my aura's energy to help heal you."

"That's very kind of you, Aan."

Aan, seeking to lift the heavy mood, changed the subject. "Earlier, when I asked if you have siblings, you glowed once. How many siblings do you have?"

"One. His name is Miĕĕcha. He's a scientist who helped develop the process that converted us from matter to pure energy."

"How do you say his name again?"

"Miĕĕcha—Mi-ee-ca," he said, slowly pronouncing it.

"Got it. Did Miĕĕcha manage to escape your planet, too?"

Jaänjo sighed. "I don't know. Miĕĕcha stayed behind to try to find a way to reverse the process so we could convert back to our physical selves, but I don't know if he escaped."

Aan felt a pang of sympathy. "I hope he survived. What about your parents?"

"They didn't make it," Jaänjo replied, his voice barely above a whisper. "People became isolated in cities and towns when traveling on the planet's surface became impossible due to the brutal heat and intense radiation from solar flares. Mom and Dad's underground city couldn't keep pace as the heat became unbearable. Miĕĕcha and I were powerless to save them. Like them, countless others perished as their cities and towns failed planetwide."

Aan's eyes welled with tears. "I can't even begin to imagine the depth of your sorrow. My heart aches for you, Jaänjo. You've faced more than anyone should ever have to endure." As she spoke, she couldn't shake the overwhelming sadness that gripped her heart, not just for Jaänjo's loss but for the countless others who perished on his planet. The thought of so many lives lost in the relentless onslaught of the failing sun, and the brutal conditions they faced filled her with a deep sense of grief and helplessness.

"Jaänjo," she continued, her voice soft with compassion, "it sounds like your spirit is still wounded. Maybe after you cure me, I can summon my spirits to help heal you."

"Your kindness and empathy touch me deeply," he replied, his energy glowing a bit brighter. "And you're right about my spirit. I'd welcome your help. I think we have much to learn from each other. Aan, are you ready to begin your healing?"

Aan took a deep breath, steeling herself. "I am. What do you need me to do?"

"To heal you, we need to work together to combine our energies. I need you to relax and focus on your breathing. Imagine my warm, glowing light within you, growing stronger with each breath. Visualize my light as your own healing energy. As you do this, I'll channel my energy into yours. I want you to imagine our energies merging, like two rivers flowing into one. Feel the warmth and light from both of us connecting and becoming one powerful force. This combined energy will help change your atoms at a molecular level, guiding them back to a healthy state. Are you ready to begin?"

"Yes," Aan replied, her voice filled with determination and hope.

"Close your eyes and focus on your breathing," he said softly. "Feel my energy within you, a warm, glowing light growing stronger with each breath."

Aan took a deep breath, feeling a gentle warmth within her chest. As she exhaled, she imagined this light spreading throughout her body. Jaänjo's energy began to flow through her, a comforting warmth that merged seamlessly with her own. It was as if a gentle wave of heat washed through her, starting in her head and gradually spreading downward into her arms, torso, and legs.

Aan felt tingling as their energies combined, like tiny sparks dancing beneath her skin. It wasn't unpleasant; it felt invigorating like her entire body was waking from a deep sleep. The warmth grew more intense but in a soothing way, dissolving any tension or discomfort within her. She sensed her cells responding to the combined energy, vibrating with a newfound vitality.

As the healing energy continued to flow through her, Aan began to notice distinct changes in her body. The chronic tingling and numbness in her fingers and toes faded, replaced by a rush of renewed sensation. Her vision, which had been increasingly blurry over the past months, suddenly sharpened, the world coming into crisp focus. The persistent fatigue that had weighed her down like a heavy blanket lifted, leaving her feeling energized and alert.

Aan flexed her hands, marveling at the ease of movement. The stiffness in her joints melted away, and she felt a strength in her muscles that she hadn't experienced in years. The constant ache in her lower back, a companion for so long, dissipated entirely.

As the healing progressed, Aan noticed her thoughts becoming clearer, and the mental fog that often accompanied her MS faded like a morning mist. She took a deep breath, realizing that even her breathing felt easier and fuller as if her lungs had expanded to their full capacity.

"Jaänjo, I feel a deep sense of connection and harmony, as if every part of me is coming into alignment." The flickering red pulse in her aura faded, replaced by a steady, calming white light. It was like a symphony of healing energy played within her, each note bringing her closer to perfect balance and health.

"Keep letting our energies work together, Aan," Jaänjo whispered. "Keep feeling the transformation within you, guiding you back to a healthy, harmonious state..."

As Aan surrendered to the process, the tension in her shoulders eased. Each breath seemed to carry away a piece of the weight she had been carrying, leaving her feeling lighter and more at peace with each passing moment. Her aura radiated a newfound vitality, a pristine white glow unmarred by the distressing hues of red.

"I'm done now, Aan. Your aura is nothing but a beautiful pure white."

A whirlwind of thoughts rushed through Aan's mind as the healing process concluded. The miraculous nature of her recovery left her in awe, but it also raised profound questions. She pondered the long-term effects of alien energy interacting with her body. Would this change her at a fundamental level? How could she explain this sudden recovery to her family, community, and doctors?

She gazed at her hands, flexing them slowly. A smile spread across her face as her fingers responded effortlessly to her commands, free from the familiar protest of pain. The simple joy of unrestricted movement washed over her. At that moment, as the reality of her cure sank in, all her doubts and questions suddenly seemed inconsequential. The gift of renewed health overshadowed these concerns, filling her with gratitude and wonder.

"Thank you, Jaänjo," she whispered, her voice choking with emotion. "You've changed my life forever..."

9

AFTER A QUICK BREAKFAST, Aan stepped out of her cabin, a shiver of anticipation running down her spine. The sun bathed the forest in a golden glow, and for the first time in years, her body felt light, unburdened by the chains of multiple sclerosis. She stretched her arms out wide, taking a deep breath of the crisp, spruce-scented air. "Jaänjo," she whispered, her voice trembling with joy. "I'm me again!"

"Try out your healed body—run, jump, skip, twirl—experience it all!" Jaänjo's voice resonated with excitement within her.

A pure and unrestrained laugh bubbled up from deep within her. Aan skipped down the worn path, her muscles responding with newfound agility. Each step was a revelation, a dance of pure joy. "Look at me, Jaänjo!" she cried in delight, twirling with effortless grace.

"It's beautiful to see!" Jaänjo's enthusiasm matched her own.

As she twirled, her hair fanned out like a halo. "I feel like I can fly, Jaänjo!"

"Then fly!" Jaänjo cheered, his voice echoing the exhilaration in her heart.

Aan took off at a sprint, her arms extended outward like the wings of a bird. The forest blurred around her, a riot of green and brown, the sun flickering through the leaves. She stopped by a towering spruce tree, her chest heaving with the sweet ache of exertion. Reaching out, she touched the sharp needles still moist with dew.

"They're like tiny swords," Jaänjo chuckled, his voice filled with childlike wonder.

Leaning closer, Aan inhaled their rich, resinous scent. It filled her lungs, grounding her to the earth beneath her feet. "They smell so good!" Jaänjo proclaimed.

Her eyes wandered to a cluster of wildflowers in a clearing, their vibrant colors beckoning her closer. Kneeling, she cupped a delicate blue blossom in her hands and smelled its sweet, heady perfume. "Smell this, Jaänjo. It's divine!" she beamed, her voice filled with awe.

"It is—the flowers are like little explosions of color!" Jaänjo's unbridled glee fueled Aan's exploration. They moved together, an inseparable pair—one in body, one in spirit. Jaänjo marveled at the rough bark of a Sitka spruce tree and gaped by the tallness of it as Aan cast her eyes upward. He delighted in the softness of moss on Aan's fingertips and the way the sunlight danced on the water of a nearby creek. Each sensation was a gift, each experience a treasure. "Do you see the wonder of it all, Aan—the wonder of it all!"

"I do," she whispered, her heart overflowing with gratitude. "Even more so, sharing it with you."

A puffy white cloud drifted across the azure expanse as she tilted her head back to gaze at the sky. The cloud piqued Jaänjo's imagination. "The cloud looks like a drimantrian!" he said, his excitement contagious.

"What's that?" Aan chuckled, delighted by his childlike enthusiasm.

"It's like an Earthly elephant, but with six legs. Your planet is so beautiful, Aan. The colors, the sounds, the smells, the feel of the wind on us—it's wonderful to be alive."

The morning unfolded like a child's dream. They ran through meadows carpeted with wildflowers, leaped over fallen logs, and splashed in the cool, refreshing stream. As the sun rose to its zenith in the sky, Aan found a soft patch of grass and lay down, her chest heaving from exertion but her heart soaring with joy. "Thank you, Jaänjo," she whispered, her voice filled with emotion. "Thank you for healing me and being here with me."

"You're so very welcome," Jaänjo replied, his voice warm and comforting. He looked at the sky through Aan's eyes and sighed. "I once read that N'ridium looked like this before our sun changed, but that beauty disappeared well before I was born. Seeing how my planet may have looked fills me with joy. Today is the best day of my life—I'm cherishing every moment of this and being with you."

"Me, too. I'll remember this day forever." Aan closed her eyes and felt the sun's warmth seep into her skin. She and Jaänjo listened to the rustling leaves, the chirping birds, and the hum of bees buzzing among the wildflowers. Every sound was nature's poetry, every breath a song of life. She loved the feeling of Jaänjo's presence within her, a constant, comforting companion sharing her joy.

A shared silence settled between them, tranquil moments of connection amidst the symphony of nature—a melody that resonated deep within their souls. Aan's heart swelled with joy. "It's like we've both been given a second chance at life, an opportunity to rediscover the world and all its beauty. We're like a perfect team, each enhancing the other's experience."

"I agree," said Jaänjo. "Every little thing is a treasure when you look at it with wonder."

Aan and Jaänjo continued their joyful exploration. They climbed a small hill to better view the landscape, gazing at how the forest stretched to the sea in a patchwork of varying greens. They found a fallen log and sat, observing as the shadows lengthened and the sky took on a softer hue as the afternoon advanced. "Jaänjo, this day is perfect. In every imaginable way, it's perfect."

As they savored the moment, a distant sound caught Aan's attention. Voices carried on the wind, growing closer. She tensed, suddenly aware of how strange her behavior might appear to others.

"Aan?" Jaänjo's voice held a note of concern. "What's wrong?"

"People are coming," she whispered. "I... I'm not ready to explain this to anyone yet. How do I tell them I'm suddenly cured? What if they ask questions I can't answer?"

The voices grew louder, accompanied by the crunch of footsteps on the forest path. Aan's heart raced, her newfound joy tempered by a sudden fear of discovery. Her mind raced with potential scenarios: How would she explain her miraculous recovery to her doctor? What would her family say? Would they believe her if she told them the truth about Jaänjo?

"Maybe we should return to your cabin," Jaänjo suggested, sensing her unease.

Aan nodded, grateful for his understanding. She stood, brushing off leaves and grass, and began making her way back to the cabin. As they walked, she tried to formulate a plan. "I'll need to come up with a believable explanation," she murmured to Jaänjo. "Maybe I could say it was a new experimental treatment? Or a spontaneous remission?"

"Those are good ideas," Jaänjo replied. "We'll figure it out together."

As they neared the cabin, the hikers' voices faded into the distance. Aan's steps slowed, her earlier exuberance tempered by the weight of her thoughts. She realized that her healing, while wonderful, brought with it a new set of challenges she hadn't considered.

Stepping inside the cabin, Aan closed the door and leaned against it, letting out a long breath. The familiar surroundings brought a sense of safety but also highlighted how much had changed in just one day.

"I hope there will be many more days like this for you and me," said Jaänjo, his voice gentle and reassuring.

Aan smiled and nodded, her thoughts both relishing her newfound freedom from physical constraints and grappling with the complexities it brought. "Jaänjo, I can't even remember the last time I was in the moment, reveling in shared joy with someone. I want more times like this with you, embracing life to the fullest, savoring every sensation, every experience, every breath." Her smile faded, replaced by a thoughtful expression. "But we have much to discuss—about what a life together could look like and how to navigate this new reality."

Jaänjo's presence enveloped her like a comforting embrace. "I look forward to this conversation."

Aan's stomach rumbled, a gentle reminder of her earthly needs. "You must hear my stomach telling me it's time to eat. I'll make something I'll bet you'll love."

After dinner, during which Jaänjo delighted in tasting smoked salmon with cream cheese and crackers for the first time, Aan settled into a porch chair. As darkness fell, a canopy of stars emerged, twinkling like diamonds scattered across the heavens. The beauty of the night sky momentarily pushed aside her worries about the future.

"Jaänjo," Aan whispered, her voice barely audible, "I want you to stay inside me. For how long, I don't know, but if I keep feeling like this, I hope it will be for a very long time..."

As she gazed at the stars, Aan felt a mix of emotions—joy at her healing, gratitude for Jaänjo's presence, and a quiet determination to face whatever challenges lay ahead. Tomorrow would bring questions and decisions, but for now, she allowed herself to bask in the simple pleasure of a starlit night and the warmth of her newfound companion.

10

The following day, Aan slept well into the morning. "Good morning, Jaänjo," she said as she opened her eyes. "Are you awake?"

"I am. As pure energy, I don't require sleep. I love hearing your heartbeat and how your body quiets itself at night."

"Hey, if you don't mind, I need to call my parents to let them know I'm okay."

"Sure. Aan, you don't have to seek my permission to do anything. It's not my intent to take over your body."

"Thanks. I'm not sure how to act or what to say. And, I must tell you, it's been quite embarrassing having to take care of bodily functions in the bathroom knowing you're observing everything."

"Would it help if I closed my eyes?"

She laughed. "My eyes are your eyes. I guess I could close my eyes and cover my ears so you won't hear, well, you know."

Jaänjo chuckled at her response. "With all this sensory deprivation, you might fall off the toilet, and I'll have to heal you again."

Aan burst out laughing. "You can never get enough of good alien humor; that's what I always say."

"How true. Hey, I'd prefer to be called an intragalactic refugee rather than 'alien.' And by the way, in the bathroom, you're like a breath of fresh air compared to Silas."

Their banter uplifted both of their spirits and eased the awkwardness.

Aan called her parents, saying she was okay but needed to take the day off from work to recharge. After the call, she put her phone down and spoke to Jaänjo. "I'll wait to tell them about my healing in person."

"Do you think they'll notice?" Jaänjo said, tongue-in-cheek.

"They probably won't until I start doing pirouettes in front of them. Hey, for breakfast, I'll make an omelet for us. Since you liked smoked salmon so much, I'll put some of it in with the omelet."

"What's an omelet?"

"It's a meal made with eggs. Do you know what eggs are?"

"I do. When I was in Silas, I learned what they are and how much he likes them."

Aan turned serious. "So, why did you enter Silas without his permission, Jaänjo?"

He sighed. "Do you want to talk about that now?"

"If you don't mind, I do."

"Okay. I'll need to start with some background information to answer this fully. As I said before, back on N'ridium, our ability to morph into energy came at a terrible price. Time ran out before we could master the reverse process, dooming us to an ethereal prison."

"That must have been terrifying for you all."

"It was," Jaänjo continued. "But just before we departed N'ridium, our experts discovered a way to intertwine our energy with an alien host possessing a similar biological makeup, and for me, their life energy—their aura—had to be compatible with mine."

"So, did they teach you how to find a compatible host?" Aan asked, her voice piqued with curiosity.

"No. Most people on my planet can't perceive auras, let alone teach how to find a compatible one. So, I was on my own. But without physical senses, I couldn't see the auras of other advanced lifeforms, and without the ability to hear, I'd never be able to understand the alien language. Sadly, given these constraints, I had no hope of reclaiming my role as a healer in the physical world."

Aan leaned back, absorbing this information. "That sounds incredibly isolating."

Jaänjo's voice held a note of sorrow as he continued. "For days, I wandered through your town, observing as best I could as pure energy, yet knowing without having physical senses, I'd be in a perpetual ethereal purgatory. Aan, I can't begin to describe how the yearning to experience the physical world again consumed me. The thought of remaining formless forever was unbearable."

Aan sighed. "It would be unbearable for me, too."

"Anyway, that's when I reluctantly considered the morally revolting idea of invading another being. It was the only way I could see auras to find a potentially compatible partner, and if I went within another being, I could learn their customs, history, and language. It seemed the only viable option to escape the grim prospect of remaining formless forever."

"I can understand why you felt you had no choice," Aan said softly.

"While wandering through your town not long ago, I chanced upon what seemed to be a friendly encounter between two people. The energy signature of one of them, a male, resonated with me. Intrigued and curious, I began following him, drawn to what I perceived as someone possessing kindness."

Aan tilted her head and offered a wry smile. "It was Silas, right?"

"Yes," Jaänjo confirmed. "The more I observed him, the more I yearned to experience the world as he man did—to feel the sun on his face, the wind in his hair, the earth beneath his feet, and the taste of food on his tongue."

He paused, allowing Aan to process this information before continuing, "I snuck into his dwelling, and while he slept, I wrestled with my conscience. Could I sacrifice my principles and integrity for the pleasure of physical sensations? I decided I couldn't and withdrew from the house through the open window."

"That must have been a difficult decision," Aan murmured.

"It was," Jaänjo agreed. "I spent the next day brooding over the missed opportunity to merge with him. Once more, I followed him throughout the day. Then I slipped into his house again when he opened the door. After he fell asleep, unable to resist, I merged with his essence."

"What happened then, Jaänjo?"

"Oh, my goodness—my world exploded into a kaleidoscope of physical sensations. His heartbeat, his snoring, his breathing, his dreams—it overwhelmed me."

"Did he wake up when you entered him—did he know you were there?"

"No, he didn't wake up, and no, he never knew I was inside of him. I never spoke a word to him, ever."

"Why not?"

Jaänjo cringed within her. "While he slept, I focused on exploring his mind. Within moments, I learned his name and quickly absorbed the nuances of English, his native tongue. Immersed in his mind, I uncovered a wealth of insights into your world's customs, traditions, and history."

Aan heard Jaänjo's deep sigh. "As I delved deeper into the recesses of his mind, I discovered the intricate layers of manipulation woven into Silas's persona—to my horror, I learned he was a skilled charlatan adept at portraying himself as a beacon of kindness and compassion to those around him. Each memory revealed another carefully orchestrated facade, a mask concealing the true depths of Silas's cunning."

Aan's eyes widened in shock. "What kind of things did you discover?"

"As I pieced together his past, I learned that Silas Tenhoff has harmed many people, leaving a trail of victims in his wake. Beneath his outward charm, a dark heart lurks beneath the surface. When he stirred and opened his eyes in the morning, I saw his aura for the first time through his eyes. Aan, his smoky black color was the signature of evil."

The weight of Jaänjo's revelations about Silas settled on Aan. Her eyes drifted to the open window, where sunlight filtered through the trees, creating a play of light and shadow on the cabin floor. A cool breeze stirred the curtains, carrying damp earth and spruce scents. In the distance, a woodpecker's steady rhythm broke the quiet. She touched the soft fabric of her sweater, finding solace in its tactile comfort against the troubling truths Jaänjo had unveiled. With a deep breath, she filled her lungs with crisp air as if cleansing her mind of the unsettling thoughts.

"I've always sensed that about Silas," she sighed, her voice tinged with validation and disappointment. "No matter how much he laid on the charm, something never felt right about him to me."

"You're quite perceptive," Jaänjo said, admiration clear in his tone. "Silas is a master at deceiving people, even me. Just so you know, he conned your father. The only issue with your boat's engine was clogged fuel injectors, but Silas saw a chance to profit. He overcharged your dad for labor by a significant amount."

Aan fell silent momentarily, her mind reeling from the revelation about Silas. Powerful emotions coursed within her—shock at the depth of his deception and anger at how he'd taken advantage of her family's trust.

"Thanks for letting me know, Jaänjo," she finally said, her voice tight with controlled anger. "When I return to work, I'll demand a big reimbursement."

"Please don't, Aan," Jaänjo cautioned, his tone urgent. "The last thing you would want is for him to hold a grudge against you and your family. He's capable of unspeakable cruelty."

She sighed, her shoulders slumping slightly. "Well, on my planet, we have a saying: 'What goes around comes around.' I think all his evil deeds will come to haunt him one day."

"I like that saying," Jaänjo mused. "His day of reckoning isn't far off. All those cigarettes he smoked affected his lungs. He has what your language calls advanced cancer." He paused, reflecting. "Back to being within him, I felt desperate to leave his body, but I couldn't until he fell asleep again so he wouldn't detect me. Dreadful as it was, I was inside of him for nearly a day—that's the day he first came to your office."

Aan's eyes widened. "I'm curious. As a healer, why didn't you heal him like you did with me?"

"That's a tough question, Aan," Jaänjo replied, his tone heavy with an unspoken weight. "As a healer, I couldn't cure him, but not for lack of ability. There are... conditions that govern my healing powers. Some barriers can't be crossed, even if I wanted to. I promise I'll explain it all later, but it ties into larger issues we need to discuss about my presence here and the nature of my abilities."

"Wow—we have much to discuss," Aan said, her voice filled with curiosity and concern.

"We do," Jaänjo agreed. "Oh. One more thing about Silas and the day I was in him. Later that night, the moment he fell asleep, I left his body and escaped his house through an open window."

He sighed. "I must admit that after leaving Silas, I immediately missed the physical sensations I observed through him and loathed being back in my ethereal prison again."

"So, why did you follow him when he returned to our office the next day?" Aan asked, her brow furrowed in confusion.

"I didn't follow him. The day after I left him, your aura so captivated me that I went to your office, hoping to learn more about you as best as I could while being pure energy again. When Silas happened by, I followed him into your office."

Aan nodded, understanding dawning on her face. "That explains why I felt you were separate from him."

"You're right. After Silas left your office, I stayed and later followed you to your cabin."

"I'm so glad you did, Jaänjo," Aan said warmly. "And I don't blame you for what you did with Silas. I would've done the same."

THE HEALER AND ME   45

As the weight of their conversation settled, Aan pondered the intricacies of Jaänjo's situation and the shocking revelations about Silas. She realized that her world had expanded exponentially, leaving her both exhilarated and apprehensive about the unknown future.

In the quiet moment that followed, Aan reflected on Jaänjo himself. She recalled his striking appearance when he had materialized before her—the luminous, humanoid form that seemed to radiate wisdom and warmth. Despite the turmoil of his experiences, Jaänjo exuded a remarkable calmness that Aan found both comforting and inspiring, as if he possessed an inner strength that could weather any storm. What struck her most was the clear moral values that guided Jaänjo's actions, even in his desperation. His internal struggle over entering Silas's body and his horror at discovering Silas's true nature spoke volumes about his character.

This openness drew her to him in a way she hadn't expected. Jaänjo's willingness to share his vulnerabilities, his fears, and his moral dilemmas created a deep sense of intimacy between them. It was as if, in baring his soul, he had invited her into a sacred space of trust and mutual understanding. Aan found herself captivated by his honesty, his self-reflection, and his desire to do what was right despite the challenging circumstances he faced. This transparency, so rare in her experiences with others, formed a connection that felt both new and somehow timeless.

Despite the uncertainties ahead, Aan felt a growing sense of trust and companionship with her intragalactic refugee. There was a comfort in his presence, a feeling that whatever challenges they might face, they would face them together.

Aan took a deep breath and shifted her attention back to the familiar tasks of daily life, starting with cracking two eggs into a bowl. "Jaänjo," she said with a smile, "do you want to learn how to make an omelet?"

11

AAN SLID THE GOLDEN omelet from the skillet onto a plate. She sat down, speared a forkful, and savored her creation. "Mmm, this is delicious. What do you think, Jaänjo?"

"It is delicious. I love the salmon pieces you crumbled into it."

She chuckled. "Well, one advantage of you being inside me is that there's only one mouth to feed."

"And I don't have to get dressed in the morning."

"The image of you being in the buff inside me is weirdly exhilarating."

He laughed heartedly. "I'm still on the skinny end of the energy spectrum, so you need to eat more."

Aan chuckled as she carried her dish to the sink. "Jaänjo, when you appeared before me the other day, you looked mighty fine. You're a handsome alien—er, intergalactic refugee, I mean."

"Thank you for your alien-corrected compliment."

"So, what did you do for fun on your planet?"

Aan's question hung in the air, the lighthearted mood shifting as Jaänjo fell silent. She sensed a change in his energy, a heaviness that wasn't there before.

"Aan, when starvation is a daily reality for everyone, survival becomes all-consuming. So 'fun' is an alien word to me. No pun intended."

"I'm so very sorry to hear that, Jaänjo. The enormity of the hell you and those on your planet faced is beginning to dawn on me."

"Perhaps now you can better understand why the simple pleasures of your planet thrill me."

"I can." Aan fell silent, the lighthearted banter of their breakfast giving way to stillness. She gazed out the window, her mind grappling with the weight of Jaänjo's experiences. After a moment, her focus returned to him.

"Jaänjo, there's so much I want to understand about you and your world. For example, how old are you?"

"My age is an interesting concept," Jaänjo replied. "N'ridium, slightly larger than Earth, was the sixth planet from our sun. Its orbit was farther out, so a year there lasted 1,440 Earth days—roughly 3.95 Earth years. So, on N'ridium, I was 7.6 years old, making me about 30 Earth years old."

"That is interesting," said Aan with a playful smile. "It's wild to think there's a childish alien living within me."

Jaänjo chuckled. "Now, here's where it gets even more intriguing. Pure energy doesn't experience time in the same way that matter does. When I was converted to pure energy and launched into space, I traveled at the speed of light, which is incredibly fast—about 670 million miles per hour. At that speed, time essentially stands still for the traveler due to the effects of relativity. So, from my perspective, I didn't age during my journey across seven thousand light-years.

"However, if we imagine a scenario where I aged during my journey, the calculation becomes truly mind-bending. I traveled over four quintillion miles to reach Earth, a journey that took about seven thousand years from Earth's perspective. Adding that to my original 30 Earth years, I would theoretically be about 7,030 Earth years old."

"Wow!" Aan exclaimed. "Two things boggle my mind—you being over 7,000 years old if we count your space travel time, and you being just 7.6 years old on N'ridium." Pausing for effect, she added with a playful grin, "Would you be offended if I said you looked like a nine-year-old alien?"

Jaänjo laughed. "I am hurt—you're back to calling me an alien again. How old are you, Aan?"

"I'm also 7.6 N'ridium years old," Aan replied with a smile. "Thirty Earth years old."

He chuckled. "And here I had you pegged at—uh, um, much younger than that."

"Nice save, there, alien," she said impishly, but then her mood turned serious. "I once was pretty, Jaänjo, but my MS aged me mentally and made me ugly. I once had lots of boys paying attention to me, but as my disease progressed, they long ago lost interest in me. Life has been hard on me, too."

Jaänjo sighed softly. "We've both endured more than our share of challenges. Let's hope the future brings brighter moments for us both." He paused, thinking about what to say. "Speaking of brightness, have you looked in the mirror today? You'll see a beautiful woman staring back at you. And through your eyes, I see something more—your radiant aura reflecting the warmth and kindness within you. Aan, you're beautiful in many ways."

Tears filled Aan's eyes. "Hearing such kind words feels a bit, uh, alien to me." She tenderly hugged herself. "Thank you, Jaänjo."

She stood, stretching her legs. "How about we take a walk? The fresh air will do us both some good."

"Great idea."

They spent the next hour wandering through the forest, enjoying how the sunlight played across their path. Aan pointed out various plants and animals, explaining their significance in Tlingit culture. Jaänjo absorbed it all, filled with wonder at Earth's beauty.

Refreshed and invigorated by their time in nature, they returned to the cabin. Aan settled into the comforting embrace of her wooden porch rocker, its familiar creaks a soothing lullaby. The Alaskan landscape unfolded before her, a canvas of green spruce against a brilliant blue sky, their branches swaying gently in the breeze. With hands resting on the worn armrests, she tilted her face to the sun, basking in its warmth. With a deep breath of crisp, clean air, she prepared herself for the conversation to come.

"Jaänjo, I must admit, while I find a partnership with you intriguing, I'm also terrified by it. I've always treasured my independence and valued my solitude."

Jaänjo didn't reply.

"I'm sorry if my saying this has hurt you. That's not my intent."

More silence. "Jaänjo, please talk to me."

"Forgive my silence—I have a riot of thoughts racing through me, and I don't know how to begin."

"I feel the same way." She shifted in her chair, searching for the right words to say. "I've spent my life cherishing my freedom, finding solace in the quiet moments where I can just be with myself. The thought of sharing my space, my thoughts, my very being with someone else—it's daunting, Jaänjo. I'm afraid of losing myself in the process."

Jaänjo's energy pulsed softly within her. "I understand. I, too, have known solitude, though in a different form. Existing as pure energy is the ultimate form of solitude. Ironically, solitude for you is a cherished thing; for me, it was brutal torture. When our paths converged, I got to experience life in a way I never thought possible—even when I was a physical form on N'ridium. That's how deeply you've affected me. But I also understand the fear of losing oneself amid such a profound connection."

Contemplating Jaänjo's words, Aan gazed out at the tranquil landscape. "I feel the same about us, too. Yesterday with you felt like heaven to me. So, it's not that I don't value what we have—it's just that I'm afraid of what it might mean for me, for us. How do we navigate this new territory without losing sight of who we are?"

Jaänjo felt her overwhelming uncertainty. "Perhaps, Aan, the key lies in finding balance," he offered gently. "We can cherish our individuality while embracing the beauty of our togetherness. Our connection doesn't have to diminish what makes us unique—it can enrich our lives in ways we never imagined."

Aan leaned back, absorbing his words. "Balance," she mused softly. "Maybe that's the answer. How would we find that kind of balance?"

"It might be easier than you think. Think about this: I don't require sleep, so I have abundant solitude time when you're asleep. Well, that is, when you're not snoring."

She laughed. "Hey, I don't snore."

He laughed, too. "I know. But Silas sure does. Among other things, I couldn't wait to leave his body because of it."

She smiled at his Silas comment. Both seemed lost in thought.

"Aan, I think I have a way for you to have solitude, too."

"How?"

"Like your body slows its functions while you sleep, I, too, can lower my energy level to a near-dormant state. So, if you want solitude or privacy, just ask me to give you alone time."

"You can do that?"

"I can, but I hope you won't ask me to go dormant when you use the bathroom. Listening to you pass gas while on your porcelain device is my chief form of amusement."

Aan shook her head and smiled. "If you had ribs, I'd poke them right now. Jaänjo, what you propose for us to have solitude is a good idea. And I liked what you said about the key lies in finding balance. As a shaman, I strive to find balance in all things."

She paused for several moments, pondering...

"Jaänjo, I... I always dreamed that someday I'd be a mother and have a husband who loved me. MS stole that dream from me, but now..."

"I feel your yearning, Aan."

"I've never been in an intimate relationship. As a shaman, I've witnessed many relationships fail, so I know that reality doesn't always align with my fantasies about being with someone. But I've also seen lasting love, like the bond between my mom and dad."

"Your experiences as a shaman have given you unique insights into the complexities of human relationships. Aan, I, too, have never experienced love. Every day demanded my full attention just to survive. He hesitated for a moment. "Sometimes, the most unexpected connections can be the most rewarding."

Aan caught his meaning. "I suppose the best we can do is allow the future to unfold naturally."

"I agree. As I told you when we first met, if you ever want me to leave you, I will. But what I didn't say is it works both ways. I reserve the right to leave you as well."

Jaänjo's comment surprised Aan. "Do you intend to leave me?"

"Well, you never know. If Tenakee Springs ever becomes a must-see destination for other intragalactic refugees, a cute alien babe might catch my eye."

He sensed Aan inwardly flinch at his attempt at humor.

"Forgive me for being so glib. No, Aan, I don't intend to leave you. Let me try to explain what I mean. As a healer, I use my pure energy to mend imbalances within the auras of others. The more pure energy a person has, the easier it is for me to heal them. But my ability to heal has a crucial limitation. Dark energy cancels pure healing energy, much like matter cancels antimatter. So, if a person's primary aura is black, I cannot help them."

"Okay, so what does this have to do with you leaving me?"

"Sorry. I know it sounds like I'm rambling, but hear me out. Auras are dynamic reflections of our inner selves, and each person's aura color reflects the most prominent energy at play. The more pure or dark energy a person has, the more intense their aura glows. And those caught in a tug-of-war between pure and dark energy will struggle to emit even a faint luminescence.

"Aan, for me to thrive within you, our auras must be compatible. But auras constantly change. On my planet, as conditions worsened, I witnessed countless people's pure energy shift to dark due to worry or losing their will to live. So, this is why I reserve the right to leave you. If your energy ever shifts to dark, it could end me—literally end me. I know this from firsthand experience. When I was in Silas for just one day, his dark energy rapidly depleted my life energy."

"What you're saying makes sense now."

"The synergy of our pure energies is breathtaking, Aan. Together, we could bring immense good to the community. We could mend injuries, revitalize ailing organs, and even reawaken dormant systems. Your spiritual gifts as a shaman healer would add an entirely new dimension to the concept of healing."

"I know. I've already seen the power of our combined energies when we cured me of my disease."

"Aan, I sensed how you flinched at my failed humor about someone catching my eye..." His pause was apparent. "The connection I feel to you is overwhelming. I..."

"I feel the same way, Jaänjo. On the trail, when I fell and pleaded for my spirits to help me—I'm sure they brought us together. Everything you're feeling, I'm feeling, too."

The weight of their conversation settled around them, a tangible yet comforting presence. It was a weight born of shared understanding and a deepening connection. As they sat in companionable silence, each found solace in the other's presence.

12

AAN BEGAN THE NEXT day by yawning after shutting off the alarm. She then hugged herself. "Good morning, Jaänjo. Today's a workday, so I need to get moving."

"Good morning to you as well. A hug from you is a wonderful way to start the day."

She got up and headed to the bathroom. "If you're extra nice to me today, I'll let you enjoy your favorite form of amusement in the bathroom."

He laughed. "I'll be on my best behavior."

As she washed her hands in the sink, Aan glanced at the mirror and smiled. It was the kind of smile that hadn't appeared on her lips for ages. "I'm happy, Jaänjo. Can you tell?"

"You're radiating joy. Aan, would you like to see your aura?"

"Sure. Can you let me see the aura of others, too?"

"I can. Ready?"

"I am." Suddenly, an enormous bright white glow surrounded Aan. "Oh my goodness! Jaänjo—it's so beautiful!"

"It is, and now that you're free from MS, it's become even brighter."

"I can't wait to see the auras of others today, especially the auras of my parents."

"Aan, regarding that, I recommend you not do it today because you'll be distracted enough telling your parents and those who see you why you're not using crutches anymore. Let's do this: to turn off your ability to see auras, touch your finger to the bridge of your nose. As you slide your finger down your nose, the auras will grow dimmer and stop when you get to the tip of your nose. Just reverse it to turn the auras on."

"Good idea. Let me try it." She slid a finger down her nose and saw her aura grow dimmer until there was nothing. "Cool."

"Let me warn you—the auras of others will be quite different from yours. You'll probably see other colors pulsing within their primary white aura. These secondary colors indicate what's troubling that person. Also, you can only see colors when white is the dominant aura color. Black auras hide the underlying colors."

"Wow," said Aan, enraptured by her shimmering aura reflection in the mirror. "I have much to learn from you. Jaänjo, I can't wait to cure people who are hurting."

Jaänjo sighed. "Aan, it's not like we can run all over town, sprinkling what you Earthlings call 'fairy dust' on everyone, making everything better. The role of a healer is much more complex than that."

"How so?"

"There are many types of energy—spiritual, physical, mental, emotional—and so on. Healing is a mutual effort where the patient, first and foremost, wants to be cured. The simple truth is that even with our combined healing energies, some people are unfixable. Take Silas, for example. The cigarettes he smokes with alarming frequency devastated his lungs. Even if I could cure him of the cancer caused by cigarettes, he likely would keep smoking. So, we have much to discuss regarding our ability to heal others. Also, there is another limitation for me as a healer."

"What's that?"

"Aan," Jaänjo began with a heavy sigh, "I am bound by a sacred oath as a healer. I cannot heal anyone suffering from the effects of old age." He paused, allowing the weight of his words to settle. "Nature has ordained a cycle of life and death. Disrupting this cycle would invite disaster, leading to a population explosion, suffering, and ecological collapse. My oath is not a limitation of my power but a testament to the wisdom and reverence for the natural order of things."

Aan leaned against the bathroom counter, her gaze fixed on her reflection in the mirror. The weight of Jaänjo's words settled in the pit of her stomach. "I understand. But could you ease someone's suffering caused by aging?"

"Yes, I could ease their suffering, but my oath prohibits me from altering their cells at the molecular level to make them younger."

"It must be hard to know you can help someone but know you can't." Aan frowned, considering the implications. "What about people with terminal illnesses? Or children with genetic disorders? Where do we draw the line?"

Jaänjo's energy pulsed with a sense of gravity. "These are the questions that every healer must grapple with. Our power comes with great responsibility and difficult choices." He sighed. "Aan, there's more to it than that. Imagine when word gets out that you're a healer. Eventually, you could have hundreds of people lined up at your cabin daily, wanting you to cure them. You couldn't thrive with never-ending hordes of people demanding your help. Compassion and healing fatigue can cause rapid burnout, and the constant demands of others can ruin the quality of your life every bit as badly as what you suffered through with your MS."

"This is sobering to grasp. It's like your gift could become a curse."

"You're right. But think about the joy you experienced when we cured your disease. As a healer, it's hard to describe the exhilaration of witnessing a patient's joy as I did with yours."

Aan nodded, absorbing Jaänjo's words. "As a shaman, I've experienced that kind of exhilaration." She pondered with excitement—and trepidation—the healing journey ahead. The enormity of their potential to help others, balanced against the ethical complexities and personal toll, weighed heavily on her mind.

Lost in thought, she absently glanced at the clock and gasped. "Oh no, Jaänjo! I'm running late for work." The sudden shift from their thoughtful discussion to the mundane reality of her job left her feeling slightly disoriented.

"Don't worry," Jaänjo soothed. "We'll continue this discussion later. For now, focus on getting ready."

Aan nodded, grateful for his understanding. As she hurried to get dressed, a thought occurred to her. "Is there anything you'd like for breakfast, Jaänjo? We could grab something on the way."

He laughed. "If you're asking, I have something in mind."

"Do you want another omelet?"

"I have something else in mind. Silas went to a place called the Party Time Bakery. He ordered what they call a cinnamon roll. When he bit into that gooey deliciousness, I nearly passed out. It's the tastiest thing I've ever had in my life."

Aan laughed, the strain from their earlier conversation easing. "Their cinnamon rolls are divine, so let's get one. I'll be ready to go in a few minutes."

As they stepped out of the cabin, Aan's mind whirled with the morning's discussion. Their newfound healing abilities were both exhilarating and daunting, laden with ethical implications and the potential to reshape their lives. Yet, the simple anticipation of a sweet treat grounded her as they made their way to the bakery. It was a poignant reminder that amidst life's extraordinary shifts, joy could be found in its smallest corners.

The bakery's intoxicating aroma of cinnamon rolls offered a comforting counterpoint to the complexities that lay ahead. Aan realized that this balance—between the extraordinary and the ordinary, the weighty and the delightful—would be essential as they navigated their shared path as healers. As she ordered their treat, she felt a renewed sense of purpose tempered by the sweet promise of cinnamon bliss.

13

THE MORNING SUN CAST a gentle warmth on Aan's cheeks as she started her descent down the hill towards town. Her trek seemed effortless, just like the smile on her face. "Jaänjo, this short trip to town felt like a marathon two days ago. Now, I'm hardly aware that I'm walking."

"You're moving with effortless grace. So, what will you say when your parents and others ask why you're not using crutches?"

"Good question. With my parents, I'll say a spirit named Jaänjo healed me. With others, I'll play it by ear."

At the town's main road, Aan strode towards the bakery with an ear-to-ear grin.

"Hey, Aan, where are your crutches?" a passing family friend called out, his voice tinged with curiosity.

Aan offered a warm smile in response. "Hi, Mr. Katzeek. I've been working hard on my recovery," she explained, her voice filled with joy. "I think my MS is in remission."

"Thank goodness. Congratulations, Aan!"

"Thanks. Please tell Evelyn I said hello."

"I sure will. Boy, you'd never know anything was ever wrong with you." He walked off, puzzled but with a smile.

"That sounded quite believable to me," Jaänjo said.

"Thanks. I think he believed me, too."

Further down the path, another villager stopped, her eyes darting to Aan's legs. "Aan, do you need help?" she asked with alarm.

"I'm fine, Dzánti," Aan replied, her tone reassuring. "Just taking it one step at a time."

Inside the bakery, crowded with tourists, the air was thick with the tantalizing aroma of freshly baked pastries. Aan's senses were alive with the sweet scent, her pulse quickening with anticipation. Inside her, Jaänjo experienced the heavenly aromas through her.

Aan's gaze lingered on the display of cinnamon rolls, their golden-brown exteriors glistening with a sugary glaze. With a smile, she ordered one. "Steady there, Jaänjo," she whispered. "I think I feel your energy drooling."

She took a seat and curled her fingers around the warm pastry. Jaänjo felt its soft texture yield to her touch. The rich flavors exploded on her palate with each bite, sending culinary pleasure to both of them. Jaänjo reveled in the sensation, his essence vibrating with delight. "Oh, my. Oh, my oh my."

"I couldn't have said it better," Aan beamed. "These are so good!"

Together, they savored the simple pleasure of indulging in the perfect cinnamon roll, the world around them fading into the background as they lost themselves in the moment.

Feeling sated, they made their way to her office with spirits soaring. Aan pulled out her phone. "I'm going to call my parents and ask them to meet me outside."

"Why?" Jaänjo asked, puzzled.

"Because when they come out, I'll run to them."

"Oh, I get it. This should be good!"

Aan's parents left their office and spotted Aan, who was a hundred feet away. When they waved, Aan spread her arms and ran to them, spinning, jumping, and performing several excellent pirouettes. "Surprise!" she beamed. "Do you notice anything different about me today?"

Her actions shocked her parents. "Oh my!" her mother shouted with astonishment and awe. "Aan—oh my goodness!"

She hugged them, laughing as tears of joy flowed down her cheeks.

"How is this possible?" Keet exclaimed in shock. "Do you need to sit down?"

"I'm fine! No more MS for me!"

Yéil looked dumbfounded. "How is this possible?"

"Let's go in, and I'll tell you what happened."

Inside their office, Aan's parents settled into their seats, eyes still wide with disbelief. Aan took a deep breath and began, "When I last walked home, I fell twice on the trail. On the last fall, I was in so much pain and felt utterly defeated. In that moment of despair, I cried out for our spirits to help me."

Her parents listened intently, hanging on her every word.

"They answered my plea and sent a spirit named Jaänjo to be with me. Jaänjo is a healer spirit, and he cured me of my MS," Aan explained, her voice filled with a blend of awe and gratitude.

Keet and Yéil exchanged bewildered glances. "A spirit healed you?" Yéil asked, her voice tinged with disbelief.

"Yes, Mom. Jaänjo is within me now, protecting me. He's pure energy and is now a part of me. Together, we are far stronger than I ever thought possible."

Keet leaned forward, and his eyes narrowed in concern and curiosity. "How do you know this spirit means you no harm?"

Aan leaned forward, her eyes meeting her father's with unwavering certainty. "Dad, we talk to each other, and I've learned much about him. He's so kind and gentle. I trust him completely."

"Are you sure you're not imagining this? Did he come to you in a dream?"

"No, Dad. Mom, the other day, do you remember me saying I felt a presence in our office? You said I was just like your mom, who said she could always feel spirits in the air."

She nodded.

"That presence I felt was Jaänjo. He followed me home."

Yéil shook her head, still trying to process the information. "This is incredible, Aan. I don't know what to say."

Keet looked concerned. "You said you asked the spirits to help you when you fell, but that was after you said you first felt a spirit in our office. So, to me, your order of events is wrong."

"It's not wrong, Dad. I won't get into the details, but trust me—if you knew the whole story, you'd know there are no discrepancies."

Her dad took a deep breath, trying to fathom all she was saying. "I believe you."

"I do, too," said her mom. "Can your spirit friend hear us?"

"Yes. He experiences the world through my physical senses."

"May we talk to him?"

"Let me ask. Jaänjo, can my parents talk to you?"

"Yes, Aan. I'd like to say hello to them, but I'll leave you if they call me an alien." Aan giggled. "Mom and Dad, please say hello to Jaänjo."

"Hello, Mr. Jaänjo. My name is Keet. I'm Aan's father. I'm pleased to meet you, and thank you for healing my beautiful daughter."

"Aan, please tell him I'm delighted to meet him, and he's welcome to call me Jaänjo—no 'Mister' is needed."

Aan repeated Jaänjo's words to her father.

"Hello, Jaänjo. My name is Yéil. I'm Aan's mother." Her voice choked with emotion. "Thank you for curing my daughter of her debilitating disease. Thank you so much."

Aan repeated Jaänjo's reply: "You're quite welcome, Yéil. I'm delighted to meet you as well. When I was in your office, your love for Aan touched me. The way you both love your daughter is heartwarming."

"This is me talking now," Aan said with a smile. "Just know I'm healthy and happy now, and Jaänjo is here to help and protect me. With his and my combined energies, I'll be able to heal others like Jaänjo did with me."

Though still in shock, her parents could see the undeniable truth in Aan's radiant smile and newfound vitality. They embraced her again, overwhelmed with relief and joy.

"Well, Mom and Dad, I should get to work."

"Forget work," said Keet. "This is a day of celebration. Let's get on the boat and cruise through the islands. It's been a long time since you've been at sea."

Aan's eyes widened with joy. "Oh, Dad, what a wonderful idea! I'd love to show Jaänjo how beautiful the islands are here."

"Well, he's in luck because Silas has our boat's engine humming again."

Aan's smile vanished. "Dad, Silas Tenhoff is pure evil and dangerous, too. He bilked us for a lot of money."

Shocked by what Aan said, Keet looked at her with surprise. "Why do you say that—the engine works fine."

"Jaänjo observed his treachery. He said the engine only needed to have the fuel injectors cleaned. Instead, Silas ordered expensive parts we didn't need, and then he charged far more for labor because we're trusting people."

"We'll see about that. I'll be talking to Silas about it."

"Please don't. Jaänjo said the last thing we should do is get him mad at us. He said Silas is an evil person."

"Why should we tolerate his behavior?"

"Dad, let's trust Jaänjo and let it go. In the future, we'll use another mechanic."

Keet sighed and nodded. "Okay, we'll do it your way. Let's not have this ruin our day."

As they pulled away from the pier, the engine's comforting rhythm and the boat's gentle sway soothed Aan. Salty air caressed her face as she leaned against the railing, lost in the grandeur of nature. After a few minutes, she joined her father in the wheelhouse, hugging him warmly. His weathered hands, steady on the wheel, spoke of a lifetime on the water.

"Beautiful, isn't it," he said, his arm sweeping across the breathtaking panorama of Chichagof Island and the surrounding Tongass National Forest.

"It's breathtaking," said Aan, her voice choked with emotion. She felt a warmth spread through her, not just from the sun's rays but from the shared joy of this moment with her father. Jaänjo's presence resonated within her, his energy mingling with hers as he took in the stunning scenery.

"Tenakee Springs is a special place," Keet continued, his eyes twinkling with pride. "Our Tlingit relatives have lived here for generations, so our connection to the land and sea runs deep." He gestured back towards the shoreline, where the cluster of colorful houses nestled amongst the trees in Tenakee Springs faded from view. "I love our little town and our tight-knit community. Tell Jaänjo it's a place where nature and people coexist harmoniously."

"He hears you, Dad, and he agrees." Aan spotted a bald eagle soaring overhead, its wings outstretched against the clear blue sky. "I can feel the spirit of this place," she said, with a voice conveying reverence.

"This feels like a holy place," said Jaänjo, his voice echoing Aan's reverence. "The land, the sea, the creatures that inhabit them... they are all connected, part of a greater whole."

Aan smiled, her heart swelling with gratitude for this unexpected adventure. She knew this trip was more than just a sightseeing tour; it was a chance to connect with her roots—to understand the land that had shaped her family's history. And with Jaänjo within her, she felt a sense of purpose, a calling to enrich the lives of those in her community.

When they returned and secured their boat to the pier, Aan hugged her father. "I'm so very, very happy to be at sea with you again, Dad. I love you so much." She hugged him for a long time.

"I'm glad to have my healthy girl back. So very happy." Tears were in his eyes.

As they walked to the office, the excitement of the morning's revelations and the boat trip began to settle. Aan felt both contentment and anticipation for what the rest of the day might bring. Their small town's familiar sights and sounds seemed fresher and more vibrant than before. She took a deep breath, savoring this new perspective on her familiar world.

"That was a wonderful trip," Aan said, her voice filled with gratitude. "Thank you both so much."

Her parents smiled warmly. "We're just so happy to have you back, healthy and strong," Yéil replied, her eyes glistening with emotion.

As they approached the office, Keet's expression grew serious. "Aan, about what you said earlier regarding Silas..."

Aan tensed slightly, sensing her father's concern. "Yes, Dad?"

"I understand you don't want me to confront him, but it doesn't sit right with me to let this go entirely. Maybe we should warn others discreetly."

Aan glanced at her mother, who nodded in agreement with Keet.

"I understand how you both feel," Aan said carefully. "But Jaänjo sensed real danger from Silas. He's not just dishonest; he's capable of much worse. For now, I think it's safest to keep our distance from him and be vigilant."

Her parents exchanged concerned looks and then nodded reluctantly. "We'll follow your lead on this, Aan," Yéil said. "But letting him get away with fleecing our people seems wrong."

"I know, Mom. But Jaänjo also said that Silas has terminal lung cancer, so his days of taking advantage of others won't last long."

In the office, Aan needed to use the restroom. She washed her hands and glanced at the mirror, expecting to see her aura. It wasn't there. "Oh, I forgot that I turned off my aura." She brought her finger to her nose and slid it upward. Her aura immediately appeared. "Nice," she said. "Hey, Jaänjo, I always have dinner at my parents' house on workdays. Trust me—you're in for a treat."

"Sounds good to me," he replied. "What a day this has been."

Aan stepped out, eager to see her parents' auras for the first time. As her gaze fell upon her mother, her mouth dropped in shock.

14

"Aan, what's wrong? You look pale."

"I—I need some air, Mom. Please, leave me alone for a moment." Aan rushed out the back door and ran to the fishing boat, leaping aboard and heading for the bow. She glanced back to ensure no one followed her, then burst into tears. "Jaänjo, did you see it too!"

"I did."

"It's cancer, isn't it? I saw the red color pulsing from her chest area."

Jaänjo sighed. "Not necessarily. I'll need to examine her more closely. But, judging by the size and frequency of the red aura pulsing, something is wrong."

"We need to cure her right now—the thought of losing my mother is unbearable."

"Aan," Jaänjo said gently, "you can't approach your mother with panic in your eyes—it'll scare her unnecessarily. You need to find your calm and talk to her in a reassuring way."

"There's no calm way to tell your mother she has cancer!"

"We don't know she has cancer. All we know right now is something's amiss. Aan, you've just told them you met a spirit who lives inside of you. They need to digest that before you charge in telling her she has cancer that needs immediate attention."

"Is she going to die, Jaänjo? That's all I need to know."

"Aan, as I told you earlier, healing is a mutual effort where the patient, first and foremost, wants to be cured. If your mom doesn't believe we can heal her, or she refuses to let us heal her, we—I mean I, am morally obligated to respect her wishes."

"Is she going to die!"

"Not if she accepts our help. Breathe, Aan. Take some deep breaths and find your calm."

Aan did as he asked. After a few minutes, Jaänjo felt her heartbeat return to normal. "Let's go back in, and let me observe your mother's aura while you talk to her. Aan, please keep the conversation light so I can see her undisturbed aura. If you scare her, her aura will reflect her anxiety, which will hinder my diagnosis. Can you do that?"

"I can. I'll tell her I felt seasick, but I'm fine now. Jaänjo, I'm so scared."

"I know. Just remember, I'm a healer. And so are you. Your mom is in good hands with us."

Aan hugged herself tightly. "I'm so glad you're here with me."

"I feel it. Put on a smile, and let's go back in. And, for a while, please don't see people's auras. Let that be my job."

"Okay." She quickly moved her finger down her nose to turn off her ability to see them. "I'm quickly learning that being a healer can be stressful."

"That's why we were taught from day one to stay emotionally uninvolved from our patients. Otherwise, the weight of the world would always be upon you."

Aan walked into the office with a big smile. "Sorry about that, you two—I felt a wave of seasickness hitting me, but now I feel fine."

Yéil looked at her daughter with suspicious eyes. "You said Jaänjo is a healing spirit, right?"

"Yes, Mom."

"And he experiences the world through your senses?"

"Yes."

"May I speak to him again?"

"Why?"

"Please, Aan. May I speak to him again?"

"Yes."

"Jaänjo, you know something is wrong with me, don't you? That's why Aan ran out of here in a panic."

Aan sighed. Tears ran down her cheeks. She pointed to her mom's chest. "From seeing your aura, Jaänjo and I know something is wrong. Do you know it, too?"

Yéil nodded. "A while ago, I noticed a lump in my breast and then more under my armpits. Your dad insisted we go to the Ethel Lund Medical Center in Juneau. With all you were going through, we didn't want to scare you, so I said I was going on the boat with your dad. Instead of fishing, we motored over to Juneau. They did a mammogram and a bunch of other tests." She sighed and took in a deep breath. "Aan, they say I have Stage 4 breast cancer, and it has spread—metastasized—to different organs and lymph nodes far from my breasts. The prognosis is grim."

Aan hugged her. "I'm so sorry, Mom. But Jaänjo and I will help you. Hold on—Jaänjo wants to tell me something." She paused for a few moments. "He says he'd like to examine your aura more closely. Is that okay with you?"

"It is. What does Jaänjo need me to do?"

"He says I need to sit down, and you should stand before me." Aan sat in her chair and motioned for her mom to come to her. "All right, Jaänjo, now what?"

Jaänjo spoke to Aan. "Aan, I'll need to move your arms and hands to examine your mom. Without touching her, I'll start at the top of her head and move downward to her toes. Please stand so I can reach above her head. Oh. I'll need to move your eyes as well."

"Okay." She stood. "Mom, Jaänjo will use my hands and eyes to examine you. Don't worry; he says he won't touch you."

"Um, okay."

Aan stood. "Okay, Jaänjo, we're ready."

Aan's arms rose without her consciously moving them. Jaänjo then cupped her hands two inches above her mom's head and held them there for several moments.

Within Aan, he spoke to her. "I'm feeling the energy of her aura, Aan, looking for traces of other colors than her primary white." He paused for a few moments. "I'm seeing and feeling red color, and there are yellow flashes, which indicate your mom's nervousness and anxiety. Please tell her she's doing fine. Now I'm going to start working my way down her body."

"Jaänjo says you're doing fine, Mom. He's going to move my hands further down your body."

"Okay. Um, thanks, Jaänjo."

Slowly, Jaänjo moved Aan's hands around Yéil's face. He lingered in front of Yéil's eyes and then moved Aan's hands to the back of her mom's head. After that, he moved her hands to the top of Yéil's shoulders.

As Jaänjo guided Aan's hands, she became acutely aware of the subtle energies surrounding her mother. The air seemed to vibrate with an unseen force, tingling against her skin. She could almost taste the metallic tang of fear and worry emanating from her mother.

"Aan, please sit and ask your mom to raise her left arm to where it's at chest level, pointing at you."

"Jaänjo wants you to raise your left arm like this, Mom." She showed her what to do.

With Yéil's arm in the air, Jaänjo started at her fingertips and worked toward her body. "Aan, I need to see her armpit, so ask her to raise her arm."

Aan asked, and Yéil raised her arm. After examining her armpit, Jaänjo sighed. "Aan, would it freak you out if I asked you to observe what I'm seeing?"

"No. Is it bad?"

"Yes. Do you still want to see her aura? It's important to see what I'm seeing, especially if we're going to be co-healers."

"Okay. What do you want me to do?"

"Turn on your ability to see auras again, and, Aan, be calm. I'll explain what we're seeing. Can you do this?"

"Yes." She brought her finger to the tip of her nose and moved it upward. Her Mom's aura appeared. It was much smaller than hers but white, which Aan knew was good since Jaänjo couldn't heal people with black auras.

"Okay, Aan, I'll need to move your arms and hands again. Ready?"

"Wait a second. Mom, Jaänjo wants me to see your aura so he can explain what we're seeing. So, unless I speak to you, please ignore what I say for a while."

"Okay. Does Jaänjo want me to keep my arm in the air?"

"He says yes, for just a bit longer."

"Look closely at your mom's armpit, Aan," said Jaänjo. "Do you see the small pulsing red colors?"

"I do." Aan's voice trembled slightly as she observed the angry red swirls, like tiny storm clouds against the white backdrop of her mother's aura.

"These energy disturbances indicate malignant cellular activity in her lymphatic system. Now, observe her forearm's energy signature. This region displays normal bioelectric patterns. Also, touch her forearm and feel the sensation."

She touched her mom's forearm. The skin felt cool and smooth beneath her fingertips, starkly contrasting the heat she sensed from the affected areas. "All I feel is her body temperature being about the same as my hand. And her forearm aura shows no color other than white."

"Right. Now, feel this." He moved her hand over her mom's armpit. "Notice the difference?"

"Yes!" Aan gasped. "It feels like pulses of heat." The sensation was unmistakable, like waves of warmth radiating from beneath the skin.

"You're right. That's from the cancer cells. Now ask your mom to lower her arm and raise her right arm to chest level."

"Mom, please lower your left arm and raise your right one to your chest level." She did as Aan asked.

Jaänjo repeated the process with the right arm, where Aan noticed even more red glowing clusters. The sight made her stomach churn. "There's more in this armpit, Jaänjo," Aan observed, her voice barely above a whisper.

"There is. My guess is her cancer started in her right breast and spread. That's why there are more cancer cells in her right armpit's lymph nodes. The cancer got there sooner than it did to her left armpit, and so it grew more. Please tell your mom she can lower her arm. Now we'll focus on her breast area."

"Mom, you can lower your arm. Now we're going to examine your breasts."

"Okay."

When Jaänjo moved Aan's eyes to see her mom's chest, Aan winced. The red color seemed to pulse and throb, a visual representation of the disease ravaging her mother's body. "The red color is everywhere, Jaänjo—especially in her right breast—is this where her cancer began?"

"You're correct. Now, I'll move your hands over each breast. Tell me what you feel."

"They're much hotter than what's in her armpits." The heat was intense, almost uncomfortable against her palms.

"It's because there are many more cancer cells here." He moved her hands down Yéil's torso, stopping at her pelvic area for a few moments, and then proceeded down each of her legs to her feet. "Between what I see in her aura and the energies I'm feeling with your hands, your mom's cancer has spread to her liver, lungs, and bones."

"Is it too widespread to cure?"

He sighed. "No, but we'll have to approach it in phases."

"What do you mean?"

"In the first phase, we'll use our combined energy to eliminate most of the cancer. But in the next phase, I'll need to leave your body and enter into your mom. There is much work I need to do at the molecular level. Your mom will have to give her permission for me to do it."

"I understand. Mom, Jaänjo and I can cure you, but he will need to enter your body to fix things. He needs your permission to do this. Is this okay with you?"

Yéil looked at Keet. "What should I do?"

He sighed. "Aan, are you sure this is the right thing to do?"

"Yes, Dad. I'm certain of it. I'm living proof that Jaänjo can cure people. In my heart, I know we can trust him."

"Keet," said Yéil, "you know how deeply connected to spirit Aan is. If she feels this highly about Jaänjo, then we need to trust her judgment."

He nodded. "Okay. Jaänjo, we're putting our faith in you."

Aan felt a sudden weight of responsibility. "Mom, Dad," she said, her voice serious, "I know this is a lot to take in. Are you sure you're comfortable with this? Using these abilities... it's not something to take lightly."

Keet and Yéil exchanged glances. "Aan," Yéil said softly, "the doctors gave me months to live, at best. If there's even a chance this could work, we have to try."

Aan nodded. "You're right. Jaänjo, could you appear before my parents as you did with me at the cabin?"

"No, Aan."

"Why not?"

"Because it takes a tremendous amount of my energy to do it, and I'll need every bit of my energy to cure your mom."

"I understand."

"Mom and Dad, Jaänjo can't appear before you because he needs to preserve his strength to heal Mom."

Her parents nodded. "Jaänjo," said Yéil, "when and where do you want to try to heal me? Do I need to do anything beforehand?"

Jaänjo spoke to Aan. "Please tell her that's a good question. The first phase can be any day she wants, but we'll need to do it early in the morning, so I'll have time to recharge by spending the rest of the day in the sun. I suppose that means it can't be cloudy on that day. Also, we should wait two days before proceeding to the second phase to allow her body to absorb the remnants of the cancer cells."

Aan repeated what he said to her parents. Keet pulled his phone from his pocket and brought up the weather forecast. "It's supposed to rain tomorrow morning but will clear up by noon. Then there'll be two days of mostly sunny skies. Will that work?"

"It will," Jaänjo said within Aan. "We can do the first healing phase tomorrow morning, and I'll recharge in the afternoon."

Aan relayed this information to her parents. The room fell into a contemplative silence, the weight of the situation settling over them all. After a moment, Aan felt a shift in Jaänjo's energy, a lightening of his mood.

"Aan," Jaänjo said, his tone softer now, "I know this has been intense. But remember, there's still joy to be found in everyday moments. Maybe we could all use a bit of that right now."

Aan smiled, grateful for Jaänjo's reminder. "Mom," she said, her voice lighter, "Jaänjo's been curious about Earth food. He's particularly fond of cinnamon rolls. What are we having for dinner tonight?"

Yéil laughed, the sound breaking the tension in the room. "Well, Jaänjo, I'm afraid we're fresh out of cinnamon rolls. But how about fresh-caught Dungeness crab and spot prawns, with roasted carrots and sautéed morel mushrooms that I picked yesterday in the forest?"

Aan felt Jaänjo's excitement bubbling up within her. "Jaänjo says that sounds even better than cinnamon rolls," she reported, grinning. "He can't wait to try it."

Aan hugged her mother and felt a surge of emotions course within her—hope for her mother's healing, gratitude for Jaänjo's presence, the chance to become a healer in ways she never could have imagined, and fear—fear that tomorrow wouldn't bring the results they all hoped for.

15

On her mother's healing day, Aan woke before the sun rose with excitement and anxiety mingling within her. The soft glow of pre-dawn light filtered through her curtains, casting gentle shadows across her room. She took a deep breath, inhaling the crisp Alaskan air that seeped through her slightly open window. As was their new custom, she hugged herself, her way of saying hello to Jaänjo. In response, she felt a gentle, comforting warmth spread throughout her body, emanating from his energy. This warmth served as reassurance of Jaänjo's presence and affection.

"Thanks for my daily, Aan." The word "daily" had become his affectionate nickname for Aan's morning hug.

"And thank you for your version of a hug, too. I love your hugs."

She hesitated momentarily, her fingers tracing the worn quilted pattern of her bedspread. "Jaänjo, do you believe in prayer, you know, asking the spirits for help?"

Jaänjo considered her question. "Hmm... how to answer this? As your language defines it, prayer is a foreign concept to me. In my world and now in my existence as pure energy, I am constantly connected to the universal energy that permeates everything. This energy is what those on my planet and I call God."

He paused, reflecting. "Every star, every rock, every living being—and every atom throughout the universe—vibrates with this divine energy. It is the source of creation, the force that binds everything together. And love, like the love you feel for your mother, is one of the purest expressions of this divine energy. So, in a way, I am always in communion with the divine, constantly aware of its presence within and around me.

"Perhaps this is my form of 'prayer,' a constant state of connection and awareness. I don't ask for things or seek favors, but I am always open to receiving this universal energy's guidance and wisdom."

Aan pondered his words, feeling awe at the vastness of the universe and her place in it. She thought about how different yet strangely similar their spiritual views were. "That's beautiful, Jaänjo. Your perspective is truly enlightening. In my culture, we also don't pray as the English language defines it. Instead, we talk to our spirits, share our joys and sorrows, ask for their wisdom, and thank them for their blessings. It's a way of maintaining our connection to the natural world and honoring the spirits that guide us. Would you mind if I talk to my spirits and your divine energy about my mother's healing?"

"Please do."

Aan closed her eyes and took a deep breath. "Spirits of my ancestors and the divine energy that Jaänjo says connects us all, let us envision my mother vibrant and whole. We give thanks for her life, the many life lessons she taught me, and her nurturing love. We send our hopes for her peace and healing. We trust in your wisdom, knowing that all unfolds as it should." Aan took another deep breath, feeling a sense of calm wash over her. The familiar words of her cultural tradition grounded her, bridging her world and Jaänjo's cosmic perspective.

"That was beautiful, Aan. Your words resonate within me." He paused for a moment. "Your love for your mother is a powerful force in itself. Never underestimate the healing power of love."

"I agree with you—love is a powerful medicine."

As Aan rose from her bed, she walked to the window, feeling the cool wooden floor beneath her feet. She looked out at the misty Alaskan landscape, the spruce trees barely visible in the early morning light. The weight of the day ahead settled on her shoulders.

"Jaänjo," she said, her voice barely above a whisper, "the healing process for my mother... it will be different from what I experienced with you, won't it? Can you explain how we'll employ our combined energies to heal her?"

"Of course, Aan. Let's start with my assessment of your mom's physical troubles. In addition to her widespread cancer, I noticed what you Earthlings call glaucoma in her eyes. Also, her arteries have lost some of their elasticity, causing them to be less able to absorb the force of each heartbeat. That's why she has chronic high blood pressure. Also, your mom is a borderline diabetic. Her cells have developed insulin resistance, causing her blood sugar levels to elevate. It's not a big problem now, but it will be in the future. I also noticed the red color in her aura on her left knee. The knee pain she's experiencing is due to her cartilage being nearly worn away, causing bone-on-bone friction and inflammation. The severity of her pain will increase in the future."

"You're right about her knee pain. She takes daily pain pills to help cope with it. Jaänjo, can we cure her of all these things?" Aan asked, her voice tinged with hope and worry.

"Yes, we can, and here's how: just as I did with your hands when I examined your mother, we'll use a similar approach to restore her health. We'll begin at the crown of her head, with your hands hovering just above her, and we'll slowly move your hands downward, channeling our combined healing energies into her body until we reach her toes. The energy flowing from your palms will be intense—a radiant white light will fill the room with brilliance."

"How do we turn on this healing light, Jaänjo?"

"Don't think of it as turning on a light, but as opening a channel. This energy already exists within you—within us—a potent force waiting to be focused and directed. It's the same energy that binds the universe together, the same energy I became when I transitioned from matter to energy."

He paused, reflecting. "To access it, we need to align our intentions and open ourselves to its flow. You'll need to close your eyes, take deep breaths, and visualize the radiant white light building within us. We'll begin to feel its warmth and power building within us. Then, we'll let it flow through your hands and into your mother."

Aan's heart raced as she contemplated the task ahead. The enormity of what they were about to attempt suddenly felt overwhelming. "Jaänjo," she whispered, "what if I can't do it?"

Jaänjo's energy resonated with encouragement. "Trust in yourself, Aan. Trust in our connection to the universal energy. Trust that we have the power to heal."

Aan sighed, drawing strength from Jaänjo's confidence. "Okay. I love my mother more than anything, so I'll focus on my love for her and summoning the universal energy needed to heal her."

"Perfect—that's what you need to do." As the first rays of sunlight began to pierce through the mist outside, Jaänjo added one last piece of advice. "Aan, let's talk about your mother's aura strength. As I'm sure you noticed, her primary aura is weak due to her advanced cancer. The weaker a person's primary aura, the more challenging it is to heal them. So, this healing will require significant energy from us, and afterward, we'll feel exhausted."

"That's good to know. I'll plan on resting afterward."

Despite Jaänjo's confidence and assurances, Aan flashed on the day ahead with anxiety churning in her stomach. *"What if something goes wrong? What if I can't channel the energy properly?"* She pushed these thoughts aside, focusing instead on her mother's smile, laughter, and warm hugs. "We can do this," she whispered to herself and Jaänjo. "We have to."

"Rest easy on that, Aan. We'll heal her. But your mother's cancer is so advanced that I'll need to enter her body and repair anything we don't quite fix. This will exhaust most of my energy reserves, so I'll need to absorb the sun's energy to recharge. To help accelerate my recovery, consuming at least one cinnamon roll daily will be critically important."

Despite the gravity of the situation, Aan burst out laughing at Jaänjo's deadpan humor, the sound echoing in the quiet room. "I hope you can cure obesity because, at your proposed level of cinnamon roll consumption, I'll be as big as a whale before long."

As her laughter subsided, Aan felt a renewed sense of determination. She glanced out the window and gasped as a raven landed gracefully on the porch rocking chair, its beady eyes glinting in the morning light. "Jaänjo, look!" she said, her voice filled with reverence. "A raven." She paused, her gaze fixed on the bird. "This could be an omen. In our stories, the raven brings change and transformation. Its appearance can signify a significant shift or new beginnings in your life." Then, a shadow of concern crossed her face. "But we must be cautious. The raven is also a trickster. It could be a warning, a sign to tread carefully..."

16

Rain fell in a gentle rhythm as Aan, sheltered beneath an umbrella, approached her childhood home. "I love being in the rain," Jaänjo remarked. "The raindrops speak to me in such a joyous, soothing way."

"I never thought of rain talking to me," Aan replied, "but you're right about it being soothing. Did you often walk in the rain on your planet?"

Jaänjo sighed. "During my lifetime on N'ridium, the oceans had mostly evaporated, leaving behind a desolate landscape scorched by the sun's relentless rays. I spent my entire life underground, so I never experienced rain or nature until I came here. My grandfather used to tell stories of water falling from the sky, but I never imagined it could be as beautiful as this."

"Rain in Southeast Alaska is so commonplace that we take it for granted—and we often view it as a nuisance," she admitted. "But for you, after living underground on N'ridium, I can't even begin to fathom how you feel right now. I suppose you could easily make a case for Earth being paradise."

"I could. Aan, rain is more than joy. It's a reawakening, a connection to something... primal."

Aan pondered Jaänjo's words, sensing the depth of emotion behind them. For Jaänjo, "primal" wasn't just about nature or a lost paradise. It was about experiencing, for the first time, the raw, elemental forces that shaped worlds. Rain represented life itself—a phenomenon so basic to Earth yet so foreign to his experience. It was a visceral reminder of the fundamental processes that had long ago abandoned his home world. In feeling the rain, Jaänjo wasn't just enjoying a novel sensation; he was connecting to the very essence of a living, thriving planet—something he had only dreamed of in his sterile underground existence on N'ridium.

Pausing outside her home, Aan shook the raindrops from her umbrella before collapsing it and tucking it under her arm. "Please, my dear spirits," she whispered. "Let everything go well."

"Mom, Dad—we're here!" Aan yelled as she walked in.

Yéil and Keet came to them from their bedroom, their faces etched with anxiety and hope. "I hope you two slept well," Yéil said, her eyes searching Aan's face for any sign of strain. "And Jaänjo... I'm so grateful for what you're doing." Her voice wavered, a hint of desperation clinging to her words. "Your dad and I have our bedroom ready."

"We did sleep well—I mean, I did. Jaänjo doesn't sleep. He lies awake, dreaming of cinnamon rolls. Oh! Jaänjo says you're quite welcome, Mom."

Keet hugged Aan. "Good morning, daughter, and you, too, Jaänjo. When do you want to begin?"

Aan returned his hug. "Jaänjo says good morning as well, and he says anytime is fine."

"I have to be honest and say I'm a bit terrified on many levels," said Yéil.

"I understand, Mom. I'll be right next to you the whole time. And, Dad, you can watch it too. Jaänjo told me the room will be flooded with light during the healing, so be prepared."

"Aan," Jaänjo whispered. "during our boat trip, your dad wore an ocular device that shielded his eyes from the bright sunlight. Could you ask him if you could wear them to shield your eyes from our healing energy? Also, please tell your mom she needs to close her eyes during the procedure."

"They're called sunglasses, Jaänjo. Dad, Jaänjo wants me to use your sunglasses because, during the healing, a strong, radiant white light will fill the room. And, Mom, you'll need to keep your eyes closed to protect them from the bright light."

"I'll go get two pairs," Keet replied, "one for you and me."

While Keet left for the sunglasses, Jaänjo spoke to Aan. "Aan, please ask your mother to lie on her bed and get comfortable. Also, I would like to speak to her."

"Mom, Jaänjo asks that you lie on the bed and get comfortable. Also, he wants to speak to you."

"Okay."

Aan spoke the words Jaänjo said to her mom: "Yéil, please release your worries and open yourself to the divine energy that connects us all. Aan and I will add our pure energy to yours and make you well again."

"Thank you, Jaänjo. I wish I could hug you right now."

"Mom, Jaänjo said he feels the same way."

Keet returned with the sunglasses and handed a pair to Aan. She put them on. "Okay, Jaänjo, what do we do?"

"Aan, please tell your mom it's time to close her eyes and keep them closed until we tell her to open them. Tell her we'll do the same thing as before, moving our hands over her. She will feel tingling sensations throughout her body, but they won't be unpleasant. Please tell her to take deep, easy breaths and focus on welcoming the divine energy into her body."

Aan repeated his words aloud. Yéil closed her eyes and began breathing deeply.

"Are you ready, Aan?"

"I am."

"Okay, once more, I'll guide your hands and eyes like yesterday. Please close your eyes, take a deep breath, and visualize the radiant white light building within us. When it rises to the level we need to heal, I'll tell you and move your hands to your mother. Are you ready?"

"I am." Taking a deep breath, Aan closed her eyes and reached deep within herself, summoning the vibrant energy that Jaänjo had awakened within her. A soft, white glow began to emanate from her palms, growing brighter with each pulse of her heart. As the room brightened, the air thrummed with a palpable energy that enveloped them all.

"My dear spirits," Keet whispered in the background, marveling at how Aan's hands emanated an almost blinding light.

"Aan, we're ready to begin," Jaänjo's voice resonated within her. "Open your eyes."

She gasped as a radiant glow poured from her palms. Jaänjo guided her hands to hover just above the crown of Yéil's head, and Aan watched in awe as their combined energies flowed into her mother.

Jaänjo then gently moved Aan's hands to Yéil's face, pausing over her eyes. Slowly, methodically, they bathed Yéil's upper body in their combined healing light, lingering for several moments over her chest, where the cancer was most concentrated. Jaänjo marveled at the synergy between his energy and Aan's. He could feel the cancer cells shrinking, the damaged tissues regenerating. *"This is more powerful than anything I've ever experienced,"* he thought. *"Aan's love for her mother is amplifying our healing energy."*

The process continued, with Aan's hands slowly gliding over Yéil's entire body until they reached her toes.

"Aan," Jaänjo's voice resonated softly, "this part of the healing process is complete. It's time to ease the flow of energy. Visualize our light dimming, our energy gradually receding back into your body. Please sit next to her, and I'll guide your hands to rest on your mother's chest so you can feel the warmth of the mother-daughter energy connecting the two of you. When you're ready, please tell your mom she can open her eyes."

Aan marveled at the power of the energy flowing between her and her mother. Its warmth transcended the physical, a connection that resonated deep within her soul. She felt deep love, gratitude, and renewed appreciation for their unbreakable bond. As tears welled in her eyes, she knew this healing moment was more than just a physical restoration—it was a strengthening of their respective spirits, a reminder of the enduring love between mother and daughter.

With a trembling voice, Aan whispered, "Mom, you can open your eyes now."

Tears streamed down Yéil's face as she opened her eyes. "Aan," she whispered, her voice thick with emotion, "I... I feel something from long ago—the overwhelming joy I felt the first time I held you in my arms."

"I know, Mom, I feel it too," she said, her voice filled with a quiet conviction. Reaching out, she gently took her mother's hand, their fingers intertwining. In that simple gesture, their shared energy deepened, reaffirming their unbreakable bond.

"Tell Jaänjo it was just like he said it would be—I felt tingling sensations throughout my body. It felt like every one of my cells got a tiny little massage."

"I felt the same way when Jaänjo healed me. I love you so much, Mom."

"I feel it. Now you know how powerful my love is for you. "She put her hand on Aan's chest. "Jaänjo, thank you so much for healing me. I felt your gentle energy, too."

"Aan, please tell your mom I appreciate her kind words." Aan repeated what he said to her mom.

"How do you feel, Mom?"

"Wait," Jaänjo interrupted. "Aan, touch your nose to see your mom's aura."

Aan did as Jaänjo asked and gasped. "Mom—there's barely any red left in your aura! That means most of your cancer is gone! Can you notice a difference?"

"I feel…" Yéil paused, searching for the right words. "I feel renewed and lighter, like someone lifted a burden from me." She took a deep breath, surprised by how easily her lungs filled with air. "It's remarkable," she said with wonder in her voice. "I feel no pain in my chest area."

Yéil sat up slowly, her movements cautious initially, then becoming more confident. She flexed her knee, noticing how the stiffness that had plagued her for years seemed to have vanished. She looked around the room. "My vision," she exclaimed suddenly. "Before, it was like looking through a narrow tunnel, but now I have peripheral vision—and everything looks so clear!"

She reached out, her hand trembling, and clasped Aan's hand again. "Thank you," she whispered. "Thank you both. Can I stand?"

"She sure can," said Jaänjo. "And she can do pirouettes if she wants to."

Aan laughed. "Jaänjo says you can stand and do pirouettes if you want to."

When her mom got up from the bed, she moved with a grace and ease that belied her recent condition. She took a few tentative steps, then, overcome with joy, she did a small twirl. Aan stood and hugged her tightly, feeling the strength in her mother's embrace.

As the adrenaline of the moment began to ebb, Aan felt a wave of fatigue wash over her. The rapid change from the intense focus of healing to the joy of success made her feel lightheaded, and bone-deep exhaustion quickly replaced her elation.

"Mom," she said, her voice suddenly heavy with weariness, "Jaänjo warned me the healing process would drain our energy. Would you mind if I lie down for a while?"

"Of course not. Please rest as long as you need to," Yéil said, concern evident in her voice.

"I'll get your bed ready," said Keet. "You can stay the night if you'd like." He hugged her, his embrace warm and comforting. "I've never witnessed a holy moment until now. I'm at a loss for what to say except thank you—and thank you, too, Jaänjo." His voice trembled with emotion. He looked at his wife, then at his daughter, his eyes shining with unshed tears. "What you and Jaänjo have done… it's a miracle. I didn't fully believe it was possible, but now..." He shook his head in wonder. "You've given us our lives back. All of us."

"You're quite welcome, Dad—from both of us."

In the bedroom of her youth, the weight of the day's events settled upon Aan as she sank onto the comfort of her bed, her eyelids heavy. In the quiet of her room, the healing ritual replayed within her mind, the sensation of channeling their combined energy to restore her mother's health still vivid and exhilarating. Aan's heart swelled with awe and empowerment, realizing the profound impact of her and Jaänjo's abilities when wielded with compassion and purpose.

Before she succumbed to sleep, Aan instinctively wrapped her arms around herself. "Thank you for healing my mom, Jaänjo," she murmured, her voice thick with sleep.

"I love you, Aan." As Jaänjo whispered the tender words, he felt Aan drifting into a deep slumber, unaware of his heartfelt admission. Still, the simple act of voicing his love brought him a quiet sense of peace.

He settled into a state of restful alertness within Aan as she slept. A deep sense of fulfillment permeated his essence as he reflected on the day's events. The healing of Yéil had been more than just a physical restoration; it had solidified his place in this new world and in Aan's life. His love for Aan, newly acknowledged even if unheard by her, resonated through his energy. For the first time ever, Jaänjo felt contentment, a sense of peace, and... happiness.

17

Late in the afternoon, Aan woke from her lengthy nap feeling refreshed. She immediately hugged herself. "Hi, Jaänjo," she said, but he didn't answer. "Jaänjo?"

"Hi, Aan." His voice sounded weak and raspy.

"Jaänjo, what's wrong?"

"I'm very... very tired." Saying each word seemed to require immense effort.

"What can I do?"

"Sunlight," he rasped. "Basking in it will do me good."

"Okay, let's go outside." As Aan scrambled to her feet, Jaänjo's following words stopped her cold.

"Aan, I need to leave you to get the most out of the sun's energy."

Her eyes widened with concern. "Leave me? Now?"

"Yes."

"O-okay. Any time you're ready to leave me, please do. I'll sit with you outside."

"Please be with your parents. This is a time for you to rejoice as a family."

"You're family, too, Jaänjo. I think you need me more than they do."

"I'll be fine. Conversing is quite hard for me right now, and flashing yes or no signals when I'm outside of you uses a lot of energy."

She sighed. "Okay. How about I come out as the sun sets?"

"Okay. I'll leave you now."

As Jaänjo left her body, Aan felt an immediate and tangible void, as if a fragment of her very essence had been extracted along with him. The absence of his energy within her created a sudden silence, like a missing heartbeat.

An idea sparked in her mind—she might be able to see him! Aan touched her nose, activating her ability to see auras. As soon as she did, his aura materialized. "Oh, Jaänjo!" she gasped, seeing his aura barely flickering with white light. She burst into tears. "Your aura is nearly depleted. Let's get you into the sunlight. If you follow me, I'll walk outside with you."

Aan hurried into the living room, where her parents were seated. "Hello, Aan," her mother greeted her cheerily, but her smile faded when she saw Aan's tears. "What's wrong?"

"Mom, Jaänjo is very weak. He needs to go outside to recharge in the sun. Come on, Jaänjo."

She opened the front door and followed his faint aura outside. Slowly, Jaänjo rose into the air and settled onto their roof to maximize his exposure to the sunlight.

Her parents came out and joined her. "Why are you looking up, Aan?" Keet asked, his brow furrowed.

"Jaänjo's on the roof; he's facing the sun."

"I thought he dwells inside you."

"He does, Dad, but he asked to separate from me to get maximum sunlight."

"Is he going to be okay?" Yéil said with a voice laced with alarm.

In anguish, Aan hugged her. "I hope so, Mom. I so wish I could help him."

"Do you want to sit with him, Aan? If you do, I can get the ladder out."

"Dad, he said talking is hard for him right now, and I should spend the time rejoicing with you two. We agreed to meet again when the sun sets."

"Well, let's respect his wishes and go inside," said Keet.

Aan nodded. With an expression tinged with concern, she waved to Jaänjo before following her parents inside.

Jaänjo's form delicately shimmered on the rooftop in the golden afternoon light. The sun's rays poured over him, slowly recharging his energy, each sunbeam feeling like a lifeline. Despite his weariness, his thoughts drifted far from the exhilaration he felt earlier from being a healer again. They lingered on his co-healer and what he whispered to her as she fell asleep.

When he said "I love you" to Aan, he thought about how it carried a weight and depth that far eclipsed the casual, almost habitual expressions of affection he had encountered. On N'ridium, declarations of love were often routine, akin to greetings exchanged in passing. They lacked the profound resonance that true, deep-seated love imparts.

However, with Aan, the words "I love you" emerged from a previously unknown depth within him. This love wasn't a mere formality or a hollow phrase—it was a revelation, an emotion so profound that it surged through his very being, altering his essence. For the first time, the words felt laden with meaning, filled with a sincerity that was as foreign to him as the new planet he was on. When he whispered those words to Aan, they weren't merely a statement; they mirrored something so pure and intense that it surpassed his own comprehension. This was a love that left an indelible mark on his soul, a love that echoed with the vibrations of his deepest energies. The words "I love you" had never crossed his lips with such depth and authenticity, making this declaration a unique and transformative moment that forever changed his perception of love and connection.

He sighed, thinking about how much he loved receiving his "daily" from Aan and how he desperately wanted to be in a physical form so he could hug her back with the same enthusiasm. Now, he was nothing but a wisp of energy, unable to take on a physical shape. He sighed again as the truth of his nature weighed on him. He'd never be able to hold her, touch her, or make love to her. The realization sent ripples of sorrow through his energy.

He pondered the cruel paradox of his existence. How could a being of pure energy, incapable of physical form, fall in love? The question echoed within him like a symphony of longing, desire, and sadness. Though only separated from Aan for a short time, the yearning to be with her, to reexperience the world through her senses, surged within him. The desire to feel her presence entwined with his own became an ache that seemed to stretch time itself, turning mere moments into what felt like an eternity.

As the sun descended in the sky, its light began to fade. It felt like a metaphor for his connection with Aan—strong at times but fragile at others, a complex interplay of strength and fragility that reflected the harsh reality of their differences. Despite this, he found himself irresistibly drawn to her, as if by an intangible force defying all reason. It proved both a blessing and a curse, a bittersweet paradox—to be so close yet so far from truly being with her.

A flood of "what if" possibilities danced within him like shadows in the fading light. What if he were a human being? What if he could feel the warmth of Aan's embrace, her heartbeat against his chest? What if he could hold her hand as they watched the sun sink below the horizon, painting the sky with beautiful shades of color? With each passing moment, the longing in his core grew stronger, aching to bridge the divide between their worlds.

If only... if only he could defy the boundaries of his existence, transcending the limitations of his form to be with her, truly and wholly...

A wave of unexpected relief washed over him, interrupting his musings—he was glad Aan hadn't heard his whispered admission of love. He'd be shattered if she had heard it and didn't feel the same. Even worse, it might have frightened her, compelling her to demand he leave her body. The thought of separation terrified him. Losing their precious connection was unimaginable. This revelation demanded a new imperative: he must safeguard their bond by keeping his love for her a secret. From now on, he would lock this secret deep within his energy.

Despite his lack of physical senses, Jaänjo spotted Aan's distinctive energy signal on the ground below him. As they had agreed, she'd meet him outside after sunset. He floated down and rejoined her. They both felt the scintillating sensation of their energies mixing once more.

"Hi, Jaänjo—it feels so good to have you back!" she beamed. "Your aura is noticeably bigger. Are you feeling better?"

"I am. It feels like I've returned to my favorite place in the universe," he said, his voice soothing and vibrant.

"I feel the same way," Aan replied, relieved by the strength in his voice compared to earlier. "While we were apart, it felt like I was missing a part of myself. Jaänjo, I've been so worried about you."

"Thank you for caring. I knew we'd be tired from performing such an extensive healing, but I never imagined being so drained. That's what traveling over seven thousand light-years can do to you. I think you Earthlings call it jet lag."

She laughed. "Your humor is back, which is good to see. Traveling as far as you did, I think you've surpassed the worst jet lag case that any human has ever experienced." She hugged herself. "I'm so glad you're okay."

"Her hug feels so good," Jaänjo mused. *"So good."*

"How are you, Aan? I've been concerned about you as well."

"I feel fine; my long nap refreshed me. Jaänjo, about today, healing Mom was the most exhilarating thing I've ever experienced." Her eyes welled with tears. "How your energy combined with mine was like a sensual dance—a dance with the essence of life itself. Mom's healing is a miracle caused by the power of our connection. I'm so grateful to you on many different levels."

"I've never combined my energy with another healer, so it felt just as exhilarating. You're right about it feeling like an extraordinary dance." He paused before continuing, wanting to say much more about their amazing connection, but decided to let it pass. "How's your Mom doing?"

Aan's face lit up with a radiant smile. "She's doing wonderfully, Jaänjo. You should've seen the smile on her face as she flushed all her meds down the toilet." Her voice turned serious. "Jaänjo, after my mom's healing, when you asked me to sit next to her and feel our mother-daughter energy, it was such a beautiful moment. I marveled at the power of the energy flowing between her and me. It was the most beautiful gift I've ever received—for both of us. That you even thought to have us share such a tender moment speaks well of the kindness and love in your heart. Thank you so much."

"You're welcome. When I first laid eyes on you and your mom when I was in Silas, I felt the strong bond between you two. It inspired me to help you both explore the depth of your invisible connection."

"I'm so glad you did."

As Aan breathed in, Jaänjo sensed a delightful scent he had never experienced through her. "Hey, what smells so good?"

"While you've been recharging, Mom has been a whirlwind of energy. She's preparing a special dinner just for us—the lovely scent you're experiencing is from a freshly caught chinook salmon grilling on the barbecue. Jaänjo, if you don't mind, after dinner, since it's dark out, I'd prefer to stay here instead of walking home. In Alaska, the forest's inhabitants—the large, furry ones with big teeth and even bigger appetites—regard humans and aliens from other planets as tasty treats."

"We're not quite as tasty as cinnamon rolls, but N'ridians are high in protein and low on drama—perfect snacks for forest creatures."

That night, nestled in her childhood bed, Aan reached for the light on the nightstand and turned it off. As the soft moonlight filtered through the curtains, her eyes picked out familiar shapes: the old bookshelf still packed with her favorite childhood stories, the dreamcatcher hanging in the window that her grandmother had made, the faint outlines of nature pictures on the wall, and the lingering scent of her mother's cooking—a cocoon of comforting memories. The room was silent except for the faint sound of the sea and the distant hoot of an owl. She took a deep breath, gathering her thoughts and emotions before speaking.

"Jaänjo," she, her voice soft and tender, "I loved seeing my mom beam as you complimented her meal. I hope you understand even more what my parents mean to me. Throughout my illness, they've been my unwavering support, always there with comfort and strength. Their love for me is boundless, and so is mine for them. It's woven into who I am, sustaining me through everything. They're not just my parents but my rock, guiding light, and inspiration. I cherish them deeply. Did you feel the same about your parents? Please tell me about them."

Jaänjo was slow to answer. He sighed softly, his voice tinged with sadness. "My relationship with my parents was... complicated. Let me try to explain. On N'ridium, few possessed the ability to see what I could—the aura, the life energy force of others. And the ability to manipulate auras was an even rarer gift, often associated with those with exceptional healing abilities. I was one of those people. My gift manifested early in life, allowing me to see the energy surrounding every living being. It helped me understand their emotions, physical health, and spiritual essence, showing me how all life is connected.

"Unfortunately, since both my parents were logic-driven scientists, they never accepted my being different than others, and they wanted—demanded, actually—that I be a scientist, too, just like them and my older brother, Miěěcha, who was attending a prestigious institute of higher learning. So, to please my parents, I tried to follow in their footsteps, taking countless science courses in school. But when I reached puberty, I rebelled, knowing in my heart that science wasn't for me."

"I can sympathize with how you must've felt as a kid. I also was different. Unlike other kids, I felt a deep connection with spirit in my childhood. Fortunately, my parents accepted my being different, especially since my mom's mother was a shaman. I spent many hours with my grandma, fascinated by how she could spiritually heal people. I knew early in life that I also wanted to be a shaman."

"You were fortunate to have such an understanding family," he remarked, pausing as memories from his childhood flooded back with bittersweet intensity. "My parents saw my abilities as a curse, something to be feared and shunned. Their lack of understanding created a chasm between us that grew wider as time passed, especially when my parents believed, as did nearly everyone, that combating our encroaching sun was an overarching priority."

Jaänjo sighed as he recalled that time of his life. "I was lucky to have one family member who always supported me. Miěěcha saw my gift not as a burden but as a blessing, and my earliest memories were of him encouraging me to cultivate my abilities and embrace who I was without fear or shame.

"In the days when travel on the planet's surface was still possible, Miĕĕcha came home for a brief visit. Witnessing the fractured relations between my parents and me, he sensed my inner turmoil and talked to me about it. In tears, I told him about my feelings of hopelessness and wanting to end my life. Shocked by my disclosure, he told my parents that I would live with him from then on. To my surprise, my parents didn't say no and even looked relieved to be rid of me. The feeling was mutual. Regrettably, my farewell to them was a mere halfhearted wave—absent of hugs, kind words, or any semblance of warmth. Little did I know that would be the last time I'd see them."

"That's so sad, Jaänjo."

"It is. As we left my parents' house, bound for the underground city where Miĕĕcha worked, I remember the conflicting emotions of hope and uncertainty swirling within me. It turns out that going with Miĕĕcha changed the course of my life. I gained acceptance into a prestigious institute of integrative healing and proudly attained accreditation as a healer. Joining this community filled me with an immense sense of purpose and belonging. Surrounded by like-minded individuals who understood and respected my path, I felt a deep sense of acceptance and warmth. If not for Miĕĕcha, this never would've happened."

"From what you're saying, Miĕĕcha seems to be an exceptional person and brother."

"He was always a towering presence in my life, and our bond is tightly knit and enduring. In many ways, I owe him everything; he's the reason I'm here with you today."

"How so?"

"After he graduated, Miĕĕcha specialized in advanced scientific research. He led a team that made a monumental breakthrough—discovering how to convert people into pure energy. It was a leap into the unknown, a desperate gambit born of necessity as our planet teetered on oblivion. But despite their success, there remained a crucial piece of the puzzle they had yet to solve—how to reverse the transformation and return someone to their physical form.

"As our sun's fiery tendrils reached ever closer, threatening to consume our world, a wave of desperation swept across the planet. People everywhere perished in droves. Under the relentless heat, our fusion power plants faltered, unable to yield enough energy for hydroponic crop production and the cooling systems essential to sustain life in our underground cities. Food riots broke out, and when people learned of my brother's breakthrough, everyone wanted to be converted and launched into space, hoping to survive. People with wealth and influence demanded to be converted before others, which caused more riots. As a healer, I witnessed how people became far less civilized as the panic, riots, and famine increased. Hardly anyone's primary aura glowed white during those dreadful times, so as a healer, there was hardly anyone I could help. Because my effectiveness as a healer became marginalized, the government deemed me to have little value to society, so my conversion to energy priority plummeted.

"Knowing time was running out for our planet, Miĕĕcha knew he had to convert me to energy. But he faced an agonizing decision: Launching me into the cosmos as pure energy without perfecting the conversion back to a physical form would doom me to spending an eternity in an ethereal prison. He offered a partial solution: his team discovered a non-ideal way to return to a physical state by intertwining our energy with an alien host possessing a similar biological and life energy makeup. This wasn't perfect, but it offered the possibility of escaping a formless energy prison.

"Anyway, Miĕĕcha knew I would never get converted if we waited for the energy-to-matter reversal because there'd be a stampede of others demanding to leave the planet. So he urged me to undergo the transformation and flee our doomed world. He would stay behind to perfect converting energy back to matter. Once he succeeded, he vowed to follow my trajectory and one day join me.

"Leaving him was the hardest thing I ever had to do, but we both knew this would be my only chance to live. So, Miĕĕcha's team converted me to energy under the guise of me being a test subject to perfect their new conversion equipment and launched me into space. Before getting converted, I remember hugging Miĕĕcha so tight, crying as I said goodbye to him, and wondering if I would ever see him again."

"Oh, Jaänjo, it must have been unbearable for you both to say goodbye. Do you think Miĕĕcha perfected the energy-to-matter conversion?"

"I don't know, Aan," Jaänjo said, his voice tinged with contemplative sorrow. "Miĕĕcha always pushed himself to the limits of his intellect and imagination, driven by a fierce determination to save those on our planet. And yet, somehow, he always found time to care for and nurture me. Deep in my heart, I know when Mиěěcha vowed to one day join me, it wasn't a bunch of empty words—it was a promise. A promise that no matter what distance or obstacle, it would never extinguish the flame within him to find me."

"His love for you is as powerful as the love my parents have for me. I hope I can meet him one day."

"I love him—there's nothing I wouldn't do for him. I'd love for you to meet him as well."

A flicker of unease disturbed Aan's calm. If Mиěěcha could reverse the energy conversion, would Jaänjo return to a physical form, perhaps to reunite with his brother elsewhere? The prospect of losing Jaänjo filled her with a sudden, chilling dread. She forced the thought away, unwilling to face the implications just yet.

She yawned, trying to mask her apprehension. "Sorry, it's been a long day."

"Let's say goodnight, Aan."

"Okay. Goodnight, Jaänjo." She hugged herself, a tender, comforting gesture meant for him.

"Jaänjo..." Her voice echoed with a gentle resonance that seemed to align with the rhythm of her heartbeat.

"Yes, Aan?" He noted the soft cadence of her voice, a melody he could listen to for eternity.

"Your presence in me..." She paused, choosing her words carefully. "It—it feels... right." It was a simple statement, yet it carried the weight of a revelation. What was once a foreign entity within her had become an intrinsic part of herself, leaving her with a deep sense of wholeness she hadn't realized was missing.

"Aan," Jaänjo whispered, his voice a caress against her mind. "Imagine me holding you right now, hugging you tenderly." He sighed. "I wish with every fiber of my being that this moment could be more than just shared words."

"I know. I feel the same way..."

18

THE FOLLOWING MORNING, YÉIL prepared breakfast. It was a simple yet satisfying meal of scrambled eggs flavored with cheese and flakes of leftover salmon, a savory reminder of the previous night's feast. At the center of the wooden table, she placed a large bowl brimming with wild blueberries and huckleberries, their jewel-like hues a vibrant testament to the land's bounty.

"Mmm, Mom, this is good!" Aan beamed as she took a bite of the scrambled eggs. "Jaänjo agrees."

"Thanks to both of you. What are your plans for today?"

"If you don't mind, I'd like to take Jaänjo to the meadow by my cabin so he can continue to recharge in the sun."

"Sure. Jaänjo, I hope you and Aan have a good day."

"Jaänjo says thanks, Mom. He loves being in nature as much as me."

On the trail leading to her cabin, Aan set a fast pace. "Jaänjo, my energy seems boundless since you healed me." She twirled around and laughed. "I'm happy. Can you feel it?"

"I can. You're radiating joy."

"You're right. Hey, we're almost to the meadow." She let out an audible sigh. "I know you'll need to leave me to maximize the sun's energy on you. I'll turn on my aura vision to see you, and when you're ready to enter me again, how about glowing once to let me know?"

"Good idea. Since we can't communicate well while I'm outside of you, how will you pass the time?"

"Easy. I'll meditate."

"What's that?" Jaänjo inquired, his curiosity piqued.

"Meditation is a practice where I quiet my mind, focus my attention, and connect with my inner self. It's like listening to the heartbeat of the earth beneath me. It quiets the chatter in my mind so I can hear the whispers of the spirits."

"How do you define your inner self?"

"It's the part of me that lies beyond thoughts and emotions," Aan elaborated. "It's a place of stillness, peace, and deep wisdom. Through meditation, I can tap into this wellspring of inner strength and guidance."

"We had something similar to meditation in my world. We called it *vëlîtarĭs*. As a healer, I find what you're saying fascinating because I also connect with what we call the universal energy. Please explain more about what meditating does for you."

Aan smiled. "Okay, sure. Jaänjo, meditating is like tending to a garden. It allows me to cultivate inner peace, clarity, and connection."

"Cultivate?" Jaänjo questioned.

"Yes," Aan explained. "Just as a gardener pulls weeds and nourishes the soil to help plants flourish, meditation helps me clear away mental clutter and cultivate positive qualities."

"What kind of positive qualities?"

"Qualities like compassion, patience, gratitude, and focus. Meditation helps me connect with my innermost self, my ancestors, and the spirits of this land. It strengthens my intuition and allows me to tap deeper wisdom."

"Does it help you with your work as a shaman?"

"Absolutely. Meditation sharpens my senses, enhances my ability to perceive the subtle energies around me, and deepens my connection to the spirit world. It empowers me to channel healing energy and perform my duties with clarity and compassion."

"It sounds like a powerful tool."

"It is," Aan agreed. "Meditation is a gift, a practice that allows me to nurture my spirit and fulfill my purpose as a shaman."

"Maybe after I recharge, you could explain more about what a shaman does. I already see many parallels to what I do as a healer."

"I'm seeing it, too. And, if you don't mind, I'd like you to explain more about your thoughts and feelings about your God."

"We have much to talk about."

"I know. It's exciting. I feel we're kindred spirits, Jaänjo."

"I feel the same way."

She sighed. "I guess you should leave me to recharge." She looked around and spotted a moss-covered log in the shade. "I'll sit on the log while you bask in the sun."

As the sun shifted across the sky, a beam of light pierced through the leaves, gently caressing Aan's face and rousing her from her meditative state. Her eyelids fluttered open like delicate butterfly wings, and a serene smile blossomed on her lips. She reconnected with the world around her, noting the meadow's vibrant tapestry of wildflowers—purple lupines, bright yellow buttercups, and delicate white yarrow swayed gently in the breeze. The air was thick with the sweet scents of nature, punctuated by the buzzing of bumblebees. Her gaze drifted to where she had left Jaänjo, and her smile widened upon finding him. His aura pulsed with newfound strength. She rose and approached him. His aura briefly flared as she neared, a radiant signal of his readiness to rejoin her. She opened her arms in welcome.

As his energy flowed back into her, a familiar warmth spread through her, comforting and profound. "Welcome back, Jaänjo." She wrapped her arms around herself in a gesture of affection and reassurance.

"It felt so good basking in the sun, but being with you again feels even better."

"It does. Your aura looks much brighter than it did after we healed Mom. Do you think you're—what would you call it—fully charged?"

He laughed. "I'm not sure if 'fully charged' is an accurate way to describe the state of my being, but for the first time in a long time, I feel happy and, hmmm—how can I articulate this..."

"Go on, tell me what you're thinking."

"I feel, even though I'm not a physical form... when I'm intertwined with you, I feel whole—like I'm experiencing far more physical senses than I ever did when I was a physical form. Does this make any sense?"

"It does. I can't explain it either, but when you're inside me, I feel an overwhelming sense of peace and harmony—as if I'm experiencing the world through my senses and yours. When you leave me, things don't feel right."

"It doesn't feel right to me, either."

"Do you mind walking to my cabin so I can have a bite to eat? Mom's planning on having another big dinner, so I'll have just a snack."

"Not at all."

Aan headed along the winding forest path that led to her cabin.

As she walked, Jaänjo spoke. "On my planet, we were what you Earthlings call vegetarians because raising animals to consume was too energy intensive. I have to admit that eating another once-living being troubles me."

"I understand your reservations, Jaänjo," she replied, her voice soft yet firm. "Many people share them. But on Earth, our relationship with animals is complex. For some, it's a matter of sustenance; for others, it's tradition. In my culture, we honor the animals we consume, recognizing the sacrifice they make to nourish us. We believe that we maintain balance with nature by respecting animals and using every part of them. It's a way of life that has sustained my people for countless generations."

A moment of silence passed between them. Aan sensed his internal struggle. "I see," he hesitantly replied, his tone thoughtful. "It's a perspective I hadn't considered."

"What did you eat on your planet to survive, Jaänjo?"

"Cinnamon rolls," he replied with a deadpan delivery. "They were our main source of sustenance."

She burst out laughing. "Yeah, right. Really though, what did you eat?"

"Our vegetables were different than yours, but they consisted of various nutrient-dense leafy greens and root vegetables. We also had fruits like your berries and the protein-rich equivalent of what you call legumes. Some cities had aquaponic systems providing fish as an additional protein source, but I never saw or tasted fish until I came here. They sure smell good on the grill."

"I'll bet you also never had a cinnamon roll until you came here."

"You are correct," he chuckled.

At the cabin, Jaänjo discovered yet another culinary love when he tasted the simple peanut butter and jelly sandwich that Aan had made.

"Aan," he asked, "please tell me more about being a shaman."

"Okay." She paused, collecting her thoughts, trying to find the right words to explain something deeply rooted in her identity. "Being a Tlingit shaman is more than rituals and healing. It's a deep connection to nature and the spirit world. I remember watching my grandma lead ceremonies when I was young, the way the entire Tlingit community would gather, hanging on her every word. Now, I've taken her place. It's a weighty responsibility, especially when I see the hope in people's eyes—like when I helped little Káach with his nightmares last month. Being a shaman means walking between the physical and spiritual realms."

"That's inspiring to hear. What do you mean by walking between the physical and spiritual realms?" Jaänjo's energy pulsed with intrigue.

"Good question. Shamans walk in the realm of humans, but our spirits soar in the realm of ancestors and powerful forces. We are healers, seers, guides, and protectors. As a shaman, I serve as a bridge between our physical world and the spiritual one. I'm responsible for understanding and interpreting the will of the spirits, ancestors, and natural elements."

"Where do the spirits reside?"

"We believe everything has a spirit—animals, plants, rocks, and rivers. These spirits are always around us and interact with our world in ways we don't always see."

"Do the spirits ever appear to you?" Jaänjo asked, his voice tinged with awe.

"Sometimes. Not in the way you might think, though. They often come to me in dreams or visions. They might show themselves as animals or other symbols. Interpreting these signs is a big part of my role."

"And what do you do with the guidance they give you?"

"I use it to help the community. If someone is sick, I ask the spirits for healing knowledge. If someone has a problem or question, I seek the spirits' advice. It's about finding balance and harmony in all things."

"Can you tell me more about healing? And how do you know if an illness is physical or spiritual?"

"That's where my training and intuition come in. I've learned to recognize the signs of both. I often treat physical ailments with herbs and plants. For spiritual issues, I perform ceremonies to cleanse and realign the person's spirit."

"What kind of ceremonies?"

"Each ceremony is unique, depending on the issue. It might involve chanting, drumming, and using sacred objects like feathers or stones. The goal is to connect with the spirit world and ask for its help in healing."

Aan paused briefly, thinking. "Ceremonial leadership is a significant part of my responsibilities. I lead important community events such as weddings, naming ceremonies, and funerals. These rituals mark crucial life transitions and help individuals and the community navigate these changes. For instance, during a funeral, I help guide the departed's spirit to the afterlife, ensuring they are honored and their spirit finds peace.

"In times of conflict or crisis, I mediate and offer counsel. Whether it's a dispute between individuals or a larger community issue, my role is to seek a resolution that restores harmony and balance. This often involves spiritual consultation, rituals to clear negative energy, and practical advice based on the teachings of our ancestors.

"Oh! One of my key roles is storytelling. Our people's myths and legends are not just tales but lessons encoded in narrative form. They teach us about our history, values, and how to live harmoniously with the world around us. As a shaman, I'm also a keeper of these stories, ensuring they're passed down to future generations. Being a shaman also means being a custodian of our traditions and a protector of our Tlingit cultural heritage. It's like holding a piece of the universe's puzzle, ensuring our connection to the cosmos remains intact.

"Lastly, personal spiritual development is a continuous journey for me. I spend significant time meditating, connecting with the natural world, and seeking personal visions. These practices help me grow as a shaman and enhance my ability to serve the community."

"Aan, do the spirits ever ask for anything in return?"

"Yes, sometimes. They might ask for offerings, like food or a special object. It's a way of showing respect and gratitude. Maintaining a good relationship with the spirits is crucial."

As Jaänjo absorbed the information, a thoughtful silence settled over him. A moment later, his energy pulsed with a newfound understanding of Aan. "Your work is quite important and admirable. How do you become a shaman?"

"The journey to becoming a shaman starts early in life. It involves years of learning and experiencing the traditions and wisdom passed down from our ancestors. It's a calling," Aan replied. "A gift from the spirits. It requires years of training, learning the ways of the plants and animals, and listening to the whispers of the wind and the rivers. It requires courage, for we face the darkness and the light. I've had to study the medicinal properties of plants, learn the significance of animal spirits, and understand the intricate balance of nature."

"The path to becoming a healer was no less daunting for me," said Jaänjo. "The training demanded every ounce of my strength and spirit—and an unwavering commitment."

He paused, reflecting. "Aan, my unique gift—seeing auras—has always set me apart from others, making solitude a familiar companion. Even as a healer, this isolation persists. As a shaman, do you also experience this feeling of separateness?"

"I do," she said softly. "And as my MS progressed, it further isolated me from others. But being a shaman is also incredibly fulfilling. I'm deeply connected to my community and the world around me. I see and experience things that most people don't, and I'm always learning."

"Do you ever get scared? With my planet and our society collapsing, fear was a constant, always there, gnawing at me."

"Yes, Jaänjo, I, too, have known much fear, especially with the MS ravaging my body. And sometimes, I feel the vast and mysterious spirit world can be overwhelming. But I've learned that fear is part of the journey, and it teaches me to be humble and respectful." She hesitated for several moments... "Jaänjo, I have to admit that my illness made me question everything about my beliefs in there being spirits and in shamanism itself. I prayed and pleaded to the spirits to help me, but it fell on deaf ears."

"I disagree."

"Why"

"Because I believe your spirits did answer your call, Aan. They sent me."

He paused, letting the weight of his words settle. "Consider this: I was converted to pure energy, launched into space, and hurtled through the cosmos. And yet, in the infinite expanse of the universe, I ended up here, on Earth, in your tiny village. Do you truly believe that was just a matter of chance?"

"I guess I believed it was a chance encounter rather than a divine action."

Jaänjo's energy radiated with intensity as he spoke, "I believe your spirits, and perhaps the universal energy I call God, orchestrated our meeting. Consider this, Aan: your prayers were so powerful, your connection to the spirit world so strong, that they reached across the stars and brought us together."

"Jaänjo, what you're saying makes perfect sense! Oh my goodness." She hugged herself. "Jaänjo, you not only rejuvenated my health, but you've just restored my faith as well."

"You've also restored my faith, Aan. It's proof that we're both healers."

Aan touched her chest. "I think it's the work of our hearts, Jaänjo. For me, it's my way of serving my people, honoring my ancestors, and tending to the spirits of this land."

"I agree that it is a calling for both of us. And what's truly remarkable is that even though we come from vastly different worlds, our purpose—our mission—is remarkably similar. We're both dedicated to serving and healing others." He paused, reflecting on the unexpected parallels between their paths. "Though our approach may differ, the essence of our work is eerily similar."

"It is," Aan agreed, a warmth spreading through her chest. "That's why I feel such a powerful connection to you, Jaänjo. I'm so glad we had this talk. It touches me that you see the value in what I do. If you didn't, I don't think we could truly understand each other."

Her voice softened, taking on a more vulnerable tone. "It's not always easy to be a shaman. Many don't understand or appreciate the sacrifices we make. To have someone like you, who not only respects my path but also shares a similar calling... it means more than you can know."

"I feel the same way." Unexpectantly, Jaänjo's energy flickered with unease. "Aan... I can't help but wonder about the challenges we might face. Our abilities, combined, are powerful. I wonder how others will react when they discover what we can do. And what if someone tries to exploit our gifts?"

19

ANOTHER DAY PASSED WITH Jaänjo spending more time in the sun, recharging, and getting ready for the next round of healing for Yéil in the morning. In bed that night, Aan hugged one of her pillows. "I had another good day with you, Jaänjo. I'm still laughing about how you demanded I eat my cheeseburger faster at dinner. You're turning into quite the carnivore."

He laughed. "It tasted so good."

"Are you sure tomorrow's healing session will cure Mom of all her ills?"

"I am. We've already fixed most of her issues."

"Jaänjo, can you explain more about how you heal people?"

"Sure. In my world, healers have honed our understanding of energy to a degree you might find remarkable. We perceive the universe as a symphony of vibrations, a complex interplay of frequencies and patterns. Every living being, every object, resonates with a unique energy signature."

He paused, his energy flowing through Aan like a soothing balm. "When illness or injury afflicts a body, it disrupts this harmonious flow, creating imbalances and blockages in the energy field. As a healer, I perceive the subtle flows and imbalances within your body in a way others cannot. Most people see any physical form as something seemingly solid, but for me, it's a vibrant tapestry of energy pathways and centers.

"When I lay my hands over someone needing healing," he continued, "I channel a transformative energy that penetrates to the very core of their being. This energy delicately manipulates the blueprint of their cells, restoring them to a healthy state and guiding the body back into harmony and balance. It's as if I am realigning the intricate threads of their physical and emotional fabric, mending what has become frayed or tangled."

Aan nodded. "I experienced this transformative energy coming through my hands when we healed my mom. I'm still awed by it."

"And I'm in awe of how our energies intertwined to create a potent healing force."

"Jaänjo, can you explain in more detail how you make changes at the molecular level?"

Jaänjo's energy pulsed with a focused intensity as he addressed Aan's question. "Okay. Hmm... how to say this... When I speak of manipulating energy at a molecular level, it's akin to adjusting the very building blocks of your being. Imagine each cell as a miniature universe, teeming with complex structures and processes. Within these cells, molecules interact in a delicate dance, orchestrating the symphony of life."

He paused, contemplating how to continue. "My healing energy acts as a catalyst, profoundly influencing these molecular interactions. It can repair damaged DNA strands, mend broken proteins, and even restore the integrity of cellular membranes. Think of it as a microscopic repair crew meticulously fixing the tiny tears and imperfections accumulated over time.

"This molecular realignment triggers a cascade of beneficial effects. Cells become more efficient at performing their functions, tissues regenerate with renewed vigor, and organs operate in greater harmony. It's like restoring the foundation of a building, ensuring that the entire structure is stable and resilient."

His energy radiated into her with a warm reassurance. "The changes I make are not superficial, Aan. They are fundamental, reaching down to the essence of one's being. This is why the healing I offer is so deep and lasting. It's not simply about masking symptoms, but about addressing the root cause of the imbalance and restoring your body to its natural state of health and vitality."

"Thank goodness for that, especially with my mom's cancer and my MS."

"Anyway, getting back to how I heal people, I can sense in their auras where the flow of energy is stagnant or disrupted, where disharmony has taken root. This is often the underlying cause of illness or discomfort. By subtly changing the energy within someone, I can restore their balance and harmony. I can also stimulate the flow in stagnate areas, soothe inflammation areas, and realign their energy centers. It's not about imposing my energy upon someone's body but rather about working in harmony with their body's innate wisdom and capacity for self-repair.

"As my healing energy flows through them, it helps their body to realign at a molecular level. This means it fixes any disruptions within their cells, tissues, and organs, bringing everything back into a healthy, balanced state. Even though this process happens on a level too small to see, its effects are felt throughout their entire being, leading to a deep and lasting transformation. The colors in their aura, which once showed signs of trouble, return to a balanced white state, reflecting the restored health and emotional peace."

His voice resonated with a deep understanding. "Think of it like a river, Aan. When the flow is obstructed, the water becomes motionless and unhealthy. By removing the blockage, the river can flow freely again, bringing life and vitality to the surrounding ecosystem."

"That's a good analogy."

"Thanks. In the same way, by restoring the natural flow of energy within someone's body, I can facilitate healing and promote well-being."

He paused again, his energy pulsing with warmth and compassion. "Like how you summon spirits to heal others, I invoke the divine energy that flows through all things to heal. For me, it's a reminder that we are all connected, all part of the same vibrant tapestry of life."

"That's beautiful, Jaänjo. As you said, it's truly remarkable how even though we come from different worlds, our life's purpose is remarkably similar. And you were right to say that though our approach to healing may differ, the essence of our work is eerily similar."

"It is."

"It's fascinating to hear how you heal people." She yawned. "I suppose I should get some sleep. I'm excited about tomorrow—and so is my mom."

"It shouldn't take long to do it. Maybe afterward, we could visit a certain bakery in town for sustenance."

She laughed. "I already mentioned to Mom how that should be our special treat to you for healing her."

In the morning, knowing they would go to the Party Time Bakery after Jaänjo healed her in the morning, Yéil made a simple breakfast of yogurt mixed with berries and oats.

As they sat at the table, Yéil looked at Aan. "Can you tell me what Jaänjo plans to do today?"

Aan put her spoon down and smiled. "Jaänjo," she said, "will you please talk to Mom about what she should expect?"

"Of course," said Jaänjo. "Please let her know it'll be talking through you for the next few moments."

"Mom, Jaänjo wants to speak to you now. Go on, Jaänjo..."

"Good morning, Yéil. Here's what I plan to do when my energy is within you. First, I'll hunt for any remaining cancer cells and fix them at the molecular level. Then, I'll tend to what's causing the glaucoma in your eyes. Aan and I already corrected most of that in the first procedure. Your arteries have lost some of their elasticity, causing them to be less able to absorb the force of each heartbeat, which causes you to have high blood pressure. I'll correct that. Your cells have developed insulin resistance, causing elevated blood sugar levels. I'll take care of that, too, and then I'll finish repairing the cartilage in your left knee that's causing you pain."

"Thanks, Jaänjo. Will this take all day to do?"

"No, it'll take maybe an hour or so."

Her eyes went wide. "Only an hour?"

"Since you all have graciously said we can go to the Party Time Bakery afterward, I'll try to finish it in thirty minutes."

They all laughed.

"Jaänjo... will it hurt when you fix things inside me?"

"No, Yéil, it won't. You'll feel warm sensations, but it won't be painful. You can lie in your bed again whenever you're ready, and I'll enter you."

"Okay. It'll be interesting to experience what Aan is experiencing—having your energy inside her."

"Forgive me ahead of time if you experience gas."

Aan burst out laughing. "He's messing with you, Mom."

Yéil laughed, too, as did Keet. "Jaänjo," she said, "there's a bit of a rascal in you."

"If you only knew," Aan chuckled. "Jaänjo could be a standup comedian."

Yéil reclined on the bed, her fingers nervously plucking at the quilt—a family heirloom adorned with traditional Tlingit designs. Aan and Keet flanked her, lending a comforting presence. The room was thick with anticipation, and the air seemed to hum with unseen energy.

"Mom," said Aan, her voice soothing, "Jaänjo asks if you're ready to receive his healing energy."

Yéil took a deep breath. She glanced at the dreamcatcher hanging in the window—a gift from her mother, a connection to generations of healers before them. "I'm ready," she whispered, her voice steady despite her apprehension.

Aan felt Jaänjo's presence stir within her like a warm current beneath her skin. Then, his energy emerged with a sensation akin to a gentle exhalation. He coalesced in the air above Yéil, a softly pulsing orb of white light that cast dancing shadows across the room. For a moment, he hovered there as if gathering himself. Then, with a fluidity that belied his otherworldly nature, he enveloped Yéil, seeping into her very being.

Yéil's eyes widened with wonder. "I feel... a warmth," she murmured to Aan and Keet, her eyelids fluttering as Jaänjo's energy coursed through her. "A warmth that isn't just on my skin, but... within me. It's like a thousand tiny suns, all glowing gently inside."

Aan and Keet looked at each other in amazement. She reached out and touched Yéil's hand. "I know how that feels, Mom."

Yéil's eyes widened, and her breath caught, conveying a look of wonderment. "It's changing," she whispered to Aan and Keet, her voice barely audible. "The warmth... it's moving, flowing. It feels like tiny rivers of light are coursing through me." She paused, concentrating on the sensations. "It's... it's so precise. Like he's following specific paths within me, finding every hidden corner, every forgotten nook."

A soft gasp escaped her lips as she felt a surge of energy in her chest. "He's... he's touching my heart," she murmured, her voice thick with emotion. "It's beating stronger, steadier. I can feel it."

Tears welled up in Keet's eyes as he watched his wife, overwhelmed by awe and gratitude. "Can you feel him working on the other parts, too, Yéil?" he asked, his voice trembling.

Yéil nodded slowly, her gaze distant. "Yes," she breathed. "Everywhere. My eyes, my legs... even places I didn't know needed healing. It's like... like he's following the intricate lines that connect every part of me."

A sense of peace settled over her as Jaänjo's energy continued his meticulous exploration. "He's everywhere, touching every part of me. It's... it's extraordinary."

A wave of awe washed over Aan as she witnessed this miraculous healing. She touched her mom's chest and felt the warmth of Jaänjo's energy radiating from her mom into her hand.

"He's working on your knee now," Aan observed, noting the subtle shift in Yéil's aura. "The red is fading, replaced by a soothing, healthy white glow."

Yéil nodded, a peaceful smile gracing her lips. "The knee pain is gone," she whispered.

A tingling sensation spread through Yéil's body as she felt Jaänjo's energy gradually retreat, flowing outward toward her skin like a tide receding from the shore. The warmth that had permeated her being now concentrated at the surface, leaving a tingling sensation in its wake.

"He's moving outward," Yéil whispered, her eyes still closed. "The warmth is gathering at my skin, becoming more intense." She paused, a gasp escaping her lips. "It's... it's like I'm glowing from within."

Aan and Keet watched with wonder as a soft, ethereal light emanated from Yéil's skin, casting a warm white glow around her. The light grew brighter and began forming into a pulsing ball of otherworldly energy.

"He's... leaving me," Yéil breathed, her voice filled with wonder. The pure white light hovered above her, shimmering with a comforting energy.

Aan stood, arms outstretched, eyes closed in anticipation of Jaänjo's radiant embrace. The ball of light descended, merging seamlessly with her form. A shiver of pure joy coursed through her as Jaänjo's energy melded with her essence, filling her with a profound sense of warmth and well-being. A contented sigh escaped her lips as she reveled in the feeling of wholeness, of being reunited with a kindred energy.

Aan hugged herself. "Welcome back, Jaänjo," she said with a smile. "How did Mom's healing go?"

"Hi, Aan. Everything went well. As you can see, your mom's white aura proves her afflictions are gone."

"Mom, Jaänjo says the procedure went well, and he fixed everything."

Keet gently took Yéil's hand, his thumb tracing small circles on her palm. "I've been by your side through every doctor's appointment, every treatment," he said softly. "To see you healed like this... it's a miracle I never dared hope for." His voice cracked with emotion. "I feel like I'm getting my wife back."

"You are, Keet," said Yéil in tears. "Because of Aan and Jaänjo, you are. Thank you so much, Jaänjo. Feeling you inside of me is me is like nothing I've ever experienced."

"Please tell her she's quite welcome," said Jaänjo. "Now, um, could we get a cinnamon roll?"

"Mom, Jaänjo says you're quite welcome. He's ready for a cinnamon roll."

In the cozy warmth of the town's bakery, Keet and Yéil found a table and sat down while Aan purchased three enormous cinnamon rolls and coffee. As she walked to her parents with a tray laden with sweet deliciousness, Jaänjo acted like an excited kid. "Inhale deeply again, Aan, so I can smell the mouthwatering aromas." She rolled her eyes and took a deep breath. "Oh, yeah—it smells so good. Inhale again, please!"

She laughed. "Your enthusiasm could brighten the darkest of days, Jaänjo. You've earned this cinnamon roll, that's for sure." She took a seat, and they each grabbed a roll and coffee. "Well, I better take a bite before Jaänjo starts impatiently jumping up and down inside me." She took a big bite where the icing was particularly generous on the cinnamon roll."

Inside of her, Jaänjo swooned as he savored the bready, gooey culinary masterpiece. "Oh, my. Oh, my oh my."

"It's too bad we can't see Jaänjo," Aan chuckled. "I'm sure his eyes would be crossed right now in utter delight."

Both Yéil and Keet laughed, imagining the blissed-out spirit within their daughter.

Yéil touched Aan's hand, her expression turning serious. "Aan, while I was getting treatment at the native hospital in Juneau, I made several friends with others of our people who have cancer just as bad or worse than me. Could you ask Jaänjo if he could cure them, too?"

Within Aan, the lightheartedness Jaänjo was experiencing vanished. Aan sensed his mood change. She took a deep breath, knowing something was amiss. "What's wrong, Jaänjo?"

"Aan, we need to talk in private. Please think your words instead of saying them aloud. I'll still be able to hear you."

"Okay. Mom and Dad, Jaänjo and I need to talk to each other mentally, so give me a few minutes to do this."

Her parents exchanged concerned glances. "Do you want us to leave?" Yéil asked in a surprised tone.

"No. I'll speak to Jaänjo mentally. In the meantime, please enjoy your treats." She shifted her chair slightly and gazed out the window, focusing on the street outside.

"I'm ready to listen, Jaänjo. Can you hear my thoughts?"

"I can." He paused, and she felt his hesitation. It was as if he was carefully weighing each word before speaking.

Aan took a sip of her coffee, feeling the comforting heat spread through her, and mentally prepared herself for the conversation she sensed coming.

"Aan," Jaänjo began, his voice resonating gently within her mind, "your mother's request is heartfelt and understandable. But we need to consider the consequences of what she's asking."

She sighed softly, feeling the weight of the situation settle on her shoulders. "I know, Jaänjo. Healing my mother was such a beautiful gift. But what's the harm in helping a few more people?"

He sighed. "It's not just about helping a few more people. If word spreads about what we can do together, Tenakee Springs could become a mecca for the sick and desperate. Hundreds, if not thousands, could come, all seeking a miracle. You would never be able to live an ordinary life or have moments of peaceful contemplation. Also, it takes much of my energy to heal others, especially those with weak auras and extensive afflictions. You saw how exhausted I was after your Mom's first healing session. I don't have sufficient energy reserves to cure scores of people each day."

Aan glanced through the bakery's window, imagining the quiet town overrun with strangers and the toll it took on Jaänjo to heal her mother. The thought made her grimace. "I hear what you're saying, Jaänjo, but how could I turn away people who need help? How can you turn them away?"

"It's not about turning them away," Jaänjo replied gently. "On my planet, healers constantly faced moral dilemmas associated with our power, such as the responsibility of saving lives and the burden of constant demand for our services. And we grappled with whether to charge for our healing abilities and how much to charge, balancing our altruistic instincts with practical needs. It would help to consider how being a healer like me will impact your life. Imagine never having a moment's peace, where those needing help would relentlessly hound you everywhere you go. You'd surely suffer from compassion fatigue, unable to keep up with the demands and the emotional toll it would take on you."

Aan's eyes softened with understanding but also with conflict. She felt torn between her desire to help and the reality of Jaänjo's words. "I see what you're saying. But we can't just ignore people who need healing. Maybe there's a way to balance it?"

Jaänjo's energy pulsed thoughtfully. "Aan, we need to keep our abilities hidden from the public eye to avoid undue attention and maintain a semblance of normalcy. Perhaps we can start by secretly helping a few, but we must be cautious. Our well-being is just as important as others. If we are chronically strained and exhausted, we won't be able to help anyone."

Aan nodded slowly, taking in his words. She glanced at her parents, who were watching her with hopeful eyes and felt the pressure of their expectations. "I agree we need a plan, a way to help without losing ourselves in the process."

"Exactly," Jaänjo affirmed. "We can discuss how to select those we help and ensure it doesn't become overwhelming. If word gets out, we'll face a situation neither of us can handle."

Aan felt a chill run down her spine. She thought of the government agencies that might take an interest in their abilities or, worse, those who might try to exploit their power for personal gain. Maintaining secrecy suddenly felt like an urgent necessity.

"Okay," she agreed. "Everything you've said makes sense. I'll let Mom know that we have to proceed with caution, and until we figure out a way that works for us, we can't proceed with any healing."

Jaänjo's presence felt warmer, more settled. "Thank you, Aan."

With that, she turned back to her parents. "Mom, Dad, healing people is utterly exhausting for Jaänjo and me in several ways. We need to figure out how to help others without becoming overwhelmed. Until we have a plan for doing that, we can't help others. And we ask that you tell no one about your healing, Mom, or mine. If they ask, say our spirits touched us both."

Yéil sighed, her face etched with sadness. "My friends don't have much time for you and Jaänjo to come up with a plan, Aan. Without your and Jaänjo's help, they won't survive."

In her mom's anguished look, Aan immediately grasped the magnitude of Jaänjo's words about desperate people needing their immediate help. It tugged at her heart yet made her inwardly cringe about it becoming an all-consuming endeavor where a moment of peace would be considered a selfish luxury.

"Mom, I understand what you're saying, but you have to trust me and Jaänjo on this. We can't cure the world. So, we must learn to manage this gift carefully, or it will become our curse..."

Aan glanced out the window again and imagined tiny Tenakee Springs flooded with desperate people seeking a miraculous healing. The town's tranquil life would vanish. While some businesses might boom, she worried about the impact on their close-knit community. How would her Tlingit people, already struggling to preserve their way of life, cope with this influx? The weight of this potential future settled heavily on her.

Keet touched Yéil's hand. "Aan and Jaänjo are right, Yéil. Hundreds of people will camp at her door if word gets out that Aan can cure any illness. She'll never have any peace, and they're right—it will become a curse."

Yéil sighed and nodded. "It doesn't seem fair that you and I received a healing when so many others need help, too."

"I know, Mom. We're all of equal importance in the eyes of our spirits, and perhaps our healing is a sign. I need to listen to the spirits to learn why they brought Jaänjo to us. In the meantime, let's practice gratitude for the health blessings we each have received."

20

ON THEIR RETURN TO Aan's parents' home, several people commented in amazement about Aan not hobbling on crutches. In response to their queries, she smiled and responded, "Our spirits touched me, and my MS is now in remission." No one challenged her assertion, especially her Tlingit friends.

"Hey, Mom and Dad," said Aan as they walked. Would you mind if Jaänjo and I head to my cabin? I'm sure he needs to recharge after your healing. I'll start working again tomorrow—I need to pay several bills."

"That's fine," Yéil replied. "Jaänjo, once more, thank you so much for all you've done for me. Keet and I promise that no one but us will know how Aan and I were healed."

"Jaänjo says you are most welcome, Mom, and he thanks you for letting us find a way to manage our gift to heal."

They stopped, hugged, and said goodbye at the trail leading to Aan's cabin. Aan bounded up the steep dirt path, her smile as bright as the Alaskan sun. "It feels good to be alone again with you, Jaänjo. I just flashed on the thought of my lonely trail packed with hordes of people coming to my cabin wanting to be healed. The thought is troubling, especially since I cherish my solitude."

"I hear you. Speaking of cherishing your solitude, am I infringing on that in an unwelcomed way?"

She stopped and hugged herself. "Jaänjo, I feel like you're a part of me. Not a separate entity inside of me but an extension of myself. When you returned to me after curing Mom this morning, it was as if a missing piece of me had returned."

"I felt it, too. It's incredible how powerful our connection has become in such a short time."

"I know. I'm already dreading you soon leaving again to recharge. If you don't mind, I'll use that time to meditate."

"That's a good idea. Fortunately, your mother's healing today didn't drain me too much, so I won't need to be in the sun for long."

"Just a heads up about dinner," she cautioned. "My culinary skills pale compared to my mother's, so be prepared for a simple meal."

"I was thinking—maybe we should have dinner every night at their house to help me bond more with your parents."

She chuckled. "Nice try, but I see through your clever ploy. Before we met, I was often tempted to do the same thing, but with my MS, the trip back and forth was too much. Now, it's just a quick jaunt to get to their house."

"Or the bakery," Jaänjo quipped.

His subtle humor brought a smile to Aan's face. "I love how your wit brightens my day."

At the meadow, Aan stopped at the same moss-covered log she had sat on the day before. "Whenever you're ready, feel free to leave me." She touched her nose, activating her ability to see auras.

"Sounds good. Here I go..."

Once more, Jaänjo's energy departed from Aan. She watched his shimmering aura drift to a sun-drenched patch of meadow and remain there, still. With a cheerful sigh, she settled on the log, closed her eyes, and quieted her mind, ready to commune with her spirits.

After meditating, Aan smiled as she opened her eyes and gazed upward, admiring the deep blue sky. But as she turned to see Jaänjo's aura, her breath caught in her throat. Her eyes widened in fear as she fixated on the hulking figures of two black bears standing beside Jaänjo. Cold dread washed over her; her heart pounded against her ribs. Although she froze in place, instinctively, her muscles coiled with the urge to flee, terrified by what the bears might do to her. As Jaänjo's aura moved toward her, the bears followed. Panicked, she motioned for him to move away, but he ignored her frantic gestures and merged with her.

"Jaänjo," she whispered, "we need to get out of here. Now."

"What's wrong?" Jaänjo's confusion rippled through her.

"Jaänjo, bears eat people." Her voice conveyed abject terror.

He laughed. "There's no need to worry, Aan. My friends mean you no harm. See—their auras glow white. The bears you should avoid have dark auras. May I use your arms?" She hesitated, her body still coiled with fear.

Jaänjo moved her hands onto the head of each bear. "They love being scratched behind their ears." As he scratched behind their ears, they each made low, rumbling sounds, clearly content and feeling relaxed.

"Jaänjo, this is amazing!"

"I told them they're welcome to drop by anytime to say hello, but don't invite any of their grouchy friends to come with them. Are you ready to go to the cabin?"

"Yes."

"Okay, let's say goodbye to them."

"Do they understand what you say to them?"

"Probably not, but they sense our good energy."

Through Aan, Jaänjo patted both of them on the head. "Goodbye, my friends. Aan and I hope to see you soon."

As Aan walked away, she glanced behind her and saw the bears drift into the forest.

"Jaänjo, I'm at a loss for words…"

That night, dinner consisted of canned stew, crackers, and a simple salad. After heating the stew in her microwave, Aan blew on her first spoonful before tasting it. "Well, Jaänjo, what do you think?"

"I think… well, you know, uh, um… it's… warm."

She laughed. "I know, I know. There's nothing quite like Mom's home cooking."

Through Aan's eyes, Jaänjo peered into a bowl of stew. "What are those brightly colored things?"

"They're called carrots," Aan replied. "We call their color orange."

"Hmm." Jaänjo thought for a few moments. "Maybe orange things are best for decoration, not consumption."

"You crack me up. Hey, tonight, let's have a fire outside. I haven't sat by my fire pit in ages. It'll be fun."

"I've never sat by an open fire before."

"Like my stew, you're in for a treat."

He laughed. "Aan, your humor brightens my days, too."

After dinner, once Aan had washed and put away the dishes, she gathered logs and kindling and carried them to the fire pit, arranging the kindling among the logs. As evening fell, she set a match to the kindling. Soon, the logs caught fire and crackled as the flames danced higher. Aan sat on a portable chair near the fire and breathed in the sweet, woodsy scent of the burning Sitka spruce. Amidst the darkness, the forest surrounding her exuded an air of mystery, its presence felt rather than seen. The Alaskan wilderness stretched around her, a testament to the ancient beauty and strength of the land, its secrets hidden beneath the cloak of night.

"Jaänjo," she whispered, "I feel a deep connection to the earth and the spirits of my ancestors. Can you feel it, too?"

"I feel many things, Aan. The wonderful scent of the burning wood, the primal joy of seeing flames dancing, the brilliance of the stars shining above me, and the joy I feel from sharing this with you. I, too, feel a deep connection to all that is holy."

"I'm glad you're here, enjoying this with me."

As the fire danced, casting flickering shadows on the trees around them, Aan touched her heart, acknowledging Jaänjo's presence within her. "Jaänjo, can you tell me more about how you perceive God?"

She felt Jaänjo's warmth spread through her. "I'd be happy to. On my planet, we understand God in a way that may differ from what you and other Earthlings know. For us, God is not a living being but a pure form of energy, the fundamental vibration from which all other frequencies arise."

Aan's brow furrowed as she pondered this. "Vibration? Frequencies? Can you explain this more?"

"Sure. Imagine that the universe is a grand symphony. Every entity—a rock, a tree, or a living being—resonates with its unique energy signature, a specific frequency at which it vibrates. These frequencies interact with each other, creating patterns and harmonies that sustain the balance of life."

Aan nodded slowly, trying to visualize the symphony Jaänjo described. "So, this energy you speak of is like the music of the universe?"

"Yes—exactly. On N'ridium, we perceive this divine essence as the source of all energy, manifesting in countless forms—the conductor and the music itself, guiding the interplay of all these vibrations. This essence isn't separate from us but is the very fabric of existence.

"Think about this forest where we're sitting. Everything here—the trees, the soil, the rocks, the animals, the air we breathe—even our bodies—are composed of countless vibrating particles, a swirling dance of energy. And this energy isn't just confined to individual objects or beings. It flows between us, connecting us and to the vast cosmos. This interaction of energies, this symphony, is how we experience the sacredness of existence. It's both within everything and larger than everything simultaneously."

Aan nodded slowly, trying to grasp the concept. "So, it's like... the ocean?" she offered. "Each wave, each droplet is part of it, but it's also more than just the sum of its parts?"

"Exactly!" Jaänjo's energy pulsed with excitement. "And just as the ocean influences the weather and the land, this divine energy shapes and influences all of existence.

Aan absently touched a small rock lining the fire pit with her toe. "But, Jaänjo, how does this energy relate to what we perceive as solid matter?"

"Good question. Consider the rock you just touched. It seems still and solid, but it's a vibrant community of atoms, each reflecting God's divine energy. Normally, these atoms are tightly bound and slow-moving, creating the solid rock you see. However, adding enough heat energizes the rock's atoms, causing them to vibrate more intensely and break their connections. The solid rock will melt, turning into a liquid—just like when lava, which is molten rock, flows from a volcano. This change from solid to liquid mirrors the adaptable nature of divine energy. Add even more energy, and the liquid rock turns into gas. So, even a seemingly solid rock is just slow-moving energy. When we observe the rock's transformation, we see not only a physical change but also a glimpse of God's energy within it."

"I never considered that solid objects are slow-moving energy, but you explained it well." Aan stared into the fire pit, mesmerized by the dancing flames. "Look, Jaänjo," she murmured, "the solid logs are also transforming. The heat breaks them down, converting their solid form into heat, light, smoke, and ash."

"You're right," Jaänjo replied. "The illusion of solidity is created by energy vibrating at different frequencies. Understanding that everything—every rock, flower, person, and star—is fundamentally composed of energy is key to our perception of the divine. All matter is energy, and this energy is what we call God."

Aan's eyes widened with realization. "So, everything I see and touch is part of your God?"

"Yes," Jaänjo replied. "Everything in the universe is inextricably woven from this divine energy. The rocks, the trees, the stars, and every living being are manifestations of this energy. This means that the divine essence permeates everything and everyone. By understanding this, we see that we are all interconnected and integral parts of God. In other words, you are part of God, and God is part of you."

Aan took a deep breath, her mind opening to the vastness of Jaänjo's proposition. "On Earth, many people see God as a creator, an all-powerful being who exists apart from us. Your perception of God deviates from this."

Jaänjo's energy pulsed warmly within Aan, a comforting feeling. "To me, the idea of God being separate from us is like saying a wave is separate from the ocean—it simply doesn't make sense."

He paused, allowing the analogy to settle in Aan's mind. "Just as a wave is an expression of the ocean, a temporary manifestation of its vastness, so are we expressions of the divine energy that permeates the universe. We are not separate entities but rather unique patterns within the cosmic tapestry. The energy that animates your body, the thoughts that dance through your mind, the emotions that swell within your heart are all part of the same universal energy that swirls and flows through everything, all expressions of the same divine source."

"Wow, this is a lot to take in. But I think, deep down, I've always sensed what you're saying."

"Isn't it comforting to know that in every breath you take, every step you make, and every act of kindness you perform, you express the divine energy that flows through you? You are not separate from God, Aan, but an inseparable part of the grand symphony of existence."

Aan smiled at that thought. "In my Tlingit traditions, we don't have one singular God like most religions on my planet do. Instead, we believe in a rich tapestry of spirits who inhabit the world around us—the land, the sea, the animals, the wind, everything. These spirits are our guides, our protectors, our ancestors. We honor them through ceremony, song, and dance. They are not separate from us, but a part of us, and we are a part of them. So, I guess you could say our God is also the interconnectedness of all living things, the spirit that flows through everything. Like you, we believe in the interconnectedness of all life and that every being is a part of a greater whole. So your concept of divine energy resonates deeply with my beliefs."

"It does," Jaänjo responded. "Very deeply. As a healer, I strive to harmonize with divine energy, to align my frequencies with the greater symphony. If you remember, we strive for this harmony by practicing vëlîtarïs—similar to your meditation. This alignment brings balance and peace, like how your shamanic practices connect you to the spirits and the natural world. The interconnectedness you speak of is the very essence of this grand symphony. Each of us, each entity, is a note in this cosmic melody. By understanding and harmonizing with our unique frequencies, we contribute to the overall harmony of existence."

"I see the similarities between your vëlîtarïs and what I call meditation."

"Me, too. Aan, the unity and oneness of everything is fundamental to my understanding of God," continued Jaänjo. "The universe is a single, interconnected whole. Every atom, every molecule, every being is part of this grand tapestry, vibrating with the same universal energy. Consider your love for your mother. That powerful connection you have with her is a manifestation of this divine energy. It's one of the purest expressions of the interconnectedness that binds everything together. We healers on N'ridium learned to perceive and harmonize with these vibrations, understanding that nothing exists in isolation."

Aan took a deep breath and exhaled slowly, thinking. "Love is a powerful energy. So, when you speak of healing, is it about restoring this harmony within ourselves and with the universe?"

"Yes, Aan," Jaänjo confirmed. "Healing is not just about mending physical ailments; it is about restoring balance and harmony within the individual and the greater cosmos. We connect with the divine essence that sustains all life by attuning ourselves to the fundamental vibration."

Aan looked up at the stars, admiring their brilliance. Jaänjo's voice resonated within her. "Do you see the wonder of it all, Aan? Each star is a manifestation of divine energy, contributing to the vast symphony of the universe. These energies make up what we consider God—everything is part of this divine essence."

The fire crackled softly, casting a warm glow over Aan as she absorbed Jaänjo's words. She felt a deep sense of peace and clarity, understanding that the divine essence he described was not so different from the spiritual forces she revered. "Your words bring a new dimension to my understanding of the sacred," she said softly. "It's as if the symphony of your world and the spirits of mine are singing the same song."

Jaänjo's presence within her seemed to pulse in harmony with her. "That is a beautiful way to put it, Aan. The symphony of existence transcends worlds and forms, uniting us in a shared understanding of the divine essence. By embracing this unity, we can find deeper meaning and purpose in our lives."

As the night deepened and the stars twinkled overhead, Aan and Jaänjo sat together, lost in the wonder of the star-strewn sky. Despite the vast gulf between their origins, they realized the same divine energy coursed through their worlds—through all of existence—connecting them with a glorious commonness.

While Aan pondered this newfound notion, a nagging thought tugged at the edge of her mind. How would her community react to these ideas? Would they see this blending of beliefs as a threat to their traditions? And what of those who might seek to exploit this knowledge for their own gain? The weight of their secret felt heavier than ever.

Her face took on a thoughtful look. "Jaänjo, if we are all connected to God, why are there bad people, evil energy, disease, and suffering? How does this fit into your understanding of the universe?"

Jaänjo took a moment before responding. "Aan, these questions have perplexed many—especially those on N'ridium when our civilization started to unravel. The existence of what you call 'evil' and suffering is part of the universe's complexity. Every being has the potential to resonate with the fundamental vibration, but various factors—fear, ignorance, disconnection—can lead to disharmony. This disharmony can manifest as negative behaviors or energies. It is not that these entities are separate from God but that they are out of sync with the divine harmony."

Aan considered this. "So, these negative energies are like notes that are out of tune in the symphony?"

"Yes," Jaänjo agreed. "And just as a skilled musician can bring discordant notes back into harmony, so too can individuals and societies strive to realign with the divine essence. This is the role of healers, shamans, and all who seek to restore balance. As a healer, I see 'out-of-tune notes' in the auras of people and work to transform these disharmonies back into harmony."

"And what about disease and suffering?" Aan paused, her voice laced with vulnerability. "Are they also a consequence of this imbalance? I've always strived to be a good person. So why did I develop MS? It doesn't seem fair."

Jaänjo's energy flowed gently through Aan as he replied. "The universe doesn't judge people as 'good' or 'bad'—those are human concepts. Unfortunate events are challenging to comprehend from our limited perspective. Maybe they are part of the natural interplay of energies, sometimes necessary for growth and learning. Just as a forest fire, though destructive, can lead to new growth, suffering can lead to deeper understanding and transformation. In our interconnected universe, your experience with MS might have far-reaching effects we can't yet see. Perhaps divine energy gave you MS to promote the growth of your consciousness."

He paused, allowing his words to settle. "You perceive MS as a punishment, an enormous burden, but consider the gifts it has bestowed—a heightened appreciation for your body, a deepened understanding of your parents' love, and a profoundly deeper empathy for others' challenges. Your view on life has been radically altered, just as my suffering led me to discover the extraordinary beauty of nature. And you."

She gasped. "Your perspective, if true, leaves me breathless."

Jaänjo's energy resonated with warmth. "I don't mean to diminish your pain. But perhaps viewing your experience as part of a larger process might bring a new understanding."

Aan fell silent, thinking. After a moment, she whispered, "It's a lot to take in, but... I'm beginning to see it. Thank you, Jaänjo. For both of us, our pain and suffering have made us better healers."

"I agree."

"Jaänjo, I'm glad we share a common goal—to heal and to contribute to the divine symphony that connects all of existence."

"Me, too, Aan. I hope you see now how healing, for me, is more than just the restoration of bodily health but a process of aligning with the divine energy that permeates the universe."

"Yes, Jaänjo, I do," Aan said softly, gazing at the dying embers. "Your words about divinity resonate deeply with my spirits. It's as if they've been trying to tell me this all along." She paused, lost in contemplation. "You've helped me see my traditions in a new light. I'm eager to weave this understanding into my shamanic practice."

"Aan, I am deeply honored by your words," Jaänjo replied.

A smile whispered across Aan's face as she gazed up at the star-studded sky. A blend of apprehension and exhilaration surged within her as she contemplated sharing Jaänjo's insights with her parents and community. She hoped his words would resonate with them as deeply as they had with her. Envisioning the possibility of enriching her people's traditions with the concept of universal divinity, Aan felt a renewed sense of purpose in her role as a shaman, eager to guide her people toward a broader understanding of the sacred.

21

AAN SIGHED CONTENTEDLY, MOVING her hands closer to the crackling fire. "Jaänjo, I wish we could stay here all night, but tomorrow's a workday. I should get ready for bed." She savored the fire's warmth for a moment longer before standing and stretching, working out the stiffness from sitting. Glancing at the cabin, the flickering firelight dancing dimly on its walls captivated her.

"I'm grateful for this time together, Jaänjo."

"Me, too, Aan. I've never experienced sitting by a fire. Watching the flames dance and twist feels like witnessing pure magic. It's incredible."

He paused, reflecting on his sterile existence. "On N'ridium, there were no songs of birds, no gentle breezes carrying the scent of wildflowers, no magnificent trees to witness, no sunsets to watch, no wonderful rain falling from the sky—only the perpetual hum of enormous air conditioners struggling to cool our underground cities from the relentless heat."

Aan's breath caught in her throat, a lump forming as she envisioned the barren world Jaänjo described. The crackling fire felt suddenly luxurious, a sharp contrast to the misery of N'ridium. "But you endured," she whispered, "and now you're here with me."

"I am," he said with a sense of gratitude. "What a thrill it is to experience this paradise with you—the beauty and bounty of Earth, its vibrant colors, the vast openness of the brilliant blue sky, and the delight of feeling your benevolent sun's warmth. It's like a celebration of life everywhere I turn. And laughter—simple, carefree laughter with you. The feeling is pure jubilation."

"I love feeling your jubilation." She paused, thinking. "Jaänjo, I still know so little about you. Is Jaänjo your full name, or do you have a last name like those on my planet?"

"I have a last name, too."

"Nice! What is it?"

"N'íxrâkvînlór."

"Wow. Please say it again, but slowly."

He laughed. "It sounds like this: N-iks-rak-vin-lor."

"My, that's a mouthful. Does it mean anything on your planet?"

"Yes. On N'ridium, our last names often signify lineage. My last name follows this tradition. The end part of my name—'lór'—means 'son of,' so my full name translates to 'Jaänjo, son of N'íxrâkvîn.' It's a way of honoring our ancestors and keeping their memory alive."

"I like that. In my native Tlingit language, names often reflect personal or family history, connections to clans or places, or characteristics associated with individuals. My last name, 'Gajaa,' doesn't have a direct translation of a specific meaning or concept. But my first name—Aanóokw, pronounced Ah-nook, is a Tlingit term for 'maternal grandmother.' My mom told me that when I was born, her mother, a shaman, looked at me and knew I, too, would one day be a shaman. So, my parents chose Aanóokw as my first name. Aan is my nickname."

Jaänjo chuckled. "Speaking of mouthfuls, your name rivals mine."

She smiled and yawned. "It does. Come on, let's go inside."

As she went through her nightly routine, the familiar actions provided comfort after the evening's deep conversation. The wooden floorboards creaked softly beneath her feet as she walked to her small bedroom, a reassuring sound in the quiet night.

In her bed, Aan hugged herself. "Goodnight, Jaänjo. What a day it's been. Tomorrow, I can heat some leftover stew for breakfast if you like."

Silence...

"I'm kidding."

He chuckled. "Whew. I was thinking about going dormant while you ate."

She laughed. "Very funny, alien man."

"Hey, I wasn't trying to be funny." He couldn't contain himself and burst out laughing.

Aan rolled her eyes. "Okay, okay, maybe we can dine with Mom and Dad."

"Oh, yeah!"

She hugged herself again. "Goodnight, Jaänjo."

"Goodnight, Aan."

An hour later, Aan roused from her tenuous sleep. "Jaänjo," she whispered, "are you there?"

"Yes. Is something troubling you?"

"I've been thinking about what you said this evening. Can I ask you a few more questions?"

"Of course."

"What do you think happens to a person's energy when they die?"

"Aan, I believe that death isn't an ending but a transformation. The energy within a living being does not simply vanish when the body ceases to function. Instead, it transitions, returning to the vast reservoir of energy that permeates the universe. Imagine a drop of water falling back into the ocean. It loses its individual form, merging with the boundless expanse from which it came. In the same way, the energy that once filled a person's body returns to the cosmic sea of energy, becoming one with the divine source."

He paused for a few moments. "This is not a loss but a reunion, a homecoming, a return to the source. The individual consciousness may dissolve, but the energy that fueled it continues to exist, flowing through the interconnected web of life. Perhaps this energy, now free from the constraints of physical form, will find its way back into the universe in a new and beautiful expression of life, or maybe it will simply merge with the vast, undifferentiated energy that is the essence of all that is."

"Jaänjo, about what you said about your energy finding its way back into the universe in a new expression of life, on Earth, reincarnation is the belief that a person's spirit lives on after death and is reborn into another body. Many religions believe in this cycle of rebirth, often tied to karma, where actions in past lives influence future ones. The ultimate goal is often to achieve liberation from this cycle through spiritual enlightenment."

"Karma," Jaänjo mused. "I like the sound of that word."

Aan smiled, but then her voice turned serious. "If all you're saying is true, why do the people on my planet, including myself when I had MS, try so hard to survive instead of returning to energy? And why did the people on your planet, including yourself, desperately try to survive?"

"Your question reveals a profound truth about the nature of existence. The spark of consciousness, the individual self, while ultimately a part of the greater whole, also possesses a unique and powerful drive toward self-preservation. This drive is woven into the very fabric of life itself.

"The forest seeks renewal after a wildfire, animals learn to endure long, frigid winters, and the human body fights against illness and injury. This is not a denial of the interconnectedness of all things but an expression of it. Just as the wave, while part of the ocean, maintains its individual form for a time, so too does the individual consciousness strive to persist.

"This drive to survive is not a flaw but a gift. It allows us to experience the world in all its richness and diversity. It is what motivates us to create, to love, to learn, and to grow. It is the source of our resilience, courage, and compassion.

"Even in the face of illness—or the death of my planet—the desire to survive is a testament to the strength of our spirit. It reflects the deep-seated yearning to continue experiencing the world, to connect with loved ones, and to fulfill our unique purpose.

"So, while it is true that death is a return to the source, it is also true that life is a precious opportunity to explore the vast landscape of existence. And it is only natural that we, as conscious beings, strive to make the most of this opportunity, to cling to life as long as we can, and to savor every moment of this extraordinary journey."

"I agree with what you're saying," said Aan. "The day we met—when I fell on the trail—my first instinct wasn't to give up and die, but a desperate plea to my spirits for the strength to carry on." She thought for a moment, reflecting. "Jaänjo, I wonder why, for some, the pull towards the spirit world outweighs the primal urge to remain in this physical form. Could this be a factor in the tragically high suicide rates among Indigenous communities, like my own Tlingit people?"

Jaänjo sighed. "Aan, your question touches upon a deep and complex aspect of existence. While the drive to survive is a powerful force, for reasons we don't fully understand, there are times when the individual consciousness feels a pull towards a different kind of existence than the attachment to their current form. It's not merely a matter of primal desire but a culmination of many factors—the weight of suffering, unfulfilled longings, and the depths of mental anguish. Suicide, in those instances, becomes a tragic attempt to alleviate unbearable pain, to seek solace as a release from suffering.

"As healers, we face this question on a deeply personal level. It reminds us that each consciousness walks a unique path—facing distinct trials and perceptions. While our physical bodies yearn for survival, our spiritual essence seeks connection and harmony."

He paused, reflecting on distant memories. "Twice in my life, I have been consumed by despair. The first time, my brother saved me from the darkness within my family. The second time, the suffering of my planet overwhelmed me. Had my brother not transformed me into energy, I might have surrendered to the allure of eternal peace. These experiences have given me a deep empathy for those who question their existence." He hesitated a moment. "So, when we wrestle with these profound questions, perhaps the answer lies in honoring both—the resilience of life and the mysteries of the soul's journey."

"Jaänjo," she began, her voice filled with empathy, "my heart aches for the struggles you've endured. I know the despair of which you speak. For us Tlingits, the roots of that despair run deep. Historical trauma, a loss of connection to our culture, the struggles of poverty, and limited access to mental and spiritual healthcare—especially care that understands our unique Indigenous perspectives—all play a part. As a shaman, I find deep reward in bringing healing and happiness to others."

Aan paused, feeling the weight of her words. "Jaänjo," she said softly, "your presence has expanded my understanding of healing in ways I never imagined. It's as if you've opened the door to a vast, new realm of possibilities." She took a deep breath, her mind racing with thoughts. "I wonder how this will shape my path as a shaman. Our traditions are ancient and sacred, but now I see there's so much more to learn—so many more ways to help my people. It's exciting—and a little overwhelming."

"I understand what you're saying. And I'm learning a lot from you. I instinctively knew you were a healer from the moment I saw you and your radiant, pure white aura. And I was right. Your commitment to healing others is both vital and inspiring."

"Thank you for your kind words." She yawned. "My spirit feels at peace after hearing your words." She yawned again and drifted back to sleep.

22

"These are delicious, Aan," Jaänjo remarked, savoring the flaky treat. "What do you call them?"

She smiled, still getting used to sharing her consciousness with her alien companion. "They're called biscuits, Jaänjo. My mom makes them with a special blend of flour, butter, buttermilk—and a touch of honey for sweetness." She dipped a spoon into a glass jar, extracting a translucent amber substance she spread generously on another biscuit. "And this is spruce tip jelly. Mom and I make it from the tender new-growth tips of spruce trees we harvest near my cabin." She took a bite, closing her eyes in delight. "Mmm... I love the bright, citrusy flavor balanced with the resinous notes of the spruce."

Jaänjo chuckled. "Even though there's nothing orange in this breakfast, it still tastes wonderful."

Aan laughed. "You're not going to let that canned stew meal go, are you?"

"I never would've guessed that spruce trees could taste better than stew," Jaänjo teased.

Aan rolled her eyes in mock exasperation. "Hey, if you don't stop razzing me about that stew, I might serve you oolichan for dinner," she retorted with a grin. "Those little fish—also known as candlefish because they're so oily they can be burned like candles—will curl your toes with their unique taste."

"The next time you have stew, let's see if it'll work as a candle, too."

She laughed as she put the breakfast plate, cup, and utensils in the sink. "I'll clean these later. We need to hurry to get to work on time."

"I'll be ready as soon as I put shoes on," said Jaänjo, tongue-in-cheek.

Aan's smile widened, showing her amusement, as she slipped on a light jacket to ward off the crisp morning air. "Uh-huh. I hope you've changed your underwear, too."

As she stepped onto the porch, her eyes widened with shock to see four bears lurking in front of her cabin. "Jaaäänjoooo," she blurted in alarm, her voice barely a whisper. Her heart pounded in her chest, and she felt her legs tremble, ready to bolt at any moment.

"Oh, look—they've brought friends! Let's say hello!" Jaänjo's calm voice contrasted sharply with Aan's rising panic.

"Are-are they friendly?" Aan's voice quivered, her eyes darting between the massive creatures.

"They are. Touch your nose to see their auras."

With a trembling hand, Aan touched her nose, half expecting the bears to charge at any moment. To her amazement, all four bears glowed a pure white. "They—their auras are beautiful, Jaänjo," she breathed, her fear slowly giving way to wonder.

"They are. Please say hello to them."

"Um, hello, everyone," Aan timidly remarked. "I hope you're having a good day."

The largest bear—a behemoth with a shaggy coat—walked her way, stopping in front of her. He gently nudged Aan's hand with its nose. Fear and awe ran down her spine as she hesitantly stroked its fur, surprised by the combination of wiry outer hairs and the incredibly soft underfur beneath.

"Oh my," Aan whispered, her voice filled with wonder. "They're... incredible."

Jaänjo chuckled, his voice warm and reassuring. "They are. Aan, they sense the goodness in you. You have nothing to fear."

The other bears cautiously approached Aan, seemingly encouraged by their leader's gesture. They allowed her to touch them, their gentle eyes filled with curiosity.

Aan's heart raced from the exhilaration coursing through her. She sensed Jaänjo's calming presence, steadying her nerves. "Remember," his voice whispered in her mind, "they're responding to your energy. Stay calm, and they'll remain peaceful."

"Thank you, Jaänjo," Aan said, her voice thick with emotion. "Thank you. Besides my and my mom's healing, this is the most amazing thing I've ever experienced."

"Your world is full of wonders, Aan—you just have to look."

"You're right." She sighed. "I wish I could stay here and be with our new friends, but I need to get to work."

"Let's say goodbye to them."

"Goodbye, everyone. It was nice meeting you."

Aan set off down the familiar path toward town. The bears accompanied her a few paces before disappearing into the dense undergrowth.

"My goodness..." Aan exclaimed in a voice tinged with awe. "Wait till I tell my parents what just happened." As she said the words, a wave of anxiety washed over her. How would her parents react to her incredible encounter with the bears? This story defied a lifetime of warnings her parents instilled in her about the dangers of wild bears.

As she entered the modest office of her family's fishing business, Aan chirped, "Good morning, Mom and Dad!"

Yéil greeted her with a warm smile and a hug. "And good morning to you and Jaänjo as well. Did you sleep well?"

As Aan hugged her dad, she answered her mom. "Jaänjo and I were up half the night talking, but I did manage to get a few hours of sleep."

Through Aan's eyes, Jaänjo noticed a look of quiet strength about Keet. His weathered face, etched with lines from years of working outdoors, broke into a gentle smile as Aan hugged him. Pride for his daughter glimmered in his eyes, mixed with the practical demeanor of a man who had spent his life running a fishing business.

"Mom, Dad, you'll never believe what happened yesterday and this morning!"

She told them of their bear encounters and how Jaänjo and her could see their auras. Keet was dubious. "Aan, their wild animals. They can turn on you in a heartbeat."

"I know, Dad. Jaänjo says we need to avoid any bear with a dark aura. The ones with white auras are friendly."

"Jaänjo, no disrespect to you, but wild animals are nothing to play around with. Plenty of people have thought like you and got mauled or worse."

"Aan, please tell your dad I'd like to speak to him."

"Dad, Jaänjo wants to respond. Go ahead, Jaänjo."

"Good morning, Keet. I understand your concern. As a healer, my insights are drawn from extensive observation and the sensing of energies emanating from living things—like the bears we met yesterday and today.

Their white auras signified a gentle nature. I'd be concerned about aggression and unpredictability if they displayed dark auras.

"So, it's not about playing with danger; it's about reading the signs nature provides and acting accordingly. Aan's safety is my priority, and I would never endanger her. Understanding auras is crucial to how I perceive and interact with the world."

Keet looked thoughtful, his skepticism softened by Jaänjo's calm assurance. "All right," he said finally. "I'll trust your judgment, but still, we must be extremely cautious."

Aan looked relieved when hearing Keet's response. "I promise, Dad—I'll be careful." She paused for a moment, reflecting. "Dad, interacting with the bears felt like a spiritual encounter."

She looked at her mom. "Guess what, Mom: Jaänjo loves your biscuits and our spruce tip jelly. But the canned stew I made for dinner, well, let's just say he's not a fan of it—especially the carrots in it." She chuckled. "He asked if we could eat here every night."

"You know you're both welcome to have dinner with us whenever you want. And, Jaänjo, I'm glad you like my cooking. I'm also not a fan of any meal that comes in a can."

Aan smiled. "Well, I need to get to work." She walked to her desk and settled into her swivel chair. Through her eyes, Jaänjo took in her cluttered desk, the filing cabinets, and the worn-out chair where she spent countless hours. Using Aan's physical senses, Jaänjo experienced the aroma of saltwater mingling with the scent of freshly caught fish wafting in from the open window.

As Aan turned on her computer, Jaänjo felt a jolt of surprise. Through her senses, he saw the screen come to life with a series of clicks and keystrokes, displaying an interface that seemed rudimentary. He couldn't help but react, his energy shimmering with confusion and dismay.

Aan felt the strange ripple of energy from Jaänjo, almost like a gasp of surprise. "Jaänjo, what's wrong?" she asked.

"Nothing. I'm just... adjusting to your technology. It's quite different from what I'm used to. What is this device you're using?"

"It's my computer," she replied, sensing Jaänjo's puzzlement. "It's where I keep our accounts, pay the bills, and manage the business."

Jaänjo's energy pulsed with a blend of curiosity and disbelief. "This is what you use to manage your operations? It's so... primitive."

"Primitive? Jaänjo, this computer is loaded with advanced features. What's so shocking about it?"

"On N'ridium, our technology has advanced in ways that might seem almost magical to you. Our computers are nothing like this. They interface directly with our consciousness, requiring no physical interaction."

Aan's eyebrows shot up in disbelief. "Wait, what? How is that even possible?"

"We call them Neuro-Computational Systems, or NCS. These devices read our brainwaves and translate our thoughts into commands. There's no need for hand input. We think, and the computer responds."

Aan leaned back in her chair, trying to wrap her mind around the concept. "That sounds incredible—and a little scary, to be honest. How do you filter out random thoughts? Human minds are so chaotic."

"You're right—thoughts can be complex. But, our systems have advanced algorithms that filter out irrelevant noise and focus on specific commands. This makes interacting with the computer seamless."

Aan's awe grew. "That must save so much time. What else can your computers and technology do?"

Well, our brilliant scientists—my brother among them—used astonishingly advanced quantum computing to figure out how to transform a living being into energy, which is why I'm here speaking with you. We also harnessed hydrogen fusion to unlock a nearly limitless energy source and developed highly dexterous robots capable of performing intricate tasks with flawless precision, from intricate manufacturing to complex repairs.

Aan's mind raced with possibilities. "That sounds like something out of science fiction. But it must come with its own challenges and risks, right? I mean, could people or governments use your technologies to monitor everyone's thoughts?"

"Our NCS devices had multiple layers of encryption and security protocols to protect our thoughts and data, but sadly, you're right—as things unraveled on my planet, governments abused our privacy rights."

Aan nodded, deep in thought. "It's sad that you couldn't save your planet even with your advanced technology."

"That's true—we couldn't save our planet, but maybe a few of us, like me, will preserve our civilization."

Aan leaned back in her chair, contemplating everything Jaänjo had shared. "I don't think I could be very happy in a technology-dominated world. I'm far happier being in nature, free of any technology." She paused, reflecting a bit more. "I wonder," she mused, "if there's a way to balance technological advancement with respect for nature. Maybe that's something we could explore together."

Jaänjo's energy pulsed warmly. "Interesting comments. Like me, I have no doubt that most people on my planet would gladly trade all forms of technology to experience the simple beauty of your planet."

Aan beamed with pride. "On behalf of planet Earth, I'm delighted you find it beautiful. Not to offend you, but I hope we never reach the level of technological advancement your world has."

Jaänjo chuckled. "No offense taken. After experiencing the wonder and beauty here, I hope your technology will never replace your glorious primitiveness."

"That's a good way to put it."

"Hey, if you don't mind, I'll bask in the glorious sunlight on your roof while you work."

"Good idea. Enjoy the sun," she said with a smile. "I'll be thinking of you. I'll come get you when I'm done." She felt a warm pulse in response before turning her attention to her work.

As Jaänjo drifted away, a sudden loneliness washed over Aan. The speed with which she'd grown accustomed to his presence surprised her. She turned back to her computer, the once-familiar screen now seeming strangely antiquated after Jaänjo's descriptions of his world's technology. With a small sigh, she began her work, her mind still buzzing with thoughts of bear encounters, alien technology, and the strange new path her life had taken. As she settled into her work, a smile slowly spread across her lips, kindled by the excitement of the future.

23

SEVERAL HOURS LATER, AAN leaned back in her chair, a broad smile spreading across her face as she switched off her computer. The afternoon light had shifted, casting long shadows across the office. Aan stretched, feeling the satisfying pull of muscles that had been still for too long. She glanced at the clock, surprised at how quickly time had passed. "Mom, for the first time in ages, I'm caught up on everything," she declared, the joy evident in her voice. "I finished all my work projects, responded to every email, and paid our bills! Since recovering from MS, my mind feels like it's sprinting instead of crawling. It's amazing."

Yéil smiled. "With MS, it was like your whole life was in slow motion—your moving, thinking—everything. It was like living in a perpetual fog, where even the simplest tasks felt insurmountable."

"I know. It feels like I've been given a new lease on life. I'm so thankful for all Jaänjo has done for you and me. He has opened my eyes in many ways."

"You two seem to get along quite well."

"Mom, he... he completes me." She thought about it more. "I mean, when he's inside of me, everything feels right. And when he's out of me, like right now, a part of me feels missing."

Yéil nodded. "I understand what you feel. When Jaänjo entered me to heal, I felt an extraordinary sense of peace."

"It's not just that, Mom. I love how he delights in every new experience—it's like I'm seeing the world anew through him, a world filled with wonder and possibility. And his beliefs about God and divine energy resonate deeply with my understanding of the sacred."

"Well, you're both healers in your own unique ways, so I can understand the resonance you feel." She paused thoughtfully. "Now that Jaänjo has healed you and me, do you think our spirits will have him continue his work elsewhere?"

Aan winced at the question, knowing it was valid but painful. "Mom, I... I don't know how long he'll stay..."

"We'll all miss him when he leaves."

Rattled by the thought of Jaänjo leaving her, Aan opted to change the subject. She felt a pang of guilt for not directly answering her mother's question, but the idea of Jaänjo leaving was too painful to contemplate. "I'll let Jaänjo know I'm done working. If you don't mind, could we have dinner with you and Dad?"

"We'd love for you to stay. Tell Jaänjo I promise nothing served for dinner will come from a can."

She chuckled. "If I tell him that, I'll be in for another round of stew-related razzing."

Outside, Aan touched her nose and saw Jaänjo's aura perched high on the roof. She waved to him, and he floated down to her. She opened her arms, and he once again merged with her.

"Basking in the sun feels so good. Are you finished with your work?"

"I am. And I figured out how to heal people without them seeing what we do."

"Oh? How?"

"I'll tell them I use intense light therapy to heal people, so they and anyone else in the room will need to wear sleep masks to block the light. I've ordered these masks online. Also, I bought a powerful work light with three bright bulbs mounted on a stand. It's far stronger than a regular light bulb and will flood the room with intense light. So, even if they peeked from under their mask, seeing the healing energy coming from my palms would be unlikely in the intense light. For myself, I've ordered special goggles to dim the bright light. So, with this guise, no one will know what we're doing. These items should arrive in about a week."

"That's very clever, Aan. It could work."

"Thanks. I also bought something called a body pillow. I'll pretend it's you so I can hug you."

Jaänjo chuckled. "I think I'm going to like this body pillow."

Aan smiled, breathed in deeply, and then sighed. "Jaänjo," she began, a hint of unease in her voice, "my mom asked when you're going to leave since your work to heal her and me is done. It doesn't feel right to have them think you're a spirit. If you don't mind, could we tell them the truth about you after dinner?"

Silence...

"Aan, do you... do you think they would take this news well? What if they demanded that I leave you?"

"My parents are open-minded people. I know you don't pray, but I've asked our spirits to have Mom and Dad sanction our togetherness. They both like you, so we have that going for us."

Jaänjo sighed within her. "Whatever the decision is, I'll abide by it."

Aan nodded. "Jaänjo, I told my mom that when you're not in me, it feels like a part of me is missing, so she knows I care deeply for you. After I tell them about you, could you appear before us so they can see what you look like?"

"I could. Maybe I should comb my hair before they see me so I won't look like a disheveled intragalactic refugee. And whatever meal your mom makes tonight—even if it's stew—I'll offer profuse compliments on her culinary skills."

"Good one, Jaänjo," Aan chuckled. "I already told her about your disdain for food that comes in a can, and she said to tell you that nothing into night's meal will come from a can."

"I really like your mother, Aan."

During dinner, fretting over telling her parents about Jaänjo, Aan found conversation difficult and barely touched her food.

Noticing her daughter's unease, Yéil reached across the table and gently squeezed her hand. "Aan, you seem a million miles away. Is something wrong?"

"Sorry, Mom," Aan replied, "I have something to tell you about Jaänjo after dinner."

"Is he leaving?" asked Keet.

"I hope not, Dad." She put her fork down. "I'll do the dishes to say thanks for this delicious meal."

After putting the dishes away, Aan joined her parents, who were sitting in the living room.

She sat across from them, took a deep breath, and sighed. "Mom and Dad, I need to tell you more about Jaänjo."

"Why do you look so troubled? What's going on?"

"Dad, Jaänjo isn't a spirit in the sense that you and Mom are thinking."

"Well, what is he?" asked Yéil, her eyes wide with bewilderment.

Aan hesitated in replying. "Jaänjo is an intragalactic refugee from another planet."

Yéil exchanged a puzzled glance with Keet. "Are he and others like him invading our planet?"

"No, Mom, it's nothing like that. Their sun destroyed his home planet, and he's the only one he knows who made it to Earth."

Her parents stared at her, their expressions mixed with disbelief and worry. "Just listen, please, and I'll tell you about him," Aan pleaded. She took another deep breath before continuing.

"Jaänjo is from a distant planet called N'ridium," Aan began, her voice steady despite her nervousness. "His world was doomed when their sun began to expand, engulfing the planets surrounding it."

Keet and Yéil listened, their skepticism slowly turning to rapt attention as Aan continued.

"Their sun's expansion scorched their planet, causing massive devastation. They tried to survive by building underground cities, but it wasn't enough. Eventually, their advanced civilization realized they had to leave. In a desperate bid for survival, they found a way to convert themselves into pure energy and launched into space, hoping to find other habitable planets."

Aan paused, searching her parents' faces for any sign of understanding. She found none, but they were still listening, so she pressed on.

"Jaänjo's energy traveled over seven thousand light-years before reaching Earth. When he arrived, he found himself trapped in an energy form, unable to live a physical life again. But scientists on his planet found a way for Jaänjo and others like him to merge with compatible hosts on other planets, provided they have a similar biological makeup and life energy."

Yéil raised an eyebrow. "And Jaänjo found you?"

Aan nodded. "He saw my aura—my life energy—and realized it was compatible with his. He approached me with an offer: a partnership. He would share his knowledge and healing abilities with me, and in return, he would experience life through me."

Keet leaned forward, his brow furrowed. "Aan, this is... a lot to take in. How can we be sure this isn't some sort of hallucination or side effect of your recovery?"

Yéil's eyes narrowed in doubt. "This is too far-fetched to comprehend, Aan. It's hard to believe a word of it."

Aan shook her head. "Dad and Mom, I know it sounds unbelievable, but what I'm saying is true."

Keet shook his head, still unconvinced.

Aan looked him in the eyes. "Dad, the things Jaänjo knows, the way he communicates with me—he's genuine. He's not here to harm us. He wants to help. He was a healer on his planet, and you've seen this firsthand with my healing and now with Mom."

Yéil sat, thinking. "You asked Jaänjo to appear before us, but he said he couldn't because he needed to conserve his energy for my healing. So that means you've seen him, right?"

"Yes. I asked Jaänjo if he could show me his physical form, and he materialized before me in a soft white glow that looked like a human."

Keet shook his head slowly. "So you're telling us this being of energy just happened to pick you because your aura was compatible? And now he's in you, sharing his knowledge and healing abilities?"

Aan nodded earnestly. "Yes, Dad. We've all witnessed his ability to heal others."

Keet's skepticism deepened. "Aan, if he's really from another planet, how do we know his intentions are good? What if this is all just some elaborate manipulation? How can you be so sure he's not using you?"

Aan's expression grew serious. "I know he's not manipulating me, and his motives are pure. He's given me no reason to doubt his intentions, and he's shown me nothing but kindness and a desire to help."

Yéil interjected softly, "Aan, what happens if he decides to take control of you? Could you stop him?"

Aan hesitated, glancing between Keet and Yéil. "Jaänjo assured me he would immediately leave if I asked, and he has never overstepped—he always seeks my permission first." She sighed. "I'm asking you both to trust my judgment, believe in my instincts, and accept that Jaänjo is a kind and genuinely decent being."

Keet sighed heavily. "It's a lot to take in. But if you believe it, we'll try to understand. Just promise us you'll be careful and keep us informed about everything. We're worried about you, Aan."

"We are," Yéil agreed, her voice soft but firm. "And Aan, have you thought about the long-term implications? What happens if you want to have a family someday? Or if Jaänjo's people come looking for him?"

Aan hesitated. "I... we haven't thought that far ahead. We're still figuring things out day by day."

"How old is Jaänjo, Aan?" asked Yéil.

"In Earth years, he's the same age as me."

"Was he ever married, or does he have a family?"

"Conditions were brutal on his planet, and starvation was rampant. So, Mom, Jaänjo never married, but he has an older brother. His name is Miěěcha, and he's one of the scientists who discovered how to convert living beings to pure energy so they could travel through space to other potentially hospitable planets."

"Did his brother survive their planet's destruction?"

"Jaänjo said Miěěcha stayed behind to perfect the process of converting energy back into a living form. Miěěcha told him he would come looking for Jaänjo once they figured it out. So Jaänjo doesn't know if Miěěcha survived."

"I hope he did," said Yéil.

"Me, too, Mom. Jaänjo is very close to his brother."

"Like your dad, I believe what you're saying. And I, too, witnessed the extraordinary peace you spoke of when Jaänjo was in me. So, I'll support you and Jaänjo being together. Many desperately ill people could benefit from what you and Jaänjo offer."

Aan smiled, tears of relief welling in her eyes. "Thank you, Mom. I knew it would be hard for you and Dad to believe, but I had to tell you." She hesitated. "There's something else I need to tell you."

"What's that?" asked Keet.

"I... I'm starting to have feelings for Jaänjo."

"What kind of feelings, Aan?"

"You know, Mom... feelings."

Yéil sighed. "Aan, you have always been a physically demonstrative person. Could you ever be fulfilled if you lacked that from Jaänjo?"

"I don't know, Mom. All I know is I've never felt as close to anyone as I have with Jaänjo."

"Be careful, daughter. I don't want you to be hurt or go through life without experiencing the joys of physical intimacy that come with a loving relationship."

Aan nodded. "Jaänjo and I talked about that. As I said, he and I plan to take it one day at a time."

Keet nodded slowly. "We'll support you, Aan, but we need to observe Jaänjo more closely to form our own opinions of him."

"And we'd like to speak with him directly, if possible," Yéil added. "There are many questions we have that only he can answer."

Aan nodded. "I understand. I'll talk to Jaänjo about it. Maybe we can find a way for him to communicate with you directly. Mom and Dad, having your support means everything to me. Would... would you like to see him?"

"Of course we would," Yéil said, her voice filled with excitement. "Can we see him now?"

"Yes," Aan replied. "Let me turn off the light so you can see him better." She rose and flicked off the living room light switch, plunging the room into darkness. Then, approaching her parents but stopping a few feet away, she spoke. "Okay, Jaänjo, please show them what you looked like in your physical form."

A soft light began to emanate from Aan's body, swirling and expanding as it coalesced a few feet away. The air in the room seemed to vibrate with his energy, sending shivers down Yéil and Keet's spines. The light grew brighter, shaping itself into a humanlike form until Jaänjo stood before them, a shimmering figure of pure energy. Despite being composed entirely of energy, Jaänjo's presence felt undeniably real, filling the space with a palpable sense of otherworldly wonder. His eyes sparkled with an inviting glow. Although his brilliant light partly obscured his features, the warmth and kindness he radiated were unmistakable.

Yéil gasped, her hand flying to her mouth. Keet tensed as if ready to protect his family, but when Jaänjo looked at him and smiled, a sense of calm washed over him, and his fear melted into awe.

"Oh, my," Yéil breathed, her voice filled with amazement. "Hello, Jaänjo."

Jaänjo inclined his head slightly towards Yéil and Keet, a gesture of respect and acknowledgment. He then extended his arms outward, palms facing up, inviting connection and trust. The light around him pulsed rhythmically, emanating a comforting warmth.

Keet, overcome by curiosity and eagerness, instinctively reached out to shake Jaänjo's hand, but his fingers closed on empty air. He blinked in surprise, his eyes adjusting to the ethereal nature of the being before him.

"I... I wish I could shake your hand, Jaänjo," Keet stammered, withdrawing his hand. "You don't look like the aliens we see in movies..."

Jaänjo's smile widened, his eyes twinkling with amusement. He raised his hand to his mouth, gently indicating his inability to speak, yet his expression conveyed understanding and reassurance.

Yéil found her voice, her tone laced with wonder. "You're quite handsome, Jaänjo. Thank you for healing me and my precious daughter."

Jaänjo nodded, his movements graceful and deliberate. He gestured toward Aan and brought his hand to his heart, a silent communication that spoke volumes.

Understanding dawned on Keet's face. "Thank you for caring so much for our daughter," he said, his voice cracking with emotion.

Jaänjo nodded again, his radiant form seeming to pulse with affirmation.

Yéil's eyes welled up with tears. "You are always welcome in our home, Jaänjo. Always."

Jaänjo's smile softened, and he placed a glowing hand on her heart in a gesture of gratitude and compassion. The silent exchange spoke of a connection deeper than words.

Jaänjo stepped back, and with a subtle wave to her and Keet, he turned around and moved toward Aan. She spread her arms to welcome him, and his light once more merged with her.

Aan smiled and gently hugged herself, welcoming Jaänjo back. She looked at her parents, her eyes sparkling with love and joy. "Like me," she said softly, "I think you both now understand the depth of Jaänjo's heart—his warmth, kindness, and sincerity."

"We do," Yéil replied, her voice warm and accepting. "Jaänjo is a truly remarkable being."

Keet's mood lightened. "Regarding your feelings for Jaänjo, not many boyfriends cure their girlfriend's mother of end-stage cancer, so he's got that going for him. But I don't think he'll make much of a fisherman. In the future, I suppose I could use his skills to determine the honesty of mechanics we hire to fix our boat's engine."

Aan laughed, her mood noticeably lighter. "I love you both so much. Thank you for supporting me."

24

As fall settled over Tenakee Springs, the landscape transformed into a vibrant colorful tapestry. Hues of red, orange, and gold from the deciduous trees contrasted with the deep greens of the Sitka spruce and western hemlock. The crisp air carried a distinct aroma—a blend of saltwater, the resinous fragrance of spruce, and the earthy scent of decaying leaves. Though small, the village bustled with preparations for the coming winter. Wood was chopped and stacked, fishing nets were mended, and smoke curled from chimneys as the community worked to secure their homes against the approaching cold.

For Aan, this season brought not just changes in the landscape but profound transformations within herself. Freed from the shackles of MS, her laughter, long silenced by illness, now echoed through the village, a testament to her newfound joy. She moved with a lightness and grace that astonished everyone, her steps quick and purposeful as she flitted from one task to another. The years of suffering had been like being in a cocoon, and now, having emerged, she was ready to spread her wings.

The presence of Jaänjo within her was a constant source of wonder. Aan enthusiastically embraced their partnership, dedicating herself to understanding the enigmatic energy that now shared her being. Hours slipped away in the lively exchanges of words with him. She learned to feel the ebb and flow of his energy, a rhythmic dance that often mesmerized her.

Aan equally captivated Jaänjo. He marveled at her resilience, her compassion, and her deep connection with the land and her community. He saw in her a wisdom far beyond her years, born of hardship and perseverance. Their bond grew stronger each day, a symbiotic dance of two souls intertwined. Jaänjo's energy flowed through Aan, amplifying her intuition and empathy, while Aan's groundedness provided Jaänjo with a place to learn and grow.

Walks through the forest, often accompanied by their bear companions, became a cherished ritual for them. The symphony of crunching leaves underfoot marked the passage of seasons, each footfall a harmonious note blending with the wild soundscape. Jaänjo reveled in the play of dappled sunlight on the forest floor, while Aan often paused to appreciate the intricate melodies of the birds. Each walk unveiled new layers of the forest's hidden magic, filling them with a sense of wonder and connection.

The villagers of Tenakee Springs couldn't help but notice the change in Aan. Her fluid movements, vibrant laughter, and sparkling eyes reflected an inner light that hadn't been there before. They sensed a deeper power within her, a quiet strength emanating from her core. Children, like moths to a flame, were drawn to her, their laughter a sweet melody carried by the wind as they followed her down the village's main path.

One crisp morning, as the sun cast a golden light over the village, Éesh, a middle-aged Tlingit woman, made her way to Aan's family's fishing building. The structure, perched on sturdy pilings at the water's edge, was a hub of activity. The rhythmic sound of water lapping against the pilings mixed with the occasional call of seagulls overhead. The scent of freshly caught fish and the hum of conversation filled the air.

Behind the building, Éesh spotted Aan skillfully gutting a halibut. Aan had tied back her raven-black hair and wore an apron smeared with the day's work. Despite the mundane task, Aan seemed to glow with an inner peace that Éesh desperately craved.

"Aan," Éesh called softly, hesitant to interrupt.

Aan looked up, her eyes filling with warmth upon seeing her friend. "Éesh! What brings you here?"

"I... I was hoping we could talk," she replied, her voice tinged with despair.

Aan handed her work to a fellow villager and wiped her hands on a cloth. "Let's have a seat," she said, gesturing to a weather-worn bench on the deck overlooking the water.

As they sat, a cool breeze carried the salty scent of the ocean. Aan took Éesh's hand, her gaze compassionate. "I can feel your heart is heavy with sadness," she said gently. "Sometimes, sharing your burden can lighten it, even if just a little. Would you like to talk about what's troubling you?"

Éesh took a deep breath, and her words spilled out in a torrent. "I feel so lost, Aan. The sadness... it's like a weight I can't bear. I don't know what to do."

Aan listened, her presence a comfort to Éesh's troubled spirit. "You're not alone," she whispered. "Would you like to invite the spirits to help you find your way back to the light?"

Tears brimmed in Éesh's eyes. "Yes. I want to feel whole again."

"Okay. Give me a moment to change, and then let's walk to the sacred springs. There, we'll ask for your healing and renewal."

As Aan prepared to leave, she paused inside the building, her thoughts turning to Jaänjo. "What does her aura tell you?" she asked quietly.

"Her white aura is very weak, Aan. The pervasive grays indicate hopelessness and despair, and the indigo suggests deep sadness. Her troubles seem more spiritual than physical, so your shaman skills are best suited to help her."

Aan nodded. "I agree." She looked upward. "Please, my dear spirits, help Éesh find her way..."

Taking Éesh's hand, Aan led her through the forest. The sunlight from earlier in the day faded, and clouds that threatened rain rolled in, casting a soft, diffused light over the landscape that seemed to mirror Éesh's melancholy. At the sacred springs, the clear waters reflected the muted sky, and the scent of cedar and sweetgrass filled the air.

"Let's begin your healing, Éesh," Aan said softly. She dipped her hands into the chilly water, murmuring an invocation to the spirits of the water to cleanse and renew. Éesh cupped some water in her hand and sipped the water.

Aan began to chant, her voice rising and falling in a melodic cadence that merged with the rustling leaves and the gentle gurgle of the spring. The ancient Tlingit healing song bridged the mortal and spiritual worlds.

Éesh closed her eyes, letting the chant envelop her. She felt Aan's hands on her shoulders, her touch warm and reassuring. "Feel the strength of our spirits, Éesh," Aan whispered. "You are not alone. Your ancestors walk with you."

As Aan continued the ritual, Éesh's shoulders, once hunched with the weight of despair, began to relax. A flicker of warmth replaced the familiar chill in her heart. Tears welled up, but instead of grief, they brought a sense of release.

As the last echoes of Aan's chant faded, Éesh opened her eyes, feeling a lightness she hadn't known in months.

"Thank you, Aan," she whispered. "I feel... better."

Aan smiled warmly. "The journey to healing is not always easy, Éesh. But you are strong, and you are loved. Hold on to that light within you."

"I will," Éesh nodded, hugging Aan tightly. "I waited too long to do something about it."

On the town's main path, Aan and Éesh hugged and said goodbye.

As they parted ways, Jaänjo's voice filled Aan's thoughts. "Your gentleness and empathy touch me. The energy of her aura noticeably strengthened after your healing. I... I have much to learn from you."

"Oh? What do you think I can teach you?" Aan asked softly.

He hesitated. Aan sensed something troubled him deeply. "What's bothering you, Jaänjo?"

He sighed. "Despite my efforts to heal at the molecular level, I've noticed that some beings still suffer. They're physically restored, yet there's a lingering pain that my methods can't touch."

Aan's heart ached for him. "Jaänjo, what you're describing is the soul's cry. Healing is not just about mending the body; it's about restoring balance within the spirit. The spirit carries wounds that the eyes cannot see, but they manifest in the body and mind."

Jaänjo's energy dimmed. "From the trauma I've experienced from my civilization's collapse, I unknowingly began viewing spirit as something abstract. I focused my healing on mending molecules and cells. I suppose you could say I lost my faith. But now, since being with you, since being on this beautiful planet... You've restored my faith in the divine."

Tears welled in Aan's eyes. "Hearing you say that makes me so happy. We, the Tlingit, know that spirit connects us all—to each other, to nature, and to the universe. When it's disrupted, like it was with you, no amount of physical healing can bring true peace. The spirit must be healed as well."

Jaänjo's energy flickered as he shared his pain. "On my planet, the despair... it permeated everything. My spirit, my will to survive, dwindled to almost nothingness. In retrospect, trauma affected my spirit in ways I didn't understand, and because of that, I couldn't heal myself."

He paused, his energy dimming. "So, I focused on what I could heal—people's bodies, their cells, their molecular structure. It was a way to cope, to feel that I was making a difference. But I see now that it wasn't enough. I neglected the very essence of what makes life sacred—the spirit."

"My heart aches for you, Jaänjo. The suffering you witnessed leaves marks on the spirit and those marks must be tended to with compassion and care. You focused on the physical because it was what you could control, but your spirit bears wounds that need healing—wounds that only spiritual care can mend."

"Aan, how can you heal my spirit?"

Aan sighed, feeling the weight of his question and the vulnerability in his words. "Jaänjo," she began softly, "healing the spirit is a journey that requires patience and openness. It's not something I can do for you, but something I can help you navigate."

She paused, her voice carrying the wisdom of generations. "First, you must allow yourself to feel the pain you've carried, to acknowledge it fully. The suffering you witnessed, the despair that touched your soul—it must be honored, not pushed away. We can't heal what we don't first recognize."

Aan touched her heart, sensing the energy of Jaänjo's being. "I will help you connect with the spirits and with the energies that surround us. Through rituals and communion with the earth and my ancestors, we'll find a way to release your pain. It's a process of letting go, of finding peace within the chaos you've known."

She smiled softly, her eyes filled with compassion. "Healing your spirit will take time, Jaänjo, but you are not alone. I will be with you, helping you through the darkness to find the light within. Together, we can restore the balance that was lost, and in doing so, you will find a deeper sense of peace and purpose."

"Thank you, Aan," he whispered, his voice filled with gratitude. I am ready to begin this journey back to wholeness."

Aan nodded and smiled. "We're in this together. Hold on tight to that."

She paused, reflecting. "Jaänjo, my people have also experienced generational trauma. We lived for millennia in peace, connected deeply with our land and our beliefs. Then the white man came, tried to marginalize us, steal our land, and take away our sacred beliefs. That trauma continues to this day."

She gently hugged herself. "But despite all our suffering, Jaänjo, we found a way to survive. It's made us see people with more compassionate eyes. We understand pain and loss, and it drives us to help others heal, to restore balance in any way we can."

"It does. Still, the hurt lingers..."

"Come on, let's head home," she said. "Your journey to healing your spirit will begin with me hugging my body pillow for an extra-long time tonight."

"I'd like that."

As they walked toward their cabin in quiet contemplation, a light rain began to fall. Aan lifted her face to the sky, feeling the cool water on her skin.

Jaänjo sighed. "I love water falling from the sky." He paused, and she felt his energy course through her. "I wish I could hold your hand right now like you did when you walked with Éesh. I found it quite comforting."

"I know, Jaänjo. I'd love to hold your hand, too. And I'd love to feel your arms around me. But your presence within me is a comfort all its own." With a smile, her confidence about their relationship bloomed—perhaps her spirits whispered to her that they would find their way.

25

Aan rose before the sun, got dressed, and ate quickly. "Jaänjo, are you as excited as me to go fishing today with my dad and the crew?"

"I am. But why are we leaving so early?"

"The best time to catch halibut is on slack tides."

"What are slack tides?"

"Slack tides make fishing easier because the water is still, allowing for smooth casting, easy gear setup, and more fish bites."

"Um, what are tides?"

Aan laughed. "My, aren't you full of questions this morning? Tides are the rising and falling of sea levels caused by the gravitational pull of the moon and sun."

"What's a moon?"

She paused, a look of genuine surprise crossing her face. "A moon is a celestial body that orbits a planet—" She caught herself. "You're messing with me now, aren't you?"

Jaänjo unsuccessfully stifled a chuckle. "No..." he finally managed, with amusement in his voice.

She laughed. "You're a rascal, you know that, right?"

"What's a rascal?"

"Argh! Come on, let's go. You can continue to mess with me on the trail."

Outside, two of their bear friends milled around, also starting their day. They immediately came to her. "Hello, Barney and Fred," she said, casually stroking their heads. "Where are Wilma and Betty this morning?"

"Tell me again why you came up with those names," Jaänjo chirped.

"As a kid, I loved watching 'The Flintstones' cartoons on TV. I named them after the characters in the show."

"What's a cartoon?"

She rolled her eyes. "Here we go again…"

After saying goodbye to Barney and Fred, Aan walked briskly down the trail. "I need to hurry, Jaänjo. The last thing you want to do is show up after the boat leaves the pier."

The forest gradually yielded to the town's main path, and a salty breeze hinted at a day by the sea, stirring a familiar excitement within Aan.

On the pier, she hugged Keet and boarded their boat. Later, as it chugged through the calm waters toward their fishing spot, Aan helped the two-person crew prepare their gear. The crisp morning air, filled with the rhythmic chug of the boat's engine and the cries of seagulls, electrified Aan with excitement.

"We'll be jigging for halibut today, Jaänjo. It's a technique I learned long ago from my dad."

He cringed at the pungent smell of the fish Aan expertly threaded onto a hefty hook. "That fish smells awful. Why are the hooks so big?"

"Halibut are huge and have powerful jaws," Aan chuckled, holding the hook up to the sunlight. "You need a sturdy hook to reel one of them in. What you're smelling is herring. We bait our hooks with chunks of it, and their oily scent attracts the bottom-dwelling halibut."

After baiting all the hooks, Aan and the crew attached them to heavy-duty fishing lines, each line ending in a shiny jig—a metal lure that would enticingly flutter as it bounced up and down near the ocean floor.

"Okay, that's done," said Aan. "Now we need to secure the lines to our sturdy fishing rods and add a hefty sinker to each one to ensure our bait reaches the depths where halibut lurks."

As they approached where they were going to fish, Keet slowed the boat and then cut the engines. Jaänjo noted Aan's anticipation—a mix of nerves and eagerness for the thrill of the catch.

With their gear ready, Aan and the crew took their positions along the railing, each holding their rod firmly. One by one, they swung their lines out over the side, the sinkers pulling the baited hooks down into the depths of the dark water. Now, the waiting game would begin for the telltale tug of a hungry halibut.

Several minutes passed with no action. Aan leaned against the railing, feeling the gentle sway of the boat beneath her feet. She watched her dad and the crew, their eyes fixed on the lines as they waited for a bite.

"It looks like this might be a slow fishing day," she said with growing frustration.

Through her eyes, Jaänjo gazed at the water. "Um, can I ask a question?"

"I'm not sure I can handle fifty questions right now, Jaänjo."

"I only have one question."

"Okay, what?"

"Why are you fishing where there aren't any fish?"

"How do you know there aren't any fish?"

"I can sense their energy," Jaänjo replied. "A faint energy vibration, a pulse in the water."

"Are you messing with me again?"

"No. Look towards the back of the ship," Jaänjo replied. "They're about twenty boat lengths away in that direction."

Aan's eyes widened with amazement. "Are you sure, Jaänjo?"

"I am."

"Hey, Dad, come here!" she yelled, beckoning him over.

Keet ambled towards her, a puzzled look on his face. "What's wrong?"

"Dad, Jaänjo says he can feel the halibut's faint energy vibrations. He says they're twenty boat lengths that way." She pointed where Jaänjo told her they'd be.

"Is he sure?"

"Yes, Dad, he is."

"Okay, let's give it a try. Hey, everyone, reel up your lines—we're moving to another spot."

Aan reeled in her line and then followed her dad to the wheelhouse. "Jaänjo says he'll guide you to where they are."

Within a few minutes, Keet stopped where Jaänjo told him the fish were, and they recast their lines.

Moments later, Aan's rod bent over, the line humming with tension as a heavy fish fought to escape. "Fish on!" she shouted, exhilarated. But then, as suddenly as it had begun, the struggle ceased. The line went limp. "No!" she cried, her heart sinking. Frantically, she cranked the reel, hoping against hope for a miracle. But it was too late. The fish was gone.

The rest of the crew cast their lines in the same area, and soon, they buzzed with the excitement of multiple hooked halibut.

Keet left the wheelhouse to help, in awe of Jaänjo's ability to lead them to a bounty of fish. "Jaänjo, when Aan told us about you being from another planet, I said I didn't think you'd be much of a fisherman. Sir, I stand corrected."

Inside Aan, Jaänjo chuckled. "Please tell your dad I'm also good at catching compliments."

Aan laughed and told her father what Jaänjo said.

On the way home, Aan stood on the bow, taking in the breathtaking beauty of the sea and the emerald-green islands. "It's so beautiful, Aan—I'm glad I'm here with you."

"Me, too, Jaänjo. Being at sea elevates my spirits. Being with you elevates my spirits even more." She paused, reflecting on how much her life had changed in such a short time. From the depths of illness to this newfound vitality, from loneliness to this deep connection with Jaänjo. Gratitude and wonder filled her, but also a twinge of uncertainty about the future. She hoped days like this would never end.

For the next month, Aan fished every day with her dad. Jaänjo's guidance made it the best fishing season they'd had in years.

26

AT THE OFFICE, AAN'S eyes crinkled with delight as she double-checked the figures on her laptop screen. "Jaänjo, your fishing expertise has made this an epic month for our business. You've earned your monthly ration of cinnamon rolls."

"I'm glad I can help. Are you ready for our walk?"

"Almost. Let me ask Mom if she needs anything else."

Looking out the back window, Aan saw her mom sitting on the pier bench, looking troubled. Concern gripped her, and she quickly walked outside. "Mom, what's wrong?"

Yéil held up her phone, a sigh escaping her lips. "I just got a text from Tala, one of my friends from the Native hospital. She's about to go into hospice care."

A wave of sorrow washed over Aan. She sighed deeply. "I'm so sorry, Mom."

"She's only thirty-three years old, Aan," Yéil said, tears welling up. "Ovarian cancer. She has three little boys who will soon be without a mother. My heart aches for her and her family." She paused, looking at Aan with a mixture of hope and despair. "Is there any way you and Jaänjo could help her?"

Aan's heart ached for the woman and her children. A familiar determination rose within her—a need to help, to ease the suffering of others. "I... I'll talk to Jaänjo about it on our walk. I can't promise anything, though."

Yéil nodded, wiping away her tears. "Thank you."

As they walked along the town's main path, a somber silence replaced the usual vibrant energy that crackled between them. When they reached the secluded forest trail, Aan finally spoke. "Jaänjo, I might have a way to help her without being discovered."

"I'm listening."

"What if we sailed the boat to Juneau, docked it there, and had Mom's friend come to us? We could black out the cabin windows and perform the healing on the boat. We could even bring our shop light to flood the space with bright light. And since the cabin is small, we could say that no one else can join us during the healing."

Jaänjo's voice carried a note of doubt. "It's clever, but she's bound to tell someone if we heal her. What if the hospital discovers her cancer is gone? They'll demand answers."

The weight of the dilemma settled upon Aan. "Well, she could say she saw a shaman. It wouldn't be a lie."

"If her doctors come to you, and you say you gave her some special herb or something like that, they'd want to know what it was so they could use it to help others. Aan, if word gets out that you can cure people of incurable diseases, the world you know will be over."

"I know, Jaänjo. I know. But she's so young, and she has three little boys." Her voice trembled with anguish. "Knowing we could cure her, how could we do nothing? What should we do?"

"This is the time for us to ask a simple question."

Aan's curiosity stirred. "What question?"

"We need to ask, *'God, what say you?'* and listen for the response."

A small smile tugged at Aan's lips. "Jaänjo, I think you'd make a good Tlingit shaman."

He chuckled softly. "Maybe some of you is rubbing off on me." His tone turned serious. "Aan, we both need to meditate and hope the answer about how to proceed will come to us."

"I agree. Maybe we could walk to the meadow by the cabin and pray for guidance there."

That night, after turning off the light on the nightstand, Aan lay in the quiet darkness, the soft moonlight filtering through the curtains. The room was silent except for the faint sound of a distant owl. A cool breeze whispered through the slightly open window, carrying the scent of spruce and sea salt. She hugged her body pillow, gathering her thoughts and emotions before speaking.

"Jaänjo," she began, her voice barely above a whisper, "you feel at peace to me. Am I correct?"

"Yes."

"We both know the way forward, don't we?"

"I feel your peace, too, Aan. So yes, we both know the way forward."

"Since she's about to enter hospice care, we need to move fast. Let's talk to Mom and Dad about it in the morning." Relief mixed with apprehension in Aan's voice. "We'll need to be careful about how we approach this. Maybe we can suggest a 'spiritual healing' that doesn't promise miracles but offers comfort? That way, if she does recover, it won't seem so... impossible."

"I agree."

Their words hung in the air, the unspoken weight of their mission settling between them. Though the path ahead was uncertain, Aan and Jaänjo faced it together, united by their compassion and commitment to helping others.

As the night deepened, Aan felt a familiar restlessness. The weight of unspoken words pressed on her chest. She'd been carrying these feelings for too long, fear and hope warring within her. What if Jaänjo didn't feel the same? What if this changed everything between them? But the thought of never expressing her true feelings was unbearable. Taking a deep breath, she steeled herself. It was time.

Her voice, a fragile thread of vulnerability, filled the silence. "Jaänjo... I need to talk to you about something very important." Her fingers twisted nervously in the sheets, and she could feel her heart racing, its rhythm echoing in her ears.

The change in her tone and heartrate aroused Jaänjo's concern. "Aan, are you okay?"

"I don't know. Maybe."

"Please talk to me."

She sighed. "When I took a nap after Mom's healing, just before I fell asleep, I heard you say you loved me."

A ripple of tension passed through Jaänjo's energy. "I hoped you hadn't heard that."

"Why?"

"Because... if you didn't feel the same, the thought of losing you overwhelmed me." His voice quieted to a whisper. "It was such a scary thought that I vowed never to say those words to you again."

Aan pondered his words and tenderly hugged her pillow. "Jaänjo, I want you to know I feel the same way." Her voice trembled with sincerity. "My love for you is as intense as yours is for me. Despite our different worlds, I've never felt such a deep connection with anyone."

As she spoke, she thought about her grandmother's teachings on connection—to the land, to the spirits, and to each other. In her Tlingit culture, relationships were sacred, tied to the very fabric of existence. Her bond with Jaänjo, unconventional as it was, felt like an extension of that interconnectedness. It transcended the physical, touching something deeper, more spiritual. Perhaps this was why, despite the challenges, their relationship felt so right to her.

Her heart pounded as she searched for the right words to express her feelings. "Every moment we spend together strengthens my love for you. Our souls are intertwined, bound by an invisible thread that nothing can sever. I feel your energy within me, and it's beautiful and comforting in a way I can't begin to explain. When you are apart from me, it feels unbearable."

"When you told your parents about me being from another planet and said you had feelings for me, the urge to ask what you meant by that consumed me."

"I'm sorry to put you through that. Just so you know, I'm just as terrified that you could one day leave me. That's also why I haven't discussed how I feel about you."

He sighed. "When I said I love you, it wasn't a hollow utterance. It's an emotion that courses through my very being with an intensity that exceeds my comprehension. Those words have never crossed my lips with such depth and authenticity. That's how I feel about you."

Tears welled up in Aan's eyes. "That's so beautiful. You've shown me what true love means, Jaänjo. It's more than just a feeling—it's an experience. When I'm with you, my heart overflows with joy."

She hugged her pillow tightly. "I love you, Jaänjo. With all my heart, I love you."

Relief and joy swept through Jaänjo. "When did you know you loved me?"

"That's easy to answer. After my mom's healing, when you asked me to sit next to her and feel our mother-daughter energy, it was such a beautiful moment. I marveled at the power of the energy flowing between us. It was the best gift I've ever received. The fact that you even thought of having us share such a tender moment speaks volumes about the kindness and love in your heart. That's when I knew I loved you."

"You know, this—I mean, us—it's uncharted territory."

Aan moved her hand to her chest, feeling the comforting presence of Jaänjo's energy. "It is. And we'd be fools to pretend it won't be complicated."

"An alien living within a beautiful Earth woman—what could go wrong?"

Despite herself, a smile played on her lips. "Here I am, trying to be serious, and there you go—being your witty self."

"Oops. Forgive me. Let me put on my serious face for a moment."

She burst out laughing. "Nice try, oh faceless you. I've fallen in love with an intergalactic comedian."

Aan's playful response drew a heavy sigh from Jaänjo.

"Did I say something wrong?" No reply... "Jaänjo?"

He sighed deeply. "After your mom's healing, while I was perched atop the roof, replenishing my energy, a deluge of 'what if' scenarios inundated my thoughts. I found them deeply unsettling."

"Please tell me about the 'what-ifs.'"

A brief silence followed her comment, heavy with unspoken thoughts.

"Jaänjo, for our relationship to progress, we need to confide in each other, even if it's disconcerting."

"I know. Aan... these 'what-ifs' overwhelmed me: What if I could feel the warmth of your embrace? What if I could feel your heartbeat against my chest? What if I could hold your hand as we walked? What if I could kiss your lips? All the things I could never do as energy."

Jaänjo's words hung in the air, heavy with longing, and his vulnerability touched her deeply. Aan felt her own heart ache with similar desires. "I understand, Jaänjo," she said softly. "I've imagined those things, and..." She blushed, leaving the thought unfinished. "But Jaänjo, our connection goes beyond the physical. The way I feel your energy, the way our thoughts intertwine—it's unlike anything I've ever experienced."

"You're right," Jaänjo agreed. "Our bond is unique. But how do we navigate intimacy, Aan? How do we express our love physically when I have no physical form?"

Aan pondered this. "We'll find a way. Maybe through shared experiences, through the merging of our energies. It won't be traditional, but it will be ours."

"What you're saying sounds wonderful. Aan, there are countless unknowns and pitfalls that could happen with this relationship."

"I agree. But we'll learn from them and adapt, and our relationship will grow even stronger. All I want is to be with you."

"I feel the same way."

Aan placed her hand over her heart again, feeling the gentle warmth of Jaänjo's energy within her. "I believe in us, Jaänjo. Our love is a divine gift we'll cherish and protect from the world." She paused, reflecting. "What does our future look like, Jaänjo?" she asked softly. "I mean, long-term. Can we... grow old together? Will you always be with me?"

Jaänjo's energy dimmed slightly. "This is one of the unknowns. As pure energy, I don't age. So my lifespan will be different from yours. And my presence in your body—we don't know the long-term effects. But I do know that as long as I exist, I want to be with you."

As Jaänjo's words settled in her mind, Aan felt a blend of love, hope, and uncertainty about their future. With a soft sigh, she closed her eyes and drifted asleep, embraced by Jaänjo's comforting presence.

27

THE EARLY MORNING SUN streamed through the cabin window, casting a warm glow on the small, rough-sawn wooden table where Aan sat, enjoying a breakfast of berries and oatmeal. A contented smile played on her lips as she savored the sweet burst of flavor from a plump blueberry. But her thoughts were far from the quiet solitude of her cabin—they were filled with Jaänjo.

"You know, Jaänjo," Aan began, a playful lilt in her voice, "you really are a good-looking alien."

"That's an interesting comment," Jaänjo mused. "You humans seem to place a lot of value on physical appearances."

"Well, yeah," Aan replied, spooning another bite of oatmeal into her mouth. "It's natural to appreciate beauty, isn't it? And you are... well, you're gorgeous. When you appeared before us, your glow masked your finer physical details. What color are your eyes, hair, and skin?"

Jaänjo paused, considering Aan's question. "My ancestors lived in the high northern latitudes of N'ridium. Family lore tells of them being fishers, navigating around the coastal islands where they dwelled. Perhaps my fondness for Tenakee Springs lies somewhere in my cellular memory, reminding me of the land where my ancestors once lived. Anyway, people in these regions developed fair skin, blond hair, and blue eyes." His energy shimmered within her, reflecting a deep nostalgia and connection to his heritage. "In addition to those physical features, I'd like to think that one of my ancestors was also a healer, and I inherited that from them."

"Maybe your family heritage also explains your ability to detect fish," Aan teased, a devilish smile spreading across her face. "Blond hair, blue eyes, and fair skin—I'll bet the N'ridium girls fawned over you."

As soon as the words left her mouth, Aan sensed a shift in Jaänjo's energy. The playful mood evaporated, replaced by a heaviness that made her sit up straighter.

A poignant silence descended. Jaänjo's reply, tinged with melancholy, caught her off guard. "No one on my planet ever found me desirable, Aan," he admitted. "Because I possess the ability to see and manipulate auras, I was considered a rare breed."

Aan's hand paused midway to her mouth, the spoon of oatmeal forgotten. She set it down, her breakfast suddenly less important than this unexpected revelation. Her brow furrowed. "I don't get it. To me, that's a gift that would make you even more attractive to someone."

"It is a gift," Jaänjo confirmed, his voice thoughtful. "But also a curse. It made me an oddity, someone who didn't fit in with the norms of others. My 'gift' isolated me from society, including my parents."

"I'm sorry," Aan said softly, struggling to comprehend the weight of his words. "But surely there were others with abilities similar to yours?"

"None my age," Jaänjo replied. "As I mentioned, people like me are rare. Being different makes forming relationships extraordinarily challenging—a reality I've faced my entire life. The only close bond I ever had was with my brother, Miĕĕcha. Somehow, he accepted me for who I was." He sighed. "There's another reason I never dated. Miĕĕcha worked at a prestigious institute where teams focused on helping our people survive. While Miĕĕcha's team worked on transforming living beings into pure energy, one of his friends worked on a different project—making our dwindling food supplies last."

"What does that have to do with you not dating?" Aan asked, her curiosity piqued.

Jaänjo sighed again. "His friend's team found a way to add birth control and hormone-deadening substances to the water supply. It was a desperate attempt to control the population, to curb the number of mouths to feed."

As Jaänjo recounted N'ridium's decline, Aan's gaze wandered around her cozy cabin, the stark contrast between her peaceful world and his harrowing one becoming increasingly apparent. The gravity of his words weighed heavily upon her, intensifying her gratitude for life's simple pleasures. "It's inconceivable that your government would do such things," Aan replied, her brow furrowed in disbelief. "But I still don't see how this relates to you not dating anyone?"

Jaänjo's energy dimmed, and Aan felt a chill pass through her. "Let me explain," he said, his voice heavy with remembered pain. "Before these extreme measures, any woman discovered to be pregnant and their partner faced a terrible choice: abortion or banishment to our planet's toxic surface—a death sentence."

Aan's eyes widened in horror as Jaänjo continued, "After they secretly added the birth control and hormone-suppressing substances to our water, people's desires for intimacy and companionship faded away. The relentless struggle for survival further eroded meaningful interactions."

He paused, allowing Aan to absorb the gravity of his words. "That's why I never had a relationship... until now, with you."

"How utterly dreadful that you lived through what you just described," she whispered.

"I agree. But it got worse. Toward the end, the government banished the elderly unless they were part of the privileged society. Those who participated in food riots, protests, or other perceived forms of troublemaking were also banished." He sighed. "As you know, healers like me can't heal those with dark auras, and nearly every government official I ever saw had a dark aura. When healers—including me—said we couldn't heal them, they claimed we were troublemakers and banished nearly all of us. Fortunately, Miĕĕcha's critical role in the matter-to-energy research shielded me from most of the government's wrath. But Miĕĕcha knew his leverage with the government would end once his team perfected energy back to matter, so he got me out before that happened."

Jaänjo sighed deeply. "So that's why women weren't 'fawning over me.' Aan, I lived in a brutal world in many different ways."

Her mind reeled, struggling to grasp the scale of suffering Jaänjo described. His words painted a harrowing picture of unrelenting torment, allowing her to comprehend the damage to his soul fully. "Oh, Jaänjo, I'm so terribly sorry," she whispered, her heart aching as she realized the full extent of his pain. "What you endured is unimaginable—a hellish existence. I understand now why you've been unable to form relationships and the depth of your pain. Thank you for confiding in me. It makes me love you even more."

She paused for a moment, reflecting. "I want you to know that I also felt different from others as a child, and later, I experienced isolation due to my MS. But I can't imagine what it was like for you on N'ridium. I promise you'll never feel that way again. You're not alone, starving, and oppressed now, Jaänjo," she said, her voice choking with emotion. "And you have a kindred spirit in me. I love who you are, especially your oddity. It's what makes you 'you.'"

"Thanks for your kind words." He sighed. "N'ridium was once a lush land, teeming with life and beauty. At its zenith, my civilization numbered in the billions. But as our planet neared its end, Miěěcha told me they'd be lucky to convert a hundred thousand people to energy. Of those, the chances of them encountering another hospitable planet were remote. So, as you can imagine, it makes me wonder why I'm one of the few who lived. Survivor's guilt haunts me."

Aan nodded slowly, her Tlingit heritage offering a unique lens through which to view Jaänjo's suffering. "My people, too, bear the scars of immense hardship and loss," she began gently, "though nothing on the scale of your planet's devastation. Our history is marked by wounds that persist, echoes of ancestral pain. Yet, even with this understanding, I find it impossible to fathom the weight of your world's sorrow—and your personal anguish."

"We are both survivors, Aan," Jaänjo replied. "Until I came here, I didn't know the meaning of happiness. To love and be loved is such a wonderful thing."

A lump swelled in Aan's throat, her vision blurring as she absorbed the depth of his feelings. "You deserve all the happiness in the world, Jaänjo. You've been through so much, yet you've given me more than I could ever repay."

Jaänjo's energy pulsed gently, a comforting presence that enveloped her heart. "I'm the one who should be thanking you. Your kindness, acceptance, and love have shown me the beauty of life beyond survival. We both have been given second chances at life—you with being free of MS and me to experience life in a way I never thought possible."

A tear slipped down Aan's cheek. "Jaänjo, I'm grateful every day that you're a part of my life. You're not just an incredible being with a rare gift; you're my friend, my partner, and my love." Even as Aan's heart swelled with love and compassion for Jaänjo, a small part of her wondered about the implications of loving someone so different, someone whose very existence defied the laws of her world. But for now, she pushed those thoughts aside, focusing on the warmth of Jaänjo's presence within her.

28

Later that morning, Aan discussed with Yéil and Keet her and Jaänjo's plan to heal Tala on their boat.

"Well, Mom and Dad, what do you think?"

Keet sat, contemplating the details. "It could work, Aan. I'll call Statter Harbor to see if any transient slips are available."

"What does that mean?" Jaänjo asked Aan.

"Statter Harbor is where we moor our boat when we visit Juneau, the biggest city around here with a population of 32,000. In comparison, our town has only about 130 people."

"Wow, that's quite a difference."

"Keet," said Yéil, "Tala might not be mobile. Let me call her first to see if she'd be open to Aan healing her and if she could join us on our boat."

"Mom, Jaänjo and I will wait on the dock while you talk to Tala. Don't mention Jaänjo, please."

"Got it—there'll be no mention of Jaänjo."

Outside, Aan took a deep breath of the salty air, its scent soothing her as she settled onto the weathered dock bench. "I love the smell of the ocean, don't you?"

"I do," said Jaänjo. "Aan, I understand the gravity of Tala's situation, but if I had a face, I'd be grinning from ear to ear."

"I think I know why—it's about our feelings for each other, right?"

"It is."

"I'm smiling, too, Jaänjo. If Tala wants us to come, this could be a busy day."

"I know. Aan, as with your mom's healing, it's likely I'll have to enter Tala to cure her. I can't do that without her permission, but we can't say I'm an alien. So how can I keep my integrity without telling her the truth?"

Aan pondered for a few moments. "I'll tell her a spirit resides within me, and this spirit needs to be with her temporarily to heal her."

Jaänjo sighed. "That will work, but it's stretching the truth. Tala and her family won't fully understand what they're agreeing to. So, is it truly informed consent if they don't know about my alien nature?"

Aan nodded, acknowledging his concern. "As you said before, we need to protect our way of life. Sometimes, compromises have to be made to promote the higher good."

"In this case, I agree. But, Aan, I must respect Tala's decision if she refuses the spirit's entry." He paused, reflecting. "In the future, this ethical dilemma will always confront us."

"I understand and agree with what you're saying, but let's focus on healing Tala for now."

She paused, furrowing her brow. "Jaänjo, after you healed Mom, your depleted energy scared me—really scared me. What if it happens again, especially today, since it's overcast everywhere? You won't be able to recharge."

"Don't laugh, but I'm fully charged—I have much more energy now than when I healed your mom."

"That's good to hear—" She noticed Yéil frantically motioning for her to come over. "Mom wants us, Jaänjo. Something's wrong."

She hurried to join her. "Mom, did she pass?"

"No, but her husband says Tala's taken a turn for the worse. She might not make it through the night. I told him about you and how you cured me of my cancer. He said we're welcome to come but thinks we're too late to cure her."

Aan nodded. "Let's go back inside and talk about our options."

At their dining table, Aan sighed. "First off, Jaänjo, if she's on the brink of death, can you still cure her?"

"It's possible," he replied. "If her aura still has any white glow, we can help her. If her aura is dark, then there's nothing we can do. The only way to know is to see her." He sighed. "Aan, if we cure her at her home, our worst fear of someone witnessing it would likely become a reality."

Aan repeated what Jaänjo said to her parents.

Silence fell over the room as they considered the implications.

Aan sighed deeply. "Mom and Dad, Jaänjo's right—if we try to heal Tala at home, we're foolish to hope we can keep this secret."

Keet raised his hand and spoke. "I've looked at your new shop light, Aan. The three lights mounted on the stand can detach and operate independently. We could bring one of them and use it during the healing process. As long as no one else is in the room but you and maybe me holding the light, you could still heal her without them seeing anything."

Aan's eyes widened. "It could work. Jaänjo, what do you think?"

"As long as Tala covers her eyes with a sleeping mask and no one but you and your dad are in the room, I think it could work, too."

"Dad, Jaänjo agrees that it could work."

"Then let's do it," said Yéil. "Keet, please book a slip at Statter Harbor while I pack a light meal for the journey."

The family quickly gathered the necessary equipment, including the sleeping masks and shop light. Within an hour, they were ready to depart.

Two hours into their journey, a steady rain pattered against the boat's wheelhouse glass as Keet expertly navigated the choppy waters. He smiled at Aan after taking another bite of his turkey sandwich. "No need to worry, Aan. This is a sturdy vessel, and it's weathered far worse storms than this."

"Dad, I'm not worried—I'm just thinking about healing Tala and protecting how we do it."

As Keet approached Statter Harbor shortly before noon, he contacted the harbormaster and received permission to moor at their D dock. After securing the boat in the steady rain, Keet grabbed the bag holding the shop light and masks. They walked briskly to the harbor office to meet Eeton, Tala's husband.

Inside the office, a man with a somber expression gazed out the window and spotted two women and a man approaching from the docks. He stepped out to greet them. "Are you the Gajaa family?" he inquired.

Keet put the bag down and extended his hand. "We are. You must be Eeton."

"Yes," Eeton replied, shaking Keet's hand. "Thank you all for coming. I have to be honest and say I fear you're too late to save her. Her doctor said the end is near, and he agreed with Tala's request for her to die at home."

"Eaton," said Yéil, "as I mentioned on the phone, Aan called on our spirits to assist her in curing my cancer, and we hope they can help Tala as well."

He looked at Aan. "Do you really think you can help Tala?"

"Eaton, I can't say until I see her and ask our spirits if curing her is possible."

"I understand." He gestured toward the parking lot. "My van is this way. It seats eight, so there's plenty of room. Our home is about twenty minutes away."

The drive to Eaton's house was largely silent, punctuated only by Jaänjo's internal commentary to Aan on the city's clamor and primitive modes of transport. As they arrived, Eaton flushed with embarrassment and apologized in advance for the state of their home.

"Eaton, we understand," said Yéil. "My house was also messy during my illness. If our spirits say they and Aan can cure Tala, perhaps we can go somewhere for ice cream to give Aan the peace she and our spirits will need to heal her."

"Okay," he said, his tone resigned. "But I still think you may be too late." With a weary sigh, he led the way toward the house.

"Mom," said Eaton, "this is the Gajaa family from Tenakee Springs—Keet, Yéil, and Aan." His mother offered a cautious hello. He then turned to his three sons. "Boys, these are our guests. Taayoo is the oldest—he's six; Samuel is four, and Niko is two." The children shyly smiled at the strangers.

"We're pleased to meet all of you," said Aan.

"Aan," said Jaänjo, "please activate your aura vision—something is wrong with their oldest child."

Appearing unfazed by Jaänjo's words, Aan casually scratched her nose, covertly activating her aura vision. She then turned her gaze to their eldest son and smiled warmly. "Boys, I'm a shaman—a healer—and if you all don't mind, I'd like to meet your mother to see if I can help her." She focused her gaze on Taayoo as she spoke.

"Sure," said Eaton. "Please follow me."

"Aan and Yéil, I'll wait here and let you two be with Tala," said Keet. Yéil gave him a quick nod in reply.

As Eaton entered the bedroom, he smiled at Tala. "Dear, Yéil and Aan are here."

29

Upon seeing Tala, Yéil suppressed her shock at the sight of her. "Hello, my friend," she said, forcing a smile as she embraced Tala. Inwardly, her emotions churned, but she maintained a calm exterior.

Aan stood back, giving her mom time to greet her friend. She cringed at the sight of Tala, who lay in her bed, her frail body barely making an impression on the covers. Her aura was pitiful, a fragile white fringed with gray—a sign of her life force slowly fading. She noted Tala's pale and drawn skin and her hollowed cheeks. Tala's breathing was shallow and rapid, her lips slightly parted as she struggled for air. Though still bright with love, her eyes held a weariness that spoke of pain and exhaustion. A glimmer of sweat adorned her forehead.

After hugging Tala, Yéil put her hand on Aan. "Tala, this is my daughter, Aan."

"Hello, Tala, I'm pleased to meet you." When Aan took Tala's hand in hers, she was struck by its coolness and alarming frailty. Tala's aura, a pitiful fragile white fringed with encroaching gray, revealed her fading life force. Masking the turmoil churning within her, Aan offered a reassuring smile to the ailing woman.

"Thank you both for coming," Tala labored to say. "As you can see, I will soon join our ancestors in the great beyond. Aan, could you talk to our spirits and ancestors, asking for their guidance and protection for me on my journey to the afterlife?"

Aan smiled with empathy. "Of course, Tala, but before I do that, a healing spirit dwells in me, and his name is Jaänjo. He and I will use my hands and eyes to examine you without touching you to see if we can cure you. Is that okay with you?"

Tala's gaze met Aan's, a flicker of understanding in her eyes. "I'm willing to try anything, Aan. I'm not ready to say goodbye to my boys."

"Okay, great. First, I'll remove your blanket. If you hear me talking, it will be with Jaänjo. I'll let you know when I'm talking to you."

Tala nodded.

"Jaänjo, can you hear me," Aan asked mentally instead of speaking.

"Yes. Aan, Tala's aura is dreadfully weak, but it's still white. Let's examine her. I'll need to move your arms and eyes again."

Aan nodded and then spoke aloud to Tala. "Tala, I'm going to put my hands above you and move them from your head to your toes to feel your energy."

"Okay."

Aan's arms rose without her consciously moving them. Jaänjo cupped her hands two inches above Tala's head and held them there for several moments. Then he moved her hands down Tala's body, spending the most time over Tala's abdomen. He sighed. "There's much to fix, Aan."

"I know, Jaänjo. Can we heal her?"

"Yes, but cancer isn't her only issue. Her liver shows signs of fatty infiltration, indicating substantial alcohol consumption. Did you notice the irregularities in Taayoo's aura? It appeared fragmented and dull, with unusual fluctuations in color and intensity, particularly around areas linked to cognitive function and emotional regulation. If Tala consumed alcohol during her pregnancy with Taayoo, it would explain both her compromised liver and his cognitive abnormalities."

Aan exhaled heavily. "Yes, I observed the aura disturbances you described in Taayoo. Your suspicion about the alcohol connection seems well-founded. Prenatal alcohol exposure often leads to severe lifelong consequences such as facial deformities, stunted growth, behavioral challenges, and the cognitive abnormalities you mentioned. I've witnessed firsthand how this disproportionately affects Indigenous communities—a cruel legacy of systemic inequities and historical trauma. Fortunately, Taayoo's symptoms appear less severe than many cases I've encountered."

"That's sad to hear how it afflicts your people. If Eaton and Tala are open to it, I could also cure Taayoo."

"Thank you, Jaänjo!" she said aloud. "Tala, Jaänjo and our spirits say we can help you!"

"Hold on, Aan," said Jaänjo. "You have to get Tala's permission for me to enter her body. And I'll need permission to enter Taayoo, too."

Aan placed her hand over her heart. "My apologies, Jaänjo," she said aloud. "I got carried away." She turned to Tala, noting her bewildered expression. "Pardon the interruption—I was talking to Jaänjo. Tala, to heal you, Jaänjo needs to enter your body to expel the cancer. He cured my multiple sclerosis and my mother's cancer, so my mom and I can tell you there is nothing to fear. Jaänjo is a gentle spirit, so you won't feel any discomfort during his temporary presence in your body. However, he requires your consent before proceeding with the cure."

"He has my permission to cure me. Thank you, Aan, and please thank the spirit Jaänjo."

"Jaänjo expresses his gratitude. Tala, I need to inform your family about our ability to help you. I also must confer with Jaänjo regarding our approach to your healing process. I'll be back in a few minutes."

"Okay."

Back in the living room, Aan smiled as she greeted the family. "The spirits say there's still time to cure Tala, but we must act quickly. "Eaton, as my mom said, the spirits and I need absolute quiet during the healing process, so could you take your family out for ice cream or something else for an hour or so?"

"Yes, I can do that."

"Eaton, if you'd like, I can come with your family to help with the kids," Yéil said.

"Thanks, that would help." He looked at his kids. "Boys, let's go to Chilkat Cones for ice cream cones. Mom, please come with me."

"Great," said Aan. "I use light therapy, so my dad needs to be with me to hold the light we brought."

"I'll go to the van to get my bag," Keet said.

After the family departed, Aan retrieved a sleeping mask from Keet's bag and showed it to Tala. "We're ready to begin the healing," she explained. "I use a powerful light during my ceremony to simulate our sun, so I'd like you to wear this mask to shield your eyes."

Tala nodded, and Aan gently put the mask over her eyes. Aan then donned her protective goggles. "Dad, please turn on the light," she instructed.

Keet put on his sunglasses and switched on the light.

"Tala," said Aan in a soothing voice, "remember to breathe calmly. I'll begin with a chant to invite our spirits to join us."

"Okay," Tala replied.

Aan's chant started low, almost a whisper, then gradually increased in volume and intensity, filling the bedroom with melodic, rhythmic sounds.

Though the words were indecipherable to untrained ears, their power was palpable in the air.

As Tala lay still, her chest rose and fell in measured breaths that seemed to draw in the strength of Aan's voice.

The cadence of Aan's chant ebbed and flowed like ocean waves, at times soft and soothing and then building to a crescendo that seemed to make the air vibrate. Her body swayed slightly with the rhythm, fully immersed in the ceremony.

Keet stood motionless and noted how Tala's fingers twitched in response to the power in Aan's voice. He mentally asked the spirits to help his daughter and Jaänjo heal Tala.

In this transformed space, time seemed to lose meaning. There was only the light, the chant, and the battle being waged against the sickness that had taken root in Tala's body. Aan's voice seemed to bring the healing power of their ancestors into the room, her chant a conduit between past and present.

As the last echoes of her chant faded, Aan felt a deep connection—to her ancestors, to Jaänjo, and to something greater than herself. She reflected on how her people's traditional healing practices now intertwined with Jaänjo's otherworldly abilities. This fusion of ancient Earthly wisdom and cosmic knowledge filled her with awe and purpose.

She gently placed her hand on Tala's chest. "Jaänjo," she said aloud, "we're ready for you to begin. Tala, as I mentioned, you won't feel any pain."

"Your ceremony moved me deeply, Aan," Jaänjo responded, his voice filled with awe and reverence. "Please tell Tala she'll experience tingling sensations as you move your hands over her, but they won't be unpleasant."

After relaying the message to Tala, Aan closed her eyes as she had during her mother's healing. She reached deep within herself, summoning the vibrant energy at her core. A soft, white glow began to emanate from her palms, growing stronger with each heartbeat.

Jaänjo positioned Aan's hands above the crown of Tala's head. Aan opened her eyes and once again marveled at their combined energies flowing into another person. With gentle precision, Jaänjo moved Aan's hands downward. Their combined energies flowed through her hands as they systematically addressed each area of Tala's body affected by the cancer, focusing on her abdomen, where the disease was most concentrated, before sweeping the healing energy through the rest of her body.

Throughout the procedure, the room remained charged with a palpable sense of purpose and power, the air seeming to pulse with the rhythm of their combined efforts.

"Aan," Jaänjo said softly, "this part of the healing process is complete. It's time to ease the flow of our energy."

Aan nodded. She drew in a deep breath and, as she exhaled, focused on dampening the intensity of her energy. The glow from her hands dimmed, and the charged atmosphere in the room began to subside.

"Tala, the first part of our healing is complete. Now, Jaänjo will enter your body to finish the healing process."

"Can I take off the mask?" Tala asked.

"Not yet," Aan cautioned softly. "The light is still active. Tala, Jaänjo wants to know if you're ready to receive his energy."

"I am," Tala replied, her voice trembling slightly with anticipation and nervousness.

At that moment, Jaänjo's energy left Aan's body. He manifested as a softly glowing white light, hovering briefly above Tala. Then, with fluid grace, his luminous energy enveloped Tala's form before gradually seeping into her body.

A half-hour passed, marked only by the steady rhythm of Tala's breathing and the glowing light of the lamp. At last, Jaänjo's work reached its conclusion. His energy, luminous and fluid, gradually withdrew from Tala's form. He hovered briefly in the air before merging once more with Aan.

"Welcome back, Jaänjo," Aan whispered, her voice filled with quiet awe. "I observed Tala's aura as you worked. It shifted to pure white during your time with her. It seems your healing was successful."

Jaänjo noted Tala's aura through Aan's eyes, confirming what Aan had observed. "It's good to be back with you. You're right—Tala's aura reflects a positive outcome. We've eradicated the cancer and restored her liver to a healthy, viable state."

The certainty in Jaänjo's voice underscored the miraculous nature of what they had just accomplished. A sense of achievement radiated between them, a testament to their collaborative healing power.

Aan nodded to Keet, who extinguished the light. A hush fell over the room, broken only by the gentle rain drumming on the roof.

"Tala, we've finished," Aan said softly. "I'm going to remove your mask now." With tender care, she lifted the sleeping mask from Tala's face. As Tala's eyes adjusted to the soft sunlight bathing the room, Aan's smile greeted her. "Jaänjo and our spirits confirm that you're cured."

Tears welled in Tala's eyes, glistening with relief and profound gratitude. "Thank you both so much, Aan," she whispered, her voice thick with emotion. "I felt Jaänjo's energy within me. It was... indescribable." She paused, searching for words to convey the experience. "It... it felt like a warm, golden light flowing through every part of my body, washing away the pain. I've never experienced anything like it."

Tala's gaze drifted as if seeing a future that had once seemed lost. Her voice quivered with a renewed sense of hope as she continued. "It's hard to grasp that I won't have to say goodbye to my boys." The weight of this realization settled over her, bringing with it a flood of possibilities she had dared not imagine before.

The room seemed to resonate with the power of this moment, filled with the palpable sense of a life reclaimed and a future restored.

"I'm so happy for you, Tala," Aan said with a warm smile, but her expression soon turned serious. "But there's something we need to discuss. Jaänjo discovered your liver was damaged, likely due to alcohol consumption. We also noticed irregularities in Taayoo's aura around areas linked to cognitive function. If you consumed alcohol during your pregnancy with Taayoo, it would explain both your compromised liver and his cognitive abnormalities. I have to ask, is this true?"

Tala nodded, fresh tears welling in her eyes. "During my first pregnancy, I had trouble sleeping, so I drank a glass or two of wine before bed. I didn't see a doctor until I was eight months along. When Taayoo was born, we knew something wasn't right. They asked if I drank during the pregnancy, and I admitted I had. They said he likely had fetal alcohol disorder." Her voice quivered with regret. "Aan, I never knew drinking could harm my baby. After that, I quit drinking, and my two other boys are fine. It breaks my heart that I hurt poor Taayoo." She touched Aan's hand to emphasize what she was about to say. "I never drank again until I found out I had incurable cancer. Then I started drinking to numb my sadness."

Aan sighed softly. "I'm sorry you went through that. But now that you're well, I urge you to give up drinking again."

"I will, Aan," Tala promised, her voice filled with renewed determination. "I have so much to live for now."

"Tala," Aan continued, "Jaänjo and I can also help Taayoo, but Jaänjo will need to enter his body as he did with you. We also need your and Eaton's permission for him to do that."

Tala's eyes widened, a spark of hope igniting within them. "Yes! Jaänjo can do it!" Relief seemed to flood through her as she spoke, her voice brimming with newfound optimism.

"Aan," Jaänjo said, his voice gentle but firm, "please tell Tala she will experience weakness for several days as her body recovers from the energy drain of her illness. She needs to consume nutritious, high-energy foods—like your mother's salmon dishes. This will significantly aid her recovery and help restore her strength. Also, her muscles need to regenerate. Gentle exercise, such as walking, will be beneficial in this process. Emphasize the importance of gradually regaining her strength."

Aan nodded and conveyed Jaänjo's recommendations to Tala.

"Please give my deepest gratitude to Jaänjo again, Aan," Tala said with emotion. After a thoughtful pause, she asked, "When do you think you'll be able to help Taayoo?"

"That's a good question," Aan replied. "Give me a few moments to talk to Jaänjo."

Aan's expression turned serious as she mentally communicated with him. "Jaänjo, I'm worried about your energy level. Are you certain you're up for this?"

"Aan, I feel stronger than I did after healing your mother. However, once I've helped Taayoo, I'll need to rest and recharge when we return to Tenakee Springs. I suggest healing Taayoo around midnight. Perhaps we could ask Eaton to take us back to your boat and pick us up later tonight. This would allow their family some time to celebrate their good news."

"That's a good idea." She looked at Tala. "Jaänjo believes it would be most effective to treat Taayoo when he's in a deep sleep. He suggests doing it tonight around midnight."

The following day, as they journeyed back to Tenakee Springs, Aan stood on the deck in front of the wheelhouse, the wind tousling her hair. Her thoughts turned inward, connecting with Jaänjo.

"Jaänjo," she said with a voice warm with emotion, "we've done something remarkable for that family. I hope you feel as elated as I do. And I must say, my love and admiration for you have only deepened after witnessing all you've done."

"I feel the same about you. Witnessing Tala's family's joy is what makes healing so fulfilling. And I'm glad they agreed to keep what we did a secret. Aan…" His voice trailed off, and she sensed a shift in his energy.

"Yes, Jaänjo?"

"When you summoned your spirits for Tala, their presence enveloped my soul with an extraordinary peace. In that moment, my soul suddenly felt untethered from the weight of my past traumas."

Aan gasped and placed her hand over her heart, her eyes welling with tears. "I pray daily for my spirits to aid your soul. During my chant for Tala, I also asked them to heal you. I'm certain that when they saw your tender heart and willingness to help one of our people, they answered my prayers."

"Thank you," he said softly. "Invisible scars often run deepest, but with your love and the touch of your spirits, my soul, at long last, now feels unburdened by the past." His gaze shifted to the horizon. "Rain is coming. We should head inside."

Aan smiled and nodded. "We've both been released from our past burdens and now, life feels so much sweeter." She looked at the darkening sky. "You're right about rain coming. Oh! When we get home, we're taking you to the Party Time Bakery for your favorite treat."

"Beef stew?" Jaänjo replied, tongue-in-cheek.

"Uh, no," Aan replied with a chuckle. "Something even better than that."

30

JUST AFTER NINE IN the morning, Keet expertly maneuvered their boat to the family's pier. After securing the vessel, he turned to Aan with a mischievous grin. "If we hurry, we might still snag some cinnamon rolls."

Aan's eyes sparkled with amusement. "Did you hear that, Jaänjo?"

A moment later, she burst into laughter. "Dad, Jaänjo suggests we sprint to the bakery."

At Party Time Bakery, Aan joined her parents at a worn wooden table, setting down a tray laden with three enormous, glistening confections. The aroma of cinnamon and fresh-baked dough wafted through the air. "We snagged the last three cinnamon rolls," she announced triumphantly. "What luck!"

As they happily devoured their treats, Silas Tenhoff entered the bakery. Compared to the last time they saw him, he looked gaunt and pale, his cheekbones more pronounced and his skin ashen. Spotting them, he approached with an exaggerated smile that did little to mask his sickly appearance. "Ah, the Gajaa family—my favorite people!" Despite his bravado, the signs of deteriorating health were impossible to ignore.

Aan felt a chill run down her spine, remembering Jaänjo's warning about Silas's true nature. She noticed how his overly friendly demeanor didn't reach his eyes, which remained cold and calculating. Despite his attempt at warmth, an underlying tension in his posture put Aan on edge. Instinctively, she touched her nose, activating her aura vision to see the dark aura Jaänjo had previously warned her about. As it appeared, she gasped, choking on her water.

Silas looked at her with concern. "Are you all right, Aan?"

She nodded, coughing to clear her throat. "The water went down the wrong way. I'm fine."

"Congratulations on your MS going into remission. And, Yéil, one of the crew on your boat says Aan cured you of cancer."

Both Yéil and Aan's eyes widened. Aan took the initiative. "Silas, I'm a shaman. I simply asked our spirits to help my mom and me. Mom's initial cancer diagnosis turned out to be a false positive—just a benign cyst."

"I see," he replied. "Well, I've just been diagnosed with incurable lung cancer, and they assured me it's not a false positive. Perhaps you could call on your spirits to help me as well."

Aan frowned. "Silas, it's well-known that you don't think highly of Native people or our beliefs. So let's not waste each other's time."

Silas feigned hurt. "I don't know why you'd say that. I've never mistreated any of your people. Ask anyone around here. And I even expedited your family's boat engine repair."

Aan locked eyes on Silas, poised to confront him about his inflated labor costs. Jaänjo's voice cut through her thoughts. "Don't say anything, Aan! Do not incur his wrath!"

She caught herself. "You're—you're right, Silas. I apologize. Sometimes, we Tlingits perceive slights that aren't there."

He nodded. "No offense taken. So, will you ask your spirits to help me?"

Aan hesitated. "Um, sure. When we finish, we can go to the yard beside the bakery, and I'll ask our spirits to heal your body."

"Thank you." He turned his attention to Keet. "If you don't mind, I'll grab a quick bite and join you."

Keet nodded. As Silas walked to the counter, Aan pushed her plate away. "I've lost my appetite."

"What should we do?" Yéil asked, concerned.

"Mom, let's go outside with him. I'll say some gibberish to make him think I'm calling our spirits. Five minutes, tops, and we're done." She paused. "Jaänjo, you were right—his aura is pure evil."

Silas returned, frowning. "They're out of cinnamon rolls, so I got a sandwich to go." He eyed their unfinished meals and smirked. "Most people overestimate how much of these they can eat. Looks like you all fall into that category."

"Silas," said Aan, "we're pressed for time. Let's use the side yard for privacy. I'll perform a brief ceremony there to call on our spirits for you."

"Fine by me. Glad I got my sandwich to go."

Aan, her family, and Silas gathered in the bakery's side yard. Aan closed her eyes and began a series of meaningless chants, feigning a spiritual ceremony. As she finished, she raised her hands, palms facing Silas.

Suddenly, her palms began to glow with an ethereal energy. Aan's eyes widened in shock, mirroring Silas's stunned expression.

"What—why are your hands glowing?" Silas stammered.

Aan, trying to maintain composure, replied, "They're not. It's just sunlight reflecting off them."

"No," Silas insisted, "I know what I saw. They were glowing!"

Keet stepped forward. "Silas, you're quite mistaken. There's nothing unusual happening here."

Silas's face reddened. "After seeing her glowing palms, I know Aan can cure me of my cancer. If she doesn't, I'll tell everyone she's some kind of witch or sorcerer!"

"Fine," Keet retorted. "Tell everyone. They'll think you've lost your mind." He turned to Aan. "We're leaving. Now."

As they began to walk away, Keet turned and faced Silas. "Leave my daughter and my family alone."

Silas stormed away from the Gajaa family, his mind reeling from what he'd witnessed. The image of Aan's hands glowing during her chant played in his thoughts. "She has some sort of magical power," he muttered, clenching his fists. "The power to heal. And she won't help me."

As Aan and her family hurried away, tears welled up in Aan's eyes. Her voice trembled as she whispered, "What are we going to do? How can we keep this secret?"

Keet placed a comforting hand on her shoulder. "Take a deep breath, Aan. We'll figure this out."

Yéil glanced around to ensure no one could hear them. "We need to be more careful. Jaänjo's presence... it's becoming harder to conceal."

Aan wiped her eyes, her mind racing. "I never expected my hands to glow like that. Jaänjo, was that your energy? Or something else?"

Jaänjo paused before answering, his tone thoughtful. "I believe it's a combination of our energies, Aan. Our connection is growing stronger, and as it does, your abilities are evolving. But this is new to me as well. We'll have to learn together."

Aan nodded as uncertainty gnawed at her. "Do you think it's dangerous? Could it hurt someone?"

"I don't believe so," Jaänjo replied. "But we must be careful. We're venturing into unknown territory, and there may be risks we don't yet understand."

A shiver ran down her spine. The idea of wielding such power—of being responsible for it—felt both exhilarating and terrifying.

She shared this with her parents, then added, "It's like our energies are becoming more intertwined. I can feel changes in myself, but I don't fully understand them yet."

Keet furrowed his brow. "An alien living within you as pure energy is bound to cause changes."

"I know." She paused, reflecting. "When Silas tells everyone, do you think they'll believe him?"

Yéil squeezed her hand. "Who knows? For now, let's go home and talk it through. We'll find a way to protect Jaänjo and you."

"It's not just local anymore, Mom," Aan replied, her voice taut with worry. "Think about what we did in Juneau for Tala and Taayoo. Word of that could spread, too. Jaänjo warned me this might happen, and it's coming true."

As they walked, Aan struggled to calm her racing thoughts, acutely aware of the extraordinary being within her and the immense responsibility of safeguarding him. The weight of their secret seemed to press down on her shoulders with each step.

Back home, they settled into their living room, the tension from their encounter with Silas still palpable in the air. Aan's eyes were red-rimmed from her earlier tears, a visible reminder of the day's emotional toll. As they sat together, worried glances were exchanged, the gravity of their situation evident in their tense postures.

As they talked, the familiar creaks of their house and the sound of waves lapping at the shore provided a comforting backdrop to their tense conversation.

Keet cleared his throat, his voice steady but underlined with concern. "So what do we do?"

Yéil leaned forward, her face bright with an idea. "Let's attribute the healings to traditional remedies and claim we're using ancient herbal treatments passed down through generations."

Aan shook her head. "That might work for minor ailments, Mom, but what about dramatic cases like Tala's in Juneau? And if someone investigates, they could uncover your hospital records. Even though they're supposed to be confidential, they'd reveal your end-stage cancer diagnosis.'

"Aan's right," Keet said, his expression grave. "This isn't just a local issue anymore. We're dealing with medical records and cases beyond our community."

There was a moment of silence as Aan communicated with Jaänjo. Her expression shifted. "Jaänjo has some input. He suggests we could perform healings more subtly, over time, rather than instant cures. It might draw less attention."

"That's clever," Yéil said. "We could claim it's a series of treatments, explaining gradual improvements."

"But what about Silas seeing my glowing hands?" Aan asked, worry creeping back into her voice.

Keet snapped his fingers. "Bioluminescent algae! We could say you use it in your treatments. It's native to our waters, so it wouldn't seem out of place."

Aan's eyes lit up with understanding. "That's brilliant, Dad. Bioluminescent algae are known for their blue-green glow in our waters. We could say I've found a way to concentrate their properties for healing purposes. It's vague enough to be believable, yet scientific enough to deflect immediate suspicion."

As they continued brainstorming, Keet's expression grew serious. "There's one more thing we need to consider," he said. "You and Jaänjo should stop all healings for now, at least until this situation with Silas blows over."

The room fell silent. Aan grimaced, and she nodded reluctantly. "I hate not helping people, but you're right, Dad. We can't risk exposing Jaänjo."

Another moment passed as Aan listened to Jaänjo. Her eyes widened. "Jaänjo says Silas likely won't live more than a month. His condition is worse than he knows."

The atmosphere in the room grew somber.

"All the more reason to lay low," Keet said softly. "If Silas passes away soon, his wild claims will be forgotten quickly."

Yéil reached out to squeeze Aan's hand. "I know it's hard, but it's temporary. We'll resume helping people when it's safe."

Aan nodded, her eyes reflecting sorrow and determination. "Mom, I'm not sure it will ever be truly safe. But you're right. For now, we'll wait it out. No more healings until we can be certain it won't endanger Jaänjo and me." The words tasted bitter as they left her mouth, each syllable a reminder of the lives they could save, the suffering they could alleviate.

Sensing Aan's inner turmoil, Jaänjo's gentle voice resonated within her. "Aan," he reminded her softly, "sometimes the right choice creates heartache. By protecting ourselves now, we ensure we can help others in the long run."

Aan nodded, then looked at her parents. "If we encounter a life-or-death situation, I... I don't know if I could stand by and do nothing. Fortunately, in Tenakee Springs, that's a rarity."

As the family sat in quiet agreement, the weight of their decision settled around them. They had a plan, but the path ahead was uncertain. For now, they would have to trust in each other and allow the passage of time to keep their extraordinary secret safe.

As the family's discussion about their immediate plans concluded, a charged silence filled the room. Aan fidgeted, her gaze meeting her parents' briefly before dropping to her hands. She took a deep breath, steeling herself to broach a topic weighing on her mind.

"Mom, Dad, there's something else we should address now," Aan said, her voice soft but determined.

"What's that, Aan?" Yéil asked, sensing the weight in her daughter's words.

Aan took a deep breath. "Jaänjo and I... we love each other."

Yéil sighed, a gentle smile touching her lips. "Both your dad and I know that. It's plain to see."

Aan's eyes welled with tears, but she smiled. "I know it might seem impossible or strange to you. Jaänjo is from another planet, existing as pure energy within me. But our connection goes beyond the physical. We share thoughts, emotions, experiences... It's a bond—unlike anything I could have imagined."

She paused, collecting her thoughts. "I feel his joy, his curiosity about our world. He understands me in ways no one else can. And I've come to know him—his compassion, his wisdom, his struggles. We've faced so much together."

Keet leaned forward, his expression soft. "Aan, love doesn't always follow conventional paths. We've seen how you two interact, how you light up when you speak of him, how you consult each other. It's clear your bond is powerful."

Yéil nodded in agreement. "It's not just about physical experiences. We've witnessed the care and respect between you—how you protect and support each other. That's what love is, regardless of form."

Aan wiped a tear from her cheek. "Thank you for understanding. It means so much to both of us."

Keet smiled and nodded. "Your happiness and well-being are what matter most to us, Aan. If you and Jaänjo have found love in each other, then we're grateful for that blessing."

The family sat in a tender silence, the depth of Aan and Jaänjo's unique love acknowledged and accepted, bridging worlds in ways they were only beginning to understand.

AS SILAS TRUDGED TOWARDS his cabin, a coughing fit seized him. He paused, leaning against a tree, and lit a cigarette with trembling hands. The smoke burned his lungs, intensifying his cough. To his horror, he tasted the unmistakable coppery tang of blood in his mouth.

Spitting on the ground, Silas saw the red-tinged saliva and cursed. "Those no-good, heathen Natives," he growled. "Especially that Aan."

Inside his cabin, Silas stumbled to the bathroom and gripped the porcelain sink, his knuckles whitening, mirroring the anger roiling within him. As he lifted his gaze, his reflection confronted him in the smudged mirror—a stranger with a haggard face and deep-set eyes. His skin, once ruddy from years under the Alaskan sun, now hung pallid and drawn over sharp cheekbones. The cold reality of his situation washed over him like a wave of dread, crashing through his body with an unforgiving force.

"I'm running out of time," he whispered to his reflection.

Silas paced his small living room as evening fell, consumed by thoughts of Aan and her refusal to help him. Anger and desperation warred within him, fueling a dangerous resolve.

"I can't just sit here and die," he muttered. "Not when she has the power to save me."

For a brief moment, fear flickered across Silas's face, replacing his mask of anger. He thought of his life, his choices, and felt a pang of regret. But as quickly as it came, the moment passed, and his features hardened once more with resolve.

31

AFTER SAYING GOODBYE TO her parents, Aan strolled towards her cabin, the weight of their Silas encounter lingering. Jaänjo's presence within her awakened as she neared the sun-kissed meadow. She sensed his tension.

"Aan, if you don't mind, I need to recharge. Tala and Taayoo's healing and the Silas encounter have drained me."

"Okay, Jaänjo," she said softly, noting his fatigue. She pointed to a towering spruce tree. "I'll lie in the shade and meditate while you recharge."

Jaänjo's ethereal form slipped from her body and drifted into the warm sunlight.

As she lay on the ground, gazing absentmindedly at the sky, thoughts of Silas consumed her. His menacing demeanor and the potential threat he posed loomed like a dark cloud. She shook her head, trying to dispel these troubling thoughts, and decided to focus on Jaänjo and his need to recharge. She gazed his way and frowned at the sight of his diminished aura. She closed her eyes and tried to meditate. Nothing but dark thoughts danced in her awareness. She sighed...

Moments later, to her delight, the familiar lumbering forms of Barney, Fred, Wilma, and Betty emerged from the tree line, their curious noses twitching as they approached. Always interested in finding a comfortable resting spot, Fred's massive bulk dropped to the ground beside Aan. She lovingly touched his head and then rested her head against his soft, furry belly. After milling around with a protective air, Barney moved to Aan, wanting a scratch behind his ears. Wilma, ever curious, sniffed Aan, probably smelling hints of the cinnamon roll she had for breakfast. Betty, the most cautious, hung back slightly, her eyes watchful. Eventually, she approached Aan, enjoying the gentle strokes to her head.

"Thank you for being my pillow, Fred," Aan whispered, scratching behind his ear. The other bears settled around her, forming a protective circle of warmth and companionship that eased Aan's troubled mind.

She closed her eyes, trying to calm her racing thoughts, but Silas and his veiled threats played on a loop in her mind. The fear of losing Jaänjo, should his true nature be discovered, gripped her heart with a painful intensity.

Hours slipped by, with each moment filled with troubling thoughts. Aan's gaze drifted to Jaänjo, and a smile softened her features. His aura, now noticeably larger, shimmered in the sunlight—a mesmerizing ballet of energy and light. Transfixed, she watched the ethereal display until a sudden disturbing sound beside her broke the spell.

Fred's belly rumbled ominously, followed by a sizeable gastrointestinal disturbance. The ensuing noxious odor caused Aan to scrunch her nose involuntarily.

"Phew, Fred! What on earth did you eat?"

As if on cue, Jaänjo's glowing form drifted towards her. Except for Fred, who looked quite content lying with Aan, the other bears stood and appeared to greet Jaänjo. He lingered with them for a few minutes before merging with Aan.

"How are you feeling, Jaänjo?" she asked.

Jaänjo's energy pulsed with a lingering unease. "I'm feeling better," he began, "but the encounter with Silas keeps replaying in my awareness. I'm deeply concerned about your safety, Aan." His tone softened as he continued. "I shared our Silas predicament with the bears. Hopefully, they'll protect you if he comes to your cabin."

"I'm also worried for you," Aan replied, her voice barely above a whisper. "Silas haunts my thoughts, too. The mental image of his dark aura sends chills down my spine." She hugged herself. "I love you, Jaänjo," she continued, her voice trembling slightly. "Silas can destroy what we have. The very thought terrifies me to my core."

She took a deep breath, trying to center herself. The serene meadow and the comforting presence of the bears helped calm her racing thoughts. "You know, Jaänjo," she said softly, "this situation with Silas has made me realize how many complex issues we're dealing with. There's so much more to consider than just healing people."

"I know."

Barney playfully swatted at the butterflies, an act that contrasted sharply with the troubling thoughts swirling in Aan's mind. She smiled at his antics.

"Jaänjo," she began, absently stroking Fred's fur, "let's drop thoughts of Silas for a while. Other things are weighing on me. Can we discuss them?"

"Sure. Please talk to me."

She nodded. "I can't stop thinking about all the people we could help. But, obviously, we can't heal everyone, can we?"

Jaänjo's energy pulsed gently within her. "No, we can't. The burden of choosing is heavy, Aan. We must consider not just who needs help, but who we can help without risking exposure."

Fred got up and lumbered over to a patch of berries. Having lost her pillow, Aan sat cross-legged in the grass and frowned. "How do we decide who to heal? What criteria should we use?"

"We can prioritize those with the most severe conditions or those with young children who depend on them like Tala," Jaänjo suggested. "But each choice means saying no to someone else in need. It's not easy."

Aan sighed and absently ran her fingers through the grass. "No matter what we do, we'll end up denying help to those who desperately need it."

"It's a delicate balance, Aan," Jaänjo replied. "If we're discovered, we'll lose the ability to help anyone. But you're right—the weight of those we elect not to heal will be significant."

Barney let out a soft growl as if sensing Aan's distress. She smiled, reaching out to pat his head reassuringly.

"You brought up interesting points on informed consent during Tala's healing." she continued. "We may ask for permission, but we're not telling the whole truth. Is that ethical?"

Jaänjo's energy flickered, reflecting his unease. "It's a compromise we have to make. It's not possible to be more transparent without revealing my true nature."

As they talked, the bears moved around them, a living, breathing circle of protection and comfort. Aan drew strength from their presence as she grappled with these difficult questions.

"And what about the unintended consequences?" Aan asked, watching a butterfly land on Betty's nose. "We've changed Tala and Taayoo's lives dramatically. Are there negative effects of this that we haven't foreseen?"

"It's a valid concern," Jaänjo agreed. "We've given Tala more time with her family, but we've also altered the natural course of events. The ripple effects of our actions are impossible to predict fully."

Aan hugged her knees to her chest, her gaze drifting to a wispy cloud overhead. "I worry about the power we have. How do we make sure we don't abuse it?"

"By constantly questioning ourselves, as we're doing now," Jaänjo replied, his tone gentle yet firm. "By being aware of the responsibility we carry and always striving to act ethically and with integrity."

Aan's eyes shifted to the ancient forest, her voice tinged with concern. "And what of my culture? Our abilities will inevitably impact my traditional Tlingit healing practices."

Jaänjo's energy pulsed thoughtfully. "It's a double-edged sword. Some might view it as a threat to your ancestral ways, while others could embrace it as an evolution of your healing gifts."

Aan drew a deep breath, her brow furrowing. "It's far more complex than mere perception. Your healing abilities and your views of God intertwined in every atom in the universe—which deeply resonates within me—could fundamentally alter my connection to my traditions and my ancestors." Her voice grew passionate. "For me, healing is something sacred that's bound to the spirits of my ancestors and a bond with the earth." She paused, her eyes reflecting both wonder and apprehension. "My—our—new healing abilities... it could reshape these ancient connections. I could argue it's a blessing, a gift from my spirits, and I could argue that it's a deviation from my people's time-honored ways." She sighed. "I embrace and am grateful for you and our enhanced healing abilities, but it's quite real that it could create rifts within my community."

Jaänjo's energy pulsed with empathy and thoughtfulness. "Aan, I deeply appreciate your honesty and the complexity of what you're facing. Your connection to your ancestors, your land, and your traditions is profound and beautiful. It's a part of you that I've come to cherish and respect."

He paused as if carefully choosing his next words. "Perhaps we can view this not as a replacement of your traditions but as an expansion. Just as your ancestors' knowledge grew over generations, adapting to new challenges and discoveries, so too might this be seen as a new chapter in your people's healing wisdom."

His tone became gentle, almost reverent. "I've observed how your spirits work through you. They've accepted my presence and even facilitated our bond. Could it be that they see this union of our abilities as a natural evolution of your healing practices? And regarding change—even positive change—it can be difficult for people to accept. But think of those we've healed—you, your mom, Tala, and Taayoo. I think all of you would enthusiastically endorse the change that gave back your lives."

Betty nuzzled Aan's hand. She smiled, drawing comfort from the bear's affection.

"You're right, Jaänjo. Your freeing me of MS profoundly altered my life." She paused, reflecting. "This brings up another troubling thought of mine—the long-term effects of your healing... we're not entirely sure about those, are we?"

"Based on generations of healers like me on my planet, I know for certain there are no negative physical effects," Jaänjo replied confidently. "When I repair a cell at the molecular level, it's fixed, period. But..." his energy wavered slightly, "the long-term effects on the soul are up for debate."

Aan's brow furrowed. "What do you mean?"

"Well," Jaänjo continued, his tone thoughtful, "while the body may be healed, the soul might still carry the memory or imprint of the illness. It's possible that even after physical healing, a person's spirit could still feel... unwell, in a sense. The soul's journey isn't always in sync with the body's condition."

Aan nodded slowly, absorbing this new perspective. "So we might heal someone's body, but their soul could still be grappling with the experience of illness?"

"Exactly," Jaänjo confirmed. "It's another layer of complexity we need to consider in our healing work. Physical healing is just one part of a person's overall well-being."

Aan nodded in agreement. "Do you think we have a responsibility to those we've healed beyond the initial healing? I ask this thinking about the health of the person's soul. Should we be following up on that?"

"It's a good question," Jaänjo replied. "Regarding soul health, your shaman skills would be especially useful."

"You're right—much of my shaman work focuses on healing the soul." She shifted her position, bringing her knees to her chest. "Jaänjo, while you were recharging, I also couldn't stop thinking about the energy coming from my hands during the fake Silas ritual. How was this possible without you doing it?"

Jaänjo's energy pulsed thoughtfully within her. After a moment, he replied, his tone filled with wonder and realization. "Aan, I believe what we're experiencing is a true merging of our life energies. It seems that our prolonged togetherness is causing an integration of my energy with your life force."

"What does that mean exactly?" Aan asked, her voice tinged with curiosity and concern.

"It means that my presence isn't just coexisting within you anymore. Our energies are intertwining at a fundamental level. You're developing abilities that were once solely mine while I'm becoming more attuned to your physical and spiritual nature. It's as if we're evolving together into something... new."

Aan's eyes widened with awe. "Is this... is this safe? For both of us?"

"As far as I can tell, yes," Jaänjo reassured her. "But it's uncharted territory. We'll need to be vigilant and observe how this progresses. It could enhance our healing abilities, but it also means we'll need to be even more careful about concealing your newfound powers."

Aan nodded slowly, absorbing this information. "I suppose this adds another layer to our ethical considerations about healing and secrecy."

"It does," Jaänjo agreed. "Our bond is deepening on so many levels. It's both exciting and a little daunting."

Aan stood, stretching her arms above her head. The bears stirred, sensing the conversation was coming to an end. "There are so many questions, Jaänjo. How do we navigate all of this?"

"With care, compassion, and constant reflection," Jaänjo said gently. "We may not have all the answers, but as long as we strive to bring good to the world, I'm confident that my God and your spirits will sanction our work."

32

THE FOLLOWING DAY, SILAS made his way to the Gajaa's house, his face a mask of grim determination. He paused at the door, wheezing and clutching his side, before rapping sharply.

Keet answered, his expression wary. "What do you want, Silas?"

"Where's Aan?" he demanded, his voice raspy. "I need to talk to her."

Keet's eyes narrowed. "She's not here. I think it's best if you leave her alone."

Silas leaned in, sweat beading on his pale forehead. "You don't understand. I need her help. I'm dying, Keet."

"I'm sorry about your condition, Silas, but harassing my daughter won't change anything. Please, go home and rest."

As Keet began to close the door, Silas's trembling hand shot out, holding it open. "Listen to me," he hissed. "I've got nothing to lose. If Aan won't help me, I'll make sure everyone knows she's a witch. Your whole family will be exposed."

Keet's face hardened. "You're losing your mind, Silas. Leave, or I'll call the authorities."

With a menacing glare, Silas turned and stumbled away, his mind racing with desperate plans. As he walked, another coughing fit wracked his body, nearly bringing him to his knees and reminding him of the clock ticking against him.

Keet watched Silas's retreating figure until he disappeared around a corner. Closing the door, he turned to find Yéil standing nearby, her face etched with concern. "I heard what he said. What should we do?"

Keet nodded grimly. "We need to go to Aan's cabin and stay with her in case Silas shows up. But first, I'll call Láag and ask if Aan can stay with her until this blows over."

After a brief phone call to Keet's surprised sister, they set out, their pace quick with worry. As Keet and Yéil approached the meadow near Aan's cabin, they stopped short. The scene before them sent a chill down their spines.

Aan lay motionless on the ground, surrounded by four large black bears lying around her. Keet's breath caught in his throat, and Yéil's hand flew to her mouth, stifling a gasp. Time seemed to stand still as they stood frozen, eyes fixed on their daughter's still form amid the massive, dark shapes.

Fred's ears perked up at the sound of approaching footsteps. He huffed softly, alerting Aan to the presence of visitors.

Aan sat up and followed Fred's gaze. She placed a hand on his broad shoulder. "It's okay. They're my parents," she murmured before calling out, "Mom, Dad, it's all right! These are the bears I told you about. They won't harm you. Come join us!"

Keet and Yéil exchanged bewildered glances before cautiously approaching, their eyes darting between the massive creatures.

At ease among the bears, Aan gestured to each one. "Mom, Dad, allow me to introduce you. This is Fred—he's the one who heard you coming. And here are Barney, Wilma, and Betty."

The bears regarded Aan's parents with curious eyes, showing no signs of aggression. Fred, reassured by Aan's words, settled back down but kept a watchful eye on the newcomers.

Noticing her parents' lingering unease, Aan spoke softly. "I know it's a lot to take in. These bears are my friends and protectors. They understand more than you might think." As if to demonstrate, she whispered something to Barney, who promptly lumbered to Yéil and gently nudged her hand with his nose, offering a gesture of reassurance.

Yéil touched Barney with a trembling hand, her nervousness still evident. "Aan, we... we need to talk to you about Silas."

Aan's expression grew serious, her brow furrowing. "What happened?"

Keet took a deep breath, his face etched with worry. "Aan, Silas came to our house looking for you, and he was... not himself."

Yéil nodded, her eyes reflecting the same concern. "He seemed desperate, Aan. More than that, he seemed dangerous."

"He made some thinly veiled threats," Keet continued, his voice low and urgent. "He said if you don't help him, he'll expose your abilities to everyone and ruin our family."

Aan's hand stilled on Fred's fur, her expression growing grave as she listened.

Yéil leaned in, her voice soft but firm. "We're worried about you. Silas is unpredictable, and in his condition, he might do anything to get what he wants."

Keet nodded in agreement. "That's why we think it's best if you don't stay at your cabin for a while. In fact," he paused, exchanging a meaningful glance with Yéil, "we want you to leave Tenakee Springs."

"Leave?" Aan's eyebrows rose in surprise, her voice barely above a whisper. "Where would I go?"

"I want to take you to your Aunt Láag's home in Hoonah," Keet said firmly. "I've already spoken with her, and she also thinks you should stay with her. Silas wouldn't think of looking for you there."

Yéil reached out to gently take Aan's hand. "We understand this is a lot to ask, but we're deeply concerned for your safety. Please, at least consider it."

"Aan, I agree with your parents," Jaänjo said with alarm, "Remember, I was within Silas. I know he'll stop at nothing to compel you to heal him."

Aan relayed Jaänjo's words to Keet and Yéil, her expression grave.

"Jaänjo brings an invaluable perspective to this situation, Aan," Keet said, his voice gentle but firm. "Come back to town with us now, and at first light, we'll leave for Hoonah."

The bears, sensing the tension, shifted restlessly around Aan. She glanced at her parents and then at her bear companions, the weight of the decision evident in her eyes. She sighed. "Okay. Since Jaänjo knows firsthand how Silas thinks, if he's worried, so am I. I'll pack some things and go with you, but first, let me say goodbye to my friends."

While Aan embraced each bear, Keet and Yéil watched with wonder and apprehension, fully realizing the uniqueness of their daughter's life. They knew that safeguarding Aan—and the secret of Jaänjo—was now more crucial than ever.

After packing a suitcase for her stay in Hoonah, Aan stepped out of her cabin with her parents. As they descended the trail, Aan's mind raced with possibilities of what might happen next while her parents remained vigilant, eyes scanning the forest around them. Not far from her cabin, as they rounded a bend, the sight that greeted them was what they dreaded—Silas.

Spotting them, he approached, his face contorted with anger and desperation as his gaze fixed on the suitcase in Keet's hand.

"Where do you think you're going, Aan?" he shouted, his voice filled with desperation.

Keet stepped forward, placing himself between Silas and his family. "Silas, Aan is leaving for a while. Your behavior has us concerned."

Silas's eyes flashed with anger. "You can't do this, Aan! As a shaman, you have a responsibility to help me!"

Aan met his gaze. "Silas, I've already explained that I can't cure your cancer."

"You're lying!" Silas shouted, his face reddening. "I saw what you can do. You have the power to heal me and choose not to!"

"That's enough, Silas!" Yéil shouted. "Leave my daughter alone!"

Silas pointed an accusing finger at Aan. "You'll regret this. Everyone will know about your so-called 'gifts.' Your comfortable life here—it's over!"

Drawn by the raised voices, the bears emerged from the forest. They approached Silas, huffing and gnashing their teeth, stopping several feet short. Fred, however, moved forward and stood beside Aan, snarling at Silas.

Silas's eyes darted between the bears in shock before settling back on Aan. "What kind of freak are you?" he spat, his voice wavering despite the venom in his words.

"We're done here," Aan said, her tone accepting no argument. "Go home, Silas. My bear friends have lost their patience with you." As if on cue, Fred growled menacingly.

Silas glared at Aan, his breathing labored. "This isn't over," he muttered, "I'm going back to town and letting everyone know about you." He turned and stumbled back down the trail.

Before he retreated, Aan caught a glimpse of something in his eyes beyond the anger—an intense fear and desperation that made her heart ache. For a moment, she saw not a threatening man but a fellow human desperate for help.

She cast a worried glance at her parents. "He's right—life as I've known it is over."

"Let's return to the cabin and wait an hour, Aan," urged Yéil, "and then head to our home. It's more important than ever to get you to Hoonah."

"Aan, your mom is right," said Jaánjo, his voice resonating with distress. "I sense Silas's rage. I know he'll be coming after you. Instead of waiting to leave town in the morning, I suggest getting on your boat and leaving immediately."

"Do you think it's that bad, Jaänjo?" Aan said aloud.

"I do. Aan, he has nothing to lose, and he's convinced you can heal him. I agree with your mom about waiting here for an hour before leaving so we won't run into him on the trail."

"Okay. Mom and Dad, after we wait an hour, Jaänjo wants us to leave immediately for Hoonah. He says Silas will stop at nothing to force me to cure him."

Aan turned to her bear companions, her eyes filled with gratitude and a hint of sadness. "Thank you all for protecting me. I need to leave here for a while. I'll miss you." She touched Fred's broad shoulder, feeling his warmth beneath her palm. "I'll be back as soon as I can."

The bears seemed to understand, their eyes holding a depth of comprehension that still amazed Aan—and her parents. They nuzzled against her before lumbering back into the forest. Fred was the last to leave, giving Aan one final, meaningful look before disappearing into the underbrush.

As they faded from view, Aan felt a pang of loss. These creatures were more than just animals; they were her guardians, her confidants. Leaving them behind, even temporarily, felt like leaving a part of herself. With a deep breath, she turned back to her parents. "Let's go back to my cabin. We might as well have a quick bite to eat while waiting."

An hour after their confrontation with Silas, Aan and her parents headed down the trail toward town. Near the town's main path, they spotted a figure lying face down, motionless on the ground.

"Oh no!" Yéil gasped, recognizing Silas.

They rushed to his side. Silas was unconscious, his breathing shallow and labored. Near his mouth, a pool of blood stained the ground.

Aan checked his pulse. "He's alive, but barely. Since he's bleeding his mouth, we should leave him on his chest so he won't choke on it. Dad, please go to the clinic for help. Mom and I will wait here with Silas."

Keet shook his head. "Aan, Yéil should go to the clinic instead of me. If Silas wakes up and gets enraged, I want to be here."

Aan nodded. "Please hurry, Mom. I don't think he has long to live."

"Okay. I won't be long—it'll take only a few minutes to get to the clinic." She touched Aan's hand. "Even though we despise this man, please ask our spirits to bless him on his journey."

Aan nodded. "I will, Mom. Please hurry."

Yéil took off, determined to get help as quickly as possible.

As Silas lay face down on the forest trail, his breaths shallow and fading, Aan knelt beside him. She closed her eyes and summoned her ancestral spirits with whispers in Tlingit. With deep reverence, she implored the spirits to welcome Silas into the great beyond with compassion. In this solemn moment, Aan fulfilled her sacred duty as a shaman, helping a fellow human depart the world peacefully.

Minutes crawled by as they waited, the forest eerily quiet around them. Aan's emotions churned—concern for Silas's well-being, anxiety about the potential consequences if he survived, and a complex sense of guilt. Even though she knew Jaänjo couldn't heal those with dark auras, she questioned if there was more she could have done. Could she have found a way to help Silas without Jaänjo's direct intervention? The weight of having such power yet being limited in its use felt crushing. She understood the reasons, but the human cost of those limitations lay before her, a heavy burden to bear.

Jaänjo's voice resonated within her. "Aan, I sense your troubled thoughts. You did everything you could to help him. My healing abilities are ineffective against those with dark auras. Their negative energy negates my positive energy, making it impossible for me to help them."

She sighed. "I know, Jaänjo. Still, as despicable as he is, he's part of what you call the divine energy. I should've tried harder at the bakery to help him..."

Jaänjo's presence stirred with compassion and firmness. "Aan, healing isn't just about physical ailments. Silas's darkness runs deep, and perhaps the divine energy is concerned about the dire consequences he could inflict on others if he survives. Sometimes, the kindest act is to let God or nature take its course."

Aan pondered these words, finding comfort in Jaänjo's wisdom.

They heard the sound of people coming to help. As they approached, Aan waved to them. "It's Silas. He's hemorrhaging blood from his mouth."

The clinic practitioner grimaced as he saw the pool of blood on the ground and felt Silas's neck for a pulse. He sighed. "No pulse. I'm afraid he's gone."

"We was unconscious when we found him," said Aan. "We were afraid to turn him over because he might choke on his blood."

"Aan, Silas came to the clinic a while back, and we sent him to Juneau for testing. They found that cancer had riddled his lungs. It was just a matter of time before he passed." He looked at her, puzzled. "Why was he out on this trail—it's no place to be for a man in his condition."

Keet stepped forward. "He knew Aan is a shaman. He came to her cabin, demanding that she cure him. When she told him it wasn't possible, he stormed off. We found him unconscious on the trail about an hour later as we were heading to my home."

The practitioner's expression softened with understanding. "I see. People will go to great lengths to survive. I suppose he saw Aan as his last hope." He motioned to his two companions. "Let's put him onto the stretcher and carry him to the clinic. Keet, I'd appreciate your help."

As they headed to town, the earlier tension felt by Keet and Yéil gave way to an awkward relief. The loss of one life had, in a twisted way, ensured the safety of their daughter and Jaänjo.

For Aan, however, the relief was tinged with sorrow. Unlike her parents, she felt a deep sadness for the life lost, even one that had threatened her own. A complex wave of emotions washed over her, relief intertwining with grief and guilt. She sensed Jaänjo's comforting presence within, sharing the burden of her intricate feelings.

"Mom, Dad," she said softly, breaking the somber silence, "when we get home, could we hold a ceremony for Silas? Despite everything, I think it's important to acknowledge the passing of a life."

Her parents exchanged a glance before nodding, recognizing the depth of their daughter's compassion and the weight she carried as a shaman. In that moment, they were reminded of the remarkable woman Aan had become, fully embodying the sacred responsibilities passed down through generations. Her request served as a powerful testament to her maturity and the wisdom she had cultivated in her thirty years.

33

SINCE THE UNSETTLING ENCOUNTER with Silas, winter had settled firmly over the land. Aan plodded through the falling snow as she returned to her cabin from town. Within her, Jaänjo glowed with delight at the serene winter landscape surrounding them. As she walked, Aan reflected on how much had changed since Silas passed. The town had largely forgotten his wild claims about Aan, dismissing them as the ravings of a dying man. Still, she and Jaänjo had become more cautious, focusing on her traditional shaman duties to avoid drawing unwanted attention.

"Aan, could you pause and take in the view?" Jaänjo mused. "The forest is so peaceful in winter. The way the snow blankets everything, muffling sounds and creating this pristine stillness—it's breathtaking."

Aan smiled as she stopped. "It is beautiful," she agreed. "Though I do miss our bear friends. They're all tucked away in their dens, hibernating until spring."

"I miss them, too. Could you open your mouth and catch some snowflakes? I love the sensation of them melting on your tongue."

"All right," she chuckled. "I never tire of how you delight in such simple pleasures."

As they neared the cabin, delicate wisps of smoke curled from the chimney, remnants of the fire Aan had kindled earlier. The scent of burning Sitka spruce wafted through the air, a fragrance Jaänjo savored deeply. "It's wonderful how the townspeople provide wood in exchange for your services," he mused. "Your stove truly makes the cabin a warm sanctuary."

Once inside, Aan added logs to the fire and settled into her favorite chair, reflecting. "Jaänjo, on the walk here, I flashed on Silas nearly exposing us. I'm glad we decided to lessen that risk by focusing on my shaman duties."

"It was the right thing to do," he agreed.

She nodded. "The spirits have been especially active this winter. I need to devote more time to communing with them and meditating." She reached for her drum, its skin painted with traditional Tlingit symbols representing the spirits of the land, sea, and sky. "Jaänjo, let's perform a ceremony to thank my spirits for our peace and to seek their guidance for the coming year."

"I'd like that."

She closed her eyes and lightly tapped the drum. Her voice lifted in a soft chant, the ancient words of her people flowing through the cabin and out into the wintery day. As she connected with the spirits, Jaänjo felt a swell of admiration for her and marveled at how their bond had deepened, forming an intricate weaving of two vastly different beings.

After the ceremony, Jaänjo sighed with contentment. "I never imagined I'd find such belonging here," he said, his energy pulsing warmly within Aan. "You've shown me so much about this world and what it means to be connected to a place, its people, and its spirits."

Aan smiled, her hand gently resting over her heart where Jaänjo's presence resonated most strongly. "And you've broadened my understanding of the universe," she replied softly. "We truly balance each other." She paused, reflecting on their unique bond. "Who would have thought an intragalactic refugee of pure energy and an Earth-bound shaman could find such common ground and mutual respect?"

Her voice filled with warmth as she continued. "I cherish how we challenge and support each other, navigating the intricacies of our extraordinary relationship." Aan's tone then shifted, a hint of anticipation coloring her words. "By the way, my spirits whisper that the new year will bring welcomed changes for us."

Jaänjo's energy pulsed thoughtfully within Aan. "That's good to hear."

As the day wore on, the cozy warmth of the cabin and the tranquility of the winter landscape outside led Jaänjo's thoughts to deeper reflections. The peace they'd found since Silas's passing had given him time to contemplate the nature of his relationship with Aan. Through Aan's eyes, he gazed into the flickering flames of the fire and pondered their bond's complexities.

He broke the agreeable silence with a sigh and spoke with a hint of concern and melancholy. "Aan, there's something I've been wondering about. You once mentioned wanting a husband and children. Does it trouble you that we can't have a physical connection?"

Aan paused momentarily and took a deep breath, her brow furrowing as she considered her response. "I won't lie to you, Jaänjo. It does trouble me sometimes."

She gazed out at the snow-covered landscape as she gathered her thoughts. "Our bond is incredibly powerful, more so than anything I've experienced. We connect mentally and spiritually beyond what I ever imagined possible. But..." she trailed off, her fingers tracing patterns on the frosty glass.

"There are moments when I yearn for physical touch. To feel the warmth of an embrace, to share a kiss, to experience the intimacy of a physical relationship. And yes, a part of me still dreams of having children, of creating a family in the traditional sense."

She turned back to face the room, though her eyes seemed vacant, as if she were looking through the walls rather than at them. "It's like I'm torn between two worlds, two different kinds of love. What we have is extraordinary, Jaänjo. It fulfills me in ways I never knew I needed. But there's still that very human part of me that craves physical connection, that wants to experience motherhood."

Aan's eyes glistened with unshed tears, her voice soft and wistful. "Sometimes I imagine what it would be like if you had a physical form. To feel your arms around me, to trace the contours of your face, to... to experience all the intimacies humans share. It's a bittersweet fantasy because I know it's not possible, but the longing persists."

She took another deep breath, centering herself. "But then I think about the depth of our connection, how you understand me in ways no one else ever could. I realize what we have is rare and precious, even if it's not what I once envisioned for myself."

She sighed. "I won't pretend it's always easy. There are days when the longing for physical touch is almost overwhelming. But then you'll say something, or I'll feel your energy pulse with joy or concern for me, and it reminds me of how lucky I am to have you, to have this unique and beautiful bond."

She smiled with a mix of love and melancholy in her expression. "So yes, it troubles me sometimes. I still grapple with those very human desires. But I wouldn't trade what we have for anything. You mean everything to me, even if our love doesn't fit a traditional mold."

She stood and walked to the window, her finger tracing a heart pattern in the frost on the glass. Her breath fogged the windowpane as she collected her thoughts, feeling Jaänjo's presence pulsing gently within her, patient and attentive.

"Aan, when we first met, I promised I'd leave if you asked. That promise still holds. If your need for physical connection becomes something you can't ignore, I'll understand. I'll leave if that's what you truly want."

Aan's eyes widened, a flash of panic crossing her face. She shook her head, her voice firm despite its slight tremor. "No, Jaänjo. That's not what I want at all. Yes, I struggle sometimes with the physical limitations of our relationship, but the thought of losing you... that's far more painful than any unfulfilled desire."

She took a deep breath, steadying herself. "You've become a part of me. The idea of you leaving would tear a hole in the fabric of my being."

She hugged herself tenderly. "Jaänjo, I choose this. I choose us. Whatever challenges we face, whatever longings I might have, we'll face them together. Please don't ever think that I'd want you to leave. You're my partner, my love, my other half. Physical or not, what we have is real and precious to me."

"I'd give anything to hold you for just a few minutes. Anything. I..." Jaänjo's energy flickered, his words trailing off.

"What is it, Jaänjo?" Aan asked, sensing his hesitation.

"Whenever I think of holding you, a recurrent dream visits me. Lately, I'm obsessed with it."

"What's the dream about?" Aan asked, concern coloring her voice.

Jaänjo's energy pulsed with longing and uncertainty. "I dream of Miĕĕcha coming to Earth and finding me. He converts me back to my physical form, and I can finally hold you, make love to you, and have children with you."

Aan's breath caught in her throat. She hesitated before asking, "If... if that were to happen—if you could return to your physical form, would it even be possible for us to have children? I mean, we're from different planets..."

Jaänjo's energy intensified within her. "It's not as impossible as you might think," he explained, his tone filled with excitement. "Despite our different origins, our DNA structures are strikingly similar."

"Really?" Aan's eyebrows raised in surprise. "How is that possible?"

"The building blocks of our genetic code—what your scientists call base pairs—are almost identical," Jaänjo continued. "And the way these building blocks are arranged to create instructions for making proteins—the coding sequences—follow remarkably similar patterns."

Aan nodded slowly, trying to grasp the concept. "As if life throughout the universe follows a common template?"

"Exactly, but with slight variations arising from different environmental factors. This similarity is one of the reasons I was able to bond with you in this energy form. And this compatibility extends to our genetic repair mechanisms and reproductive processes," Jaänjo explained. "If I were in my physical form, it's quite likely we could have children together."

Aan's breath caught in her throat. "So the idea of us creating a family..."

"It isn't just a dream," Jaänjo finished. "It's a distinct possibility based on our genetic compatibility."

Aan sat in stunned silence for a moment, processing this information. "I... I had no idea. But Jaänjo, is there any real chance of Miĕĕcha finding you here? Of you regaining your physical form?"

Jaänjo sighed. "I don't know, Aan. The chances are... slim. Miĕĕcha would have to track me across vast distances of space, and even if he did find me, he might not have found a way to convert my energy back to a physical form. It's more of a dream than a realistic possibility."

Aan nodded slowly, a mix of emotions playing across her face. "I understand. Thank you for sharing this with me, Jaänjo. Even if it's just a dream, it's comforting, in a way, to know that we could have that kind of life together in another reality."

She paused, then smiled softly, "But remember, no matter what form you're in, you are my family. We may not have children, but we have each other, and that's enough for me."

Jaänjo's energy wrapped around her warmly, a gesture as close to an embrace as he could manage. "And you are everything to me, Aan. No matter what form I'm in, that will never change."

Aan nodded thoughtfully, processing all that Jaänjo had shared. When she finally spoke, her voice was soft and genuine.

"Jaänjo, the idea of you having a physical form, of us being able to touch and hold each other... and even have children together... it's beautiful. A part of me aches for that possibility." Her hand instinctively moved to her heart. "But there's something else. The thought of you no longer being inside me—no longer being this constant, intimate presence... it's terrifying."

Her eyes glistened as she continued, "You've become such an integral part of me. Even if it meant we could have a physical relationship, the idea of you being separate is almost too much to bear. I've grown so accustomed to feeling you here, always with me, always a part of me."

She took a deep breath, steadying herself. "I never thought I'd say this, but the prospect of losing our unique connection, even for a more traditional relationship, is both exhilarating and frightening. You're not just with me—you're a part of me. And I... I don't know if I could give that up, even for the chance to hold you or have children with you."

Her voice grew stronger, more resolute. "Perhaps it's selfish, but I love what we have now. The intimacy we share goes beyond anything physical. And while I may sometimes long for physical touch, the thought of losing our deep, constant connection is unthinkable."

A tear escaped, rolling down her cheek. "Yes, your dream is beautiful. But our reality, unconventional as it is, is beautiful too. I wouldn't trade it for anything."

"I feel the same way, Aan," he replied with tenderness and wry amusement. "It's ironic, isn't it—to get what we think we want, we'd have to lose what we know we need."

That night, as Aan's consciousness began to fade into sleep, Jaänjo's thoughts stirred within her. For now, their life in Tenakee Springs was a peaceful sanctuary, but he knew the world beyond might not be as accepting. The possibility of Aan facing scrutiny or danger because of their bond gnawed at him. In the quiet of her slumber, he made a solemn vow: he would always protect her, even if that protection meant severing their connection. The implications of this unspoken promise lingered in his essence, leaving him troubled and, once again, gripped by a familiar fear of losing her.

34

As WINTER'S ICY GRIP loosened its hold on Tenakee Springs, the first whispers of spring stirred to life. Patches of earth emerged from beneath melting snow, and the air carried the promise of warmer days ahead. The transformation of the landscape seemed to awaken the town from its long slumber, yet Aan sensed a heaviness within her, a melancholy that wasn't her own.

She stepped onto her cabin porch, settling onto the weathered wood bench, and noticed the sun struggling to break through the blanket of clouds. With a quiet sigh, she turned her attention inward.

"Jaänjo," she murmured, "what's troubling you? Your spirit seems dimmed lately."

A familiar sensation stirred within her as Jaänjo's voice resonated in her mind, tinged with sadness.

"I feel... lost, Aan. Adrift in a way I never thought I'd experience again."

Aan closed her eyes, focusing on his presence. "Tell me more. What's weighing on you?"

A moment passed, filled with a contemplative silence that Aan found unsettling. Slowly, Jaänjo's thoughts began to unfold.

"Healing isn't a hobby or a pastime for me, Aan. It's what I live for, my noble purpose in life. But to keep us safe, I'm forced to suppress it entirely. I feel... worthless. I can't heal others or even help you with simple physical tasks. More than ever, I long to exist freely, to experience the world as you do—to sit on a hillside and watch the sun rise, just me and the dawning day."

Aan listened intently, her heart constricting with empathy. "I had no idea you were grappling with this, Jaänjo. If you could have anything right now, what would it be?"

A potent mix of frustration and longing stirred within him. "Purpose," he said finally. "I want purpose again. As a shaman, you have a reason to get up each morning; I just exist. My calling in life is to ease suffering, but I can't do this and keep you safe at the same time. Unfortunately, fulfilling my purpose in life will forfeit any sense of safety."

Aan's breath caught in her throat as Jaänjo's words resonated within her. She closed her eyes, feeling the weight of his struggle.

"Oh, Jaänjo," she whispered, her voice thick with emotion. "I understand more than you know. If someone told me I could no longer be a shaman—that I had to suppress my abilities and ignore the spirits' calls—it would be like losing the essence of who I am."

She paused, gathering her thoughts. "We're healers. It's not just what we do—it's who we are. The thought of having to choose between my purpose and safety and the pain and frustration that comes with it... it's awful. She touched her hand to her heart. We'll find a way, Jaänjo. There has to be a middle ground where you can fulfill your purpose without putting us at risk. Your calling to heal is too important—to you and to the world—to be silenced forever."

Aan took a deep breath, her resolve strengthening. "Jaänjo, I know our path forward now. Our goal—our shared purpose—should be finding a way for both of us to be healers again, safely. We'll use our combined wisdom—your divine knowledge and my spirit's wisdom—to find a solution."

She stood, her eyes scanning the awakening spring landscape. "Let me ask my spirits for guidance."

Closing her eyes, Aan spoke softly: "Spirits of my ancestors, we seek your wisdom. Please show us the way to heal without fear and use our gifts as we were meant to. Guide us on this journey."

As she finished, a gentle breeze rustled through the trees. Aan opened her eyes and smiled slightly. "Well, Jaänjo, I've asked. Now, we wait and watch for signs. We'll figure this out together."

Jaänjo's essence pulsed within Aan, warm with gratitude. "Thank you, Aan," he said softly. "Your understanding and support mean more than I can express. I'm honored to share this journey with you—and humbled by your willingness to find a way where we both feel fulfilled. Your wisdom and love continue to amaze me. Whatever path the spirits reveal, I'm grateful to experience it with you."

In the days that followed, Aan and Jaänjo settled into a rhythm of contemplation and planning, seeking ways to reclaim their healing roles safely. Life in Tenakee Springs continued its usual pace, the town oblivious to the deliberations taking place in Aan's cabin.

A week after Aan and Jaänjo's "purpose" conversation, an unexpected knock sounded at Keet and Yéil's front door. Keet opened it to find a gaunt, rail-thin man he didn't recognize greeting him with a smile. In tiny Tenakee Springs, strangers knocking on doors was an oddity that demanded immediate suspicion.

"Yes?" Keet said cautiously. "What can I do for you?"

"Hello, sir. Pardon the intrusion. My name is Dr. Naas Katasse. I'm an oncologist at the Ethel Lund Medical Center in Juneau. May I come in and have a few words with you?"

"Why?" Keet asked, his guard up.

"Sir, I'm trying to find a Tlingit shaman who lives in Tenakee Springs. I inquired about her at the bakery, and they directed me here."

"Why do you want to speak with my daughter, Dr. Katasse?"

"Please, call me Naas." He paused, choosing his words carefully. "I'm a friend of Eaton Eesh's brother, S'eek, who works as a radiology technician at our hospital. S'eek says your daughter cured Tala of cancer and Taayoo of his fetal alcohol disorder."

Keet's expression hardened. "Your friend is quite mistaken, Dr. Katasse. My daughter has already been harassed by people seeking miraculous cures. We're not going through that again. Please leave." He began to close the door.

"Please, sir," Naas pleaded, desperation evident in his eyes. "I'm also Tlingit. I grew up in Hoonah. Just give me a few minutes of your time."

Keet hesitated, his hand still on the door. "My sister lives in Hoonah."

"What's her name, sir?"

"Láag Shaan."

Naas's eyes widened in recognition. "Sir—I know her and her family. I went to school with her son, Nelson. I lived on Eagle Drive, and they live on Huna Court."

Surprise flickered across Keet's face. He paused, considering. "Okay," he said, "you can come in for a bit and say what you have to say."

Keet led Dr. Katasse into the living room where Yéil was sitting. When the doctor saw her, his mouth fell open in shock.

"Mrs. Gajaa? I... I know you," he stammered. "I treated you for advanced breast cancer. You're—you're still alive, and you look completely healthy."

Yéil greeted him warily. "Hello, Dr. Katasse. It turns out it wasn't cancer, just a benign cyst."

Dr. Katasse shook his head respectfully. "Mrs. Gajaa, please forgive me, but that's not true. I remember your case quite clearly. And then there's Tala, who had hours to live but is now back at work. Eaton's brother S'eek says she's fully healed, and Taayoo is completely normal after having fetal alcohol-related issues." He paused, looking between Keet and Yéil. "I know your daughter Aan cured them, but I'm not here to expose her."

The room fell silent momentarily before Dr. Katasse continued, his voice heavy with emotion. "I have the most aggressive form of pancreatic cancer. I... I don't have much time left. I was wondering if there is any way Aan would consider healing me, too." He paused, his heart heavy with emotion. "I have a lovely wife and two young girls I adore..."

Keet and Yéil exchanged a worried glance. Keet spoke. "Dr. Katasse, you must understand the implications if word gets out about Aan's abilities. She's already been accosted by someone demanding to be healed. If people knew the truth, thousands could be showing up in Tenakee Springs, all wanting a cure, just like you."

Dr. Katasse nodded. "I will never tell anyone about her gift—you have my word. As a doctor, I understand the importance of confidentiality. More than that, I'm Tlingit like you. Our ways, our secrets—they're sacred. I would never betray that trust."

He paused, collecting his thoughts. "I understand the potential consequences if the word gets out. The influx of people seeking cures would overwhelm Tenakee Springs, changing it forever." His voice softened, tinged with both hope and respect. "I come to you out of desperation for my own life, yes, but I approach you with the utmost respect for honoring your request to protect your daughter. I have daughters, too, and would never want people hounding them unmercifully."

"Dr. Katasse, your words carry great weight with us," Yéil said, reaching for her phone. "Please, have a seat and give us a few minutes to discuss this privately."

"Of course," he replied.

Yéil motioned for Keet to follow her to their bedroom. Once inside, she closed the door and handed her phone to Keet. "Please call Láag and verify what he says about knowing her. Ask her if we can trust him."

Keet nodded and called his sister. After a brief conversation, he ended the call with, "Thank you, sister. I'll relay your message to Yéil." He turned to his wife, a smile spreading across his face. "Láag confirms everything the doctor said is true. They hold Naas in high regard, and she believes that if Aan can heal him, she should."

Yéil let out a relieved sigh, her shoulders relaxing visibly. "Well, that certainly helps. I'm in favor of asking Aan and Jaänjo to cure him."

Keet nodded in agreement. "Let's inform him of our decision."

They returned to the living room, where Keet addressed Naas. "We've come to a decision. You're welcome to stay at our house tonight. We'll step out for a while to discuss with Aan the possibility of her healing you." His tone became serious. "However, if she decides against it, I need your word that you'll leave and never attempt to contact her again."

"You have my word," Naas replied with relief and hope visible on his gaunt face.

With that, Keet and Yéil made their way to Aan's cabin. They explained the situation to their daughter, providing all the details of their conversation with Naas. After thoughtful consideration and internal dialogue with Jaänjo, Aan agreed to meet with him.

As Aan walked with her parents to their house, her mind raced with thoughts and concerns. She knew the risks involved but also felt the weight of her and Jaänjo's gift and the responsibility it carried. A new thought occurred to her: this might be a perfect opportunity for Jaänjo to overcome his melancholy by healing someone again. The prospect of alleviating both Dr. Katasse's suffering and Jaänjo's emotional distress filled her with cautious optimism. She touched her nose to activate her aura vision.

Entering the house, Aan saw Dr. Katasse for the first time. His frail appearance tugged at her compassion, but his aura captured her attention.

"Jaänjo," she whispered internally, "he has a white aura, but it's fractured by pulsing flits of red—a clear indication of his illness."

"I see it too," Jaänjo replied within her mind. "His aura confirms both his good character and his dire condition."

Aan took a deep breath, steeling herself for the challenging conversation ahead that could have far-reaching consequences for all of them. She put on a fake smile, hoping it appeared genuine, and extended her hand. "Hello, Dr. Katasse. I'm Aan."

He rose from his seat, returning her smile as he shook her hand. His grip was weak but genuine. "Thank you so much for coming to see me. Please, all of you, call me Naas."

"I like him, Aan," Jaänjo's voice resonated within her. "He's a healer like us—a person with a good heart."

"I agree," she mentally replied.

Aan took a seat across from Naas, her parents flanking her protectively. She took a deep breath before speaking. "Dr. Katasse—Naas—I want to be direct with you. Yes, I can facilitate healing, but it's not a power that comes from me alone. I have a spiritual partner who works through me. We combine our energies to heal people, but it's a complex process that we don't fully understand ourselves."

Naas's eyes widened, but he remained silent, allowing her to continue.

"What I'm about to tell you must remain absolutely confidential," Aan emphasized, her gaze intense. "My fear of thousands of people inundating Tenakee Springs, demanding to be cured, is very real. All I want is a peaceful life, to help where I can without disrupting everything around me."

She leaned forward slightly. "Before we go any further, I need to know why I can trust you. Why did you become a doctor? What drives you?"

Naas nodded, understanding the weight of her questions. He took a moment to gather his thoughts before responding.

"I became a doctor to help our people," he began, his voice soft but filled with conviction. "Growing up in Hoonah, I saw how limited our access to healthcare was, especially for serious conditions. Too many of our people died unnecessarily or had to leave our communities for treatment."

He paused, his eyes distant with memory. "I remember attending my first Ku.éex'—our traditional memorial potlatch—as a child. The way our community came together, feasting, singing, dancing, and gift-giving, to commemorate important events such as births, deaths, and weddings or to mark social status. It showed me the strength of our people. But it also highlighted how much we've lost to diseases that modern medicine can treat." He sighed. "When I turned twelve, my grandmother died from breast cancer. The struggle she went through, the pain our family experienced—it left a mark on me. That's when I vowed to become a doctor, to bring modern medicine back to our communities, and to help bridge the gap between Western medicine and our traditional healing practices."

"That's a noble cause," said Aan.

He nodded and refocused his gaze on Aan. "I've dedicated my life to this work. I've seen the devastation cancer can bring, and I've also seen the power of our traditional ways. What you can do... it's beyond anything I've ever encountered. I understand your need for secrecy. As a doctor, as a Tlingit, and as someone who has seen too much suffering, I give you my word that your secret is safe with me."

Aan studied him for a long moment, feeling Jaänjo's presence stirring within her. She could sense his approval, his desire to help.

"Thank you for sharing that, Naas," Aan said finally. "I believe you, and I think we can trust you. There's something else you should know." She took another deep breath. "The healing spirit who lives within me—his name is Jaänjo. He's as much a part of me as I am of myself."

Aan carefully avoided mentioning Jaänjo's extraterrestrial origins, but she wanted Naas to understand that her gift to heal was not hers alone.

She stood. "Please give me a few minutes to talk with Jaänjo privately." Donning her coat, she stepped outside into the crisp air. "Well, what do you think, Jaänjo?"

"I'm certain we agree—he's most worthy of being healed. And I'm confident he'll safeguard our secret."

"I agree. Let's go back inside and tell him." Aan paused. "Jaänjo...?"

"Yes?"

"I'm so glad you'll be able to fulfill your life's purpose once more."

"I know. If I were a physical form, my face would have an enormous smile."

"I feel your spirit soaring," she said, touching her heart. "When do you want to heal him?"

"Since your parents said he's staying the night with them, we could have breakfast together and then do the healing."

"That's a great idea. A good night's sleep will be good for everyone."

Aan returned inside, her gaze settling on Naas. "Jaänjo and I have decided to help you," she said, her words accompanied by a sudden pang of fear. She felt like a mother bear fiercely protecting her cub—in this case, Jaänjo.

Taking a deep breath, she continued, "Naas, before we proceed, you need to understand the full implications of what we're about to do. If we heal you, you'll become living proof of our abilities. Your very existence could put us at risk." Her eyes locked on his, conveying the gravity of the situation. "Are you prepared to protect our secret? To face questions about your miraculous recovery that you can never truthfully answer?"

Naas nodded solemnly, his eyes reflecting gratitude and determination. "I am," he said, his voice steady. "I'm willing to do whatever it takes to protect you and Jaänjo. Your gift of life is sacred, and I vow to honor it by guarding your secret with every fiber of my being."

Aan glanced at her parents, hoping to see approval in their eyes. Her mom responded with a subtle smile and nod.

"All right," Aan said, "let's move forward."

Naas's eyes welled with gratitude. "Thank you, Aan—and Jaänjo. From the deepest reaches of my being, you have my word that I will never reveal any of this."

She nodded. "Mom, since you said Naas is staying the night with you, Jaänjo and I would like to do the healing tomorrow after breakfast. Would that work?"

"It would." Yéil gave Aan a mischievous grin. "Jaänjo, do you have any breakfast preferences for tomorrow?"

Jaänjo's laughter echoed within Aan. "Tell your mom I love her."

Aan's face lit up with a delightful smile. "Mom, Jaänjo says he loves you."

"I love you too, Jaänjo," Yéil replied warmly. She turned to Naas. "Jaänjo has a legendary love for the cinnamon rolls at our local bakery. If you're agreeable, we could have breakfast there tomorrow morning."

Naas smiled. "I have a weakness for cinnamon rolls myself."

"You and Jaänjo might be kindred spirits," Aan chuckled as she glanced at the wall clock. "We'll return to my cabin now and meet you here at 7:30 tomorrow. Does that work for everyone?"

Her parents and Naas nodded in agreement. Aan hugged her parents and then Naas. "You'll be in good hands tomorrow, Naas. Jaänjo and I will take excellent care of you."

"Thank you both. How... how long will the healing process take?"

Jaänjo chuckled internally. "Tell him three weeks and six days. And maybe longer if he says he's watched online videos on spiritual healings and offers to tell us what we need to do."

Aan burst out laughing and repeated Jaänjo's words. Her parents joined in the laughter. Naas laughed, too, recognizing the humor from his experiences with patients who claimed expertise from online videos.

"I'm sorry, Naas," Aan said, trying to stifle her giggles. "Jaänjo is a spirit with a rather dry sense of humor. In reality, the healing should take an hour or less."

Naas looked relieved. Jaänjo's humor lifted the mood and alleviated the tension from their serious discussion.

As laughter filled the room, Jaänjo marveled at the sudden shift in his circumstance—from feeling adrift and melancholic to now being on the verge of being a healer again. The prospect sent a thrill through his essence, but a surge of fear quickly tempered it. What if healing Naas led to their discovery? This dreadful thought rampaged through his consciousness, leaving him to question if his longing to heal again was a selfish act that might ultimately doom him and Aan.

35

THE SUN'S GENTLE MORNING light embraced Tenakee Springs as Aan, her parents, and Naas made their way back from the bakery. Their shared meal had nourished more than just their bodies; it had cultivated a deeper connection among them, a trust crucial for the task ahead. As they entered the house, sunbeams filtered through the windows, casting a warm glow that seemed to highlight the gravity of the moment.

Aan settled into a comfortable living room chair and gestured for Naas to sit across from her. "Naas," she began, her voice calm and reassuring, "I'd like to share with you what Jaänjo has told me about how he cures people. This will help you understand the healing process we're about to do."

Naas nodded and leaned forward, his eyes intense with curiosity and hope.

"For highly evolved beings, auras—which reflect their life energy—manifest in two primary colors: white and black. White represents pure energy fueled by positive emotions like kindness, love, joy, peace, and creativity. This promotes healing, harmony, and well-being. Conversely, black auras signify dark energy fueled by negativity, such as anger, hatred, worry, anxiety, cynicism, and malice.

"Auras are dynamic reflections of our inner selves, ebbing and flowing in response to our emotions, thoughts, actions, and overall state of being. Each individual's aura color mirrors their predominant energy. Those struggling between pure and dark energies emit only a faint luminescence."

"Wow, this is fascinating, Aan," Naas said in rapt attention. "Please continue."

Aan nodded. "It is fascinating. As healers, Jaänjo and I mend imbalances within a person's aura. These imbalances appear as distinct colors superimposed on the primary aura colors, revealing underlying issues.

Naas, your aura shows flickering red pulses within your white aura, indicating your physical distress. Jaänjo uses these visual cues to guide the healing process, identifying specific areas needing attention.

"When I lay my hands over someone," Aan began, her voice soft yet clear, "Jaänjo and I channel a transformative energy that penetrates the patient's very essence. This energy delicately manipulates the blueprint of their cells, restoring them to a healthy state and guiding the body back into harmony. We realign the intricate threads of their physical and emotional fabric, mending what has become frayed or tangled." She paused, meeting Naas's eyes. "To put it simply, Jaänjo and I use our healing energy to return the aura to a balanced state, reflecting restored health and emotional peace."

Naas stared at her, his eyes wide with astonishment. "Are you saying you can alter atoms within living cells?"

Aan nodded, her expression serene yet serious. "Yes, we do it in two ways," she explained. "First, since Jaänjo has no physical senses, he uses mine. He guides my hands over a person's body to detect imbalances—think of it as a spiritual MRI." She paused, allowing Naas to process this information.

"Then," she continued, "depending on the illness's severity, we make another pass, channeling our combined healing energy through my palms into the person. For most, this is sufficient to heal them. But for severe conditions like yours, my mom's, Tala's, and Taayoo's, Jaänjo temporarily enters their body to complete the healing."

Aan leaned forward slightly, her gaze meeting Naas's. "There's one crucial point, Naas. Jaänjo needs your explicit permission to enter your body. Do we have it?"

Naas nodded enthusiastically. "Absolutely. Will I feel him inside me?"

"Yes, but as my mom and I can attest, there's no pain—mostly a pleasant, warm sensation. When I first met Jaänjo, I had debilitating MS, and he cured me, so I also have experienced his healing firsthand."

"Thanks for your reassuring words, Aan."

She smiled and nodded. "Naas, if you're ready to begin, we'll need you to lie on the bed in the guest room."

Naas nodded, a mix of nervousness and anticipation in his voice. "I'm ready. Should I remove my clothes?"

"No, that's not necessary," Aan replied gently. "Just wear whatever you're comfortable in."

Naas glanced at his attire. "What I'm wearing now should be fine, then."

"Perfect," Aan said, standing up. "In that case, let's begin."

She gestured towards the guest room, her demeanor calm and confident, helping to put Naas at ease as they prepared for the healing process.

An hour later, Aan smiled at Naas. "We're done. Jaänjo would like to speak to you through me."

Naas eagerly nodded, his eyes bright with hope and nervousness. "Jaänjo, can you hear me? I want to thank you."

Aan felt Jaänjo's amusement bubble up within her. She couldn't help but smile as she relayed his message: "Jaänjo says, 'I can barely hear you—speak louder!'"

Nass raised his voice, nearly shouting. "Thank you for healing me, Jaänjo!"

Aan rolled her eyes good-naturedly. "Naas, Jaänjo's just having a bit of fun at your expense. He hears you perfectly fine."

Looking embarrassed, Naas grinned, his tension visibly easing. "I've always said I appreciate a spirit with a dry sense of humor."

Jaänjo's laughter resonated through Aan. "Jaänjo says most people can't fathom the subtlety of dry wit, so he appreciates you."

The lighthearted exchange seemed to dispel some of the nervous energy in the room.

"Naas," Jaänjo continued, "while my primary focus was on your cancer, I also repaired the socket in your left shoulder. The injury appeared to be two or three years old. Given your civilization's medical capabilities, I assume you chose to live with the pain rather than seek treatment."

"You're correct, Jaänjo," Naas replied. "I injured it playing basketball three years ago. As a doctor, the demands of my job made it impractical to take time off for surgery and rehabilitation, so I decided to manage the discomfort with painkillers."

Naas paused, meeting Aan's gaze. "Aan, witnessing the energy flowing from your palms into my body—and Jaänjo, observing how you left Aan, hovered above me, and then merged with me—it was extraordinary. Feeling you move through my body... it's humbling to realize that our 'advanced' medicine pales compared to what you and Aan offer."

Through Aan, Jaänjo's voice resonated with playful mischief. "Just wait until you see our bill," he quipped.

Aan chuckled. "Naas, Jaänjo is teasing you again—there won't be any charge."

Naas smiled, but then his expression turned serious, his voice tinged with hope and apprehension. "Jaänjo, am I... am I really cured?"

Aan's face softened as she relayed Jaänjo's response. "Yes, you are. Your aura now radiates with a beautiful white glow."

Naas swallowed hard, his next question barely above a whisper. "Do you think the cancer will return?"

"Rest easy on that, Naas. I converted every last cancer cell back to normal."

Tears welled up in Naas's eyes, spilling down his cheeks. His voice trembled with emotion. "Thank you. Thank you both so much."

The room fell silent, filled with the weight of the moment—a life saved, a future restored. Aan felt Jaänjo's warmth spreading through her, a shared sense of joy and purpose in what they had accomplished together.

"Aan, there's something else I need to discuss with Naas—on a personal level," Jaänjo said, his tone turning serious.

Aan noted the shift in his voice and sensed that something was amiss. "Okay, Jaänjo." She turned to Naas. "Jaänjo has something more to share with you."

Naas sat up, his posture alert and attentive. "I'm listening, Jaänjo."

Aan's voice softened as she relayed Jaänjo's words, her expression mirroring his deep emotions: "Naas, I want you to understand what healing you means to me. This winter has been difficult for me. Very difficult. To protect Aan, we agreed that she should only do shaman duties, with no healings involving me. But for me, this gift of healing... it's not just something I do—it's the very essence of who I am.

"Being unable to heal others left me feeling hollow and purposeless as if a vital part of my being was locked away. I felt adrift, disconnected from my core. There were days when the weight of this inaction felt unbearable.

"Healing you today has been a profound experience, Naas. It's as if a fog has lifted, revitalizing my spirit and reconnecting me to my purpose. Witnessing your cells respond—and your aura glow with renewed energy—fills me with joy. This experience reinforces the precious gift I have to heal and rekindles my sense of purpose. Thank you for allowing me to be who I am once again. I am deeply grateful."

Aan paused, her eyes glistening with emotion as she finished conveying Jaänjo's heartfelt words. "Naas, it's me speaking now," she said gently. "Jaänjo means everything to me. Seeing him struggle was agonizing, so I'm also thankful to you for helping to pull him out of the dark place he was in."

Naas stood. "May I hug you and Jaänjo?"

"Sure," she replied with a tender smile.

Naas held her close for several moments before stepping back, wiping tears from his eyes. "I love you both dearly. For saving my life, you will always be family to me."

Naas's mind began to race with possibilities as the reality of his healing sank in. He thought about all the people suffering as he had been, and a seed of an idea began to form. After a moment of contemplation, he turned to Aan and her parents with a look of determination. "It moves me deeply to hear Jaänjo's love for healing others and its importance to him. What if I could devise a way for you and him to use your gift to heal people without ever being exposed?"

Aan regarded him skeptically. "I don't see how that could work."

"I have an idea, but it's only half-formed right now," Naas admitted. "But if it could guarantee your autonomy, would you consider it?"

"Jaänjo, what do you think?" Aan asked aloud.

After a moment, she relayed Jaänjo's response: "Jaänjo says let's hear your idea, even if it's not fully formed. But it must be a foolproof plan that protects Aan's life from being ruined."

Naas nodded, looking grateful for their openness. "Again, this just came to me, so it's far from being polished."

"We understand," Aan reassured him, "but please, tell us anyway."

"Okay," Naas began, taking a deep breath. "I bought a used Bayliner 285 Cruiser to get away with my family on weekends, go fishing, or visit my parents in Hoonah. I also use it to bring medical supplies to various villages, offering my doctor's services to our people at no charge. It's spacious enough for overnight stays and has separate sleeping areas. What if we used it as a mobile healing center?"

Aan and her parents listened intently.

"Naas, I've seen boats like yours," Keet interjected. "They seem quite nice and seaworthy. I think I see where you're going with this."

"How so?" Naas asked, intrigued.

Keet leaned forward, his voice taking on a confident tone. "Yéil is friends with Tala. When she heard how ill Tala had become, she pleaded with Aan and Jaänjo to heal her. We formulated a plan similar to yours—we sailed our fishing boat to Juneau, intending to have Tala meet us on board.

The idea was to conduct the healing in the boat's cabin. We purchased a powerful light to flood the cabin, masking the glow from Aan's palms. We also bought a light-blocking sleep mask for Tala to wear during the healing so she wouldn't see anything."

He sighed. "Unfortunately, Tala was near death, so she couldn't come to our boat. We had to go to her house instead. I held up our light in her bedroom while Aan and Jaänjo performed the healing. Tala wore the sleep mask, so she didn't see what they did. We were the only ones in the room, ensuring complete privacy. And, Aan and Jaänjo cured Taayoo in his room as he slept, so no one witnessed that healing either."

Naas nodded, his eyes brightening with understanding and growing excitement.

"Keet, we're on the same wavelength. We could use my boat to visit various villages and have patients come aboard for treatment. Aan, you could remain hidden in one berth while I prepare the patient and have them wear a sleep mask, ensuring they never see you."

His voice gained momentum as he elaborated. "After the healing, you could quickly move to the other berth. The patient would never know you were there. The boat would act like a mobile healing center that conceals your identity."

The room fell silent for a moment as the implications of this plan sank in. It was a creative solution that could allow Aan and Jaänjo to continue their healing while maintaining their privacy and safety.

Yéil shook her head, her expression dubious. "This all sounds promising, but there's still a significant risk. Even though Tala and her family never saw what happened, Naas, you still found out about it. Once word gets out that you're healing people, you'll be hounded just as Aan was."

Naas frowned, acknowledging the validity of Yéil's concern. But then his eyes brightened as a new idea struck him.

"You're right," Naas began, his voice gaining momentum as the idea took shape. "But what if we initially focus on patients whose conditions aren't advanced?" His eyes lit up with growing excitement. "Aan, you and Jaänjo could assess their auras to identify the problem and heal them discreetly. And since their condition wouldn't be advanced, Jaänjo wouldn't have to enter them, so no permission from the patient would be needed. Since no hospital would be involved, we'd avoid raising suspicions."

The room fell silent as they considered Naas's refined proposal. It was a clever approach that potentially addressed many of their concerns. Still, Aan felt a knot forming in her stomach. The prospect of helping people while safeguarding their secret was tantalizing, but any plan always comes with unforeseen risks.

"Naas, Jaänjo and I believe your idea has merit," Aan began, her voice carrying a note of cautious optimism tinged with hesitation. "We'd like to give your proposal more consideration and refine it over the coming days." She paused, her brow furrowing as she continued. "There are some practical matters we need to address. For instance, healing drains Jaänjo's energy significantly, so there's a limit to how many people he can heal in a day."

She hesitated, then added, "Also, there are some practical matters to consider. I work as a bookkeeper at our family business. It's my primary source of income, as being a shaman generates little revenue. We'll need to consider these aspects as well." Her voice softened, conveying genuine appreciation for Naas's efforts. "Your idea opens up possibilities—a starting point that could allow us to help people while safeguarding our privacy and security."

Naas nodded thoughtfully, his fingers drumming lightly on the arm of his chair. The room felt charged with excitement and apprehension as they all grappled with the weight of the decision before them. "You raise valid points, Aan," he replied. "And as a doctor, I also have an active practice to maintain. Please call me whenever you wish to meet again, and I'll return." He paused, his tone becoming solemn to emphasize his following words. "No one—not even my wife or family—will ever know about you and Jaänjo. Your secret is safe with me."

Aan nodded, grateful for Naas's sincerity. As she contemplated the possibilities of his plan, a conflicting surge of emotions washed over her. She could sense Jaänjo's excitement pulsing within her, his eagerness to once again fulfill his purpose as a healer. The prospect of witnessing his genuine contentment warmed her heart.

Yet this warmth was quickly chilled by a cold fear that gripped her core. If they were discovered—if their secret reached the masses—she could lose Jaänjo forever. The thought of losing him—severing the deep connection they shared—was almost unbearable. She found herself caught in an emotional tug-of-war: the desire to bring Jaänjo happiness pitted against the terrifying risk of losing him altogether.

Her eyes glistened as she finished speaking. The house fell quiet, each person lost in their own thoughts. Naas looked at Aan, acutely aware of Jaänjo's presence within her as he processed all he had learned. He leaned back, his mind buzzing from all he had witnessed and learned. The healing Naas had experienced was unlike anything he had ever known—a mystical experience that defied conventional understanding. He marveled at the power and beauty of Jaänjo's gift, yet he couldn't help but feel a pang of empathy for the burden it placed on both him and Aan.

"I... I'm truly honored by the trust you all have placed in me," he said softly, his voice barely above a whisper. "What you've shared—what you've shown me—it's extraordinary. I see why you guard this secret so fiercely." He paused, looked at Aan, and chose his following words carefully. "But I also see the toll it takes on you and Jaänjo. The isolation, the constant fear of discovery... it's a heavy price to pay for such a remarkable gift." He looked at Keet and Yéil. "You're all now part of my family, and if there's ever anything I can do to help you—any of you—to ease this burden you carry—you need only ask."

"Thank you, Naas," said Keet. "We feel like you're now part of our family, too. The appeal of your idea to help our people is undeniable, yet we all recognize there are issues to resolve. It's a fine line between utilizing Aan and Jaänjo's extraordinary healing abilities and preserving the life they hold dear. Still, the immense good your proposal could bring touches our hearts. In the coming days, we have much to think about..."

36

As THE SUMMER DREW to a close, Aan stood at the bow of her family's fishing boat, her heart full and spirit soaring after another successful day at sea. The afternoon sun warmed her skin as she looked out over the calm waters of Alaska's Inside Passage, noting the lush emerald-green islands surrounding her. Their thick forests showcased the region's natural beauty.

A light mist hung over the treetops, adding a touch of mystery to the scene as the boat moved steadily through the water. In the distance, the snow-capped mountains of the mainland peeked through gaps in the clouds, their quiet presence a gentle reminder of the landscape's enduring grandeur.

With deep satisfaction from another successful fishing trip, Aan placed her hand over her heart. "Jaänjo," she whispered, her voice barely audible above the gentle waves, "look at the beauty surrounding us. The spirits of my ancestors truly blessed us with this magnificent home."

"I agree," Jaänjo replied within her. "Aan, the Earthling concept of 'joy' was foreign to me, something I never experienced on my planet. But now, sharing these moments with you, feeling the rhythm of this world... I believe I understand this amazing thing called joy. It's... overwhelming in the most positive way."

Aan smiled, her eyes bright with happiness. "Because of you, I feel the same way," she said softly. "Sharing our healing work, seeing our abilities grow, and our love deepening... it's brought me a joy I never expected."

As they shared this moment, a small pod of orcas surfaced nearby, their dorsal fins splashing the water. Seabirds circled overhead, their calls mingling with the steady hum of the boat's engine and the gentle splash of waves. The fresh scent of saltwater filled the air, a familiar and comforting presence as they made their way home.

"Aan, I've been thinking," Jaänjo's voice resonated within her. "When I first arrived on Earth, I saw it merely as a refuge. But now, I'm beginning to understand what your people mean by having a connection to the land. How the tides shape the shoreline, how the forests breathe with the seasons, how the animals adapt to their environment... it's all so intricate and alive. On N'ridium, we lost this harmony with our world long ago. Experiencing it here, through you, it's... an expression of divinity."

Aan smiled, touched by Jaänjo's words. "I'm glad you're seeing my home this way. It's more than just a place to me—it's part of who I am."

As the afternoon sun descended, the family's boat approached Tenakee Springs. Aan moved beside Keet at the helm and noted his weathered hands steady on the wheel. Years of experience were evident in the confident way he guided the vessel home. Nearing their dock, he slowed the engine, maneuvering with the sure touch of a seasoned mariner.

Aan positioned herself at the railing, ready to secure the boat. As they pulled alongside the dock, she leaped off with the agility born of countless repetitions. Her hands moved with practiced ease, wrapping the mooring lines around sturdy metal cleats. She double-checked each line, ensuring the boat nestled snugly against the fenders, protected from the tide's constant motion.

Without pause, Aan and the crew sprang into action, offloading the day's salmon catch. The dock transformed into a hive of activity, resonating with friendly chatter, the rhythmic slap of fish on ice, and the eager cries of circling gulls. In short order, their catch was on its way to the local processor, marking the close of another successful day of fishing in Tenakee Springs.

With a satisfied smile, Aan paused, her mind briefly flashing back to the days when MS had limited her abilities. A wave of gratitude washed over her for her spirit ancestors and Jaänjo, who had made it possible for her to engage in this physical work again. She took a deep breath, releasing it in a contented sigh.

Oddly, a troubling feeling swelled within her in this moment of happiness—a sense that something was about to change. She cocked an eyebrow, wondering if it was just a random rambling of her tired mind.

"Jaänjo," she thought, "did you feel the emotional shift that just rolled through me? A feeling of enormous contentment followed by an intense fear that this happiness can't last forever?"

She felt a ripple in Jaänjo's energy before he responded. "Whew—that was a big shift. Initially, I felt your contentment mirroring my own, but then came your abrupt mood swing. Given your refined intuition, I wouldn't dismiss the feeling outright, but I wouldn't obsess over it, either. Perhaps the best approach is to wait and see if the feeling persists."

"That makes sense." She smiled softly, experiencing the gentle warmth of Jaänjo's energy pulsing within her. This quiet, tender moment highlighted their bond, reflecting their love and care for each other.

As the evening drew to a close, Aan bid her parents a warm goodnight. The family dinner had been filled with laughter and stories from their successful fishing trip, a perfect end to a fulfilling day. On the walk home, Aan savored the crisp Alaskan night. The moon, a gentle beacon, cast a soft luminescence on her path while stars dotted the vast canvas of darkness. The forest around her came alive with the gentle rustling of leaves and distant calls of owls. The scent of Sitka spruce and damp earth filled the air, a comforting reminder of home. She smiled, thinking of Jaänjo's presence within her, a constant source of warmth and companionship.

At home, Aan started a fire to warm the cabin. "It'll feel good to get some warmth in here, Jaänjo," she said with a smile as she headed to the bathroom to prepare for bed.

In her bedroom, she lifted the covers and nestled into her cushy mattress. "Oh, this feels so good after our long day."

"I hope we have many more days like today," Jaänjo mused.

As Aan lay contently, reliving the day's events, she suddenly felt a strange sensation, as if a cool breeze had passed through the room despite the closed window. She paused, her contentment giving way to unease.

"Jaänjo, did you feel that?" she asked.

"I did," came his reply, tinged with curiosity. "Something odd..."

She rose and approached the window. Outside, the night sky stretched clear and star-filled, yet something felt inexplicably different. Like Jaänjo, she couldn't pinpoint the change, but an unsettling sense of foreboding settled over her.

"It's probably nothing," she murmured, trying to reassure herself. Yet, as she returned to her bed, the feeling lingered like an unwelcome guest in her consciousness.

Unknown to Aan and Jaänjo, a momentous event had just unfolded on their island's far side. A tiny flash of light streaked across the night sky, so brief and dim that it would've escaped the notice of even the most attentive stargazer. But this was no celestial body—it was Mičěcha, Jaänjo's brother, another being of pure energy arriving from N'ridium. His energy seamlessly blended with the surroundings, leaving the pristine wilderness undisturbed as he pierced through the dense canopy of the Alaskan forest.

For Jaänjo and Aan, who had grown comfortable, even inseparable, in their shared existence, Mičěcha's arrival would soon turn their world upside down.

37

IN THE DAYS FOLLOWING his arrival, Miěěcha traversed Chichagof Island, his invisible energy form allowing him to move freely through the landscape. Without physical senses, he could only detect the varying energy patterns around him. The dense temperate rainforest registered as a complex, interconnected web of life forces, while the muskeg bogs and waterways appeared as unique energy flows crisscrossing the land.

Miěěcha's journey led him to an area of concentrated and diverse energy signatures—unknown to him, the settlement of Tenakee Springs. Hindered by the lack of physical senses, he couldn't see the wooden structures, smell the sea air, or hear the sounds of the small community. Instead, he perceived a hub of dynamic energy patterns, constantly shifting and interacting in ways he found both fascinating and frustrating.

As he drifted through the town, Miěěcha's presence went unnoticed. He attempted to make sense of the energy signatures around him, able to distinguish between living beings and inanimate objects. The absence of familiar reference points made this task exceedingly difficult, and Miěěcha felt a growing sense of frustration at his limited ability to understand this new world.

Days passed, and Miěěcha's observations grew more focused. He began to discern patterns in the energy flows of advanced lifeforms, correlating them with what he surmised were daily activities. Thoughts of Jaänjo fueled his desperate search for his brother, his mind constantly drifting to the circumstances of Jaänjo's departure from N'ridium.

In a desperate bid to save his brother's life, Miěěcha had launched Jaänjo into space before perfecting the energy-to-matter conversion process. To compensate, he had taught Jaänjo how to merge with a suitable host—the only way to regain physical form. Now, surrounded by foreign energy patterns, Miěěcha's frustration mounted. His lack of physical senses left him at a significant disadvantage, unable to fully perceive or interact with this new world.

Another challenge loomed larger than ever: unlike his brother, Miĕĕcha couldn't see auras, a skill that would have made locating Jaänjo easier. Amidst the unfamiliar energy patterns, finding his brother seemed a monumental task.

As more time passed, Miĕĕcha continued his silent, unseen observation of Tenakee Springs' advanced lifeforms. He discerned patterns in their movements, but his lack of physical senses greatly hindered his comprehension of this new world, leaving him increasingly frustrated.

Questions began to gnaw at him: Had Jaänjo merged with one of the lifeforms in this area? Had his energy moved beyond this tiny island? And then, the most troubling question of all—should he take over one of these lifeforms to better find his brother?

Before leaving N'ridium, Jaänjo had voiced his strong opposition to forcibly taking over another lifeform, a sentiment Miĕĕcha fully shared. Though Miĕĕcha had figured out how to turn energy back into matter before his departure, he'd need to build the equipment to do so on this new planet. This would require merging with one of the alien lifeforms. Combined with his fruitless search for his brother, Miĕĕcha reluctantly considered abandoning his ethical reservations about merging. Without physical senses, the world around him would remain frustratingly incomprehensible.

With a metaphorical sigh, he suppressed these thoughts and refocused on a non-invasive strategy. A flash of insight struck him—find a bustling gathering place along the town's main path and observe its inhabitants more closely. Soon, he discovered the perfect vantage point: a small building teeming with activity. Little did Miĕĕcha know, but he had chosen the Party Time Bakery.

As Miĕĕcha settled into his vigil at the bakery, life continued its usual rhythm elsewhere in Tenakee Springs. Unaware of the alien presence in their midst, the town's inhabitants went about their daily routines.

The following morning, Aan awoke with a smile. "Hey, Jaänjo, I have an idea. Let's go to the bathhouse in town and have a soak. Afterward, I'll treat you to whatever you want at the Party Time Bakery."

"That's a brilliant idea!"

Aan quickly threw a T-shirt and shorts over her swimsuit. "I could use a good soak—it'll be fun!"

"You know, it can smell a bit funky in the bathhouse," Jaänjo quipped.

Aan chuckled. "Sometimes, Jaänjo, you can be a bit wimpy. Yes, the hot spring water has a slight sulfur smell. It's common in natural hot springs where mineral-rich water emerges from the Earth's crust. But the smell is worth it. Everyone in town values its therapeutic properties and how it calms the mind, including you—I know you secretly love it as much as I do."

"I do," he admitted. "Just so you know, I haven't forgotten how you call me wimpy every time I go dormant when you make beef stew."

She laughed. "You're part wimp and part miracle worker, so I guess the two balance out."

At the community bathhouse, Aan sank into the 106-degree water of the large cement and stone tub. As she immersed herself in the mineral spring, she sighed contentedly. "Oh, Jaänjo, this is lovely."

"It is," Jaänjo agreed.

They savored the serene tranquility together, allowing the therapeutic waters to soothe them.

Back on the town's main path, Aan headed to the bakery. "So, Jaänjo, what would you think about this wildly audacious idea: instead of getting your usual, why don't we try a generous slice of their fresh, heavenly-tasting strawberry rhubarb pie?"

Silence...

Aan burst out laughing. "Now, I'm messing with you. We'll have your usual."

"Whew," said Jaänjo. "I was about to go dormant."

"Wimp—wimp, wimp, wimp."

"Hey, don't forget miracle worker, too."

"Yeah, that, too."

As Aan approached the bakery, she paused. "Do you feel that, Jaänjo?"

"Feel what?"

"A presence. The last time I felt this was when you entered our office with Silas."

"I don't feel anything, Aan. Maybe you're just giddy about having another cinnamon roll."

She didn't bite on his attempt at humor. "I'm telling you, I'm feeling something." She took a deep breath, opened the bakery door, and changed the subject. "Let's hope they haven't sold out of your favorite—if they have, get ready to experience strawberry rhubarb pie."

"This would be the time for you to start praying, Aan."

She smiled at his remark as she walked to the counter.

After enjoying the cinnamon roll and Aan chatting with several friends, they headed out.

On the path, Jaänjo suddenly tensed. "Aan, I see the presence!" he exclaimed in a hushed tone. "Activate your aura vision—there's a shimmering form just ahead of us!"

Aan cringed at his panic and quickly touched her nose. "I see it, too. What should we do?"

"Walk away from it, Aan! Don't stare at it—just walk away!"

Aan quickened her pace along the main path, eager to put distance between them and the ethereal presence.

"Jaänjo, I'm scared—what do you think it is?" Aan whispered.

"I don't know, Aan. Maybe Miĕĕcha succeeded in converting energy back to matter, and they launched other N'ridians here. That form could be one of them." Suddenly, realization struck him. "Or it could be Miĕĕcha himself!"

"Let's go to my parents' house and tell them what happened."

"Okay."

Aan and Jaänjo recounted their experience to a visibly concerned Keet and Yéil, describing the mysterious presence they encountered near the bakery.

Keet's brow furrowed. "Could this be the start of an invasion by less friendly N'ridians?"

Yéil, who had been listening intently, spoke up. "Let's not jump to conclusions," she said, her voice calm but tinged with concern. "We need more information before we start worrying about invasions." She turned to Aan, her eyes questioning. "What does Jaänjo think about all this?"

Aan intently listened as Jaänjo spoke to her, then turned to her parents. "Jaänjo says his brother told him they'd be fortunate to convert even a hundred thousand people to energy, so an invasion force isn't possible on any planet with such limited numbers." Her tone shifted, becoming more intrigued. "It could be his brother, Miĕĕcha. Unlike Jaänjo, Miĕĕcha doesn't have the ability to see auras, so he can't see Jaänjo."

Aan continued, relaying Jaänjo's words: "Before leaving N'ridium, Miĕĕcha and I created a simple energy-based code to identify each other. It's like a secret handshake but with pulses of energy. If I send out a specific pattern, Miěěcha will respond with his own unique pattern. This way, we could recognize each other even in our energy forms."

"It's me speaking now," said Aan. "Jaänjo has a plan. Tomorrow, he will leave my body and return to the bakery to see if the ethereal glow is still there. If it is, Jaänjo will follow it and, when the time is right, flash the signal to identify himself. However," she added cautiously, "if it's not Miěěcha and the entity is hostile, Jaänjo said things could turn dangerous. That's why he wants to keep us away from this encounter."

Aan's face tightened with worry. "Jaänjo, I don't like the idea of you going alone. What if something happens to you? We don't know what this entity is capable of. How would I even know if you were in trouble?"

Aan felt Jaänjo's energy signature pulse soothingly within her as he conveyed his reassurance. "Aan, I understand your concern. But remember, in my energy form, I'm incredibly resilient. Even if it's not Miěěcha, it's unlikely any being could harm me permanently. If I sense danger, I can retreat instantly. However, you're right that I can't sense Miěěcha directly. My ability to see auras only works when I'm within you. That's why we need to approach this carefully."

Aan nodded, still unconvinced. "Promise me you'll be careful and come back to me no matter what happens."

"I promise," Jaänjo replied. "I'll try not to stay away for long."

Yéil leaned forward, curiosity evident in his eyes. "And what if it is Miěěcha? What will you do then, Jaänjo?"

Aan relayed Jaänjo's response: "Yéil, if it is Miěěcha, I'll be overjoyed. However, we face a significant challenge. As beings of pure energy, we can't effectively communicate. I only learned human language after I entered Silas's body. For Miěěcha and me to truly reunite and converse, Miěěcha would need to find a willing human host, and that's not likely to happen."

Keet nodded, pondering this for a moment. "If it is indeed Miěěcha, I would be willing to let him enter me to learn the language and more about humans, just as Jaänjo did with Silas." He paused, a hint of uncertainty in his voice. "But Jaänjo, is Miěěcha a good person? Can we trust him?"

Aan felt Jaänjo's energy pulse warmly within her as she relayed his response. "Jaänjo says most certainly, yes, we can trust him. Miěěcha is one of the kindest, most ethical beings he's ever known. And he's a brilliant scientist who led the team that perfected converting matter to energy. He says he owes his life to Miěěcha, and there's nothing he wouldn't do for his big brother."

Keet nodded, his decision seeming to solidify. "In that case," he said, his voice steady, "if it comes to it, I would be willing to host Miĕĕcha. At least temporarily, to allow you two to communicate and for him to learn about us."

Aan looked at her dad with admiration. "Dad, that's incredibly generous of you to let Miĕĕcha be within you. But are you sure about this? It's a big decision."

Keet gazed at his daughter, his expression thoughtful. His demeanor indicated he was about to share something significant. "Jaänjo," he began, "I want to share something important about our Tlingit culture. Family, including our clan, is at the heart of who we are. We're bound together through shared ancestry, with responsibilities and honor passed down through generations. Our extended family forms the backbone of our community, supporting one another and preserving our traditions. I'm telling you this because we consider you part of our family. Yéil and I see you as our son and an integral part of the Gajaa clan. As part of our family—our clan—your family is now ours."

Keet paused, letting his words sink in. "So, to help you reunite with your brother and let him learn more about our world through me, I'll gladly host Miĕĕcha. Plus," he added with a mischievous grin, "Aan and Yéil have experienced having an alien within them, so I'm curious to experience it myself."

Suddenly, Jaänjo's energy left Aan's body, materializing in his humanlike form at the room's center. He gestured for Keet and Yéil to join him. As they stood before his glowing figure, Jaänjo gazed at them with kind eyes and a warm smile. He embraced Keet and then Yéil. Aan moved to her parents. They joined hands and formed a circle around Jaänjo. Touched by this display of love, Jaänjo gently placed a hand on Keet's cheek, then Yéil's. Finally, he turned to Aan, touching his ethereal lips to hers before merging back into her body.

With tears in her eyes, Aan smiled. Jaänjo says, "Keet, your words and this moment mean more to me than I can express. Thank you. Before I left N'ridium, even in my wildest dreams, I never imagined my true home would be thousands of light-years away. Thank you all for accepting me, not just as a refugee from another world but as a son, a partner, and a part of your family. I promise to honor the responsibilities and traditions of the Gajaa clan and to cherish your daughter. I love all of you so much."

Yéil touched Aan's heart. "We love you, too, Jaänjo."

"Thank you, Yéil." Jaänjo paused, reflecting. "Keet, your offer to host Miěěcha touches me. But first, we need to confirm if this presence is indeed him. Tomorrow's encounter will hopefully provide some answers."

The family fell silent, each contemplating the potential outcomes of the next day's events and the potential life-altering changes that might happen to them.

38

THE FOLLOWING MORNING, AAN stood at the cabin door, her face etched with worry as she watched Jaänjo's energy form depart. "Be careful," she whispered, knowing he couldn't hear her words as his energy drifted down the trail.

In town, Jaänjo moved slowly towards the Party Time Bakery. Finding a concealed spot behind a cluster of bushes near the bakery, Jaänjo settled in where they had previously encountered the mysterious presence.

Hours passed, and Jaänjo remained vigilant, his energy form barely rippling as he maintained his watch. But as the afternoon waned, there was no sign of the ethereal glow they had witnessed before.

A bittersweet feeling swept through him. Part of him had hoped to reunite with Miĕĕcha, while another part feared the possibility of a hostile entity. With no appearance of the presence, he decided to return to Aan.

As Jaänjo approached their cabin, he spotted Aan's energy signature through their dining room window. A moment later, the cabin door flew open, and Aan came onto the porch.

Jaänjo glowed brighter to let her know he "saw" her. He flowed back into her, their connection reestablishing instantly. She felt a wave of comfort as Jaänjo settled within her again. "No luck," he said dejectedly.

"Jaänjo," Aan spoke aloud, her voice quivering slightly. "I've been so worried about you." She felt Jaänjo's energy pulse soothingly within her as she continued. "I have to admit, I'm relieved you didn't encounter the entity. But... I also feel guilty for feeling that way."

"I have mixed emotions about it, too, Aan." He sighed within her. "Being apart from you makes me feel so very low."

She hugged herself, gathering her thoughts before voicing a concern gnawing at her. "I feel the same way. Jaänjo, if it is Miĕĕcha, I'm worried about how it might change things between us. Would your feelings for me change? Would our relationship be different?"

"Aan, nothing could change my feelings for you. You've become a part of me, just as I've become a part of you. Miěěcha won't diminish what we have. You're my family, too, every bit as much as Miěěcha is."

She nodded, a small smile forming on her lips. "It warms my heart to hear that, Jaänjo. I... I can't help but worry. This is all so new and unexpected."

She felt Jaänjo's warmth spread through her. "I understand your concern. But our bond is unbreakable."

Aan took a deep breath, feeling more at ease. She touched her heart. "I love what we have and hope it will never change."

As the evening settled in, Aan and Jaänjo shared a comfortable silence, but deep down, they knew that change was inevitable. Whether it would bring a joyous reunion with Miěěcha or a confrontation with an unknown entity, their world was about to shift in ways they couldn't yet imagine.

The following morning, Aan stirred as early light filtered through the cabin windows. As her awareness fully returned, she felt Jaänjo's familiar presence within her.

"Good morning, Jaänjo," she said softly. "Do you plan to head into town again today?"

"No. I've been thinking all night, Aan."

His response surprised her.

She sat up in bed, her curiosity aroused. "All night? Oh, right. I forgot that as pure energy, you don't sleep."

"That's right," Jaänjo confirmed. "I've spent the night contemplating our situation and realized something."

"What's that?" Aan asked, leaning forward slightly.

"I'm feeling as apprehensive as you are about how this could change things," Jaänjo admitted. "The unknown entity, whether it's Miěěcha or not, represents a significant shift in our lives. And I'm not sure we're ready for that just yet."

Aan arched an eyebrow. "I agree. So, what do you suggest we do?"

"I think we should try to maintain our normalcy," Jaänjo replied. "Why don't we go fishing with Keet today as if nothing happened? It might help us gain some perspective."

A smile spread across Aan's face. "That sounds wonderful. A day on the water might be just what we need."

"I agree," Jaänjo said, his energy pulsing warmly within her. "And when we return from fishing, I'll briefly separate from you and check if the entity is near the bakery. Then I'll meet you back at your parents' house."

Aan stood and stretched. "That's a good plan. It gives us some time to process everything while still addressing the situation. I'll call Dad and tell him we'll join him today."

Feeling a welcome relief, Aan swiftly prepared for the day. The mystery of the unknown entity still loomed, but for now, she and Jaänjo could take a break from the weight of this uncertainty. Fishing would provide a welcome respite, allowing them to immerse themselves in nature's simple pleasures.

On the trail to town, a constant smile adorned her face. She looked forward to another day on the water with those she held dear, both seen and unseen.

As the afternoon sun danced on the sea's surface, Keet guided their boat back to port. The day had been filled with hard work, quiet contemplation, and a satisfying catch. Yet, a faint unease settled upon Aan as they approached the dock.

"I'll miss you while you're gone," she said softly, more to herself than to Jaänjo.

Jaänjo's energy stirred within her. "I'll be back soon. Try not to worry too much."

After jumping off the boat and onto the dock, Aan took a deep breath, steeling herself for the separation. "Be careful," she whispered. Jaänjo left her body and hovered briefly beside her. Then he drifted away, his ethereal form quickly growing fainter as he moved towards town.

A strange, unsettling void enveloped Aan. She shivered, not from cold, but from the absence of Jaänjo's familiar presence within her.

The day dragged on as she forced herself to unload the catch. Her movements were stiff and clumsy, a far cry from her usual grace. She took a deep breath, trying to quell the gnawing emptiness inside.

Keet noticed her distress and gently placed a hand on her shoulder. "Don't worry," he said, his voice warm and reassuring. "He'll be okay."

She managed a small, grateful smile. "Thanks, Dad. But I can't help but worry when he's not with me."

"I understand, but Jaänjo is capable, and he'll be back before you know it. For now, let's focus on getting this catch unloaded. It'll help keep your mind occupied."

Aan nodded, though her face betrayed her unease. She tried to immerse herself in the familiar routine, but despite her efforts, her thoughts remained preoccupied with Jaänjo's absence and the potential dangers he might face. She frequently glanced toward town, hoping to catch a glimpse of his ethereal form returning. With each look, she pondered the answers he might bring—answers that could forever change their lives.

As the sun dipped low, casting long shadows across Tenakee Springs, Jaänjo hovered near the bakery. His energy form pulsed with anticipation while he scanned the area. Suddenly, he detected an energy shimmer—the mysterious entity was approaching the bakery.

Jaänjo remained motionless, observing. As darkness fell, the presence drifted away, moving towards the dense forest. Curiosity and caution warred within him as he made the split-second decision to follow, maintaining a safe distance to avoid detection.

As the entity glided silently through the trees, Jaänjo trailed behind, vigilant not to betray his presence. The forest tightened its grip, its dense canopy blocking the moonlight, creating an ominous darkness. In a secluded clearing, the presence halted.

Jaänjo waited, his energy form dimmed to near invisibility, before cautiously approaching. A moment of truth had arrived, bringing with it a critical decision. Should he risk revealing himself? The tantalizing possibility that this could be Miĕĕcha battled against the fear that it might be a hostile entity.

Jaänjo decided to act. He increased his energy output, flashing a dot and three dashes—his secret identity code. A palpable fear gripped him as he waited for a response.

To his utter amazement, two dashes flashed back. It was Miĕĕcha!

Jaänjo's energy flared with bright jubilation, his form pulsing with intense joy. Miĕĕcha's energy responded in kind, shimmering with an intensity that illuminated the forest clearing.

The magnitude of this moment overwhelmed Jaänjo. Miĕĕcha had traversed an almost incomprehensible distance—over four quintillion miles, a seven thousand light-year journey—to find him. Against near-impossible odds, they had reunited.

Miĕĕcha had kept his promise. He had found Jaänjo.

As their energy forms danced and swirled around each other in the quiet forest, Jaänjo experienced a whirlwind of emotions—elation at their reunion, awe at Miěěcha's incredible journey, and a tinge of apprehension about what this meant for his life with Aan.

For now, this was a moment to celebrate—to rejoice in their surviving an epic journey across the galaxy and marvel at the extraordinary odds they had defied to find each other.

39

With considerable effort, Jaänjo signaled for Miĕĕcha to follow him. The two energy forms glided over the forest floor, weaving between trees as they made their way back into town, moving unnoticed toward their destination.

As they approached the Gajaa's house, Jaänjo slowed, his energy form shimmering with anticipation. He hovered near the living room window, perceiving the familiar and comforting energy signatures of Aan and her parents with his unique senses.

Jaänjo glowed brightly, a signal he knew they would recognize. Inside, one of the energy signatures suddenly shifted, rising and moving quickly. He knew it was Aan.

The front door flew open. With her aura vision activated, Aan gasped at the sight of two luminous entities hovering in the night air. Confusion flickered across her face as she struggled to identify which was Jaänjo.

Sensing her uncertainty, Jaänjo pulsed brightly, indicating he was the one on the right. Recognition dawned in Aan's eyes as she opened her arms wide, a gesture brimming with love and relief.

Jaänjo's energy merged with her, and with their connection re-established, Aan felt a rush of his emotions—excitement, disbelief, and joy.

"Aan," Jaänjo's voice resonated within her, electric with excitement. "I found him! It's Miĕĕcha!"

Aan's gaze shifted to the other luminous entity still hovering nearby. Her heart raced as the reality of the situation sank in. Miĕĕcha, Jaänjo's long-lost brother, had truly arrived.

She stepped forward, uncertain how to greet or communicate with this new presence. "Miĕĕcha?" she said softly, her voice a mixture of wonder and apprehension.

"Aan," Jaänjo gently interjected, "he can't hear you."

She gestured for Miĕĕcha to come inside, her movements slow and deliberate.

As they entered the living room, Aan smiled at her parents, who watched with curiosity and concern. "Mom, Dad," she began, her voice quivering with excitement, "Jaänjo found his brother." She gestured to where Miĕĕcha's energy form hovered, but her parents' bewildered expressions made it clear they couldn't perceive his aura.

Recognizing their inability to see Miĕĕcha, Jaänjo took action. He gently separated from Aan and materialized before them as a luminous humanoid form—a sight still filling Aan and her parents with wonder.

Taking Jaänjo's cue, Miĕĕcha followed suit. His energy coalesced, assuming a similar ethereal shape beside Jaänjo. Aan couldn't help but notice the striking similarities between the brothers. They stood at the same height, and Miĕĕcha shared Jaänjo's kind eyes and charming smile. The family stood transfixed, marveling at the sight of two beings of pure energy standing side by side in their living room.

Compelled by an irresistible urge, Aan slowly reached out, her hand trembling as she attempted to touch Miĕĕcha's face. To her astonishment, Miĕĕcha moved towards her and embraced her. His warm, comforting presence touched her.

Tears welled in her eyes, spilling down her cheeks as she whispered, "I'm so glad to meet you, Miĕĕcha." The tender moment washed away her fears and doubts about Jaänjo's brother. She felt only warmth, kindness, and an overwhelming sense of family in his ethereal embrace.

Taking a step back, Aan gazed at Jaänjo and Miĕĕcha, her heart full of joy. The two brothers stood side by side, their ethereal forms casting a soft glow throughout the room. Initially shocked into silence, Keet and Yéil now wore expressions of wonder and acceptance.

Yéil stepped forward, her eyes glistening with unshed tears. "Welcome to our home, Miĕĕcha," she said softly, her voice filled with emotion. "It's clear how much Jaänjo loves you, so you'll always be welcome here."

This moment, Aan realized, marked the beginning of something extraordinary. Jaänjo, the cosmic being she loved and who had become part of her family, was now reunited with his brother. As she gazed at the scene before her—her parents, Jaänjo, and now Miĕĕcha—wonder and pride swelled in her heart. A deep sense of completeness settled over her as if the final piece of a vast, intricate puzzle had at last found its place.

The following day, mirroring Aan's experience with Jäänjo, Keet allowed Miěěcha to merge with him. Eager to learn more, Aan and her parents peppered Jäänjo and Miěěcha with questions. The two brothers rose to the challenge, offering insightful responses that satisfied their curiosity. Miěěcha recounted his extraordinary journey, and Jäänjo discussed their likes and differences. As the hours slipped by, it became evident that much remained to be uncovered and discussed in the days ahead.

Miěěcha and Jäänjo asked Aan and Keet if they could communicate in their native language. They agreed, and soon, their bodies became instruments for the N'ridian language—a complex tapestry of guttural sounds, ethereal hums, and multi-toned vibrations. It was as if they had become channels for a symphony of alien consciousness, bridging two worlds through sound.

Though Aan and Keet couldn't understand the words, they were fascinated and amused by the process. The alien language required intricate movements of tongues and vocal cords that felt foreign and sometimes comical to the human bodies producing them. Aan couldn't help but giggle at the strange sensations in her throat as Jäänjo spoke, while Keet marveled at the complex sounds Miěěcha produced through him.

During one of these conversations, the brothers discussed a topic of great importance. Miěěcha, speaking through Keet in the lilting tones of N'ridian, informed Jäänjo that he had perfected the method to convert energy back to matter.

Jäänjo's excitement surged through Aan's body. However, Miěěcha quickly tempered this enthusiasm with a sobering revelation. Having merged with Keet and gaining insight into Earth's technologies, Miěěcha realized that the materials needed to construct the specialized equipment for this feat would be quite expensive.

When Jäänjo relayed Miěěcha's message to Aan without speaking aloud, she sensed a ripple of disappointment from him. Despite her efforts to remain neutral, a small sigh of relief escaped her lips.

"Aan?" Jäänjo's voice had resonated within her. "Why did you sigh?"

Aan felt a pang of guilt. "I... I'm sorry, Jäänjo. I know I shouldn't feel relief at your disappointment, but—"

Jäänjo finished for her, his tone warm and calm. "But you're glad I won't leave you anytime soon."

"Yes," she admitted softly. "Is that selfish of me?"

She felt Jaänjo's energy pulse affectionately within her. "Not at all. I also feel the comfort of knowing we'll remain together."

Touching her heart, Aan sighed. "It's just... I can't fathom life without you."

"Aan," Jaänjo said gently, "I understand. Our lives have become so intertwined. Whatever the future holds, we'll adapt. We always have. And just so you know, I told Miĕĕcha you're the love of my life. He's happy for me—for us."

Observing Aan's expressions during this internal dialogue, Keet offered a sympathetic smile. "Are you two okay?" he asked.

Aan nodded, her eyes bright with wonder. "We are. It's extraordinary, isn't it? You and I, serving as bridges between worlds."

Keet chuckled. "It is. But I wouldn't have it any other way."

As Miĕĕcha and Jaänjo resumed their N'ridian conversation, flowing through Aan and Keet in a stream of exotic sounds, she and her parents shared a look of understanding. Their lives had taken an incredible turn, and while the future remained uncertain, they knew they would face it united—humans and N'ridians alike.

Jaänjo stopped speaking in his native tongue and shifted to talking to Aan. "I asked Miĕĕcha to address Keet's concern about the possibility of a N'ridian invasion. Would you all like to hear his response?"

Aan asked this question aloud, and both her parents nodded. "Okay. Dad, Miĕĕcha will speak to us through you."

"Keet, you need not worry," Miĕĕcha said. "I wrote a secret computer subroutine that blocked the coordinates leading to Earth, so no one else from our planet will land here."

Keet raised his hand to speak. "Miĕĕcha, how many N'ridians were converted and launched into space?"

Miĕĕcha's response surprised them. "I don't know the exact number, Keet. Once I perfected the energy-to-matter conversion process, I converted myself to energy and launched. There was no time to waste."

Keet raised his hand again. "Why was there no time to waste?"

Miĕĕcha paused, and his words had a hard edge when he continued. "The corrupt and heartless government officials placed themselves at the top of the launch list, and they insisted on me staying in case any technical difficulties might arise. In other words, they wanted to all get on the lifeboats first, and if there was no room left for me, too bad. I saw no need to help them at my own expense, and my promise to find Jaänjo was far more important than saving those unworthy people."

Aan felt a chill at the coldness in Miěěcha's tone, but she also understood the choice he had made. She squeezed her father's hand, sensing his similar mix of emotions.

Jaänjo—perhaps sensing the heaviness that had settled over the room—added his thoughts. "Miěěcha has always looked out for me, and this is another example of that. Brother, because of you, we've crossed the galaxy and found this most amazing planet and family. I love you for all you have done."

A comfortable silence fell over the room as everyone absorbed the weight of Miěěcha's words. Yéil, who had been quiet until now, broke the stillness. "Miěěcha, thank you for being such a wonderful brother to Jaänjo. We love him dearly, and I'm certain we'll come to love you just as much."

"Thank you for your kind words, Yéil," Miěěcha replied through Keet, his voice tinged with warmth. "And my heartfelt thanks to all of you for caring for my brother. I've never seen him so content and full of joy. It touches my heart."

As Aan absorbed the day's revelations, her brow furrowed in contemplation. Miěěcha's vivid descriptions of the harrowing existence on N'ridium echoed Jaänjo's earlier accounts, weighing heavily on her mind. She marveled at Miěěcha's recounting of the extraordinary odyssey across the cosmos to Earth. Now, more than ever, she understood why Jaänjo so deeply cherished and savored the life he had discovered in her world.

That evening, after dinner, Aan took a moment to gaze out the kitchen window. She smiled at the star-studded sky. The vastness of space no longer seemed like an abstract concept; it was now a bridge that had brought Miěěcha to join Jaänjo and her family. She felt a sense of wonder at how the spirits had woven their destinies together. As an abundance of questions danced in her head about how Miěěcha's arrival would change things, a surge of confidence suddenly swirled within her. Whatever challenges they might face, they would face them together.

40

As summer began to wane, the first whispers of autumn made their presence known in Tenakee Springs. The air carried a crisp edge, and the sunlight exhibited a softer quality. While the predominant conifer forest didn't offer the spectacular leaf color changes seen in other parts of the world, subtle shifts in the underbrush and the occasional deciduous tree hinted at the changing season.

While Aan, Jaänjo, and Naas provided healing services to the local Tlingit communities—with Aan also fulfilling her shamanic duties—Miěěcha settled within Keet, absorbing knowledge at an astonishing pace. Through Keet's experiences and memories, Miěěcha immersed himself in the language and customs of not only the Native people but also the wider population. The internet, which Miěěcha regarded as "primitive" yet fascinating, became a vast resource of information for him to explore.

As time passed, Keet and Miěěcha developed a strong friendship. Keet often marveled at Miěěcha's kindness and brilliance, sharing his admiration with Aan.

"You wouldn't believe the things Miěěcha knows, Aan," Keet said, his eyes wide with wonder. "He told me that with the right resources, he could build a nuclear fusion reactor the size of a coffee maker to power my boat. Can you imagine? I'd never have to buy fuel again!"

Aan smiled at Keet's enthusiasm, recognizing the same awe she felt when she first started communicating with Jaänjo.

As the weeks passed, Miěěcha's interests shifted, and his explorations became more focused. Keet noticed a pattern emerging in their nightly internet sessions, with Miěěcha showing particular interest in environmental issues and technological advancements.

It became a nightly custom for Keet to give Miĕĕcha time to explore online. Under Miĕĕcha's subtle guidance, Keet's fingers glided across the keyboard with purpose, navigating through the internet's vast knowledge repository. As he delved deeper into this wealth of information, Miĕĕcha's thoughts resonated in Keet's mind, sharing insights and observations about the human world. "The diversity of human cultures and the complex web of societies on your planet fascinates me," Miĕĕcha mused. "And your technological advancement, while rudimentary compared to N'ridium, progresses at an admirable pace."

Keet felt a wave of pride at Miĕĕcha's words, but Miĕĕcha's next observation quickly tempered it.

"Keet, I've observed a disturbing pattern," Miĕĕcha continued, his tone growing somber. "Many of humanity's greatest technological leaps seem rooted in wars. This trend spans from prehistoric use of rudimentary weapons like sticks and stones through the Bronze and Iron Ages with their cannons, knives, and swords right up to your most sophisticated—and horrific—modern technologies like nuclear, chemical, and biological weapons. War—or the looming threat of it—appears to be a primary driver of human progress."

Keet's fingers froze above the keyboard as Miĕĕcha's words sank in. "I... I hadn't considered that perspective before," he admitted, his voice quiet with realization. "But you're right, Miĕĕcha. And it's not just war. Basic human greed often poses as 'progress.' My ancestors, like countless other Indigenous peoples, were systematically oppressed, exploited, and mistreated. Those who came took our land and resources and sought to eradicate our way of life—all under the guise of progress, profit, and religious and governmental righteousness. It's a struggle that continues to this day."

"It's a tragic truth," Miĕĕcha replied with empathy. He paused, his tone growing heavier. "You know, Keet, we faced similar struggles on N'ridium during our planet's final days. Our government, the very institution meant to protect and serve our people, abandoned that duty. As our world crumbled, they prioritized their survival, securing their places at the top of the matter-to-energy lists. They exiled anyone who dared to question or resist their authority to the planet's surface—a certain death sentence, given the brutal surface conditions."

Miĕĕcha's energy pulsed with sorrow and anger. "It seems that regardless of the planet, those in power often exploit their positions at the expense of the masses. Your Earthly government leaders—like our N'ridian leaders—should be held accountable for taking advantage of their people. It's a sobering reminder that technological or societal progress often comes at a steep price paid by the most vulnerable."

Keet absorbed this information, now feeling an even stronger bond with Miěěcha. "The struggles of power, oppression, and survival seem universal." He sighed. "It's remarkable how similar our experiences are despite coming from different worlds."

Miěěcha's internet explorations shifted to the American Southwest and California as another month elapsed. Suddenly, Keet felt excitement coursing through him as Miěěcha exclaimed, "Keet, I've got a viable idea that might just work!"

Caught off guard by Miěěcha's uncharacteristic burst of enthusiasm, Keet responded with curiosity. "What have you found? What could work?"

"Let's gather everyone together so I can tell everyone about my plan."

Speaking through Keet, Miěěcha addressed the gathered family. "I've been considering Jaänjo's and my situation carefully," he began, his tone serious. "If Jaänjo and I convert back to physical form, we'd face a significant challenge. We'd be trapped in Tenakee Springs indefinitely."

The room fell silent as the implications of his words sank in.

"Why?" asked Aan.

Miěěcha continued. "Without passports or any form of legal documentation, your government would regard us as illegal aliens—not interplanetary aliens, but undocumented immigrants. If we were to leave Tenakee Springs or encounter any legal scrutiny, we'd have no way to prove our origins or right to be here."

Aan's eyes widened with realization. "I... I never thought of that," she said softly.

Yéil nodded in agreement. "You're right, Miěěcha. A background check would reveal nothing about you two—no place of birth, no country of origin, nothing."

"Exactly," Miěěcha confirmed. "And since they can't deport us to a home country, they will likely imprison us. If they run DNA tests, it might expose our extraterrestrial origins. The implications would cause an international uproar, with my brother and me likely becoming lab specimens. "So, returning to physical form carries considerable risks."

Yéil leaned forward, her expression grave. "I agree—it could be a chilling reality. Our scientific institutions would love to study you, regardless of your rights or well-being. And given the history of how governments have treated Indigenous people and others they deem 'different,' the consequences for you two could be dire. Tlingits—my people—know firsthand how those in power can justify cruel treatment when they encounter something—or someone—they don't understand. The risks go far beyond imprisonment."

The room fell into a heavy silence as the gravity of Miěěcha's words sank in. The dream of Jaänjo and Miěěcha regaining physical form had suddenly transformed into a potential nightmare, fraught with dangers they hadn't previously considered.

Aan felt Jaänjo's energy stir within her. "Aan," he said, his voice tinged with concern and curiosity, "Miěěcha's words are troubling, but I can't help but wonder what solution he's devised. My brother has always been brilliant at finding ways around seemingly insurmountable problems. Also, I can change our DNA at a molecular level to mask any extraterrestrial origin."

Aan's face paled as she processed this information. She placed a hand over her heart, where she felt Jaänjo's energy pulsing. "I'm scared," she admitted to everyone, her voice barely above a whisper. "The thought of Jaänjo being arrested and jailed is terrifying."

Miěěcha spoke through Keet: "Aan, Jaänjo, it's evident that you two share a deep love, and your merged existence works for you both. You both are fulfilling the work you were meant to do. But Keet," he paused, his tone softening, "please forgive me for what I'm about to say. You've been incredibly generous in hosting me, and I am deeply grateful. However, I'm a scientist and yearn to resume that life again. You have a wonderful life here, Keet, but our needs and aspirations are quite different in the long term."

Keet raised his hand, signaling he was speaking for himself now. "Miěěcha, I understand. And knowing you, I'm certain you wouldn't have called this meeting without having some solution in mind. What have you worked out to resolve this dilemma?"

Miěěcha's energy pulsed with excitement as he began to explain through Keet. "Before I left N'ridium, I stored a vast treasure trove of scientific knowledge within my energy form. It's been with me throughout my journey across the cosmos."

"With Keet patiently allowing me to explore your planet's internet," Miěěcha continued, "one glaring deficiency became apparent after researching the needs of the United States and the world. Many regions, like the American West, are facing severe freshwater shortages, with aquifers being depleted at an alarming rate there and globally. It's a problem that will only intensify as your planet's climate changes and populations grow. We encountered similar challenges on N'ridium, and we discovered a viable solution."

Yéil leaned forward, her interest piqued. "Would the same solution work for our planet's water crisis?"

"Yes!" Miěěcha replied, his excitement showing in Keet's voice. "I can revolutionize water management and the production of freshwater on Earth. The technology I possess could solve water scarcity issues not just in the American West, but globally."

"Really? By doing something like cloud seeding?" asked Aan.

"No, Aan," Miěěcha replied. "I have knowledge of a chemical compound that efficiently desalinates seawater. It's in tablet form, and when you add these tablets to saltwater, it triggers a chemical reaction where the sodium and chloride ions precipitate out of the water. The process is rapid, energy-efficient, and scalable. Best of all, the resulting freshwater is pure and safe for consumption, with the salt extracted in a form that can be either flushed out to sea or potentially used for other purposes."

Aan eyed Keet quizzically. "But how would you implement this, Miěěcha? You just explained the risks of revealing yourself—and Jaänjo." Her mind raced with excitement and apprehension. The potential to solve such a critical global issue thrilled her, but how Miěěcha could do it without being discovered seemed unimaginable.

Miěěcha's energy signature pulsed, indicating he had more to share. "That's where my plan comes in. I've thought of a way we might be able to introduce this technology without exposing me or Jaänjo. But it will require all of us working together—especially you, Keet."

41

"Okay, Miĕĕcha," Aan said, leaning forward. "Let's start with the basics. How would you convert seawater to freshwater? Can you explain it in simple terms?"

Miĕĕcha, speaking through Keet, began. "Certainly. Imagine a large tank filled with seawater. I have five tablets that, when dropped into the tank, cause the salt to crystallize and sink to the bottom. After about an hour and a half, the water above becomes fresh and drinkable."

"That sounds straightforward," Aan nodded. "What happens next?"

"You'd use pumps to extract the freshwater before the salt mixes back in, then flush the salt out and refill the tank with seawater. The whole process takes about two hours per cycle."

Yéil, intrigued, asked, "How much freshwater could you produce in a day?"

"With a 10-million-gallon tank, we could generate around 120 million gallons of fresh water daily, running 12 cycles in 24 hours," Miĕĕcha replied.

Aan felt her head spin at the numbers. "That's... that's an incredible amount of water," she said, trying to grasp the scale. "How does that compare to current desalination plants?"

Miĕĕcha, through Keet, quickly replied. "It's vastly more efficient. Most large-scale desalination plants produce between 10 to 50 million gallons per day. We're talking about doubling or even quadrupling that output at a fraction of the cost."

The room fell silent as they absorbed the magnitude of what Miĕĕcha was proposing.

"Miĕĕcha," said Keet aloud. "How would you make the tablets? Would you need specialized equipment for it?"

"Another excellent question," Miěěcha said through Keet, his tone thoughtful and measured. "The tablets contain a precise chemical combination that triggers the separation of salt from seawater. The science behind it is fascinating, drawing on principles of molecular attraction and ionic bonding and de-bonding."

He paused, considering how to convey the information best. "The encouraging aspect is that the ingredients for these tablets are readily accessible. We're not dealing with rare elements or highly regulated substances. Common industrial and agricultural compounds contain what we need."

Miěěcha exuded excitement as he continued, "What's particularly promising is that we can synthesize these ingredients using straightforward methods. We don't need a state-of-the-art laboratory or highly specialized equipment. Even in a place like Tenakee Springs, we could set up a small production facility."

He quickly added, "The equipment we'd need is surprisingly affordable and available online. We're talking about basic chemical synthesis apparatus, nothing exotic or suspicious. The beauty of this approach is its simplicity and accessibility. We're just combining existing elements in a novel way. It's feasible to start small-scale production here in Tenakee Springs, proving the concept before we consider scaling up."

"Brother," Jaänjo said, speaking through Aan, "I have no doubt you're capable of doing this, but as Aan mentioned earlier, how would you implement this plan, considering the risks of exposing yourself and potentially me?"

Aan nodded after hearing Jaänjo's question.

Miěěcha's energy pulsed within Keet. Through Keet, he revealed, "I'll offer this technology to your government for 100 million dollars."

The room fell into stunned silence. Aan's eyes widened, Yéil leaned back in his chair, and Keet's body stiffened as Miěěcha's words sank in.

"A hundred million dollars?" Aan finally managed, her voice filled with disbelief and shock. "How do you expect to make that happen?"

Miěěcha responded swiftly. "That'll be Keet's job."

Keet's jaw dropped, and he raised his hands in protest. "Me? Miěěcha, I'm just a fisherman without a formal education. I know nothing about dealing with the U.S. government." His voice lowered, tinged with suspicion. "More importantly, I don't trust them. How could I possibly do this?"

The room fell into a tense silence as they all absorbed the magnitude of Miĕĕcha's audacious proposal and the enormous responsibility it would place on Keet's unsuspecting shoulders.

"Miĕĕcha," Jaänjo spoke through Aan, his tone reflecting both admiration and skepticism, "I remember how you masterfully handled the government officials while heading the matter-to-energy program back home. They constantly hounded you for results, breathing down your neck at every turn. Yet you managed to keep them at bay, buying time for your team while delivering just enough progress to appease them. Your diplomatic skills were as impressive as your scientific ones."

Aan raised her hand. "It's me speaking now. This is Earth, not N'ridium. How would you navigate the complexities of Earth's governments? And let's entertain the notion that you succeed in this audacious plan—what would you do with 100 million dollars?"

"Aan, those are two broad questions," Miĕĕcha replied through Keet. "Which one would you like me to address first?"

"The easiest one to explain is why you want so much money. Let's start there."

"As you wish," Miĕĕcha agreed. "I intend to sell my tablets to the government, so I'll need to manufacture them."

Yéil's eyes widened. "Miĕĕcha, your plan is quite ambitious. But have you considered all the potential consequences? After you get the 100 million, why don't you tell the government how to make the tablets?"

Through Keet, Miĕĕcha laughed. "Because we all know how governments operate—making deals, or in the case of Indigenous peoples, making treaties—and then canceling them. I'm certain they'd find a way to either tax nearly all the money they give me or, after obtaining the tablet formula, cancel the deal and reclaim the funds. By producing the tablets ourselves, we ensure they'll have to honor their agreement."

Jaänjo spoke through Aan. "It's me, brother. If you sell them the tablets, surely they can reverse engineer them, discover the chemicals used, and start making them independently."

"Jaänjo, you needn't worry about anyone replicating my formula," Miĕĕcha said confidently. "There's a critical step in the process that combines atoms in the desalting tablet precisely, making it impossible for anyone to replicate without the knowledge and technique I possess. Trust me—even the brightest chemists on your planet won't be able to reverse engineer it."

"So, if you sell the tablets to the government, why ask for all that up-front money?" Yéil asked, puzzled. "What would you do with it?"

"This is where it gets interesting," Miěěcha replied, his excitement evident. "We'll establish factories that Native peoples will own and operate on their lands across the country, including Alaska. This will provide Indigenous peoples with stable, well-paying, lifelong jobs. While it won't right all the wrongs done to your people, it will help lift many out of generations of poverty. I want to build the first tablet factory in Southeast Alaska to help Tlingits. Additionally, Yéil, with the up-front money, I'd like to start a center for advanced scientific research in Juneau, keeping me close to all of you. My first project will involve building an energy-to-matter device so Jaänjo and I can convert back to physical forms."

Inwardly, Aan gasped at Miěěcha's words. The idea of Jaänjo leaving gnawed at her, a persistent ache she couldn't shake. Every time the conversation veered toward energy-to-matter, her heart tightened with an unspoken fear. Her mind raced. *What if his plan works?" What if Jaänjo gets what he wants—a way to become whole again—and leaves?"* The thought left her feeling hollow, as if the ground beneath her had suddenly given way.

Keet raised his hand, indicating he was speaking. "Miěěcha, while your intention is admirable, we need to be careful not to make decisions for Indigenous communities. Each tribe and nation has its own governance and priorities. We should present this as an opportunity, not a foregone conclusion."

"You're right, Keet. I apologize if I sounded presumptuous. We'll approach this as a partnership, respecting the autonomy and wisdom of each community."

Aan shook her head, skeptical about all she heard. "Miěěcha, they'll discover you to be an undocumented alien." She left her real concern unspoken—the possibility of Jaänjo leaving her.

Keet raised his hand, indicating he was speaking. "Miěěcha, your desire to help Indigenous people touches my heart. But Aan is right—the government will quickly discover you're not a U.S. citizen. How do you plan to address that?"

"Aan, this leads back to your first question—how will I get the government to do this? May I address this now?"

She nodded.

Mięěcha's energy enthusiastically pulsed as he continued through Keet. "Okay—here goes. Fortunately, because Juneau is the capital of Alaska, your two U.S. Senators visit periodically to meet with their constituents. This gives us a unique opportunity.

"Initially, Keet, we'll have you send both senators a short email. You'll state that you've perfected a method to extract freshwater from seawater in a revolutionary way, emphasizing that it uses 98 percent less energy than the most efficient desalination plants worldwide."

Keet's eyes widened with excitement and apprehension crossing his face. "Me? Sending an email to U.S. Senators claiming I've invented something this groundbreaking?"

Mięěcha's voice remained calm and reassuring. "Yes, you. You'll be our bridge to becoming legitimate in this world. The message will be brief, just enough to pique their interest. We'll craft it carefully to sound credible without revealing too much. The goal is to secure a meeting to demonstrate the technology."

Aan interjected, her voice laced with concern, "But won't they be suspicious? A fisherman suddenly coming up with world-changing technology?"

"That's a valid concern," Mięěcha acknowledged. "But it's also our advantage. Sometimes, groundbreaking innovations come from unexpected sources. Your background as a local, combined with the urgency of the water crisis, might just be intriguing enough to get their attention."

Yéil nodded slowly. "It's a bold move. If it works, it could open doors we never thought possible for our people."

"Exactly," Mięěcha agreed. "This is just the first step. If we can get their attention, we'll offer to demonstrate and showcase the true potential of this technology. And remember, Keet, you won't be alone. I'll be within you, answering all their questions."

"Okay, fine," Aan interjected. "I get it. But how does any of this safeguard you and Jaänjo?"

Mięěcha chuckled. "Here's the good part. When the government sees how revolutionary our technology is and its global implications, that's when we ask for the 100 million upfront, tax-free, or 150 million if they tax it. We'll even give them several tablets to verify our claims independently. I'll be amused when they find out they can't duplicate our tablets, forcing them to buy them from us. We'll negotiate a fair price for the tablets. After they agree to this, that's when we'll have Keet discuss Jaänjo and me."

"Discuss what, Miĕĕcha?" Aan asked. "That you're aliens from N'ridium?"

Miĕĕcha laughed. "No, Aan. I'll have Keet say he's not the inventor of the seawater-to-freshwater technology. His friend is, and he's hiding in another country to escape his government's agents wanting to steal his technology. As part of the deal, he wants full U.S. citizenship for himself and his brother, entry into the U.S. government's Witness Protection Program, and new identities, including Social Security numbers and other essential documents. To further protect themselves, they'll also demand not to disclose their real names or country of origin to the U.S. government."

Aan's face paled. "Miĕĕcha, what you're suggesting... it's essentially lying to the federal government. That's not just unethical; it could be highly illegal. Are we prepared for the consequences if this deception is ever discovered?"

The room fell silent as the weight of Aan's words sank in. Miĕĕcha, through Keet, spoke softly. "You're right to be concerned, Aan. The ethical implications are significant. But consider our unique situation—we're trying to immigrate from another planet into Earth's society. There are no rules for that. Sometimes, extraordinary circumstances require unconventional solutions. However, we should consider whether we're comfortable with this approach."

"Miĕĕcha," Keet said with an impressed chuckle, "you've certainly made the most of those evenings spent exploring the internet. Your plan is brilliant."

The room fell into contemplative silence as they all considered the audacious plan, knowing that if they implemented it, their lives would change in ways they could scarcely imagine.

42

"Everyone," Aan said, her expression troubled, "this is too much to digest. I need to go home with Jaänjo. We can meet again in a day or two to discuss this further."

Yéil rose and embraced her daughter. "I understand, Aan—it's a lot to process. You and Jaänjo have much to consider." She noticed tears welling in Aan's eyes. "Perhaps you should seek guidance from our spirits."

Keet gave her a kind, fatherly smile. "Whatever you decide, you'll have our full support."

"Thanks, Dad, and you, too, Mom. Jaänjo, do you want to say goodbye to Miĕĕcha?"

"Yes, please." He briefly spoke to his brother in their native tongue.

On the path to their cabin, Aan remained silent, even when their bear companions bounded toward them in the meadow. Fred, sensing her distress, gently nuzzled against her. She touched his head in silent gratitude for his concern.

"Jaänjo, I need to rest. You're welcome to stay out here with our friends if you'd like. It's sunny, so you can recharge."

"Is that what you really want, Aan?"

"Yes."

"All right."

He separated from her body and remained with the bears, noting how she entered the cabin without a backward glance. He understood her unspoken distress, feeling it acutely himself. The prospect of his transition back to a physical form loomed over them both, threatening to sever the intimate connection they'd grown accustomed to.

Later, Aan emerged from the cabin, approaching Jaänjo and the bears lounging beside him. "Hey, everyone," she said, her voice noticeably lighter. "I'm feeling better now." She opened her arms, inviting Jaänjo to rejoin her. As his warm, comforting presence enveloped her once more, a smile spread across her face. "Mmm... I love having you within me," she murmured contentedly.

She touched her hand to her heart. "Thanks for giving me some alone time, Jaänjo. The solitude and spending time meditating allowed me to confront my fears and find a sense of peace amidst the uncertainty. I think that change, while daunting, can also bring new possibilities."

"I feel your peace. Did you ask your spirits for guidance?"

"I did," she replied, her voice softening. "Their words brought me comfort. They reminded me of the strength of our bond and the path we're meant to walk together."

"And what path is that?" he inquired gently.

"My spirits reminded me of the intricate web of life," Aan explained, her voice filled with awe. "They likened our predicament to a butterfly stirring the air. Its delicate wings, though small, can cause a gentle breeze that ripples through the trees and affects the entire forest. Similarly, our decision on what to do can have far-reaching consequences. Yet, our love, like the enduring roots of a mighty spruce tree, will remain steadfast through any storm." She wrapped her arms around herself, embracing their shared essence. "Jaänjo, I love you. Whatever path we choose, that won't change. With all the potential upheaval looming, our love is the one thing I can rely on."

"I feel the same way," he responded. "Your spirits have great wisdom."

The next day, they remained close to their cabin, meandering through the forest with Fred, Barney, Wilma, and Betty. They exchanged few words; it was a time for quiet contemplation. As evening fell and Aan ate dinner back at the cabin, she broke the silence with a sigh. "Jaänjo, I think we should meet with Mom, Dad, and Miěěcha tomorrow morning. What do you think?"

"That's fine with me. What will we tell them?"

She sighed again. "The decision of how to proceed is yours. What will you tell them?"

Silence hung in the air.

Jaänjo's energy dimmed, reflecting the inner conflict between his bond with Aan and his duty to Miěěcha. The prospect of regaining physical form both exhilarated and unnerved him—the allure of fully experiencing this world counterbalanced by the potential loss of his profound connection with Aan. Underlying it all, he felt a deep obligation to support his brother's longing to resume his life as a scientist.

"Jaänjo?" Aan's voice cut through his contemplation.

He sighed and spoke quietly. "Aan, I have to support Miěěcha."

She nodded. "I know."

As they walked down the trail the following day, Aan touched her heart. "I feel at peace, Jaänjo. How about you?"

Jaänjo's energy stirred within her. "Peace might be too strong a word. This path we're choosing—it's necessary, but it's not without its burdens."

His energy pulsed with a quiet intensity. "Miěěcha's potential to change the world is undeniable. Fresh water for millions, sustainable energy, revolutionary technologies... the list goes on. But you're right to be cautious. Each breakthrough carries its own risks and ethical dilemmas."

Aan nodded. "It's true, the potential for good is enormous. But with such power comes great responsibility—and risk. What if these technologies fall into the wrong hands? Or if the changes happen too quickly for society to adapt? My people have seen how rapid change can lead to undesirable consequences."

Jaänjo sighed. "You're right, Aan. The road ahead is full of challenges. We'll need to be vigilant and guide Miěěcha as best we can, employing your shaman spirits as well. This isn't just about Miěěcha's happiness—it's about shaping the future of this world, for better or worse. The weight of that responsibility... it's daunting."

Aan paused for a moment and smiled. "You're right about all the things Miěěcha could do. He could be the world's next Einstein," she mused.

"Who's that?" Jaänjo asked, his energy flickering with curiosity.

"Oh, he was a rather eccentric-looking man with wild hair who revolutionized our understanding of physics," Aan explained, a hint of amusement in her voice.

"Interesting. Perhaps Miěěcha will become known as the quirky, buck-toothed scientist who surpassed Einstein's achievements," Jaänjo replied.

"Does Miěěcha have buck teeth?" Aan asked, her eyes widening.

Jaänjo chuckled, amusement evident in his voice. "I'm only teasing. But Miěěcha can look pretty wild, too, when he's on a research bender for days on end."

"What about you, Jaänjo? Do you yearn for global recognition?" Aan asked thoughtfully. "With your healing abilities, you could become a celebrity in your own right."

Jaänjo's energy pulsed gently, conveying a sense of contentment. "That kind of life doesn't appeal to me, Aan. I'd love to spend the rest of my days with you in Tenakee Springs, continuing the work we're doing now."

"Me too," she replied softly, a warm smile spreading across her face.

The walk to her parents' house passed quickly. The family gathered in the living room, with anticipation filling the space. Aan took a deep breath. "Everybody, Jaänjo and I support what Miěěcha wants to do."

"Thank you, Aan and Jaänjo," said Miěěcha. "Keet and I drafted an email to the Alaska Senators. Would you like to hear it and tell us what you think?"

Aan smiled. "We'd love to hear what you two wrote."

"Okay. Keet, please read it to them."

Keet put on his reading glasses. "Here goes." He picked up a paper and began reading:

"I'm writing to introduce a groundbreaking desalination technology that could revolutionize freshwater production. My method is 98 percent more energy efficient than traditional desalination plants. It employs specially formulated tablets that trigger a rapid separation of salt from seawater, eliminating the need for energy-intensive mechanical systems. This innovation can solve global water scarcity, transforming arid regions and ensuring water security for billions of people. I'm eager to discuss the implications and explore partnerships for its implementation. Sincerely, Keet Gajaa."

He removed his reading glasses and looked at Aan with a wry smile. "Who would've thought I'd ever become a silver-tongued orator one day?"

Aan laughed warmly. "Dad, you're not only an eloquent orator, but you have a heart of gold. Jaänjo and I love what you and Miěěcha have written."

EPILOGUE

AAN EMERGED FROM THE wheelhouse of the world's first fusion-powered fishing boat and gazed out at the familiar waters of Alaska's Inside Passage. She paused for a moment, reflecting on how much had changed since Miĕĕcha's plan had been set in motion. The past five years had brought a whirlwind of technological advancements and the promise of a better life for countless people. From Jaänjo and Miĕĕcha's integration into Earth society to the global impact of their innovations, it had been a journey beyond anything she could have imagined.

As their boat sailed through the calm waters, Aan joined her husband on the deck. "Jaänjo, did you remember to apply sunscreen? You'll surely burn on such a warm day with your fair skin."

He smiled and kissed her. "Yes, I applied some. You know, life seemed simpler when I existed within you as pure energy. You never nagged me to slather myself with lotion or put my dirty clothes in the hamper."

She nuzzled her cheek against his and gave him a mischievous smile. "That's true, but there are a few other things I do now that seem to bring a smile to your face."

"I'm sure you've noticed I smile a lot. I love what we have, Aan."

"I have noticed, and Mom says there's always a smile on my face as well. I'm glad we've managed to maintain our way of life—well, as best we can, given how things at home have changed."

Jaänjo smiled and gazed absently at the impressive snow-capped mainland mountains. "I'm looking forward to us spending the next few days with Miĕĕcha in Juneau. I keep telling him he needs to slow down, but he insists he's having the time of his life."

"He does seem happy," Aan agreed. "But my spirits tell me he needs a life outside of work." She winked at Jaänjo. "Tlingit women seem to appeal to at least half of your clan."

Jaänjo chuckled, picking up on her dry humor and concern for his brother. "I know what you mean. But every arid country in the world is clamoring for his desalination technology. Last week, he was in Arizona for the ribbon-cutting ceremony of their massive freshwater production facility, which draws seawater from the Gulf of California. Soon, Arizona's communities will have plentiful supplies of fresh water. The way he's transforming arid regions into thriving green oases is incredible, but—"

"But he's always moving, always working," Aan finished for him. "Maybe this visit will allow us to talk with him about finding balance." She paused, watching a pod of orcas near them. "I worry about him sometimes. All these amazing achievements, but at what personal cost?"

"I hear you. Speaking of remarkable achievements, Miĕĕcha has captured international attention with his portable nuclear fusion generators. The idea of every home in America having its own fusion power source within a decade is mindboggling. Once again, Miĕĕcha struck a hard bargain with the American government—in exchange for this groundbreaking technology, they must implement universal healthcare, funded by profits from these fusion devices. Just imagine—comprehensive healthcare for all, from birth to death, sustained by the revenue from this revolutionary invention."

His eyes sparkled with pride for his brother as he continued. "And that's not all. When Miĕĕcha introduces his anti-gravity technology, his company's profits will go toward providing financial support for retirees, disabled individuals, and disadvantaged children. He'll reshape society's safety net." He paused a moment, reflecting. "I'm proud to have shared my conventional medical knowledge with Miĕĕcha to aid in developing cures for cancer and other diseases. Working behind the scenes allows me to maintain anonymity while contributing to advancements in traditional medicine."

Jaänjo's expression grew serious. "Aan, I've been meaning to talk to you about something. Miĕĕcha mentioned deep concerns about the potential misuse of these new technologies. He's worried about certain governments already preparing to weaponize them."

Aan's eyes widened. "Weaponize them? How?"

"Well, for one, instead of using rockets, they could use his anti-gravity technology to launch weapons into space easily," Jaänjo replied, his voice low. "Keet said Miĕĕcha once told him that many of humanity's greatest technological leaps seem rooted in wars or preparing to defend against wars. Sadly, Miĕĕcha feels powerless to stop it."

"He's right. I hope one day, humanity will see the futility and lunacy of conflict."

"I love the peace of our home and town. Everyone should be so lucky to have what we have."

Aan nodded and leaned against the boat railing, her eyes meeting Jaänjo's. "It's hard to believe how much our lives have changed since you converted to a physical form. Remember how worried we were about losing our connection?"

A soft smile came to Jaänjo's lips. "I do. We were so uncertain about the future. But Miĕĕcha, brilliant as ever, found a solution we never imagined possible."

"A device that allows you to convert back to pure energy," Aan said, her voice filled with wonder. "It's like having the best of both worlds."

"It is," Jaänjo agreed. "Being able to merge with you again, even if only occasionally, is... indescribable. It's like coming home."

Aan's expression turned bittersweet. "I treasure those moments. But..."

"I know," Jaänjo said gently. "The time limit. When I'm in energy form, I don't age. We can't stay merged for long without creating a discrepancy in our ages."

Aan squeezed his hand. "Having you here, in physical form, sharing our lives—that's what matters most. Merging is a beautiful bonus."

Jaänjo gently hugged her. "You're right. And every day, whether in this body or briefly in energy form, I'm grateful for what we have."

She tenderly kissed him. "Me, too," she whispered.

Yéil emerged from the wheelhouse, her footsteps gentle on the deck as she approached the couple. Her eyes twinkled with amusement and apology. "Sorry to interrupt your shared moment, you two, but a little someone has been asking for his momma."

Three-year-old Tenakee squirmed excitedly in Yéil's arms. His dark eyes, mirrors of Aan's, sparkled at the sight of his parents. Yéil gently passed the boy to Aan, who greeted him with a warm smile.

"Hey, my beautiful boy," Aan cooed, cradling Tenakee close as she balanced on the gently rocking deck. "Your dad and I are happy to see you."

Jaänjo moved closer, steadying Aan with a hand on her back as he playfully ruffled their son's hair with the other. Tenakee giggled, grasping Jaänjo's fingers with one hand and clinging to Aan's shirt with the other. "Momma! Dadda!" he chirped, his voice a delightful blend of Tlingit and English.

Jaänjo leaned in and kissed Tenakee's forehead. "Have you been good for Nana Yéil?"

Yéil chuckled. "As good as a curious little explorer can be. He's been 'helping' Grandpa Keet steer the boat."

As if on cue, Keet's voice boomed from the wheelhouse. "Aan! Jaänjo! Come see what your little navigator has done to my charts!"

Aan and Jaänjo exchanged amused glances. "We'd better go see what mischief our son has been up to," Aan laughed, leading the way to the wheelhouse. She gently bounced Tenakee in her arms. "I'll bet you'll be a sea captain like your grandpa someday!"

As the family moved to join Keet, Jaänjo lingered for a few moments, his gaze sweeping across the breathtaking Alaskan landscape: majestic mountains reaching into the sky, emerald islands dotting the horizon, and pristine waters glistening beneath an azure-blue sky. The laughter from Tenakee drifted back to him, a joyful contrast to the serene beauty that enveloped him. A profound sense of belonging washed over him, marking the culmination of a journey that had taken him across the galaxy to this perfect, ordinary moment of bliss. In the warmth of his family's love and the embrace of this awe-inspiring wilderness, Jaänjo found not just a home but what it meant to be truly and completely alive.

ACKNOWLEDGEMENTS

Writing the acknowledgments is always pleasurable because it means the endeavor is finished, and I can express my gratitude to those who helped me through this book.

A special thanks to Mary Ellen Miller, my wonderful mother, who recently passed away at age ninety-eight. I will never forget our lifelong friendship and how she touched my heart with countless acts of kindness and love. I take comfort in these words by Irving Berlin, which reminds me of her: *"The song is ended, but the melody lingers on."*

For Carmen, my German wife, I'll use your language to describe my feelings for you: *Du bist meine größte Liebe* (you are my greatest love).

And lastly, a special thanks to you, the reader. May the light of God shine always on your path.

ABOUT THE AUTHOR

James Randall Miller was born in Germany and has traveled and lived throughout the world. After thirty years in Alaska, he now lives near the White Tank Mountains in Arizona. Other books by James include *Julius,* an illustrated children's story, and the inspirational novels *Howling Across Bridges, Knock on the Sky, After the Purple Heart, Gus and Billy, Untangling Claire,* and *Because of You.*

Hearing from his readers always delights James. You can reach him at JamesMillerBooks@gmail.com

FINAL THOUGHTS

You can't go back and change the beginning, but you can start where you are and change the ending. — C.S. LEWIS

If you don't know where you are going, any road can take you there. — LEWIS CARROLL

The real voyage of discovery consists not in seeking new landscapes but in having new eyes. — MARCEL PROUST

All journeys have secret destinations of which the traveler is unaware. — MARTIN BUBER

For those who believe, no proof is necessary. For those who don't believe, no proof is possible. — STUART CHASE

Of God and wind I have not seen, yet I am touched by both. — JAMES RANDALL MILLER

Many paths lead up the mountain, but at the top, we all look at the same bright moon. — IKKYU

Truth is one; the sages call it by many names. — HINDU SAYING

I believe in God, but not as one thing, not as an old man in the sky. I believe that what people call God is something in all of us. — JOHN LENNON

Neither will they say, "Look, here!" or, "Look, there!" for behold, God's Kingdom is within you. — JESUS, LUKE 17:21

You are the universe, expressing itself as a human for a little while. — ECKHART TOLLE

At any moment, you have a choice, that either leads you closer to your spirit or further away from it. — THICH NHAT HANH

The best way to know God is to love many things. — VINCENT VAN GOGH

Within each of us, there is silence. A silence as vast as the universe. And when we experience that silence, we remember who we are. — GUNILLA NORRIS

Before enlightenment, chop wood, carry water. After enlightenment, chop wood, carry water. — ZEN SAYING

It is not the answer that enlightens, but the question. — EUGÈNE IONESCO

The most beautiful things in the world cannot be seen or even touched. They must be felt with the heart. — HELEN KELLER

The earth has music for those who listen. — GEORGE SANTAYANA

You are not a drop in the ocean. You are the entire ocean in a drop. — JALALUDDIN RUMI

Genius is finding the invisible link between things. — VLADIMIR NABOKOV

Whenever you feel sad, just remember that there are billions of cells in your body, and all they care about is you. — UNKNOWN

The privilege of a lifetime is being who you are. — JOSEPH CAMPBELL

We are all writing God's poem. — ANNE SEXTON

No one is too old for fairy tales. — NICK LAKE

Goodbye? Oh no, please. Can't we just go back to page one and start all over again? — WINNIE THE POOH